Praise for *The Bones*

"Witty, sharp and surprisingly engaging . . . It takes a fairly manic imagination to come up with an animatronic walrus in the first place, and it takes real talent—and something like compassion—to get the reader to care about the guy who's riding it . . . Greenland has serious skills."
—*Washington Post*

"Here's a novel to unite America."—*Baltimore Sun*

"Greenland's touch recalls Carl Hiassen: eviscerating; yet strangely tender."—*Village Voice*

"A fun romp with some simple lessons about taking risks and unmasking your pain."—*Cleveland Plain Dealer*

"Greenland is chucklably witty in dozens of passages, alive to verbal music, rhythmically gifted, and exceedingly knowing in skewering his fellow show folk."—*Seattle Weekly*

"Greenland's wickedness and his pungent observations render the familiar fresh and entertaining . . . tart, amusing . . . quite gratifying."—*New York Newsday*

"The relationship between Frank and Lloyd is one of the book's finest surprises; sometimes idol and idolater, sometimes bitter enemies, sometimes partners in crime—literally—their bond is always fresh, always interesting, and never what would you expect."—*Daily Californian*

"An on-point spoof that validates everything you thought was ridiculous about L.A."—**Black Book**

"A darkly funny tale set at the corner of Hollywood and Whine . . . Seth Greenland will probably earn a new legion of admirers, even among the Hollywood types he has skewered with such perfect pitch."—**Buffalo News**

"*The Bones* is a genuine, unabashedly old-school Hollywood romp, with enough insider references to keep even the cagiest entertainment aficionado clawing the carpet. The novel evokes the classic glitzoid rough-and-tumbles of Nathanael West and the great Terry Southern. Like West and Southern, the author packs a weird genius for finding the single most lamentable detail in any scene. Greenland owns the rare— and for a reader, profound—ability to suffuse his most disturbing evocations with love for the very show business tropes he loathes the most."—**Jerry Stahl, author of *I, Fatty* and *Permanent Midnight***

"Greenland's showbiz evisceration is so cynical, it makes *Curb Your Enthusiasm* seem like Barney."—**Philadelphia Inquirer**

"A pitch-perfect setup of Hollywood's endemic self-importance . . . brilliantly acid narrative . . . the book's pace is fast, furious and fun . . . the pace of this raucous thrill ride never slackens."—**Publishers Weekly (starred review)**

"Greenland takes readers on an entertaining, behind-the-scenes tour of sitcoms and their socially maladroit, dyspeptic creators."—**Booklist**

"*The Bones* overflows with a wicked wit, gallows humor, heavy ache, and a survivor's perspective on an industry that can kill its creators' souls while tickling audiences' funny bones."—**Pages**

The Bones

A Novel

Seth Greenland

BLOOMSBURY

For Susan

Published by Bloomsbury Publishing, New York and London
Distributed to the trade by Holtzbrinck Publishers

All papers used by Bloomsbury Publishing are natural, recyclable products
made from wood grown in well-managed forests. The manufacturing processes
conform to the environmental regulations of the country of origin.

The Library of Congress has cataloged the hardcover edition as follows:

Greenland, Seth.
The bones : a novel / Seth Greenland.
p. cm.
ISBN 1–58234–550–3
1. Comedians—Fiction. 2. Comedy programs—Fiction. 3. Television
authorship—Fiction. 4. Self-destructive behavior—Fiction. I. Title.

PS3557.R3952B66 2005
813′.54—dc22
2004016084

First published in the United States by Bloomsbury Publishing in 2005
This paperback edition published in 2006

Paperback ISBN-10: 1-59691-031-3
ISBN-13: 978-1-59691-031-7

1 3 5 7 9 10 8 6 4 2

Typeset by Hewer Text Ltd, Edinburgh
Printed in the United States of America
by Quebecor World Fairfield

Prologue

Frank Bones is pissing on the world.

From the fifth-floor window of the Elysium Theatre dressing room in downtown Cleveland, his eyes, bloodshot behind dark glasses, follow the stream of urine as it arcs gracefully and splashes five stories down where it lands in the backseat of a red convertible. Pleased with his aim, he lifts the bottle of tequila he's holding and takes a celebratory swig.

He's dressed head to toe in black, not having received the fashionista fatwa proclaiming its obsolescence, junior high school girls wearing all black these days. Tight black jeans, black belt with small silver buckle, black silk long-sleeved shirt, the whole ensemble saying I'm forty-four years old but I rock all night. Not rock literally, since Frank isn't a musician, but rock in the sense that he can still have lots of sex with multiple partners and no day gig.

The door opens and Lou Nova, the guy promoting tonight's show, steps into the small room. Frank turns to Lou, lurching a little, the tequila evening out in his stomach. Adjusts his gyroscope and straightens his back. Tilts focus from the promoter's gut, barely contained by his too snug satin tour jacket, up to his pudgy, middle-aged face with its attempt-at-hipster stubble to his thinning hair pulled back into a short, greasy ponytail. Taking in the whole picture. Frank's voice rumbles up from his insides, over his tongue, and through his lips, from which it emerges in full snark.

"Guy's gonna regret leaving his top down."

Frank doesn't want to be in Cleveland, backstage at the Elysium Theatre with this man he hopes he'll never see again. He wants to be back in Los Angeles at his West Hollywood bungalow, in bed, under the covers, alone. Well, not alone, exactly. He'd enjoy the company of a bottle of tequila, like the one he is holding right now in Cleveland, the one making the ordeal his road life has become bearable. "Frank, five minutes," says Lou.

Frank looks out the window, feeling the humid June air fat in the room. To Lou:

"All the cars in the parking lot are Japanese. Why is that?"

"Maybe you wanna drink some coffee."

"Don't need coffee. It's showtime."

Lou shrugs, inebriated performers nothing new. He grabs Frank by the arm and steers him out of the dressing room into the hallway. Frank takes a billfold from his pocket, peels off an oily five and hands it to Lou as the two of them move toward the stage.

"Camel filters, Lou. I'm trying to lower the nicotine intake. Kind of on a health kick."

"You remember your set?"

Frank, pointing to his head, nods sagely. "It's all right here."

The Elysium Theatre: vaudeville to jazz to rock to punk to hip-hop. Seats two thousand people when the balcony's open and they don't drop a curtain behind row RR. Tonight, maybe eight hundred ticket buyers in the place. Frank and Lou stand at the side of the stage. The audience hums in the background, anticipating an evening of mirth with America's number one bad-boy comedian.

"You okay, Frank?"

No response, he's concentrating. Over the PA comes the voice of someone who sounds like the Bible: "Ladies and gentlemen, please welcome Frank Bones!"

"They're waiting." Lou gesticulates toward the stage, Frank's commitments, his life.

"How's my hair look?"

Not waiting for an answer, Frank, talking to everyone like they're an audience, all questions rhetorical, strolls onstage. The spotlight hits him

2

like a truck, slams through his dark glasses, his already shrunken pupils contracting to a degree barely measurable by precise optical equipment. Big applause, which Frank does not acknowledge. Not that he doesn't appreciate it, he's just preoccupied. Steps to the mic. Takes it off the stand. Hoods his eyes with his hand.

His opening line—

Lou, where are those Camel filters?

They laugh because they're supposed to. Paid $25.50 to $45.50, plus a handling charge, to be here and this guy's a comic so they laugh. Even though Frank is dead serious, the nicotine craving baying at the moon. Frank looks over at Lou, who shrugs, thinking he's joking, being a comedian. Annoyed, Frank turns to the audience.

Good evening, Detroit.

Someone shouts, "You're in Cleveland!"

Not if I can help it.

Frank's comeback is received with laughter and jocular booing. He squints into the electric sun searing his eyes from the balcony. Moves to the right, as if that will get him away. The beam follows him, an escapee scuttling along the prison wall.

Could you turn up the light, please? I feel like I'm lying on an operating table and a thousand doctors are getting ready to boost my kidney.

He waits. The crowd shifts. The light is adjusted slightly.

That's better. Now it just feels like I'm having LASIK surgery. How is everybody tonight?

The audience members, knowing their part in the ritual, join their voices to create a swell of approval for this man, this avatar, this comedy deity beamed in from Los Angeles to make them forget their troubles— come on, get happy for the next hour. Frank peers at them through the wall of lights, sees fat people stuffed into too tight T-shirts, bad skin, trowel-applied makeup, big hair, bad hair, awful facial hair, dreadful clothes, porcine faces rank with pent-up frustrations exacerbated by dead-end jobs, looking up at him in smiling anticipation, all desperately in need of release. He feels sick. Surges forward.

3

The show must flow on.

I'm not feeling too good myself. You know why? Because black people are really steamed and they're steamed because whitey is always ripping them off. The stereotype is the reverse, you know, it's the black guy in the Kangol hat running down the street with the television set he's just looted—but it's not true.

Elvis stole rock 'n' roll from black people but Elvis gets the credit. He gets the statues. He gets Elvis soap and Elvis shampoo. The guy steals rock 'n' roll from black people, OD's on fried peanut-butter sandwiches, then dies facedown on the bathroom floor in a pool of his own vomit and the white man—that's us, ladies and gentlemen, guys and gals—the white man puts him on a postage stamp!

They like where that one went, laughing as they arrive at the destination.

I say that as the poster child for Acquired White Guilt Syndrome, which I've been suffering from since the 1960s. I'm thinking about having a telethon. Everyone in the business is going to have to perform so pretty much everyone's . . .

And here Frank's brain blips, trips, skips a beat. He narrows his eyes, trying to remember where he is. What are all these people doing in my living room? he wonders. Then he recalls, maintaining equanimity.

You ever lick an Elvis stamp? Tastes like Vicodin.

Big laugh, drug references cheap and dependable.

I want to be a postage stamp. I want the whole world licking my ass.

Most of the audience follows Frank, already forgetting he dropped a thought in midsentence, left it hanging, twisting like a seventeenth-century felon on a creaky gibbet. They're relating to the Elvis material but feeling slightly ambivalent about the white guilt premise; this being a crowd of paychecks who work too hard to worry about what Elvis did or didn't help himself to at the smorgasbord of African-American culture. But there's one guy, there's always one, who's taking exception to Frank's surprisingly lucid train of thought. He's in his thirties, a Chicago Black Hawks hockey jersey draped over narrow nonhockey shoulders.

"Elvis didn't steal it!"

He's the Heckler. Too much alcohol and now he wants to be part of the show, make his friends laugh, hunt a story for the office or the factory floor, Frank Bones paid attention to me.

Frank thinking, Christ on a cracker, just let me get through my set. *I work alone, pal.*

Wanting to go easy, not eviscerate him like a fat bass, flesh on one side of the dock, bones, as it were, on the other. But the guy won't leave it.

"Take back what you said!"

Or what?

Rising to the challenge, the atavistic comedy urge to destroy kicking in.

You're gonna come up here and instruct me on the finer points of Elvis's many diverse musical influences?

The trap laid, the fish biting, the cotton high.

"I'll come up there and kick your ass."

Whoa, whoa, whoa.

Raising the ante.

Turn on the houselights.

After a moment the lights come on and Frank stares into the crowd.

What death-wish motherfucker said that?

The guy stands up as audience members jeer him. He's four red-white-and-blue cans of Pabst tall boys into the evening, and his friends, at once mortified and titillated, egg him on.

"I did, Bones. You ain't shit." Said with a laugh, not angry, the guy just drunk, having fun.

With what he imagines to be great savoir faire, the kind that comes from being truly and righteously stoned, Frank produces a revolver from his pocket—yes, a sidearm, a gun, a gat—and aims cool cylindrical metal at Hockey Jersey. The crowd isn't sure if this is a joke, some surrealist attempt to carry them to new and more dangerous heights of amusement, Duchamp with a microphone, Comedian Descending a Staircase. Some think it's part of the show, Frank testing the limits again. A man in seat GG 108, manager of a Foot Locker store in Parma, begins to experience heart palpitations.

You know the only thing I hate more than Elvis? And I'm talking about the post–Ann-Margret period 'cause everything he did until then was cool even if he stole it from the brothers . . . the only thing I hate more than fat, bloated, Nixon-hugging, white rhinestone jumpsuit Elvis are his fuckin' fans.

Hockey Jersey can't contain himself and the Pabsts are talking. "You're gonna wish you hadn't said that!"

Really?

Frank squeezes the trigger, firing the gun into the ceiling, once, twice, three times; plaster flakes and falls like dry, lead-encrusted snow from the sky as everyone dives for cover under the seats, their fear mixed with old chewing gum.

Frank is a lot harder to book after that.

Book One

Good-Bye, Babylon

Chapter 1

Four years later.

Frank sits on a buttery brown leather sofa in the Beverly Hills waiting room of Nada Entertainment paging through that day's edition of the *Hollywood Reporter*. Nada is one of a new breed of companies that represent actors and comedians *and* produce their movies and television shows, thereby bleeding the clients coming and going. They have names like Acme, Nameless, Intrinsic, names designed to blend, be discreet, self-abnegate to the point of invisibility.

It's ten in the morning, early for Frank given he's been up most of the night fighting with his girlfriend. He didn't have much use for sleep lately, caffeine and blow doing most of the heavy lifting.

Nada isn't really a new company. Under its original name of De Meo Entertainment, it was the private fiefdom of one Jolly De Meo, legendary Hollywood producer-slash-manager who had parlayed the success of a single client's awful but wildly popular mid-1970s sitcom into an entertainment empire comprising movies, TV shows, and personal management that brought in enough money to get Argentina out of hock to the World Bank. Jolly, unpretentious, overweight, bearded, from Brooklyn, was an avuncular figure, beloved by his clients, whom he fawned over with a solicitousness befitting a liver en route to a transplant. But, recently and on the sly, having experienced certain prostate-related tribulations ("I got fucked in the ass one too many times," he joked to the few intimates with whom he shared this dangerous information, even the *potential* for cancer viewed as a character flaw in Hollywood), Jolly had been having intimations of his own mortality, God whispering in his ear, "Even a big swinging dick like you can't bestride Wilshire Boulevard like a Roman colossus forever."

This revelation had led Jolly into a partnership with the much younger Robert Hyler, who had answered to *Bobby* growing up in Cedarhurst on the South Shore of Long Island. Bobby-soon-to-be-Robert had come to Hollywood right out of Adelphi University in 1982, all Sassoon jeans and Members Only jackets, a look he sustained past the years it was culturally relevant. He had a couple of clients, one of which, a young comic who could actually act, played a doctor on a prime-time hospital show. The show became a hit and Robert found himself on the set one day standing at the craft services table being served penne arrabiata by an illegal alien when he heard a gravelly voice asking if the green beans could be sautéed in olive oil, not butter. He looked up and gazed upon the biblical visage of Jolly De Meo, manager of choice to those in the comedy stratosphere. Robert contrived to get next to him at lunch, and a year and sundry meals later they were cylinders in the same show business engine.

A male client who had done some modeling prior to becoming an action movie star casually suggested to Bobby he might want to consider bringing his wardrobe out of the mirrored-ball era, and Bobby, realizing the impact a more sophisticated sartorial approach could have on his cash flow, dropped twenty thousand at Barneys one Saturday afternoon trading in the disco look for Hugo Boss. So from the tips of his Brioni shoes to the knot of his Hermès tie, Bobby became Robert, who became the modern Hollywood package—sleek, tasteful, a human Lexus. Jolly, seeing the future, anointed the erstwhile Bobby his partner. It was Robert's idea to change the name of their company from De Meo Entertainment to Nada, and Jolly, whose ego, unlike others of his ilk, was not his largest body part, signed on to the adjustment after listening to Robert explain the self-abnegation concept.

Now Robert was more than a flesh peddler. He was a strategic thinker, a big-picture guy, a guy who read the *Wall Street Journal* and *Barron's* over his yogurt and fruit every morning before picking up

Variety and perusing the journalistic coverage of his latest triumph. But he still handled a few clients, guys with whom he'd started out, guys whose whiny, needy, chemically fueled calls he'd take at two in the morning to the consternation of his wife, Daryl, who would turn her back to him and grumble (but not audibly object because, after all, what was paying the mortgage on their 5.7-million-dollar Bel Air house with ocean and city views, not to mention the preschool tuition for the twins?) as he whispered comforting words into the receiver.

Frank has remained one of Robert's guys. They've known each other since the early eighties when Robert was a young agent hanging around with the comics, getting high in the parking lot of the Comedy Shop, Robert always lipping the joint, too Machiavellian to actually inhale. If most of those guys were to try to get him on the phone now, their calls would go unreturned, Robert playing exclusively in the big leagues these days. But for the chosen few, those whose talent had led to accomplishment, cultural approbation, and successful network shows, Robert was unswervingly loyal: cards at Christmas, congratulatory phone calls and big hugs sincerely bestowed. Frank, however, was not a traditional success story. How then to explain Robert's continued devotion?

To those with refined taste in comedy, a group in which Robert accurately claims membership, Frank is among the most talented of all the comics. That he has never been able to harness his ability in a way that translated into mainstream American success did not mitigate this gift. Yet, despite the failure (and *failure* is a relative term since Frank has been making a good living as a comic for most of his adult life; he's just never been a beloved star, a starry star, a star who gets his own series), Robert continues to believe in him. And when, after nearly twenty years of working together it has become apparent Frank might never achieve the level of stardom comedy savants believe he is worthy of, Robert stays with him out of a sense of mission, a core belief that Frank deserves the highest level of comedy prominence. A colleague with a fancier education once told him that van Gogh had never sold a painting in his lifetime and Herman Melville died in obscurity. Robert holds to this knowledge in his dealings with Frank because, although it is about the money with virtually all of his other clients, he truly believes Frank Bones is an artist in the true sense of the word and it is a privilege to represent him.

The receptionist, a stylish black woman whose wardrobe suggests an income separate from the pittance Nada is paying her, looks up from a picture of some It Girl she's been studying in *US* magazine and says, "Robert's ready for you," everyone in show business on a first-name basis.

Frank rises, a little quickly, and feels light-headed for a moment. He steadies himself in his black Capezio jazz shoes and walks through the double doors leading into Nada's inner sanctum; he strides down the center aisle of the Nada office past the assistants' desks that line either side. These youthful strivers are accustomed to celebrities and only one or two of the younger females even look up and smile as he passes by. Frank chooses not to read the indifference of the others to mean this-guy's-barely-B-list-why-should-I-bother since no one is B-list in his own mind.

So with the purposefulness of a Golden Globe nominee on the red carpet in front of a phalanx of rabid international paparazzi, Frank struts past the human widgets tending their phones and faxes and resentments.

At the end of the corridor is Jolly's corner office, which he has held on to as one of the perks due him, given his role as founding father. The door is open, and as Frank glides past, he sees the old schmingler and bingler leaning back in his chair, belly bursting through the top of his sweat suit and cantilevered over his lap, rictus grin bisecting his graying beard, an Italian rabbi drawing on a long cigar, crooning smoky blandishments into the phone.

Jolly sees Frank and gives a distracted half wave before returning to his conversation. Frank interprets Jolly's immobility, his failure to hoist himself out of his seat and embark on the pilgrimage across the office for the ceremonial hug, to mean he must be talking to an entertainment figure of celestial status and can't possibly interrupt their conversation. The reality is Jolly tolerates Frank mainly because Robert likes him, but lately the comic is not enough of an earner to get Jolly to press the hold button.

Making a right at Jolly's, Frank heads down another hall, glancing in other offices as he does. Men and women, fashionable, polished; *how corporate this world has become*, he's thinking. Then at the end of the hall, the end of the line, the place where the real power lies, Jolly's corner office notwithstanding, the lair of Robert Hyler.

Frank walks past the assistant's desk, temporarily abandoned, and steps into Robert's doorway. His eyes do a quick pan of the office: muted tones of off-white and taupe, large handcrafted maple desk sitting atop a capacious Oriental rug, matching credenza and bookshelf, a wall lined with framed posters of the myriad movies produced by Nada, among them *Dad's a Dog, Johnny Casino*, and *Peer Gynt,* a property Robert got the studio to pony up for as a reward for his client, who wanted to direct it, reprising his starring role in the sequel to the action blockbuster *Lethally Dangerous*. Robert sits behind the desk, his small body swallowed in the vastness of his baggy linen suit, running manicured fingers through tightly curled hair as he barks into the phone.

"That he was the best man at my wedding is not relevant. If the guy is suing me for a hundred million, I have no choice but to countersue." Robert puts up a finger indicating it'll just be a minute.

Tessa, Robert's willowy English assistant, who appears to have wafted in from a Laura Ashley catalog, is at the door, smiling at Frank.

"Can I get you something to drink?"

"I'll have a mai tai." She laughs reflexively. Frank pleased, the laughter of a beautiful woman so lovely, so exquisite, so often a prelude to acts illegal in the state of Kentucky. As her features relax, Frank says, "Black coffee, please."

She disappears, trailing the barely discernible scent of Pear's soap.

"I dunno," Robert is saying. "The same amount, right? A hundred million?"

Frank looks up at the framed photograph of Robert with Bill Clinton on the wall behind his desk; remembers Robert stayed in the Lincoln Bedroom when that was news; wonders how many rooms in the Clinton Library Robert financed.

"File the papers then," Robert says, and hangs up. He turns to Frank.

"Bobby," Frank greets him, never having bought into the Robert concept. "What was that about?"

"Barry Bitterman, can you believe it, is suing me for a hundred million dollars."

Barry Bitterman is a comedian whose immense wealth, accumulated in a series of deals orchestrated by the fulminating Robert, has recently landed him on the cover of *Fortune*.

"Why?"

What Frank really wants to ask is how a bowl of oatmeal like Barry Bitterman managed to get his own television show, much less ride it for five years into the Valhalla of syndication and a nuclear bank account, but "Why?" is all that comes out.

"Because he is suffering from the delusion he helped . . . no . . . strike that . . . that he was instrumental . . . his word . . . *instrumental* in building Nada Entertainment into a powerhouse, never mind that Jolly was doing pretty well before this place became Nada. Okay, he fattened the coffers, but he's claiming he was the magnet that drew other talent here as if Jolly's forty years in the business and my own small contributions had nothing to do with it. Anyway, fuck the guy. We're going to bleed him so badly when this is over, he'll be three inches tall and living under a toadstool."

Robert takes a breath and switches from dark wizard to good fairy as Tessa floats in, places a cup of black coffee in front of Frank, and wordlessly departs. "How're you doing?"

"I'm good."

"How's Honey?" Robert asks, bracing himself for the ritual.

"The only thing worse than living with an actress who's working is living with one who's not working." A line Frank's used enough times to

14

retire but it's too early in the day for him to be generating reliable new material.

"It's tough out there."

"All she booked last year was some direct-to-video thing." The direct-to-video thing is a movie called *Hot Ninja Bounty Hunters* and it features Frank's girlfriend in several full frontal nude scenes that found their way to the Internet, where they have been among the most downloaded images of the previous several years. As a result she has catapulted to cult-figure status within a certain segment of the home-entertainment-consuming public.

Frank has been living with Honey for nearly five years. A sloe-eyed bottle blonde with legs from here to San Bernardino, she has been trying to make the leap from the cheapie action market to more legitimate fare, with discouraging results. That she is turning thirty soon does not contribute to sanguinity regarding her career path, and the tensions recently arising on the domestic front, when not caused by Frank's perceived infidelities, are often traceable to time's brutal march.

"I would think she could build on *Hot Ninja*, but what do I know?" Robert disingenuously offers, knowing plenty. He and Frank have an understanding. Frank doesn't ask Robert to help Honey, and Robert doesn't point out that, from what he's heard, Lassie was a better actress. "She's lucky she hooked up with you."

"She's got a lot of talent. The town doesn't appreciate her."

"But they do appreciate Frank Bones."

This artful segue moves Frank out of banter mode and into the mode where he is riveted to Robert's words as if by a soldering iron, all without changing expression.

"Oh, yeah?"

"I talked to Harvey Gornish at the Lynx Network this morning. The boss, okay? He wants to give you a show." Robert watches for Frank's reaction, expects to see his entire life played out in the subtle shifting of facial planes; the striving, the sure things that became near misses, the struggles, the envy wrought by the ascent of those, like Barry Bitterman, perceived to be less talented, the thoughts of quitting but to do what? And now . . . cool water on hot skin, pie and coffee in the stomach of a hungry man, sweet, sweet fulfillment. But Frank remains impassive. He's been there. Expectation management.

"What's the premise?" Chilly.

"You're a dad. You've got a wife, two kids, and you live in the suburbs of Minneapolis."

"Me?"

"You like it?"

"Bobby, I'm not a dad, I'm the fuckin' Antichrist!"

"What do you think?"

"It's too early in the day. Is this a joke?"

"Yes."

"Funny."

"Okay, okay. They want to do a show that's going to cut through all the crap that's on, breakthrough television."

"They said that? 'Breakthrough television'?"

"Pam Penner said that, the head of development at Lynx, who loves you, by the way."

"She's gay, isn't she?"

"So?"

"So she doesn't love-love me."

"To get you to sign, she might."

"We'll see about that."

"Do you want to hear it?"

"And the premise is . . . ?"

"You're an Eskimo."

"An Eskimo?"

"Kind of a hip Eskimo."

The pain starts behind his eyes, a dark beast stretching thick muscles, heaving awake, still sleepy. Then it moves slowly, lumbering, one giant foot, then the next, across the constricted tissue, until it lurches into the

16

ocular nerve. Frank closes his eyes hard and rubs his temples roughly with the tips of his index and middle fingers, inhaling deeply through his nose. Unexpectedly, the beast retreats, glowering, awaiting further provocation.

"Are you fuckin' kidding me?"

"They're very high on this concept."

"Or they're just fuckin' high. They want me to play an Eskimo? Can the Bones have a little dignity?" Frank occasionally refers to himself in the third person, particularly when trying to objectively discuss his career. Now he's warming up. "Would that be possible? Could I retain an ink stain of self-esteem? Are you telling me I finally get my personal shot on TV and I'm going to be dressed in animal skins bangin' a polar bear?"

Robert sits there, impassive, letting Frank vent.

"Why don't I play a priest?" he continues. "That'd make as much sense. I mean, who thought this was a good idea?"

"So I should tell them no?"

"I am not gonna play an Eskimo."

Now a Vesuvius of smoldering frustration, Frank gazes out the window, his brain lava boiling. Only by exercising the most exquisite self-control is he able to keep from erupting and rendering the tasteful Nada offices a latter-day Pompeii. It's the perceived disrespect that is unbearable. He wonders, *do they think I'm a clown?*

Tentatively, Robert looks up at Frank, assessing his mood. His violent dissatisfaction is, to be fair, justified. Unfortunately, this is the best offer Frank has had in a long time. In the parlance of his blinkered world, Frank has become a road monkey, a wandering practitioner of the comedy arts making his bread and butter in places like Gigglemeister's and the Snicker Shack, places that fizzed up like carbonation in a glass of happy-hour Budweiser across the American landscape in the early Reagan era.

The problem with this career path in the fresh century is that comedy is over. Not over per se, but the boom of the eighties, when someone dubbed comedy "the new rock," has ground to a halt, killed by the proliferation of cable television shows featuring a brick wall and a microphone and the sheer number of bad comedians in the clubs. Guys like Frank can still get bookings in most of the larger cities, but there just isn't the general interest anymore in comedy, its mainstream moment having passed, and what remains is a young man's game. Frank is in his late forties now, looked upon by his contemporaries with a weird combination of admiration and pity; admiration for having stayed true to his vision and pity for the exact same reason.

And why stay true to a vision? goes the reasoning of the successful television stars Frank came up with back east; guys with whom Frank used to split cab fare between Catch A Rising Star and the Improv so they could do several sets in one night, and now live in designer homes in the Hollywood Hills where they pretend to miss New York. Who needs a vision?

What the American public wants in a comedian is a toothy smile and a nice haircut. Cuddly. Bereft of genitalia. The rules are different for black comics, but Frank could not, alas, trace his ancestry back to Africa. So "vision," well, that is not necessarily a good thing.

Frank, however, is encumbered with a vision. He has a worldview, and it is, needless to say, dark. Simply: people are evil. Straightforward. Hobbesian. Not that Frank had read Hobbes during his stint at a state college in Texas where he had briefly enrolled, but that makes it no less so. If he were to elaborate, he would say people are also greedy, slothful, meretricious, covetous, lustful, violent, and dumb, but evil pretty much covers the waterfront. Frank's point of view regarding humanity makes him a direct lineal descendant of a cadre of bomb-throwers stretching from Juvenal to Ben Jonson to Lenny Bruce, but in the world of network television, Lotto Pick 6 to Frank and his peers, these names carry no weight.

Frank is proud of his vision; it gives him an identity, something to cling to as others, to whom he perceives himself superior in the talent department, outpace him in the race for public approbation and the pornographic amounts of money that now accompany it. Yet, despite this, Frank is consumed by envy. Actually, he is not just consumed by envy; he has been chewed, devoured, and excreted by it.

He once suspected if he toned his persona down, greater success might come. Along these lines, when starring in his own HBO special, he had allowed Robert to talk him into wearing a red, crew-necked sweater and losing the sunglasses he always wears so the audience could see his eyes and the network executives could see his potential to headline a series. But he had never felt so ridiculous and, when the hoped-for series didn't materialize, vowed he would on no account ever again do something so inexcusably lame. If his misanthropic outlook was going to get in the way of his success, then, fuck it, he'd rather be true to his philosophical school.

That was seven years ago and Frank's career has been stuck in an increasingly disturbing neutral. In his view, the sun should already have set on the era of cold pizza in Cincinnati after two shows at the local Comedy Casbah. Escape from the Island of Touring Comics, where all one could look forward to were an endless series of one-nighters, life as a renter, and no health insurance, came in a single form—a successful television series. Frank has hewed to the man he knew himself to be. It has paid off. An offer is on the table.

But they want him to play an Eskimo.

"Will you at least take the meeting?" Robert asks.

"Can we sell them something else?"

"They're taking pitch meetings year-round. We can do whatever we want."

"Then let's make it about me."

Frank savors that thought a moment, the notion that he, Frank Bones, is a sought-after performer; a performer a television network would allow, no, *encourage* to create a vehicle for himself; a show to let him finally claim his rightful place in the pantheon.

Robert bursts in on Frank's reverie by saying, "You mean like the *Fleishman* thing?"

The *Fleishman* thing to which Robert is referring is *The Fleishman*

Show, which starred the popular comedian Charlie Fleishman (toothy, nonthreatening, bereft of genitalia). It is a show about a fictitious version of the real Charlie Fleishman (a meta-Fleishman, if you will), a suburban dad with an attractive wife, two rascally kids, and a well-remunerated job in television, and it has recently finished an extremely successful seven years on the front page of the zeitgeist. Although Frank could admit Charlie Fleishman was not entirely lacking in talent, he in no way considered him to be in his own class. Fleishman's extraordinary success was the bête-est of bêtes noires for Frank, who took it as confirmation of his worst suspicions about the Velveeta-like taste of the American public. So to compare what Frank is suggesting to anything having to do with Charlie Fleishman is unwise.

"No, not like the *Fleishman* thing," Frank virtually explodes. "Why is it like that? I don't live in the burbs. I don't have kids. Bobby, you're comparing Picasso to a guy who paints on velvet!"

"I'm not saying you're like Charlie," Robert says, backpedaling quickly. "I'm just saying he's a comic, you're a comic, certain people might see some overlap." As Frank masticates on this, Robert leans back in his leather chair. Inhales slowly through his nostrils. *How do I put this? How do I tell this man, this friend, this potential multiyear meal ticket, the likelihood of an American television network finding sponsors for a show about the life of a middle-aged, perpetually high, beak-nosed comic in dark glasses who has had significant legal trouble is, not to put too fine a point on it, nil?*

Robert's answer to himself is *I don't.*

He knows the Law of Capitalist Entropy, whereby virtually nothing happens unless someone with a far larger bank account than yours wants it to, will combine with Frank's inherent sloth to produce the desired result.

"We can absolutely pitch a show about you," Robert says to Frank, coddling, massaging, misleading, knowing people hear what they want. "Let's just give it a slightly different spin."

"Don't worry about the spin. No one's going to confuse me with Fleishman."

"You're absolutely right," Robert declares, and he's not lying.

Frank is so delighted when he leaves the meeting he doesn't even wait until the parking valet brings his tan '87 Cadillac with the chipped paint before lighting up a joint.

Chapter 2

"Take the swatches with you, Lloyd."

The speaker is Stacy Melnick, running out the front door of a house in Mar Vista, a middle-class neighborhood in west Los Angeles. Her husband, Lloyd, is backing his new Saab out of the driveway, cursing to himself and hitting the brakes as he sees Stacy, wearing blue nylon sweatpants, a tight maroon Lycra top that clings to her small but well-formed breasts, and a pair of Adidas cross-trainers, descend on the car brandishing a handful of fabric samples over her head like a soldier waving a flag on the battlefield.

Their four-year-old son appears in the doorway, a tousled-headed moppet dressed in SpongeBob underpants and a red cape he wore last Halloween. "I'm hungry," he announces, ignoring Lloyd's imminent departure. "When's lunch?"

"Honey, you had breakfast an hour ago," Stacy reminds him. "Now go inside and put some clothes on. Mommy'll be back in a minute." Lloyd waves at his son, who ignores him and heads indoors.

It is a cool November morning, and the soft light, diffused through the palm trees lining their street, is flattering to Stacy. Waxed and buffed, she is an agreeable-looking woman. In Des Moines she would inspire epic poetry, but this being Los Angeles, world capital of female pulchritude, pleasant is what she rates. She has been successful at postponing middle-age droop, but the sexual thoughts Lloyd often found himself having about his wife have recently been trumped by a desire not to be in her presence. Oddly, for a man who had been married ten years, he masturbates to images of his spouse; it is actually having sex with her that he no longer finds appealing.

Lloyd Melnick met Stacy Schiff on a rainy, black-and-white evening in New York City after having overcome his congenital shyness and striking up a conversation with her at the P & G Bar on West Seventy-third Street, where she was waiting for a female colleague. He told her he had just come from the birthday party of a friend who'd recently joined AA. In the Big Book tradition, everyone had had too much coffee, no one could stop talking, and the whole thing had made him so nervous he had to go out for a drink, which made her laugh, and explained his presence in the bar. She told him she'd been a dietitian but had recently switched careers and now was a junior account executive at a public relations agency working on launching a new Swedish vodka called Strindberg. He told her all vodkas were the same. She offered to buy one for him at the bar and give him a taste test. He accepted, drank a Stoli and a Strindberg, couldn't tell the difference, but found himself drunkenly falling for this girl when she confessed that she couldn't tell the difference either and touched his hand when she said it. When Stacy realized she recognized his name from *Vanity Fair,* to which he had contributed a few short pieces, she was already selecting china patterns.

On their third date, driving from Manhattan to Coney Island in Lloyd's battered Toyota, she performed fellatio on him in the front seat as they rolled across the Brooklyn Bridge. Stacy hadn't wanted to go to Coney Island. Dancing at some swanky nightclub would have been far preferable, but she was thirty, unmarried, and Lloyd had all his limbs, no visible sores, and a highly developed sense of humor, all qualities she found attractive. If she had to suffer through a few excursions to godforsaken places like Coney Island as the price of standing in front of her family with a clergyman and Lloyd Melnick, then she would grit her caps and persevere.

What Lloyd did not realize at the time, or willfully did not acknowledge, her proclivity for autoborne blow jobs aside, was the degree to which Stacy hewed to convention, the beaten path, the middle of the middle of the road. This woman was the easy-listening format personified. Stacy preferred American movies to foreign ones, swimming pools to the ocean, and she'd never wear sandals if she hadn't had a pedicure in the last week. Lloyd's view of himself was more avant-garde, but every time he stared at her ass encased in tight jeans, he became weak in the knees, so he overlooked the obvious and proposed.

Taking Lloyd's measure and mistakenly sensing a tabula rasa on which she could paint her own picture, Stacy also overlooked the obvious and accepted. He might not be a big success right now, she reflected, but Lloyd was amusing, personable, and industrious—a good horse on which to bet—and they were married a year after their first date. Having vowed to keep working after the nuptials, the newly minted Mrs. Melnick faxed her resignation from the Bermuda Hilton on the third day of the honeymoon so she could devote herself full-time to her new husband's temporal advancement. That his temporal advancement continued in a holding pattern led her to beg for her job back six months later. Yet despite Lloyd's less than rapid progress, she continued to believe in his talent.

They'd had a fissureless, vanilla marriage, but when Lloyd, at Stacy's urging, made the transition from struggling freelance journalist to Hollywood comedy hack and then, through a series of fortuitous circumstances, to successful Hollywood comedy hack, Stacy took the opportunity to transform from a New Jersey–bred dietitian/junior PR executive with Formica aspirations into a Wife of an Important Guy who was going to live in a veined-marble world. Never mind Lloyd didn't see himself that way, his Bronx-bred self-loathing not allowing for personal aggrandizement. To Stacy, he was Important, she was his wife, and they needed to send out certain signals as a couple. Her chosen mode of transportation in Los Angeles was a Chevrolet Suburban, a cross between an SUV and a tank, and she ranged over the city, ear glued to a cell phone, inspiring fear in everyone not driving a military transport vehicle, as she craftily plotted their ascent. She insisted they give large amounts of money to the pet charities of people with whom she aspired to socialize: Heal the Bay, Families in Crisis, Kids Need Art, etc., were among the myriad organizations receiving generous contributions from the ever-expanding coffers of Mr. and Mrs. Lloyd Melnick.

When Lloyd began making serious television money, Stacy decreed they must live in a stately pleasure dome commensurate with their new fiscal circumstances. To this end, she has recently purchased a lot in Brentwood, where they are erecting a Mediterranean villa. All of this makes Lloyd vaguely nauseous. But only vaguely because he cannot pinpoint the cause of the disconnectedness he is feeling, the sense of not actually being Lloyd Melnick but, rather, playing the part, since no one, save for some Marxist spoilsport, could judge the accoutrements of his life, the pretty wife and attractive son, the big SUV and the soon-to-be-built mansion, to be anything less than jake. Oh, he'd wanted a family, but these other things, things that seemed to multiply and become more things in front of his eyes as larger amounts of money came in the door, aren't what he'd aspired to. He feels guilty for liking them, something he is perversely pleased with since it lets him know the old Lloyd's heart is ticking in there somewhere, but still, how can he not melt into life in a tub of butter? It is almost as if he is suffering from a form of survivor's guilt. What has he done to deserve his good fortune? Not terribly much, in his mind. Lately, he finds himself ruminating on the phrase *an embarrassment of riches*, never before having fully realized what it meant: the anxiety of affluence.

Lloyd hasn't stopped viewing himself as a journalist, even though the last time his name appeared in print was almost ten years ago. He stays current culturally and politically, subscribing to the *New Republic,* the *New Yorker, Harper's,* the *Atlantic Monthly,* and the online rags *Slate* and *Salon.* He can hold his own at any local gathering of the intellectually inclined. But he is troubled by the notion that he has abandoned the road of real life at the last rest stop. He senses something slightly ludicrous about his position. Then he wonders if the feeling that something is ludicrous is actually what is ludicrous. Truly, what haunts Lloyd is the fear he is far more conventional than he wants to admit, that he has entirely evolved out of his previous incarnation as a man to whom the bangles and baubles that now surround him meant nothing and morphed into someone who is going to live in Brentwood and have to feign being tortured about it.

Every time Stacy drags him to the construction site and he beholds the rising skeleton of an edifice more befitting a minor prince in the Saxe-Coburg-Gotha line than Lloyd Melnick, late of the Bronx, he wonders why his existence, seemingly so perfect, feels so out of control.

Lloyd had set out to become an artist and has instead become rich. His ambivalence regarding this condition sparks inchoate feelings of confusion manifesting themselves in an absence of interest in sex with his wife, whom he blames for his loss of the platonic ideal of himself.

His lone act of rebellion is his wardrobe or, rather, lack thereof, since it consists entirely of baggy khakis, T-shirts, and sweatshirts, all of which exist in varying states of degradation. In his one concession to fashion, however, Lloyd always wears the latest Nike high-top basketball shoes to remind himself he used to play before he tore his ACL in a game at the Hollywood YMCA and ended his athletic career.

Lloyd, dressed today in an ensemble that appears to have spent the previous two years in a desert sandstorm, accepts the fabric samples—red paisleys, yellow velvets, blue linens, a carnival of colors and textures—from Stacy. She kisses him good-bye, quickly, unsexually, on the proffered cheek.

He fakes a smile and backs his car into the road. Briefly considers heading to the 10 freeway and driving east to the desert, to a motel where he could plan his descent into Mexico and eventual disappearance. But Frank Bones has called him, and not having spoken to the man in years, Lloyd is curious what he wants. So, postponing the abandonment of a lifetime's worth of obligations, he points his car north and heads for Sunset Boulevard.

Lloyd sits at one of the long Formica (the very material his wife was attempting to rise above!) tables in Duke's Coffee Shop on Sunset, a few doors down from the Whiskey, nursing his third cup of decaf, wondering if Frank is going to show. Frank was habitually on Stevie Wonder time, Lloyd recalls, and it was not unusual to wait over an hour after the agreed-upon moment for him to arrive at a confab. They had known each other years ago in New York but hadn't communicated since Frank had moved to Los Angeles, Frank not being one to send Christmas cards and Lloyd being preoccupied with Stacy and then the kid.

Back in New York, Lloyd had been a writer for the *SoHo Weekly News,* a so-called alternative paper featuring leftist politics and elitist arts coverage, read by the members of the south of Fourteenth Street cognoscenti for whom the *Village Voice* was too mainstream. He had been doing a piece on young comedians (this was back when there was cultural significance in the topic), and having seen Frank do fifteen inspired minutes one summer night at an East Side club riffing Charlie Parker–like on the contents of a woman's purse he had purloined from an audience member, Lloyd realized Frank was the most talented drop in the new wave. But more than that, Frank was so masterful, audacious, charming, and funny onstage that by the time he said *Thanks, you've been a great crowd. Please remember to tip your waitress,* Lloyd was smitten in a heterosexual way. So after writing the traditional "10 to Watch" piece about the freshest prop comics, guys with guitars and mannish women, Lloyd approached Frank about doing a Boswell for an upscale glossy, Frank being the Dr. Johnson in the equation.

Mostly, Lloyd wanted an excuse to hang out with him. Frank, needless to say, craved the media validation Lloyd promised, and the two of them spent a series of afternoons and evenings together walking and talking, a pair of flâneurs drifting through the teeming metropolis.

Lloyd envied Frank the life he embodied. Lloyd would have liked to have been able to climb on a stage at a time and place not of his own choosing and make a group of strangers laugh (Frank's definition of a comedian, which Lloyd had duly quoted in his article—*GQ,* January 1987), but he lacked the gene that prevented utter terror at the prospect. Instead, he watched with fascination and then awe as Frank walked the

27

tightrope each night at the showcase clubs, departing from his act at any provocation, searching for laughs in topics as diverse as the role of Torquemada's eating habits during the Spanish Inquisition (his alleged taste for gefilte fish creating suspicion on the part of his henchmen) or the proclivity of UFOs to appear in the American South ("Why do they always land where IQs are below shoe sizes?"), usually connecting them in a mad rush of cascading thought that tumbled from his brain in seemingly random patterns—Torquemada's culinary intake leading to the paucity of UFO sightings in medieval Spain, leading to the cuisine served on alien spacecraft, leading to the presumed taste for grits and ham hocks on the part of UFO occupants (Did the spacecraft have fuzzy dice hanging from the rearview mirror?), leading to their regular visits to the American South, leading to the unpopularity of the pope in Alabama, leading, finally, back to Torquemada—a thrilling, vertiginous ride for a nightclub audience that had been listening to other comics riff on airplane food or the difference between New York and California.

What most impressed Lloyd about Frank's act, this ability to spontaneously detonate in front of a roomful of civilians and rain shards of merriment everywhere, was its demonstration of Frank's ability to exist, no—thrive!—entirely in the present. Frank didn't reflect, and *plan* was not a verb with which he was familiar. He was simply a forward-moving object, a jet-propelled, no-prisoners comedy machine indifferent to whatever detritus, human or otherwise, wound up in the slipstream. Lloyd, on the other hand, was so conscious of his own internal machinations it was as if he went through life with a personal heckler, a guy who sits in the third row of his cerebral cortex saying things like *That didn't really just come out of your mouth, did it?*

Frank told Lloyd about the detective novel he was writing featuring a character not-so-loosely based on himself, the band he was going to hire to back him during his act (he did impressive impressions of popular singers), and how his father, Norman Bronsky, a shoe-store owner given to bouts of depression, had came home from work one day, drunk a glass of milk, gone down to the basement of their home in a Houston suburb, and blown his brains out. This last nugget, parceled out judiciously by Frank and known to few people, emerged one day in Frank's Second Avenue apartment after a particularly long pull on a large bong. Frank trusted Lloyd and asked him not to mention what he had told him in whatever article he was going to write and was pleased that Lloyd complied.

When Lloyd first met Frank, Lloyd had been out of college a few years and was living with a melancholy, out-of-work actress in a basement apartment on East Sixty-fourth Street so noisy he had to take the telephone into the hall to tell the bill collectors the check was in the mail. The actress, whose name was Sonia Hopewell, would spend entire days in bed reading *Vogue* and eating Tiger's Milk carob bars, unable to face waiting tables and open casting calls where she would be forced to audition with four hundred other ingénues who had seen the same ad in *Backstage*. She would rouse herself from her torpor long enough to engage in titanic battles with Lloyd, occasionally threatening to kill herself before retreating back to her magazines, candy bars, and pervasive sense of woe. Lloyd's idea of a satisfying relationship was something else entirely, and had he not been in her erotic thrall (the sex after their fights was incredible), it would not have lasted the two years it did.

He told Frank about Sonia and her bleak moods; used it to connect with him, really, since he thought his girlfriend might be clinically depressed and could end up doing what Frank's father had done. Frank advised Lloyd to jettison her and, when Lloyd hinted he had nowhere to go if he bailed, generously offered his own stained couch as a temporary refuge. The desire to bond with Frank was as strong as his need to leave Sonia, so shortly after Frank threw him the lifeline, Lloyd moved out while she was at an audition for a student film (his escape planned so he would not have to face her wrath in person) and spent a week in Frank's living room before finding his own place in deepest Brooklyn. They weren't friends exactly, their cohabitation being mostly a matter of the exigencies of Lloyd's domestic situation, so Frank more or less ignored the young journalist while he was his houseguest. Lloyd didn't mind, proximity to the Bones being its own reward at that point.

Lloyd checks his watch and again looks at the door. He's beginning to wonder if Frank is going to show. Slightly sick after three cups of decaf, he ponders the distance he's traveled since his New York days. That he finds himself at the age of forty-two as a writer of situation comedies in Los Angeles is a source of no little dismay. Lloyd has spent the last seven years working on *The Fleishman Show,* which was spawned and run by the cranky misanthrope Phil Sheldon, with all of its scripts masterfully composed by the same Phil Sheldon. The job of the overpaid writing staff essentially consisted of coming to work, eating lunch, avoiding Phil Sheldon, and going home. Lloyd had had virtually nothing to do with the triumph of the endeavor.

This did not stop other television studios, desperate to re-create the otherworldly success of *The Fleishman Show* and not understanding it was sui generis, from throwing piles of money at *Fleishman Show* writers, whose primary, often sole, qualification was having been in a room with Phil Sheldon. Lloyd Melnick is one of those people, like Rockefeller or Onassis offspring, a possessor of undeserved wealth. What is he doing fingering swatches of plush fabric for a quintet of sofas, for it is five they are buying, that will cost more than his father, the comptroller of a medical supplies company in Queens, has ever made in a year? How did he go from being a penurious print hack to well-remunerated television one?

Lloyd had been eking out a living as a freelance writer in New York when he noticed his thirty-third birthday approaching with alarming speed. The thirty-third year had always held a mystical aspect for Lloyd. He'd long been aware that Jesus, Alexander the Great, and John Belushi all prematurely perished at thirty-three, and these were men who led lives of remarkable achievement. Whenever Lloyd thought about his own modest accomplishments, he was often overcome by feelings of deep inadequacy. He'd had the first chapter of an autobiographical novel in the desk drawer of his apartment for several years at that point, but never seemed to find the time to write the second chapter, much less finish the book. Like virtually everyone of his generation with literary aspirations, he'd written a screenplay, a romantic comedy about an actress and a playwright that stole so extensively from Woody Allen, three of the people he showed it to told him he would be sued in the unlikely event it was produced.

Stacy, to whom he'd been married for two years at this point, was encouraging him to get a job as an advertising copywriter. She had been working as a junior account executive at a downtown PR agency whose loftlike office seemed a beacon of cool capitalism, and she thought Lloyd might thrive in a similar environment. Lloyd, however, wanted no part of the advertising business, believing it to be the graveyard of literary ambition. Then one cold winter night he was invited to a party at Neil Levin's studio apartment on West Eighty-sixth Street.

Lloyd played basketball with Neil Levin every Tuesday night in the tiny gym at PS 6 on the East Side. A comedy writer who had spent a couple of years in Los Angeles, Neil had decided to leave that city after the riots in '92. Currently making peanuts directing a series of shorts for a children's show on PBS, he told Lloyd there was much money to be made writing sitcoms in L.A., if one could stand living there, Neil taking the point of view that civilization collapsed west of Hoboken, New Jersey. Also participating in this conversation was Neil's friend Phil Sheldon, a stand-up comic who had starred in one of the shorts Neil had directed. Phil didn't care particularly for either New York or Los Angeles. He was pretty much miserable wherever he was. But that said, he was about to fly to L.A. to finish work on a pilot he had written and produced, and it seemed as if he was going to emerge from the experience relatively unscathed. "It's all a shiny penny," Phil said. "A very shiny penny."

Phil told Lloyd to call him if he came to L.A.

Emboldened by his discussion with Neil and Phil, Lloyd told Stacy he wanted to move. Her agency was opening an L.A. office at the time, and

31

they were happy to transfer her out there. Three months after the party at Neil Levin's, the Melnicks were ensconced in a Spanish-style courtyard apartment in the Fairfax district surrounded by a jumble of hipsters and Hasidim, who would mingle on the sidewalks turning the sunbaked avenues of Lloyd and Stacy's new neighborhood into an MTV shtetl.

Lloyd didn't feel comfortable calling Phil Sheldon, selling himself in such a personal way not being his strong suit, so he found himself writing a spec script for a show called *Friends,* which had debuted that year. Easily capturing the pseudo-hip urban banter that made that show so phenomenally popular, Lloyd took less than a week, and the first agent he sent it to, Irv Drossman, an old-timer whose name he got from a Writers Guild directory, was only too happy to sign him. Irv got Lloyd an entry-level gig as a writer on a sitcom starring an obese comedienne with the personality of a scorpion, and by the time he was fired six weeks later for not pulling his weight in the writers' room (a comedy abattoir, to be sure), he'd found the confidence to call Phil, whose project, now known as *The Fleishman Show,* had been picked up. Phil loathed talking to agents, which was the way most show-runners usually found writers, so Lloyd's timing could not have been more propitious. He came in to meet with Phil, they talked about the New York Knicks for an hour, and he was asked to join the staff the next day. Even Irv Drossman couldn't believe it.

From that moment, Lloyd's rise was so unimpeded, it was almost as if he were mocking those whose struggles were more Sisyphean. Lloyd knew this and tried to be sensitive to it. He developed a line of self-deprecation people found winning, always careful not to take credit for the success he'd experienced, ascribing it to a combination of luck and, well, luck.

It all seems rather silly to him as he contemplates Stacy's fabric samples. *If upmarket fabric samples have a consciousness,* he's thinking, *surely they would want to be with someone who deserves them more than I do.*

This is the very thought preoccupying him as the door to Duke's opens and Frank enters, trailed by a young man with short black hair, a soul patch, three earrings, and a video camera. The cameraman pans to

Lloyd, catching him waving back, and Lloyd thinks, *Is this a fan or does Frank have a personal videographer now, his life a perpetual bar mitzvah?*

Frank walks over to Lloyd, who rises, smiling.

"Babe!" the universal greeting, familiar yet distancing. Frank embraces Lloyd, who, temporarily forgetting their positions on the food chain have been reversed, feels flattered and embraces Frank.

"Bones!" Lloyd using the last name immediately, paradoxically more intimate than *Frank*.

"You look rich," Frank says, letting Lloyd know he's been following his northerly career trajectory.

"Yeah, I'm all right." Lloyd tries to ignore the camera recording their every twitch, uncomfortable performing.

"The guy with the lens pointed in your face is Otto Duhamel." Lloyd looks at Otto, nodding. Otto fails to acknowledge the introduction. "He's making a documentary. It's gonna be in Sundance," Frank hyperbolizes, unable to not blow smoke, referring to the snowbound Utah film festival where Hollywood agents outnumber pinecones. "You can sign a release later, Babe, 'cause you're in it."

That he's forty-five minutes late is never mentioned as Frank sits down and looks at the laminated menu, Lloyd following suit, returning to his decaf. Otto lowers himself into a chair, continuing to videotape them. While Lloyd pretends to read the waffle choices, he considers his relationship with Frank. They knew each other once, and as we have seen, there was a short interlude when Lloyd planted himself in Frank's living room. Lloyd would have liked to maintain contact, but once he'd moved into his own place and his article on Frank had been published, he found the Bones somewhat less available. So much less available, in fact, that it had occurred to Lloyd perhaps Frank had played him. Not in a malicious way, certainly. Not in a way meant to diminish Lloyd. Just in a way intended to maximize the benefit to Frank.

The false familiarity that is the lingua franca of the entertainment business would lead the casual observer who had watched them greet each other to believe Frank and Lloyd were two old pals with a genuine fondness for each other. The truth is, they have never been friends, just a couple of guys who knew each other during an earlier time in another city.

The aspiring celebrity whose job it is to serve them, black roots, pink lip gloss, and a rose tattoo on her neck, places a cup of coffee in front of Frank and takes their order, Otto getting it all on tape, including Frank's desultory flirtation. She leaves; Frank turns to Lloyd and asks, "How's Phil?" Frank and Phil Sheldon had started together back in New York, and whatever Frank thinks of toothy Charlie Fleishman, he respects Phil Sheldon, whose exacting standards are well-known to everyone in the comedy universe.

"All I know is when the show went into syndication, the mint in Washington had to print extra money so there'd be enough to pay him," Lloyd says, not wanting to get into a psychological exegesis of his former boss, a complicated man, going for the reductive response.

"So, what's it been, like, ten years?" Frank asks.

"Longer, I think. We had that one dinner after I moved out here . . ." Lloyd trails off, remembering the night he and Frank had met at a Japanese place up in the Hollywood Hills. The Melnicks had just moved to town and Frank was one of the only people Lloyd knew. At the dinner, during which Lloyd consumed copious quantities of raw fish and saki as he listened to Frank discourse on all things Bones, Frank told Lloyd he was going to do a set later that night at a club on Melrose. If Lloyd wanted to come, he should shadow him in his car. After splitting the bill, Lloyd climbed into the first of several Saabs he would own in Los Angeles and followed Frank, who lost him in traffic on Hollywood Boulevard. Lloyd was never sure whether Frank had done it on purpose (Frank was lighting a large joint as he climbed into his car), but Lloyd had his suspicions. They ran into each other a few times at the Comedy Shop in the ensuing years, but Frank was always about to go onstage or he had just come offstage; he was never in the state of mind necessary to focus on someone else, and Lloyd, being older than he was when he'd first met

Frank in New York, was considerably less comfortable in the role of acolyte.

"So now you're the king of comedy," Frank says, smiling. Lloyd's facial muscles reflexively demur, but Frank continues, "I saw the article in the trades."

The article to which Frank is referring appeared the previous week and read as follows:

Fleishman *Scribe Inks Multiyear Pact*
Fleishman Show *scribe Lloyd Melnick, a veteran writer-producer on the eponymous hit skein, has inked a multiyear deal with the Lynx Network. "We're very excited to have Lloyd aboard," said Lynx prexy Harvey Gornish. "His talent and vision will be a welcome addition to the Lynx family."*

    The three-year, 12-million-dollar pact calls for Melnick to create and executive-produce network comedy series. The deal was brokered by Josh Goetzman at CAA. Melnick is managed by Marty Lavin at Invisible Entertainment.

"It's good to be the king," Frank offers.

Lloyd, noticing deference in Frank's tone, something never apparent back in New York, says, "I'm just the dauphin."

"The dauphin. That's funny," Frank says, not laughing. "I like that. I'd laugh if I didn't hate the fuckin' French."

"How long has"—Lloyd angles his head, trying to indicate the camera, which is close enough to photograph his pores—"Otto been following you around?"

"About a month. His father works at Nada. I'm his independent-study project. When he's done, we're gonna sell it on the Internet."

"Cool," Lloyd says, wondering if Frank is going to bring up the reason for their meeting. At that moment Frank notices the book of fabric swatches and picks it up.

"What's this, babe? Calvin Klein's napkin line?"

"A little item I picked up in the gift shop at the Oscar Wilde Handkerchief Museum," Lloyd effortlessly keeping up with Frank, almost forgetting Otto and his video camera. "The piecework of Lord Alfred Douglas," now, waxing esoteric. "We're building a house so we're buying some furniture. My wife's channeling her inner gay man. You know, the whole outdated interior-decorating stereotype I'd never stoop to reference. The whole thing's a point of contention in our marriage."

"Marriage itself is a point of contention, babe," says the twice-married Frank.

"I could live in a refrigerator carton, but my wife"—here Lloyd shakes his head wearily in the universal male bid for sympathy—"she thinks she's Charles Foster Kane. We're building Xanadu in Brentwood. I want to get a dog just so I can name him Rosebud. She's out of control. Whenever I leave the house, I have to remember to ask for my balls back."

"She doesn't want to wrap everything in plastic? I'd cover my whole house in clear plastic if I could. It's condoms for furniture."

"Once a week you have the maid Windex the place."

"I can't understand how that went out of style. Who doesn't like furniture you can see yourself in?"

Lloyd looks at Frank as he riffs on furniture trends, notices his hair is flecked with gray. Frank's been at this a long time, he realizes.

"The only problem," Frank continues, "is if you like to lie around in your underwear. Then you can get stuck to the couch. You fall asleep, the doorbell rings, you get up to answer it and leave a patch of flesh on the Barcalounger." Then, turning to Otto's lens and leaning toward it: "On the Barcalounger, ladies and gentlemen!"

"I'd like to cover the whole goddamn house in plastic sheeting, then inflate it with helium and watch it float away," Lloyd remarks, a little surprised at the level of vitriol in his words.

"We build our own cages."

Lloyd has a horrifying moment when he remembers Otto is taping his every word, but relaxes when he remembers the likelihood of anyone actually seeing what he's shooting.

After a few more minutes of ruminating on marriage, escape, and plastic furniture covering Frank comes to the point as he Jackson Pollocks his eggs-over-easy with hot sauce.

"Lynx wants me to do a series."

"That's great," Lloyd says, figuratively whacking himself on the forehead, thinking, *That's the best I can do after pulling the Oscar Wilde Handkerchief Museum out of the ether?* Not noticing Frank's last sentence was a simple declarative and didn't need to be one-upped.

"And I'm thinking maybe you should write the pilot. That's where your deal is, isn't it?"

This was not Frank's rent-controlled Second Avenue apartment with a bong on the table and the future spread out before them like a buffet at the Trump Taj Mahal in Atlantic City, where earlier in his career he had opened for the seventh incarnation of the Beach Boys. This was Los Angeles and some very real expectations glittered, holiday lights on the desire tree.

"What's the idea?"

"It's about me."

"Lynx signed off on this?"

"No, they signed off on a show where I play an Eskimo." Lloyd laughs, not realizing it isn't a joke. "I'm not kidding. A fuckin' Eskimo. So you want to write it with me?"

"The Eskimo show?" Lloyd, confused now.

"No. What am I, fuckin' Nanook? Fuck the Eskimo show and the fuckin' arctic elk it rode in on. I'm not doing the fuckin' Eskimo show. We're"—Lloyd noting the use of the plural, as if he's already been enlisted in Frank's cause—"we're doing a show about the Bones, babe. It's a show about *M* fuckin' *E,* okay?" Lloyd nods in a way intended to convey that Frank should continue, not *I'm with you.*

"We're gonna get together, smoke a blunt . . ." Frank goes on in this vein and Lloyd politely listens, wondering how to handle the situation.

On the one hand, he respects Frank. He is as talented a nightclub act as exists at this time. On the other hand, he is Frank: a dark, brooding, junkie-looking guy who does not appear headed for success in a traditional American television context. "We'll pitch it together, then you can write it."

Lloyd is trying to nod thoughtfully as if he's weighing Frank's suggestion, wondering, *How do I get out of this?* when Frank asks "Have you ever met Honey?"

"Frank, I haven't seen you in almost ten years. I have to think about it." Not bothering to address the Honey issue.

"We all should go out." Frank ignores, or chooses not to get, the implication of Lloyd's remark.

They push through the rest of the meal discussing the Kennedy assassination, a current obsession of Frank's, and talk about meeting at the LAX Gun Club, where Frank claims to have persuaded the manager to allow him to test the veracity of the single-bullet theory with a mannequin he found in a Dumpster behind Neiman Marcus.

Chapter 3

Lloyd's Saab is stuck in traffic heading west on the 10 freeway. It's early evening on a Saturday, and the Santa Anas have blown the smog away, making the sunset less colorful without the usual chemical enhancement.

"We got those tickets four months ago," he says, clearly not thrilled.

"This is important," Stacy informs him, impatient with what she perceives to be his male obtuseness.

"So is Elvis Costello."

"Elvis Costello is going to come back to L.A."

Lloyd liked Elvis Costello very much, believing him to be an artist who had held fast to his integrity and still managed to be successful, although he probably wouldn't live in Brentwood. "I can't believe we're missing him for some charity event where we could discharge the whole obligation by just sending a check. Why did I sign off on this? Explain that to me. Why?"

"Are you serious?"

"Extremely."

"Because it's important for us to go to this kind of thing," she says in that drink-your-milk tone he loathes, "if you want people in the industry to think of you as more than a writer."

"Why do I have to be more than a writer? What's wrong with being a writer?"

"Lloyd, do you have to be stupid?"

"You know, that's a rhetorical flourish I just love. 'Lloyd, do you have to be stupid?' That gets me paying attention."

"I don't mean it." Looking over at him to make sure he's mollified before continuing. "You have this big new deal now where you're supposed to be producing, and you don't want people to think you're still some schmuck writer. I don't want to argue, okay? I'm gonna get mascara in my eye."

Stacy is applying makeup in the rearview mirror as Lloyd drives through the gloaming toward the home of Robert Hyler. It's a few days after Lloyd saw Frank, and Stacy, through her relentless networking, has arranged for them to have the privilege of writing a huge check at a fundraiser for Save Our Aching Planet, the pet charity of power spouse Daryl Hyler.

Stacy saw her chance to insinuate herself into the orbit of Daryl Hyler and become a power spouse under her tutelage when she learned a year earlier, while getting a seaweed wrap at the Burke Williams Day Spa with Marisa Pinsker, her friend from Mommy and Me, that Daryl and Robert sent their twins to the Tiny Tuna Pre-School in Santa Monica, universally acknowledged to be the first step on the path to either Harvard or the William Morris mailroom, depending on the proclivity of the child or, more to the point, the child's parents. Marisa had tried and failed to get her three-year-old in there, a fact Stacy correctly ascribed to her friend's lack of social connections. A flurry of phone calls and a few discreet donations later and Dustin Melnick, four years old, son of Stacy and Lloyd, was blindly leading the family on their charge up the social ladder by relinquishing his place in a local Montessori program and matriculating at Tiny Tuna.

Unfortunately for Stacy, the Tiny Tuna Pre-School was not in the migratory pattern of Daryl Hyler, who, being busy making the world a better place, always sent one of her two Salvadoran nannies to pick up the twins. Yet every day, Stacy was stationed on the sidewalk in front of the adobe building on Colorado Avenue that housed the tiny tunas, chatting with the other caregivers as she patiently waited for Daryl Hyler to appear.

Months had gone by with no sign of her until the previous week, while standing in front of the school in a gaggle of women who were discussing their kitchen renovations with a fervor you would more typically associate with medieval kabbalists parsing a particularly arcane passage in the *Zohar*, Stacy finally spotted her quarry.

Daryl Hyler was driving a pint-size electric car, a kipper can Stacy could crush into a tin pancake with her Suburban and not notice. Stacy's first thought was *How can a woman with all that money drive something that looks like it should be used to make toast?*

The other mothers, lost in the minutiae of tiles and trash compactors, didn't notice as Daryl, her tall and slender frame accentuated by a tailored pantsuit and topped with a helmet of straw-textured blond hair that looked as if it could stop bullets, got out of her four-wheeled appliance, cell phone jammed to her ear, and marched toward the school, a Prada battering ram.

"Tell the senator to blow me!" were the first words Stacy could discern. "If the plant gets built near that beach, I'm holding her personally responsible and she better not come to Los Angeles thinking she's going to raise a fuckin' dime for her next campaign." Daryl snapped the phone shut like an angry clam, saw a friend, another mother, not part of Stacy's group, and waved, calling, "Hi, hon. You coming Saturday night?" flipping the charm switch. The friend, wearing a too tight, midriff-exposing, black T-shirt and white cotton pants doing nothing to hide a turquoise thong, nodded, waved a manicured hand, and went back to her own cell phone conversation.

Wasting no time, Stacy approached.

"I love your car. It's so cute!"

Daryl looked at her, head tilted. Smiling, ingratiating, Stacy lifted her hand and indicated herself with her fingers. "Stacy Melnick. Dustin's mom."

"Are you Lloyd Melnick's wife?" Daryl thinking, *Forget the icing, who's the cake?*

"Yes." Recognition. That's good.

"Wasn't he on *The Fleishman Show*?" Stacy liking the specificity, a hit show powerful currency.

"All seven seasons."

"I loved *Fleishman*. My husband and I always watched." A direct hit!

"Lloyd enjoyed doing it." *And before you start thinking he's unemployed and pathetic, Daryl, let me point out,* "He just signed a new deal with Lynx."

"That's great." Totally uninterested, Daryl looked over Stacy's shoulder. The kids were about to be sprung.

Thinking she'd better breach the walls of the fort, Stacy charged ahead: "Lloyd signed this new deal, like I was saying, and we're looking for a charity to get involved with . . ."

And the change that came over Daryl was almost like one you'd see in a cartoon character, an animated figure whose physical transformation embodied her thought process. Suddenly, dollar signs were in her eyes as the tumblers clicked into place and the ding ding ding of a Las Vegas jackpot could be heard heralding a river of silver. Daryl cocked her head and grinned at her new best friend, her bosom pal, her Santa Monica soul sista.

"Really?"

"I know you do a lot of work for Save Our Aching Planet . . ."

"Yeah, I help them out." Falsely modest. Then, unable to contain her essential nature for more than a brief moment: "I break my ass for that organization, but it's all good."

"Well, it's really . . . you do really valuable things."

"I have to because, you know, if people like me don't get involved . . . they're raping the planet, these corporations. It's criminal and somebody has to tell them it's not acceptable." Now Daryl was on a roll, ignoring the point that many of these same corporations advertised their wares on shows her husband produced, thereby allowing her a platform from which to denounce their perfidy. "I can't get past the front page of the paper anymore without having a seizure! Robert hates it." Stacy thought, *I just met this woman and it's like I'm hosting a radio show and she's an irate caller.*

"We'll be sitting there at breakfast and I'll see something about a developer wanting to pave a wetland area and just go ballistic, but then I think, 'What else should I do with my life?' How many times a week can you get your legs waxed? That's a really cute sweater you're wearing. Fred Segal?" She reached past Stacy's ear and lifted the label from the back of the collar.

"It's a Donna Karan."

"Love her! She's given us a shitload of money. Love-love-love her! What did you say your name was? I know you're married to Lloyd."

"Stacy?" She said it with a question mark as if doubting her own identity.

"Why haven't we met before? You look familiar. Did you work at Endeavor?"

"No."

"You look like someone there. Do you have plans Saturday night?"

Stacy knew Lloyd had bought the Elvis Costello tickets from a broker a week before they went on sale, that he'd mentioned the show was this weekend every day for a month, but out popped, "No. I don't think so."

"We're having a little get-together at our house this Saturday. The governor's going to be there. Why don't you and Lloyd come?"

"We'd love to."

"Write down your address," she said, the woman very comfortable speaking in orders. "I'll have my assistant send you an invitation."

As Stacy fumbled in her purse for a pen and paper, Daryl surveyed the area with her guardtower gaze. "What kind of car do you drive?"

"A Sub . . ." And Stacy nearly blew the whole thing. But with the lightning quickness of a major league shortstop adjusting for a bad hop before it can rocket into the outfield, she grabbed her mistake (". . . urban." Gotcha!) in her well-oiled glove. "A subcompact."

"Good for you. But you have to"—not *should*, because that would imply choice, but *have to* because she was willing it—"get an electric. They're the best. I have three."

"We're going to," Stacy quickly replied, and thought this should end it for now. *It's exhausting talking to this woman. And yet, somehow exhilarating.* She scribbled her address on a soiled Post-it.

"Where's it parked?" Stacy was stricken with the fear that Daryl was going to ask to see the nonexistent subcompact.

"Around the corner," Stacy lied.

"Look at that thing," Daryl said contemptuously, pointing at Stacy's Detroit mastodon, formerly the pride of the Melnick fleet but soon to be consigned to the scrap heap, parked twenty feet away where it glowered at her like a prehistoric beast. Raising her voice slightly for the benefit of the anonymous malefactor with the temerity to buy it, Daryl demanded, "How can anyone with a brain in their head drive a car like this now? Don't they know what they're doing to the planet? I see one of those things and I just want to scream." Then, catching Stacy off guard, she turned to the mothers, now engrossed in the subject of window treatments, and gruffly inquired, "Who owns the Suburban?"

Stacy held her breath, praying no one would betray her and reveal the colossal automotive faux pas she had made.

At that moment, the gates of the Tiny Tuna Pre-School opened and humanity's hope for the future poured forth. No one was paying attention to Daryl's question as Stacy pressed the Melnick address into her hand and a sea of sticky faces surged onto the sidewalk.

"See you Saturday," Stacy said to Daryl as she scooped Dustin up and walked toward the corner.

"Where are we going, Mommy?" Dustin asked, reasonably enough, since he noticed their car was in the other direction.

"Mommy'll tell you later."

Lloyd is pulling the Saab up to the valet parking stand in front of the Hyler home for the Save Our Aching Planet event, Stacy turning to him.

"If anyone asks, we have an electric car," she says.

"Why?"

"Just say we do."

"I don't even want to be here. I'm not moving until you tell me why I'm supposed to prevaricate."

"Prevaricate?" It annoyed her when he used words she didn't know.

"Lie."

"Because I ordered one and if anyone asks—"

"What do you mean you ordered one?" he interrupts. Traditionally, all large purchases have been joint decisions in the Melnick marriage. This breach of protocol does not please Lloyd.

The parking valet is leaning into the window now, wondering why Lloyd's not getting out of the car. But he's not moving. He's staring at his wife. Tries one more time. "Stacy, what do you mean you ordered one? Without telling me?"

"We're getting involved in the environmental movement now." Waiting for that to sink in as he stares at her. "Lloyd, hello, the valet parking guy is waiting for us."

Fuming, he gets out of the Saab, hands the keys to the young Mexican who risked his life climbing into an oil drum to be driven north across the border so he could make $5.50 an hour parking cars, and follows his wife toward the house, a vast, recently built hacienda-style home, the architectural love child of Louis XIV and Cortés, Versailles by way of Taco Bell.

"Stacy!"

"Can we discuss this later?" Her heels concussive on the imported flagstone as she moves toward the huge oak front door. "And don't mention the Suburban."

"Why not?"

"Because they'll look at you like you're a freakin' war criminal."

The door is slightly ajar and Stacy pushes it open and enters, Lloyd right behind her still masticating over the surreptitious purchase of the electric car. What did that portend? A new streak of independence for Stacy? A further manifestation of her profligate spending habits (the Suburban being barely a year old)? A burgeoning social conscience, reaching blindly, like a baby bird, toward the newly esteemed source of solar power.

From the threshold of the Hyler hacienda Lloyd, dressed in his usual combination of aggressively untrendy cottons and Nike high-tops, surveys the spacious home and sees a gumbo of fashionable Hollywood producers, agents, lawyers, managers, and directors, with a sprinkling of celebrities known to favor progressive causes tossed in to flavor the broth. In one corner he sees überagent Yuri Klipstein, a man reported to make 150 phone calls a day, talking to a woman who has written a movie about a talking vagina. In another, a well-known hyperactive comedian/actor whose movies Lloyd finds grotesquely sentimental is conversing with an acerbic talk-radio personality. Standing at the sunken wet bar being handed two *mojitos* by the female bartender is a former starlet who parlayed a series of early-career nude scenes into marriage to a studio head and a home in the Malibu colony.

Lloyd is filled with the urge to turn around, go back to his car, and drive home. He thrusts his hands into the pockets of his frayed khakis and prepares to denounce the entire event quietly into Stacy's ear.

"Shrimp puff?"

An attractive aspiring actress in black pants, yellow coat, and white shirt holds a silver tray where shrimp puffs are arranged like colors on the palette of a tidy painter. Lloyd smiles and takes one, briefly considering how much simpler his life would be if this purveyor of hors d'oeuvres were his wife.

"Thank you," Lloyd says, attempting to smile but only managing a halfhearted showing of teeth. She's already looking for her next customer and moves on just as Lloyd is realizing the financial ramifications were his projected betrothal to Shrimp Girl to end unhappily.

Stacy, oblivious to Lloyd's libidinous ruminations, takes his hand and leads him into the room as if he were a shy llama at a child's animal-themed birthday party. She leans into his ear and puts her arm over his shoulder, pantomiming a devoted spouse.

"Can you believe who's here?"

"How long do we have to stay?"

"There are two studio heads, the guy who hosted the Grammy's last year, the star of a huge sitcom . . . this is totally major."

"I'm getting a headache."

At that moment, Daryl Hyler excuses herself from a conversation she's having with a director of television pilots—who has come to this event hoping to be seen by someone who will hire him to do a feature film—and fixes Lloyd and Stacy in her crosshairs. As she moves toward them, Lloyd has the image of her torso on the prow of a ship.

"Thanks for coming," Daryl says to Stacy, docking in front of them. Then, sticking her hand out to Lloyd: "I'm Daryl."

"Lloyd Melnick."

As he shakes her hand, Lloyd notices they are now the sole occupants of an imaginary tunnel from which all other human life has been banished. Stacy is a dim memory as Daryl bores her brown eyes into Lloyd like concrete pilings into a beach. "I am so glad you could come. I'm such a fan of *The Fleishman Show*."

"I wish I could say I had something to do with it."

"Hello! You wrote on it for seven seasons!" This from Stacy, whom Lloyd and Daryl ignore.

"And congratulations on the Lynx deal."

"Now I have to work for a living."

"You want to meet the governor?"

Lloyd looks over and sees the governor of California standing near the kitchen nibbling on a soy meatball as an earnest housewife in four-hundred-dollar calfskin loafers lectures him about offshore drilling.

"Maybe in a little while," Lloyd replies, teasing an errant piece of shrimp puff from his gum with his tongue.

"Robert," Daryl calls, beckoning her husband, who is deeply engaged in a conversation with his lawyer about the white-water-rafting expedition they are planning in Idaho with Tom Cruise. "Get over here and meet the Melnicks."

Robert dutifully excuses himself, wades through the assembled guests, and greets Lloyd and Stacy with an extended hand. "Thanks for coming. Has Daryl hit you up yet?" His attempt at jocularity is met with a swift punch in his arm from his wife, who clearly takes exception to this characterization of her fund-raising techniques.

"Not yet, but"—Lloyd pats his chest—"I've got my checkbook right here."

"Mine has skid marks," Robert remarks. Stacy laughs too loudly; then catches herself. Lloyd smiles, notes that it's probably not the first time he's used that line.

"Robert loves that I do all the work so he can make fun of it but still feel good about himself," Daryl says with a frankness Stacy finds both alarming and intoxicating. As for Lloyd, whatever lofty illusions he has spun about men like Robert, leaders of their communities, titans of industry, holding dominion over their spouses, come crashing to earth. Daryl to Robert, "But you love it, don't you?"

"I married Eleanor Roosevelt."

Lloyd's thinking *this guy has a whole act.*

"You didn't have to dress up," Robert adds, looking over Lloyd's homeless-man-at-Venice-Beach ensemble.

"It's his trademark," Stacy says, trying not to sound defensive and failing.

"Next time I'll wear the jodhpurs and riding boots," Lloyd assures his host. "By the way, I like your house. Is it all in the same area code?" Choosing to work benign rather than saying, "I didn't know whether to check into the Napoléon Suite or order a burrito," Daryl and Robert taking the area-code joke as a compliment, smiling.

"We like it" is all Robert can manage by way of response.

Daryl takes Stacy by the arm. "The headmaster of Horizon is here. Let me introduce you."

"Horizon?" Lloyd innocently inquires. "What's that?"

"Is he for real?" Daryl asks Stacy. Then, to Lloyd, "It's, like, the best progressive private school in Los Angeles. The twins are going there next year. Come on over and talk to him. Make a contribution, we'll write a letter for you . . . maybe you'll get lucky." She tugs Stacy by the arm and, as she's leading her away, turns to Robert, suggesting, "You two can talk about golf."

"Where do you belong?" Robert asks.

"What do you mean?"

"What club?"

"Club?"

"What am I, talking Chinese? What country club?"

"We don't. I'm not a golfer."

"Well, what good are you, then?"

Lloyd immediately notices Robert is afflicted with the need so common in those who deal with funny people in their professional lives but are not funny people themselves: the never-ending desire to be humorous, too. For someone like Lloyd, who has the gift, it is always slightly aggravating in a conversation when a person who is not amusing on a professional level stumbles off the clear path of simple communication and lurches into the thickets of comedy. *I don't tort with the lawyers. I don't quark it up with the astrophysicists. Why must these people try to make me laugh?* It always ends unhappily, with a pained, if polite, smile from the intended beneficiary, followed by the fervent wish that the entertainer manqué would please cease and desist. On top of everything else, Robert's riposte "What good are you then?" rather than injecting levity into the exchange, only managed to sound vaguely hostile. But Lloyd's so uncomfortable and this guy's trying to be his version of pleasant so, *let's keep it going,* Lloyd's thinking, *before I have to fend for myself in this catered hell.*

"Do I look like someone who could get past a membership committee?" he remarks, self-deprecation always the default setting.

"They look straight through the pants and right into the wallet," Robert says, clearly something he's thought about. "You like the Lakers?"

"Sure."

"Nada has courtside seats at Staples. I'll take you."

Amazing what the announcement of a lucrative deal in the trades will do for a former nonentity with a receding hairline, tattered clothes, and no previous social cachet.

"Did Frank talk to you?"

"I saw him last week." Lloyd deciding how to play it. He knows

Robert represents Frank, and wherever this is going, it's intended beneficiary is Robert's client.

"Did he tell you about the pilot Lynx wants him to do? The Eskimo thing?"

"He mentioned it."

"He's concerned it may not be the best vehicle for his talents. Have you read it?"

"No."

"Would you mind if I sent you a copy?"

"Yeah, sure. Send it."

"If you think it's any good, maybe you can come on as a show-runner."

"I'm developing my own stuff."

"What are you working on?"

"Nothing yet. I just got the deal."

"Okay, so if you're not busy with anything else right now, you can take a look at this for us." Lloyd gets the picture that he is an ankle and Robert a pit bull who has sunk his jaws into the flesh.

"Send it to me," Lloyd surrenders.

The loud clinking of a spoon against a wineglass cuts through the moneyed hum. Lloyd looks toward the source of the sound and sees Daryl Hyler standing on a chair, towering over the tanned and prosperous crowd.

"I want to welcome everybody to our home," she honks. "Robert didn't want to have this shindig here but I made him, so let's all thank Robert, too." All eyes turn toward Robert and Lloyd. There are some nervous laughs at Daryl's lack of guile (not to mention judgment) and a smattering of applause, Lloyd thinking, *The poor bastard's fuck-you rich and his wife still breaks his balls in public.*

Daryl goes on to make a speech about how important the environment is and how the oceans are garbage dumps and the ozone layer is the size of a G-string and everybody should write a big check because they are the leaders and need to set an example for the rest of the country. But what is strange to Lloyd is the way Stacy watches Daryl. It is clear she has a new hero. Stacy, who had never evinced an interest in anything that didn't involve the betterment of her own place in the world, nods with the earnestness of a Berkeley freshman at an antiwar demonstration as she gazes upon the solemn visage of Daryl Hyler, Lady Bountiful of Los Angeles, haranguing her guests. Lloyd rolls his eyes as subtly as possible and prepares to be separated from a large chunk of his checking account.

Not that he doesn't agree with everything Daryl is saying.

Certainly, pollution is bad and humans, as curators of the planet, need to take better care of it. But something about Daryl Hyler makes him want to trade in his Saab for a large SUV in which to drive to the job she is inspiring him to get as a distributor of toxic waste. From the way things look, this Goddess of Goodness has a new disciple in Stacy, and Lloyd, who understands fully the depths of his wife's superficiality (which has increased in direct proportion to the size of their tax return), notices another chink in the marriage.

Later, Daryl introduces them to the governor, who informs Lloyd he is a big fan of *The Fleishman Show*. Lloyd manages a smile but thanks to having consumed more iced tea than he'd intended finds himself in the nearest bathroom while Stacy nervously makes small talk with the state of California's top official. As he prepares to relieve himself, he notices a sign over the toilet bowl reading SAVE WATER PLEASE. USE AT LEAST THREE TIMES BEFORE FLUSHING. That is when he knows it is time to go.

On the way home that evening, heading south on the 405 freeway, as Stacy prattles on about her prospective life as a philanthropist, a Rage Against the Machine song comes on the radio, an industrial boogie of alienation and dislocation that so perfectly articulates what Lloyd is experiencing he cries out in recognition.

No, not really.

Sad to say, it doesn't come on the radio, the Rage Against the Machine song, and no crying out is done, at least not externally. That song's appearance would have been entirely too serendipitous, and what's on

51

the car radio only reflects the inner life of an individual when that individual is in a bad movie. Lloyd simply wishes it had roared from the speakers and believes himself entitled to just such an unexpectedly perfect moment, since his life seems devoid of them recently. The music that really fills the car comes from a Barbra Streisand CD his wife had purchased; yet another of her sins, which are becoming too myriad for Lloyd to enumerate.

"What were you and Robert talking about?" Stacy demands gently.

"He asked me to work on this show with Bones."

"And you're going to, right?"

"Why would I? I have my own stuff."

"Like what?"

Why was he being asked this so regularly today, he wonders, as if he needs to justify himself to anyone other than the people who were overpaying him at Lynx.

"Like I'm working on it and why should I do some piece of crap that Robert has?"

"Maybe because Robert wants you to and he can make a lot of things happen," Stacy says, looking at him in a way meant to convey finality.

Lloyd focuses on the traffic coming toward them and tries to form descriptions of the oncoming headlights: a perambulating pearl necklace, the eyes of nocturnal electric snakes, a starry parade. Finds his powers of description wanting, although he thinks *starry parade* shows promise in a 1930s MGM kind of way. Makes a mental note to get cracking on the metaphors, maybe start keeping a notebook. He no longer wants to write television. He must be taken more seriously, he thinks, by people he respects.

He glances at his wife, who has relaxed now that in her mind their argument has been settled. Her lips are moving as she quietly sings along to the CD. Then she stops and turns to him. "You don't want me to get involved in SOAP, do you?"

"You can do what you want," he says, noncommittal.

"You'd like me to spend my days driving Dustin around and having lunch with my friends and getting my legs waxed and my nails done, wouldn't you?"

"What makes you say that?" *Where is this coming from? Where is it going?*

"For one thing, I'll be easier for you to control if I lead that kind of life."

"Stacy . . ." Lloyd's confused now. He's formulating a response but nothing is coming.

"You're making a ton of money, honey, if you haven't noticed," she reminds him. "And if you think I'm just going to be the happy housewife, you're wrong. You heard Daryl. The planet's a mess. You're too wrapped up in your career to care, which I think is fine, actually. You're the breadwinner, you have to win the bread. So I'm going to do the caring for both of us. I hope you don't have a problem with it. Whatever we donate is tax-deductible, and you can feel like you're doing something for someone besides yourself."

Lloyd is too flummoxed to answer. So he just says, "Okay," and keeps driving.

The next day, Lloyd arrives home from a meeting with his lawyer to find a three-foot-tall, cellophane-wrapped gift basket dominating the kitchen table. It contains smoked salmon, cheeses, olives, muffins, cookies, and two expensive bottles of wine, a chardonnay and a Bordeaux. The note attached reads:

Dear Lloyd,
   It was a pleasure to meet you. Here's to Frank's show. Hope you'll spread some of the Melnick magic around our house!
   Best wishes, Robert Hyler

Lloyd is eating a chocolate macadamia-nut cookie and rereading the note when Stacy walks in and says, "Robert Hyler is one classy guy."

"Who doesn't like a gift basket?" Lloyd neutrally replies.

"Lloyd, I think you should do the show."

"I don't think so," he says, finishing the cookie. "And I don't want to talk about it again."

Stacy restrains herself from responding, Lloyd's massive increase in earning power having brought him significant respite on the grief-from-the-wife front. "How was your meeting?" she inquires casually, busying herself around the kitchen.

"Joel thinks I should start a production company." Joel Gruber is Lloyd's lawyer and automatically takes five percent of his income. For this substantial piece of change, he reviews Lloyd's contracts and provides him with access to anyone in the entertainment business.

Were he to want it.

Which he doesn't.

"You're going to be a mogul, Lloyd! Your own production company?"

"So don't worry about me, okay? I know what I'm doing."

Lloyd issues this proclamation with such self-confidence, Stacy has no doubt she has hitched her wagon to the correct star. Not that she ever did. She loves Lloyd, admires him, and sincerely believes this embryonic comedy god will zoom her directly toward the light.

Chapter 4

Honey Call is standing at the microwave wearing nothing but a silk camisole that stops several inches above her navel, the twin half-moons of her gravity-defying bottom bobbing lightly as she impatiently shifts her weight from side to side. A spaghetti strap bisects a tattoo of a dragon curled along her right shoulder.

Moving with a leonine grace developed during a brief early foray into the world of exotic dancing, Honey reaches into a pressed-wood cabinet to remove two plates. She pulls two servings of macaroni and cheese out of the microwave, places them on the dishware, and turns to face Frank, the paleness of his smack-daddy physique adorned with the briefest of blue bikini underwear, sitting on a kitchen chair reading the *Los Angeles Times*.

"Breakfast, baby."

Frank looks up from an article on the situation in the Middle East and sees Honey walking toward him bearing carbohydrates. Notices her pussy, shaved in the shape of a heart, Honey a great romantic.

"Is the coffee ready?"

"It's coming," she says, placing the yellow food in front of him and turning to the coffeemaker. A moment later, Frank is ingesting the necessary caffeine.

"Can we pray first, please?" Looking at him sweetly, she puts out her hands. Frank, smiling indulgently, *my little religious nut*, lightly takes her delicate fingers and looks at Honey's bowed head, the barely visible roots of her expensive dye job infinitesimally extruding. "Dear God, thank you for this food we are about to eat and all the blessings you have bestowed upon us, especially Frank's show. Amen." Smiling at Frank. "Now you can eat."

They'd had a particularly gymnastic fuck that morning, Honey reanimated by the prospect of Frank's show jump-starting her career and wanting to demonstrate her profound appreciation as acrobatically as possible.

The two of them eat in silence as Frank continues to read the newspaper. Honey runs through the coming day in her mind: morning yoga class followed by a manicure, then lunch with her friend Amber (a starlet currently appearing at the checkout counter of Tower Records), maybe an afternoon movie, and finally her once-a-week acting class where she is currently working on a scene from *Five Easy Pieces* with a twenty-four-year-old rental-car agent from Culver City who is trying to seduce her by promising unlimited access to a Ford Eclipse.

Honey fervently hopes, in the new life as a television star that surely awaits her, she is going to be hit on by a far higher class of sleazebag. It isn't that she has any intention of relinquishing her place at Frank's side, she just wants someone to laugh at her jokes, to pay her a better quality of attention, to support her hopes and dreams. For she thinks in phrases like that: *hopes and dreams*.

The utter banality of what Frank perceives to be her interior life is one of the reasons he avoids talking to Honey about anything other than himself. He would have preferred having dinner with Elisabeth Kübler-Ross or Margaret Mead and engaging in esoteric conversations about the five stages of a Samoan's coming of age, but ultimately his libido dictates his social arrangements, so his consort is chosen accordingly. And he treats Honey well. Frank gives her spangles and bangles and escorts her to expensive watering holes, where she happily nibbles steak tartare and sips fine wine, but to her increasing chagrin, all their conversational roads invariably lead to Frank and all their behavioral roads to the bedroom. Her talents there are protean, to be sure, but she is beginning to feel like the actuary who has been crunching numbers for endless days and now finds herself increasingly impatient for the gold watch and new meadows in which to gambol.

After five years of cohabitation in the rented West Hollywood bungalow with its small backyard pool, Honey is starting to show incipient signs of dissatisfaction. Recently, they'd had an argument about his habit of consistently returning home at four in the morning. He would explain it was part of his work, that the clubs stayed open late and he needed to hang out and be seen, but Honey made it clear she was tired of going to bed night after night bathed in the dim cathode rays of a talk-show host. Frank pretended to listen, but Honey, despite her limited intelligence, could sense he was humoring her.

Honey wants to develop her self, to evolve, to become, if not scintillating, then at least someone who is able to have a conversation about something other than Frank's position vis-à-vis the rest of the entertainment business. To that end, she is taking a course on twentieth-century painting at the Los Angeles County Museum of Art and, having overheard two women there discussing something they'd read in the *New York Review of Books*, decided she should join their ranks and so subscribed herself. But all of her self-improvement was having no effect on Frank, who, when it came to Honey, remained far more interested in getting high and having sex than in discussing abstract expressionism or the poetry of Philip Larkin.

Still, in her mind, being humored by Frank Bones was a far, far better thing than having, say, one of the wealthy Persian brothers who owned the rug emporium on La Brea pay her rapt attention. And why? Because Frank was famous. He may have been B-list but, dammit, he'd appeared on *Hollywood Squares*. And, no, he hadn't been the center square (that honor having been reserved for the sparkling Whoopi Goldberg), but he was on the top left and an awful lot of people had seen him.

Being Frank Bones's girlfriend elevated Honey Call to a level that eluded most of the hopefuls who annually washed into Los Angeles on a warm wave of misplaced optimism. It was a leg up, a shortcut to the bright lights she had yearned for while growing up on a sod farm in

Washington State, Honey having spent her childhood literally watching grass grow. Circumstances may have rendered her obscure prior to her association with Frank, but their romantic association served to illuminate the shifting shadows in which people like her usually dwell until the end of their days. She is an appendage on the arm of someone who has had an HBO special and the huge billboard on Sunset Boulevard that goes with it; no small accomplishment in a town where being an ex-wife of Rod Stewart's carries significant social weight. Perhaps it hasn't gone so well for Frank lately, maybe he'd been spending too much time working dives in towns like Lincoln, Nebraska, and Portland, Oregon; maybe he hasn't had the breakthrough role that will catapult him to the forefront of national consciousness. But now the elusive bauble of a network show twinkles on the horizon like an early-evening star, and Honey feels as if she can nearly reach out and pluck it from the sky.

She draws an almost palpable strength from the prospect, believing that her prayers have been answered. The Lynx offer to Frank is surely a testament to God's power.

Even if they want him to play an Eskimo.

"I read the script," she says, having noticed him turning the pages of the newspaper, indicating the search for a new article to read is on and a conversational opening exists.

"What script?" Not looking up, his eyes having already lit on something in the Metro section about a gang shooting in Pico Rivera.

"Kirkuk." This is the Eskimo project to which Lynx is attempting to get Frank to plight his troth.

"What'd you think?" Still not looking up.

"I want to play Borak."

Frank has known this moment has been coming from the instant he read the script and has been dreading it. The situation needs to be handled with great delicacy lest he find himself sharing the same fate that befell the Athenian men in *Lysistrata:* that is to say, a suspension of coitus until the political situation transmogrifies into something more convivial to the distaff side.

"Borak is the female lead," he reminds her in a tone intended to convey the inappropriateness of her ambition.

"I know."

"Then let me tell you, before this goes any further, I'm not doing *Kirkuk*," Frank volleys, hoping to yank this weed before it takes over his garden.

"You're not? I thought you were kidding when you said you weren't doing it. You *have* to do it." The fear in her voice is noticeable. To be this close to having a boyfriend who, with a little luck, could ride his show to the promised land of the A-list, which, needless to say, would accomplish untold things for both of them, and then have her dreams dashed by Frank's petulance is unbearable.

"I met with my friend Lloyd," Frank says, his definition of *friend* expanding in direct proportion to his self-interest, "and we're talking about doing a pilot together. So pack up the mukluks, babe. No one's playing an Eskimo." And with that, Frank turns his attention to the homicide rate in South Los Angeles.

Honey's thinking, *This is different. Things may not be as dark as I anticipated.*

"What's the pilot about?"

"The Bones."

"So there's a part for me, right? I mean, if it's about you, then I have to be in it since I'm your girlfriend."

"Yeah, sure, babe. There'll be something for you to do."

The dismissive tone. *Like what? Answering your fan mail?*

"Frank . . ." Plaintive.

"There will be something for you to do," he assures her, looking up from a headline reading HONOR STUDENT GUNNED DOWN and into her limpid pools of nascent vexation. "You feel like knockin' boots?" The sight of Honey's slightly erect nipples pushing against the sheer silk of her camisole is causing a patriotic stirring as Frank's red blood cells begin to salute the flag.

"I'm going to yoga." She gets up, places her coffee cup and empty bowl in the sink. "Oh, by the way, I scheduled the surgery for next

59

Wednesday. So don't make any plans for that day." Frank nods barely discernibly as Honey exits.

"Babe"—calling after her—"I want to go out with Lloyd Melnick and his wife in the next few days so let me know what night works for you."

Honey sticks her head back in the door. "Who?"

"Lloyd Melnick. The friend I just met with."

"Who is he?"

"A writer who's hotter than Satan's balls right now."

"Why do you want to go out to dinner with a writer?" As she says *writer* her voice curdles. Apparently, her subscription to the *New York Review of Books* is doing nothing to lessen the disdain the word *writer* engenders in certain precincts of Los Angeles.

"Melnick is someone everyone wants to be in business with, and I want to get into bed with him in a figurative way because a guy of his abilities working with a guy of my abilities could put me in the position to buy you a very big house."

Honey likes the sound of that. Suddenly she is slightly less dismissive of this Melnick person, whoever he is. And she can work on him to write a part for her.

"I'll buy something new to wear," she says, disappearing with an impish grin.

Frank selected Portmanteau, an elegant French restaurant on Melrose, because the owner owed him a favor and Frank knew he'd let him skate on the bill. He and Honey, who is wearing a clinging angora sweater (purchased for the purpose of making Lloyd want to have sex with her, a desire she is fervently praying will be channeled into his writing her a particularly juicy part), are waiting at a corner table when the Melnicks arrive, Frank on time for once in his life. When Lloyd shakes Honey's hand, he works hard to not visualize her in the latex bondage outfit she wore so well in *Hot Ninja Bounty Hunters* and fails utterly. Frank greets Stacy, whom he has never met, as if she were about to give him a suitcase filled with cash, and the women exchange uncomfortable smiles.

Lloyd and Stacy settle into the table, steeling themselves for the evening. The dinner had been a bone of contention, Stacy not wanting to go. Now, Lloyd is concerned that she enjoy herself.

Frank orders a bottle of Château Lafitte from the waiter, an actual French person, a young man with Gypsy features Lloyd notices Stacy looking at a little too intently. When the waiter departs, Frank says, "So . . . ," as if inviting someone, anyone, to step into the conversational breach.

"They still chasing after you for the Eskimo thing?" Lloyd says, knowing any question about Frank's career will lead to an answer guaranteed to fill up at least the next twenty minutes of the conversation.

Three bottles of Lafitte into the evening Honey is saying, "I was thinking about doing porn for about five minutes after I did the ninja thing because I got tons of calls, people loved that movie. It sold, like, millions of DVDs. I mean, I have fans up the yin-yang. It's so funny, you pretend-fuck some guy in a movie and everyone thinks you're, like, porn girl. And we're talking simulated, you know? It's not like I was really fucking him!"

Honey's voice has risen with her level of blood alcohol, and Stacy looks nervously around to see who might be listening. A couple two tables away, the man in a conservative suit, the woman in an elegant silk dress, have stopped in midconversation. As Honey continues, Stacy shrinks into her seat. Lloyd, meanwhile, is fighting an erection. "I wouldn't do anal or two-girl or gang-bang or even two-guy, and the producer said if I was going to limit myself with what I'd do, then I wasn't going to go that far in the business." She looks over at Frank and smiles, placing her hand on the back of his neck, massaging it with the tips of her fingers.

Lloyd is now looking over at Stacy, whose jaw has literally dropped open.

Honey, oblivious to the effect she is having, continues, "I got offers for foot fetish because I have really beautiful feet, but I thought that was kind of creepy, don't-go-there, right? But the girls who do it? They market their shoes on the Internet, okay? Guys pay an incredible amount of money for girls' shoes if they're into the girl."

"You could've had a hell of a mail order business, babe," Frank says, swirling his wine around in the glass, not looking at Honey, having heard this monologue before.

"Do you guys ever watch porn?" Honey asks.

Stacy's "No" does not entirely cover Lloyd's "Yes," although it is uttered at a slightly louder volume. Lloyd's drunkenness allows him to turn to his wife and say, "Remember the hotel in San Francisco . . ." But she won't even make eye contact, pretending instead to focus on the watercolor of a Provençal landscape on the stippled wall.

Frank's had it with Honey's rambling, the conversation having detoured too far from the subject of himself. Not even bothering with a segue, he turns to Lloyd and says, "I like the way a gun feels. Have you ever fired one?"

But Honey, who would ordinarily pull over to the shoulder and let the Frank Bones eighteen-wheeler roar past, is having none of it tonight. She turns to Lloyd and says, "So are you going to write me a good part?"

"Excuse me?" Lloyd is having trouble following the conversation at this point. He glances at Stacy, who is trying to steal a peek at Honey's feet, which are encased in a pair of simple black Manolo Blahnik stilettos.

"In the pilot you're doing with Frank."

"What pilot?" Lloyd trying to think through the Lafitte haze.

"*My Life and High Times,* babe," Frank reminds him.

"We haven't exactly . . ." Here Lloyd pauses to consider his words, not wanting to offend his host. "We're still talking about it."

"I'm going to be the girlfriend," Honey says with a big smile, sticking out her chest, which Lloyd notices is not as impressive as he'd fantasized. Not that it matters. He's been thinking about peeling the angora off for the last two hours.

"Yeah, babe. You're always the girlfriend," Frank asserts ambiguously. As Honey considers this, Frank turns to Lloyd. "Have you ever fired a gun?" he repeats, reestablishing control of the conversation, confident he can still reel Lloyd in.

Stacy pours herself another glass of wine.

"Write down your home address," Honey purrs to Lloyd, in a tone that implies a house call from Dionysus himself if he complies. "I want to send you a DVD of my movie." Lloyd hastily jots it down and hands it to her.

"Here's the new one. We're moving," he tells them.

"To?" This from Frank as he takes the scrap of paper from Honey and examines it.

"Brentwood," Stacy proudly says, thinking, *And you people are going to need a passport and* shots *to get into the neighborhood.*

"Four twenty-one Carmeliiiiina, Frank says lubriciously, drawing out the vowel.

"You have to have us over," Honey tells Stacy.

"How could you discuss our sex life like that? We don't even know those people."

Lloyd is at the wheel of his Saab and driving slowly since there is some doubt in his mind as to his ability to pass a sobriety test if he is pulled over. There was no chemistry between the couples at the dinner, and because she had not had a good time, Stacy is intent on punishing Lloyd.

"Would you loosen up, please? I was trying to enjoy myself, which I have to tell you is not the easiest thing when Doris Day is my date."

"That woman is disgusting!"

"Doris Day?"

"Ha ha, Lloyd. I expect better from you."

"Since when are you such a puritan? I thought she was pretty cool."

"Cool? You think *that* is cool? She's a professional slut. I want to take a shower when we get home."

"A golden shower?" Lloyd says as oleaginously as he can manage, attempting to leaven the moment with a joke both bad and tasteless. Stacy does not fail to rise to the bait.

"You're disgusting, too," she says, arms folded in front of her, sculpted

63

nails digging into cut biceps as she stares straight ahead. "Were you ever really friends with that guy?"

Lloyd takes a moment, the answer rather painful to say out loud since Frank is a man of undeniable talent, and talent is the one thing Lloyd genuinely respects. "No."

This seems to come as a great relief to Stacy, who takes time to breathe before unloading her next salvo. "And what was all that talk about guns? You'd think a guy who's been arrested on a gun charge would be a little more discreet."

"He invited me to go shooting with him."

"You're not going."

Three days later, Lloyd holds a Tec-9 pistol in his hand with all the comfort he would have exhibited wielding a sea cucumber. He and Frank are standing in the waiting area of the LAX Gun Club, a one-story stucco building on the outskirts of Los Angeles International Airport, accompanied by the department-store mannequin Frank pilfered from the Dumpster behind Neiman Marcus. Otto, wearing a T-shirt with a picture of Lenin on it, is taping them. The soft pop of muffled gunfire, no more threatening than firecrackers, can be heard in the background.

"We got Berettas, Colts, Smith & Wessons, too." This litany of firepower from the clerk, a young guy with a wispy goatee and an American-flag button on the lapel of his nylon jacket next to another one reading KILL, 'EM ALL. LET GOD SORT IT OUT.

"I like the Tec-9 myself," Frank says. "Good trigger action."

"Which one you want?" The clerk's getting a little impatient, trying to get back to *Soldier of Fortune*, the only magazine in America where you can hire a killer in the classifieds.

"Take the Tec-9," Frank advises. Lloyd, having no basis for comparison, is silent. He notices Otto pointing the lens at him and worries that if anyone ever sees this tape, Lloyd will look unmacho to the point of feminity.

"He'll take the Tec-9." Frank, helping out.

"Rockin' choice," the clerk says, happy to close the deal. Then looks at his watch, grabs a microphone, flips a switch, purring in a suddenly smooth baritone, "The range will now close for the next half hour. Please return all rental guns. Clear the range, please." To Frank, in nonbroadcast tones: "You got half an hour, dude."

Lloyd looks through the Plexiglas wall separating the waiting area from the gun range and sees a young, denim-wearing couple, two middle-aged guys with beer guts, an Asian housewife, and a black guy in a security-guard uniform start to pack up their firearms.

Frank and Lloyd, trailed by Otto, step into the range. There are fourteen booths, all now empty. Frank is holding the mannequin, a business-suit-clad male he has christened Stu, short for Stunt President. He turns to Lloyd and issues what is a conversation-stopper to the nonobsessive: "Are you interested in the Kennedy assassination?"

"Sure," Lloyd responds, in the identical tone Frank often uses when talking to Honey. *Why didn't someone shoot Oliver Stone?*

Frank is now walking into the range with Stu under his arm, looking around for a place to set him down.

"The Zapruder film is my screen saver," he tells Lloyd.

Lloyd takes that information, holds it at arm's length, hard light glinting off the serrated edge of the concept. The Zapruder film as a screen saver? Perverse beyond measure, yet brilliant. Lloyd's screen saver is a photograph of Yosemite National Park. In a moment of insight clear as a cold vodka shot, he realizes how trite and hackneyed his own choice is, how utterly boring and predictable, just the screen saver a middleaged guy whose wife fixated on kitchen countertops would be pleased with. He might as well have a litter of kittens or a sailboat flickering on his computer screen.

The Zapruder film as a screen saver reveals a mind inured to the ordinary psychological pain protracted exposure to grotesque violence normally induces, not to mention the pain caused by repeatedly witnessing the morbid public suffering of national icons. But it struck Lloyd as something challenging, exciting, provocative, very shock-the-monkey;

in short, something a true artist would do. He makes a mental note to develop a purer worldview of his own. And to lose the Yosemite picture when he gets home.

"Every time I boot up, Kennedy's head explodes," Frank casually offers, placing Stu the Stunt President twenty feet away from the booths, his back to Lloyd. Frank carefully arranges the mannequin's right arm so it appears to be waving. Now, walking toward the booths: "I want to put Stu in a Cadillac to get the full effect, but the service door of this place isn't big enough." Lloyd wonders why Jackie's not figuring into the fantasy, but then Frank says, "I'd use a Jackie mannequin, too, but it's no good if she's not crawling around the car."

"I can see how that wouldn't work for you," Lloyd assures him.

"Okay, first of all, bullet number one nails Kennedy as the motorcade is passing a forest of trees, which completely eliminates Oswald's ability to hit him from the Book Depository unless he's got X-ray vision, ladies and gentlemen. The third shot knocks Kennedy backwards and blows out the right side of his head, completely ruining his hair and throwing him back in his seat, which, if you're a rational person, tells you it came from the front. Oswald, remember, was behind him. Zapruder himself testified shots came from behind him on the grassy knoll, but, hey, he was only there right when it was fuckin' happening. What does he know?"

Frank goes on in this vein for another few minutes as Otto rolls tape. While Frank talks, he takes a joint from his pocket and lights it, drawing deeply and then using it as a baton while he conducts a symphony of conspiracy and paranoia: the New Orleans mob states a Sicilian brass theme, which joins a Latin melody being played by the anti-Castro Cubans, leading into the dissonant crescendo of Oswald-was-a-patsy and there was a second gunman back in Dealey Plaza. Finally, the resolution: the Warren Commission is all lies but the American public is too docile to know or care. Fade-out. Bow. Applause. "Having grown up in Texas, you understand, this is all very near and dear to me."

It's an impressive rant not without a certain internal logic, but Lloyd is snapped out of his role as passive listener by the loud bang of a gunshot. Frank is shooting Stu. He squeezes off three rounds in rapid succession, all hitting the dummy in the back. The sudden spasm of violence is shocking to Lloyd, but then, he thinks, *What did I expect? I'm in a gun range.*

Then Frank says, "Let's see you shoot."

Lloyd looks down at the Tec-9 in his hand, which suddenly feels heavy. Frank senses in Lloyd an ingrained sociocultural antipathy toward firearms.

"Babe, have you ever fired a gun?"

"A popgun."

"But never a real one?"

"I shot a BB gun at Camp Mackinack."

"What was that, a bunch of Jewish kids in a tepee? My parents didn't send me to camp. They wanted to abuse me twelve months a year. Okay, grip, point, shoot." Frank demonstrates, pulling the trigger again and sending another bullet into Stu, who takes it stoically.

"Remind me why we're doing this."

"I'm working on a bit about the assassination, and for me to be able to connect the dots between all the elements, I act everything out. You know . . . get a sense of how the players felt. One day I'm Kennedy, another day I'm Jackie; then I'm Governor Connally . . ."

Lloyd is aware he's being handed a key to Frank's inner world, a pass that will potentially provide a glimpse into what he is at that moment thinking of as the hidden poo poo platter of Frank's thought process. *I'm accessing the hidden poo poo platter with its selection of savory . . .* and then catches himself. Hidden poo poo platter is a ridiculous image, he's realizing. *Never, never say that aloud or no one will ever take you seriously*, Lloyd admonishes himself as he reenters the exchange.

"And today you're . . . ?"

"Babe, are you paying attention? I'm the second gunman. We're standing on the grassy knoll."

Lloyd looks around the tacky environs of the LAX Gun Club.

67

Through the Plexiglas he can see the clerk still reading *Soldier of Fortune*. Empty shells lie at their feet. Otto's camera seems close.

"Okay."

"Don't patronize me, babe."

"I'm not." The man very thin-skinned for someone who dishes it out the way he does. Lloyd is too busy revering Frank at this juncture to remotely consider patronizing him, but Frank, never able to see into anyone else for more than a moment, does not read the subtle signs.

"So why do you want me to shoot again?"

"Do you need your husband's permission?"

Lloyd can't abide having Frank think of him in a less than masculine light. So while he recognizes the emotion he is feeling, the youthful suffering the atavistic school-yard taunt calls forth, he can't control his response.

Violence must ensue.

Now.

Picking up the gun, Lloyd aims at Stu, closes his eyes, and squeezes the trigger. The bullet hits the back of the range, wide of the Stunt President by the wingspan of a pterodactyl.

"Lloyd, if you ever want to kill yourself, stick your head in the oven because I don't think a gun would work for you. Wanna try again?"

Lloyd's feeling his stomach dropping millimeter by millimeter as Frank looks at him. There's judging going on, Lloyd knows, and he is not looking good to the panel. They're holding up scores: 2, 2, 1. And the final judge holds his panel aloft: *Fag*.

Lloyd blinks, swallows. His mouth is dry. Aims the gun once more and squeezes another shot off with the same lame result.

"Here. Watch," Frank orders. Raising the gun, he aims, shoots, and Stu takes one in the back of the head. Turns to Otto, leans into the lens. "I killed the Stunt President." Otto as serene as a day at the beach behind that lens. In a final fusillade, Frank empties the remainder of the bullets in his gun, causing the mannequin's skull to shatter and his body to vibrate for a few moments before collapsing onto its polymer chest, where his torso rocks gently from side to side for a couple of moments before settling into the eternal stillness of mannequin death. Lloyd notices a disembodied plastic nose pointing to the ceiling.

"If Stu had been riding in the limo that day, the entire course of history might have been different," Frank's theorizing. "You see Stu's hair?"

Lloyd takes a look at the broken head and sees the thick plastic hair adorning the broken pieces.

"Stu has presidential hair. A bald man can't be elected president in this country. The French might elect a bald man, but Americans won't. If Roosevelt had been a bald man, he never would have been elected, we wouldn't have bailed England out in WWII because the Republicans were isolationist, and the Nazis would have taken over in London, which means no Beatles or Stones because they would have been considered degenerate by the German cultural commissars, you know, guys who thought Benny Goodman was depraved. Never mind the Beatles and Stones *were* degenerate. That's beside the point. The point is we have the Beatles and Stones because Roosevelt had hair. He didn't have good hair, it wasn't Kennedy hair, but it was hair. You see the connection? It's a sobering thought." Frank regards his gun, as if surprised to find himself holding it. Then, to Lloyd: "Are we done here or do you want to shoot some more?"

Lloyd, for his part, is still absorbing Frank's riff about hair and liberty. It's an impressive connection. Without realizing it, he reaches up and lightly touches his own thinning pate. "Is that a bit?"

"What?"

"The thing you did just now about presidential hair."

"Nah, it just came. I was looking at the pieces of Stu's head . . . Think I should do it onstage?"

"Yeah. It's good."

"Otto got it. I'll look at it later." Frank very laissez-faire when it comes to his act. "So you want to shoot some more?"

"I think I'm done for now," Lloyd says, thrilled at having not sustained a gunshot wound. He makes a silent vow to take shooting lessons and then ask Frank for a return engagement. For a reason Lloyd cannot entirely discern, it has become important that Frank perceive him as a good shot.

"So let's talk about the pilot," Frank says.

The three of them, Frank, Lloyd, and Otto, are standing in the shadow of the fifty-foot doughnut marking Randy's, a piece of Los Angeles kitsch visible from space and a short walk from the LAX Gun Range. Otto tapes Lloyd and Frank, who right now looks incredulous, holding his cruller in midair.

"Don't patronize me, babe." More of an edge than usual.

"I'm not patronizing you, Bones. The opposite, in fact."

"You don't want to do this?"

"I can't. This is what I've been saying."

"So what am I supposed to tell the people at Lynx? I called up Harvey Gornish myself and said you and I were gonna do this thing together, and he was so jazzed he forgot to kick his dog before he left for work. Now I have to go back to him and say, what, you're doing other stuff?" Frank shakes his head and looks into the distance. The late-afternoon traffic is starting to jam up on La Cienega. The belly of a large airplane appears above them silently gliding into LAX.

"I don't particularly even want to do TV right now. It's not that I don't want to do your thing."

"*Bones Alone.*"

"Whatever you're calling it. I signed this deal, which on the one hand is a really good thing since they have to pay me a lot of money but . . . remember back in New York, like a hundred years ago, you told me you were writing a detective novel?"

"I was?"

"That's what you told me."

"Maybe I was that week."

"I think I'd get a lot more satisfaction if I could do that than I could from doing some"—he was going to say "piece of shit" but he catches himself—"show for Lynx."

"Can't you be pretentious on your own time?"

"If you want, I'll help out on the one they're trying to get you to do. I'll come to the studio when you're shooting and I'll punch it up. But I don't want to write *Bones Alone* at this point in time, not that I don't have the utmost respect for the comedy stylings of Frank Bones." Realizing he has just offered an exit line, Lloyd decides to make his getaway. "I gotta go. My wife has her book club tonight and I'm babysitting." As Lloyd walks toward the Saab he actually has the thought that Frank could shoot him in the back. He turns and faces Frank, who is not looking at him.

"Call me if you want me to come to the studio for lunch."

"For *lunch*?" Incredulous. "Patronize me more, babe."

Lloyd turns around and walks away, feeling that, while he might not have an iota of Frank's true talent, he's the one with more currency in the business. Then he remembers what he thinks of the business. The doughnut repeats on him, leaving a sickly sweetness in his mouth. Like Lot's wife, Lloyd is unable to resist turning to look over his shoulder, and while he doesn't turn into a pillar of salt, he does notice Otto is taping him.

"Hey!" Frank says to the kid, whacking him on the arm and causing the lens to jiggle. "Who's this movie about, babe?" When Otto swings the camera back in his direction, Frank looks into the lens and says, "Fuck Lloyd Melnick."

Late that night, Lloyd sits slumped in a chair in his home office, his laptop open on the desk Stacy had purchased for him at Restoration Hardware when she felt his old, nondescript model was no longer worthy of his increasingly successful television endeavors. On the computer screen is a white Ford Bronco rolling slowly down the 405 freeway in Los Angeles with a phalanx of police cruisers in lugubrious pursuit. He watches, staring at the screen as the SUV goes down the same stretch of freeway again and again.

"Did Dustin go to bed okay?"

Stacy, wearing black tights and a clinging tank top, is standing at the door nibbling on a celery stick, a copy of *One Hundred Years of Solitude* under her well-defined arm.

"He watched *Finding Nemo*." Not looking up.

"Again?"

"Stacy, what do you want? It's not like he's interested in having a conversation with me. He kept asking when you were coming home."

She takes this in, not entirely unpleased. Dustin clearly prefers his mother to Lloyd, and although Stacy will not admit this to her husband, she finds the vote of confidence from their four-year-old affirming. It allows her to look at Lloyd with sympathetic indulgence.

"What are you doing?"

"I'm changing my screen saver."

"Oh, yeah? To what?"

"The O.J. freeway chase."

"Why would you want to watch that?" The disbelief in her voice exactly what he expects as she walks over to check it out.

"I got tired of Half Dome."

"So you want to look at O.J.? Lloyd, that's kind of weird."

"Bones has the Zapruder film as his screen saver."

"The what?"

This is one of those excruciating marital moments for Lloyd. He shrinks a little inside as he is forced to acknowledge he has spent the last ten years married to a woman who has no idea what the Zapruder film is. On the other hand, she *is* reading García Márquez, which suggests a degree of cerebral engagement not necessarily congruent with someone who has seven active credit cards. If Lloyd were more honest, he would realize that the aspects of Stacy he has grown to dislike are those he secretly worries are developing within him.

"It's a home movie taken by this private citizen who was in Dealey Plaza the day Kennedy got shot. It's pretty famous."

"Why would I want to know about that? It's sick, anyway, if that's his screen saver." Lloyd has no answer that won't spark a conflagration, so he remains silent. Stacy looks down at the screen where O.J.'s SUV rolls along the same strip of asphalt in a perpetual loop. She places a hand gently on his shoulder. "So how did the meeting go? Are you going to work on his show?" He had told her the shoot-em-up with Frank was a standard business lunch.

"No."

Stacy tightens her grip on Lloyd's shoulder without being aware of it.

"Even after Robert asked you?"

"I told you I'm going to pitch my own show and I don't want to do something with Frank that I know is going to crater before we begin."

"But Robert asked you to, Lloyd. That's a good thing. And his wife called today. She wants me to be on the fund-raising committee for Save Our Aching Planet."

"Are you going to do it?"

"It's not going to be so easy if her husband requests a little favor and you blow him off."

"Well, I'm gonna bail. I hope that doesn't interfere with your plans."

"Fine. Do whatever you want."

She turns around and walks out, leaving Lloyd to stare at the Ford Bronco, trapped in an endless circle beneath the Los Angeles sky. There's something about the Bronco chase that's not working for Lloyd. He knows the Zapruder screen saver is better.

Chapter 5

So the reason we have the White Album *and* Beggars Banquet *is because Franklin D. Roosevelt had hair.*

Frank is saying this to the crowd at the Comedy Shop on Sunset Boulevard the next evening. He has worked his stoned, gun-range riff from the previous day into the relatively coherent rant with which he is about to end his set.

Never mind FDR had to walk with an Erector set in his pants. Polio is not what matters to the voting public. What matters, what's important, what's meaningful to the American electorate is the man had hair. We'll elect a gimp but we don't trust the bald guy. The only time we ever elected a bald man president was Eisenhower, and he got elected because his opponent was what? ANOTHER BALD MAN! Never mind Eisenhower was the greatest American general of the twentieth century. If Adlai Stevenson had hair, Ike would have spent the fifties drinking martinis at the driving range. Because we're a deep people. We care about what's important, and let's face it, hair is important. Here's a thought: What if Jesus was bald? You know what that means? No more Christianity. The whole belief system would have been out the window before the Sermon on the Mount. Jesus would never have been booked to work the Mount if he were a bald man. He'd've been playing the lounge. The Mount was the main room. To work the Mount you needed hair. You think the apostles could have sold a religion to the world where the poster boy was a bald man? You know why you never see pictures of Muhammad? It's because he looked like Phil Silvers. The Muslims aren't stupid. All those pictures of Jesus on the cross and he's got extensions, right? That long, thick rock 'n' roll hair. It's a great image. But if Jesus were bald, it'd look like someone nailed Murray the Pickle Man up there. I could see back in Jerusalem if

74

Jesus was developing male-pattern baldness, Jonathan saying to him, "Uh, Jesus, babe, we're losing disciples to the Zoroastrians. The Essenes are outrecruiting us. Lord, maybe you oughta think about plugs. You wear a hat for a week, we establish the Kingdom of God on Earth, and everyone says, 'He looks good. Did he lose weight or something?'" Thanks, you've been a great crowd. Please remember to tip your waitress.

The set is vintage Bones. Offensive to sensitive palates, but to discerning ones, entertaining, illuminating, and, finally, to his colleagues, inspiring, Bones a comic's comic, the ultimate getter of what are known in the trade as band laughs. Tonight he kills the room. With the Jesus-gets-plugs material, the comedians in the back, a cadre notoriously penurious with their approval, are most appreciative; their amused exhalations of air causing the arms, folded tightly across their chests in a permanent pose of make-me-laugh, to shake slightly.

What had begun the previous afternoon as rumination about the plastic hair on the shattered head of a Neiman Marcus mannequin has emerged from its gunpowder-begrimed chrysalis to flex its gossamer wings and float delicately over the inebriated nightclub crowd, darting, swooping, and landing finally in Frank's set, a fresh and lovely brand-new three minutes of material. It is the best thing he's done in months and it makes him feel unambiguously good.

Frank is on his third lemon vodka at the bar in the back of the club. He's in the middle of a conversation about the sinking of the *Lusitania* with a young comedian who had gone to Harvard and was now working as a writer's assistant on a game show, when he is approached by a slender, young redhead in a tight black T-shirt with the Comedy Shop logo, the mask of Greek tragedy being spritzed by a seltzer bottle, emblazoned across the front. She's an aspiring famous person, a future nobody whose ripe sexuality will serve to open enough doors to keep her dreams alive long after a more realistic individual would abandon them; ladies and gentlemen, please welcome the new waitress, Candi Wyatt.

"Hi, I'm Candi."

"Frank Bones."

"I know. I spell it with an *i*."

"*Bones?*"

"Candi! I love your act." Getting right to the point.

"That's just the one the public sees. The private shows are better."

Frank notices Harvard Game Show looking her over, trying to decide whether to make a play. If Frank wants to accept the tribute, HGS needs to look elsewhere. Candi has no idea the young gagman was born.

"I just started last night. I can't believe how lucky I am to have this job."

"Serving overpriced drinks to cheap tourists who get drunk and forget to tip? It doesn't get better that that, does it?"

"As long as I can audition during the day." Incapable of a snappy comeback in this situation, Candi is trying to keep her heart palpitations, a thrumming caused by this new proximity to a semicelebrity, something she has scant experience with, from becoming obvious. "Anyway, I just wanted to say I thought you were really special." Another lead balloon. Not that it matters, her job not to be the funny one but the minx.

"Sam Schlegel," says Harvard Game Show to Candi, attempting to call attention to his fading presence. Candi and Frank both ignore him.

"My shrink lets me charge him a two-drink minimum. That's how special I am," Frank tells her. Sam Schlegel takes his Harvard degree and goes to refill his drink.

Candi smiles at Frank, not up to the sodden repartee, the *soi-disant* romantic-comedy crapola he reflexively launches into whenever a possible sexual conquest presents itself, but nonetheless thrilled to continue this conversation with a person she's seen on television. When Candi was fifteen, Frank's HBO special was the subject of a particularly animated school-cafeteria conversation with three of her drama club girlfriends; the nature of the debate: Would any of them ever have sex with a famous person? Frank was not traditionally handsome but he exuded a confident cool that worked to cancel out whatever was keeping him from a career as a male model, a quality that made it possible for theatrically inclined teenaged girls who had seen his act on HBO to discuss fucking him.

"I can't believe I just said that."

"What? That I'm special? Babe, you can call me special all night and then make me breakfast."

This volley leaves her literally without words other than "I'd better get back to work." She turns around and backs away from Frank a few steps before bumping into Debbie, a thirtyish waitress Frank slept with six months ago, who looks at him and shakes her head as if to say, I know you will once again bring shame upon your gender.

"Come out to the parking lot on your break," Frank says to Candi. "I've got some Thai stick that's burning a hole in my pocket."

The following morning, Honey is dressed in a hospital gown lying on a gurney near an elevator in Cedars-Sinai Medical Center. The tranquilizer she ingested fifteen minutes earlier is starting to take effect, and whatever trepidation she had been feeling over the imminent surgical enhancement of her breasts is beginning to ease into hazy anticipation. Honey has been a 34B since high school and is convinced her inability to ascend to the glittering heights of international stardom is directly tied to what she perceives to be the meagerness of her bust. That the mammary-centric view of female Hollywood success, whereby a woman's professional advancement correlates directly to the size of her breasts, is about fifty years out-of-date is entirely lost on her; for Honey's view of glamour has not evolved past images of smoky cocktail lounges and stiletto-heeled shoes. It is of little importance to a mind rooted in the fifties-era mountainous iconography of Jayne Mansfield that the last ten winners of the Oscar for Best Actress had breasts smaller than Arnold Schwarzenegger's. Never mind Honey was born in 1975 when Jane Fonda towered lithely over world cinema, a flat-chested goddess, idol to a nation of women who had incinerated their bras, rejecting en masse patriarchal notions of female beauty. Honey hasn't read the manifesto. She has specific retro notions of what works for her,

Honey Call, and a D cup is going to work. Hence the impending scalpel of Dr. Nasrut Singh.

An orderly, young and black, wearing headphones and quietly moving his shaved skull to an unheard beat, stands by the elevator door waiting for it to open.

Frank is next to the gurney reading that day's *Variety*. An article on page three announces his deal with Lynx, and he is not happy about its contents.

"I told Robert not to release this. They're saying I'm doing the Eskimo thing," he informs the woozy Honey.

"How long did Dr. Singh say I'd be under?"

"I specifically told him, I don't know how many times, I'm not taking any job where I have to wear an anorak."

"You don't remember?"

"What?"

"What Dr. Singh said?"

"About what?"

"How long I'm going be out?"

"I don't know. Let's remember to try to get extra Vicodin, okay? It's very important not to forget that."

"Okay." Honey's on the ledge, about to slip into sweet nothing. "Frank?"

"Hmm?"

"Am I pretty?"

"You're fantabulous, babe. Every day I ask myself how I got so lucky."

"Really? You do?"

"Straight up."

"And you think this is going to help me?"

"Maybe when you're in there you can get Dr. Singh to do a little eye work."

Honey is startled out of her reverie. Her body tenses as much as the drug she's taken will allow. She focuses on Frank's face, upside down from her perspective on her back.

"Eye work? What do you mean? Do I have crow's-feet?" The panic is palpable.

"I'm kidding. You're perfect. And in a couple of hours you're going to be perfect with bigger breasts," he tells her, his eyes on the article about his pilot.

The elevator door opens and the orderly steps to the gurney. "This is as far as you can go."

Frank, wondering if they'd let him go farther if he were more widely known, leans over and kisses Honey's glossed lips.

"You've got to love a woman who makes an effort to look good when she's going into surgery."

"You didn't smudge me, did you?"

"I don't think so."

"Are you going to be in the room when I get out?"

"With a bottle of Dom Pérignon. We'll have an unveiling."

The orderly wheels Honey into the elevator and Frank is already walking in the other direction before the doors have closed. Honey tries to look over her shoulder at him but her neck can't do the angle.

Frank climbs into his motley Caddy in the Cedars-Sinai parking structure, pays the attendant, and heads east to Fairfax, his thoughts far from Honey and her current medical adventure. Making a left onto Highland, he slips an early Springsteen CD into the player and cranks the volume. Frank truly loved the young Bruce, the Bruce who wrote of fast cars and highways and hot summer nights on the boardwalk. The later Bruce, the one so concerned with the plight of the voiceless in the heartland, the pain of AIDS sufferers, and the horror of 9/11, he had little use for, preferring to get his pleasure from pop and his reality from CNN. It wasn't that he didn't respect the older, more serious Bruce. But music for Frank was about sex, and it was difficult to get a hard-on when the guy was singing about a plane slamming into the World Trade Center.

Cranking the volume another notch as he turns onto Cahuenga and heads toward North Hollywood, Frank recalls the period when he was making enough money to hire a band to back him up. Although Frank viewed impressionists as being fairly low on the food chain (below guys who worked with guitars but above prop comics), his own not-so-latent desire for rock stardom led him, almost against his will at first, to introduce impressions of certain favorite rock stars into his act. He would do adept and crowd-pleasing renderings of the voices and mannerism of these singers and could certainly have serviced that part of his act a cappella, but his income had spiked so he hired his own band of mostly session musicians, whom he dubbed Killer Bones, and gave vent to his fantasies during a handful of gigs in New York and Los Angeles. The ability of Killer Bones to vamp like the Famous Flames while Frank did an impression of a thirteen-year-old James Brown chanting the haftarah at his bar mitzvah lived in the memory of those who saw it long past the few times it was performed. Everyone agreed Killer Bones had serious musical chops, chops to the point where they could credibly have backed up any number of actual singers, but Frank found the financial drain of paying real musicians ultimately wasn't worth the ego gratification he received capering in front of them, so he reluctantly returned to working with only a microphone and the harmonica he would use to do his Dylan-at-the-dentist bit.

Frank glides the Caddy into a space across the street from an old, Spanish-style, two-story apartment building on Ardmore. Crosses the street, not bothering to look around since there's no one he knows who could possibly see him in this neighborhood, and in a moment he's standing in the entryway pressing the button for apartment 2C. The buzzer squawks, granting him entrance, and a few seconds later the chipped green door of 2C swings open revealing Candi Wyatt in shorts and a University of Texas sweatshirt a few sizes too large. Frank sees a fat, hairy cat chasing another fat, hairy cat up and over a sofa.

"Hey, come in," Candi says, holding *An Actor Prepares* by Constantin Stanislavski, the binding uncracked since she purchased it forty-five minutes ago in a hasty attempt to suggest seriousness of purpose.

Frank enters, looking around the one-bedroom apartment, the décor early thrift shop, but he's not there to critique the interior design. A piece of diaphanous, red material hangs over the window filtering the late-autumn light and lending a hint of Tijuana bordello to the premises.

Candi had given him her phone number the previous evening in the parking lot of the Comedy Shop after he had feigned an interest in her embryonic career, and his trip to North Hollywood today is ostensibly to coach her for an audition she had managed to get for Charisma, a new feminine hygiene product.

"You want something to drink?"

"You have any beer?"

"I made margaritas."

"Very spring break in Baja."

"Never been to Baja but we used to go down to San Padre Island and get hammered for a week straight"—trying to convey she's a big girl, all grown-up as she walks into the kitchen, leaving Frank wondering, *What's with the loose sweatshirt?* "You're from Texas, too, aren't you?" she innocently inquires.

"Don't remind me. I moved to New York as soon as I had the money for a bus ticket." Frank not one of those cowboy-boot Texans who revels in his geographic origins, more *landsman* than cattleman, a Texas Jew who never bought into the whole long-necked-beer-drinking, rhinestone-wearing, football-loving, cheerleader-worshiping culture whose apotheosis is a large, air-conditioned home in a boiling suburb hewn from the harsh mesquite plains equipped with a big-screen television, three kids, and a God-fearing spouse who believes in active church membership and a generous defense budget. That was never his personal vision and he left the state before Austin emerged as a plausible alternative.

Candi's gone to the refrigerator and removed a pitcher of margaritas. She takes two empty Flintstone jam jars out of the cupboard and pours the drinks, Frank looking her over in the daylight for the first time, wondering if she's old enough to drink alcohol legally in the state of California. Not that it would make any difference in his plans.

Handing one of the makeshift glasses to him, Candi raises the other in a nervous toast: "Mud in your eye." She wishes she could have come up with something more original, but there it is.

"I like my drinks fruity during the day in case I forget to eat," Frank tells her, sipping the pale green liquid, thinking she must have poured half a bottle of tequila in there.

"Thanks for coming."

"You already thanked me."

"I know, I know. I'm a little nervous is all."

"I didn't have anything going on today." A short silence ensues during which Frank briefly flashes on Honey lying unconscious at Cedars-Sinai less than ten miles away while Candi hopes he will say something amusing. "You went to the University of Texas?" Not bothering.

"Graduated in June," she says, inadvertently answering Frank's unasked question regarding the legality of her beverage choice. "Packed my stuff in the Datsun and drove to L.A."

"And now you're working at the Comedy Shop fending off the unwanted advances of your new show business friends."

"Everybody's been real nice so far."

"Just wait. They're a backstabbing bunch of amoral jackals. And those are just the waitresses."

Laughing, Candi gestures they should sit on the couch, where the cats have taken up residence. She shoos them off and sits at one end, knees together and ankles crossed. Frank sits across from her in a yellow wing chair she'd found on the sidewalk in front of the building the day she moved in. It has a large stain on one of the arms.

"You like cats?" she asks.

"Love 'em," he lies, allergic.

"That's Andrew and the other one's Brian," she says by way of introduction.

"Human names. Love that." Frank is not a pet person and can't bear the anthropomorphic thought process implied in giving something as

82

disgusting as a cat a person's name. Yet he realizes expressing this opinion today will not be helpful.

"Thanks for coming over. It's my first audition and I'm really nervous. I know, I already said I was nervous, but this is, like, a big deal for me."

"Charisma makes me feel fresh all day," Candi's saying for perhaps the hundredth time as she sits on the worn sofa in her cramped living room beneath the unframed poster of *Sleepless in Seattle* she had picked up for ten dollars at the Rose Bowl flea market the previous Sunday. Frank has now moved from the wing chair to the couch, ostensibly to correct her posture by placing a hand in the small of her back as she delivers the line. One of the cats has disappeared but the other sits on the arm of the couch next to Candi and stares malevolently at Frank, who feels his sinuses closing as a result of the feline presence. Frank's looking at his watch. Honey has probably gone from a B cup to a D cup by now, and eventually his absence is going to be noticed.

"You've got it down," he says. "If I'm a chick, I am definitely going to be douching with Charisma after I see your commercial. I'm digging it so much I'm using it on days I don't need it. Guys are going to be buying it for their girlfriends because it'll bring them closer to you." Frank laying it on fairly creatively.

"You think so?"

"I'm ready to order a case and I don't even have a girlfriend." Honey, being wheeled into post-op as he's saying this, her new breasts bursting skyward beneath their bandages, awaiting his loving touch. "I wish I was a chick so I could use it."

She laughs, tossing her head back, and looks at Frank as the laugh trails off in an appreciative giggle.

"You're just like you are on TV."

Frank gazes into her eyes, knowing the meter's running. He kisses her gently on the lips.

"And you're beautiful."

"What a line."

"We can keep talking about Charisma if you want."

"No."

He kisses her again, and in a moment her tongue is probing the nether regions of his throat. They tear at each other's clothes and Candi, standing in front of a naked and tumescent Frank in matching teal bra and panties, which combining forces wouldn't cover a challah, quickly tosses cushions helter-skelter onto the hooked rug and unfurls the foldout bed. They fall upon it like a couple of drunks at Mardi Gras, and after a hurried course of cunnilingus with a side of fellatio, Frank is inside her, weighing whether the nearly ninety minutes spent giving Candi performance pointers was worth the effort. But her pneumatic enthusiasm, combined with sets of well-developed abs and glutes rendered even more efficient by daily hikes in the nearby hills, soon makes Frank banish conscious thought altogether and allows him to make sweet love to this avatar of youth and innocence with a fervor that causes him to forget he will one day die. That is, until he ejaculates, at which point conscious thought returns at Mach 5. Christ! Honey's probably out of surgery by now.

Candi is nestled into Frank's shoulder dreamily wondering which of the friends with whom she shared that long-ago high school cafeteria conversation she is going to call first. *Tonya, it's Candi. Guess whose face I just sat on? And I was fresh as a daisy down there because I used Charisma, a company I'm going to be working for thanks to my famous new boyfriend.*

She isn't really naïve enough to think that just because she'd had sex with Frank he'd be her boyfriend. But she ardently hopes that now that she had, she will at least occupy a more prominent place on his radar. And then there was the career-enhancement aspect of the whole endeavor. Candi Wyatt is feeling good. She's only been in Los Angeles a few months and already managed to have sex with someone who's been on TV.

Frank, the effect of the margaritas sweated out of his system by the recent exertions, is feeling parched and tense, the got-to-goes having arrived. Still lost in her youthful reverie, Candi goes to kiss his neck just as he sits up, causing inadvertent contact between male shoulder and female nose.

"Ooooww!"

"Oh, no. I'm sorry."

Frank sees plasma seeping from a nostril. Shit, he thinks, this is going to slow my exit. Candi, who put her hand to her face immediately upon contact, removes her fingers from her leaky proboscis and sees blood.

"I haven't bled after sex since I was a virgin." Smiling. "I'm young again." Making Frank laugh. He almost regrets he's about to shoot out of there.

"I gotta go, so let's get you fixed up." No explanation necessary. "Let me get you some tissue for that." Ever the gentleman.

Frank moves toward the bathroom, where, out of habit, he takes a quick peek in the medicine chest—birth control pills, Mylanta, nothing worth borrowing—before grabbing a handful of toilet paper and giving it to the naked girl, who is sitting on the foldout. She presses it to her face. The two of them pull their clothes on in silence. Frank, who is now wearing pants and shoes but hasn't put his shirt back on, wants to make a gesture that will reflect well upon him and augur encore performances. Unable to think of anything else to do, he folds up the folding bed. As soon as this is accomplished, they hear an agitated mewling emanating from an unseen place. Candi looks around the apartment, does a quick calculation, and realizes she is one cat short.

"Where's Brian?" Frank doesn't want to deal with this, thinking, *I just folded up the bed without being asked and now I have to help find the fuckin' cat?* But Candi is worried, and Frank wants a return engagement, a need that forces him to feign concern.

"Where could he be? Here, Brian . . ." Frank feels himself cringing as he says the embarrassing words, the master performer finding it hard to deliver those lines with anything approximating actual concern.

Candi's eyes dart around the room as the mewling becomes louder and more frantic. Then, realizing what's happened, she says, "Frank, he's in the bed. You folded him into the bed!"

The two of them simultaneously reach for the metal bar to pull open the unit. With a focused intensity that belies what was occurring on the same piece of furniture mere moments earlier, they yank the bar toward them, unwittingly causing the cat to shoot out of the unfolding mattress in a frenetic parabola of anxiety, propelling him directly onto Frank's shoulder, where his sharp claws make themselves at home in the soft skin.

"Fuck!"

Frank pries the hysterical beast off his back, resisting the urge to throw it out the window.

Laughing, her own burst nasal blood vessel now forgotten, Candi looks at Frank's torn flesh. It appears as if a spastic child has dragged the tines of a fork over his shoulder and down his flip side.

"Do you have any Bactine or something?"

In his horror and discomfort he had already forgotten he'd performed a Dun & Bradstreet on her medicine chest and no traditional tinctures would be forthcoming.

Thirty seconds later Candi is pouring tequila into a wad of toilet paper and pressing it against Frank's wounds. He winces in pain as her Cuervo says hello to his ripped hide.

"Is it still bleeding?"

"Just a little."

"Do you have an old towel I could borrow?"

"Frank, I'm really sorry."

"Just get me a towel." Done playing.

Frank spends the drive back to the hospital with a Wal-Mart towel pressed against his throbbing back thinking about how he's going to explain his wounds to Honey and wondering whether he can conceivably avoid appearing shirtless in front of her for the time it's going to take them to heal. He worries he's going to have a hard time elucidating how he'd been attacked by a wild animal while in the waiting area of the Seymour and Rivka Tublitz Pavilion at Cedars-Sinai, heretofore known primarily as a habitat of nervous family members, not feral beasts, for this was where he'd assured her he'd be during her procedure.

Such are the hazards of the wayward life. It won't be the first time he'll have made up a story.

Chapter 6

A toxic piecrust of pollution hovers above the San Fernando Valley as Lloyd drives over the crest of Coldwater Canyon toward his new office at the Lynx studios the next morning. The Saab is filled with the soothing tones of an NPR report about unspeakable violence in an unpronounce-able place, but it seems far, far away to him as he crosses Mulholland Drive and begins his descent from the apex of the gilded hills toward the hurly-burly of Ventura Boulevard and his new life as the target of every comedy writer in town.

Comedy writers are a notoriously vitriolic bunch of dyspeptic mal-contents who often build lucrative careers channeling noxious emotions into the socially acceptable outlet of sitcoms. The goofy-seeming fellow in the casual clothes who writes all those funny things the cute black kid says in the hit show is more often than not consumed with a rage that, in another context, would lead to flying fists, broken glass, and the burning of Atlanta. But in the fluorescent rooms where sitcoms are brought to life by these socially maladroit young men and women, the boundless irritation felt by the shtickticians will undergo an alchemic process resulting in entertainment palatable to the viewing public. This is the magic of television comedy writing. The latent anger exuded by these practitioners of the laugh-inducing arts, all of whom, like the U.S. senators who think they should be president, believe they deserve their own shows, is tamped down by the egregious amounts of money they're paid; but it will still occasionally flare, when properly provoked, and manifest as derision and disdain.

Such were the emotions engendered by the contract bestowed on

Lloyd Melnick by Lynx among those who labored in the comedy vineyards cultivating the japes of wrath. All of them may have been overpaid, but Lloyd was now being overpaid to the tune of eight figures over three years, which was absurd even by the ridiculous standards of this business. It's one thing to rain crazy money on Phil Sheldon, went the aggrieved reasoning. He is the creator of *The Fleishman Show,* success extraordinaire, liner of wallets and builder of mansions, not to mention second homes on beachfront property, all praise be upon him. Phil Sheldon had made an extraordinary amount of spinach for many people involved in his show and clearly deserved to feast at the table of massive ancillary sales and the ensuing Niagara Falls of residuals. But Lloyd Melnick, the vox populi held, had done nothing, repeat nothing, repeat once again to make sure you really get the point, *nothing* to deserve the riches that had been conferred on him. Making it worse still in the eyes of those who judged him and found him so annoyingly wanting, not only had Lloyd done nothing to merit his new wealth, he had given interviews to newspaper and radio outlets where he failed to sufficiently distance himself from the creative accomplishments of *The Fleishman Show* cash cow, which, so clearly to everyone, belonged entirely to Phil Sheldon and Charlie Fleishman. That was the tipping point for the Melnick-watchers, the nocturnal breed of gainfully employed hacks often seen scurrying rodentlike to their imported cars at three or four A.M. after gangbanging a rewrite on a hapless script for a show beyond repair even before it was sold, the point conversations about Lloyd downshifted from "Can you believe how lucky Melnick is?" to "What an asshole."

To be fair, Lloyd was not deserving of this disparagement. His media foozle had been entirely unintentional. No publicist had been retained to launch his name into the ether, nor did he care terribly much about being known to the general public. It was simply that Phil Sheldon and Charlie Fleishman didn't want to give interviews after the show had become a cultural touchstone and journalists were left to seek the secondhand insights of those whose presence had been announced in a more obscure part of the credits. Lloyd, by virtue of his ability to unconsciously ape Phil Sheldon's attitudes, political opinions, philosophy, and, finally, his ramrod-straight physical posture, had endeared himself to his boss to a degree no other staff member could understand or approach. This talent, this ability to project an essential Sheldon-ness to Phil Sheldon led to a term of longer duration than that of any other writer on the series, most of whom were sent packing after one unhappy season of trying to discern their enigmatic boss's obscure needs.

So Lloyd became the default sound bite of choice for anyone chronicling the *Fleishman* phenomenon because who was he, the son of Estelle and Bernie, middle-class parents in the Bronx, people who vacationed at a bungalow colony on Lake Kiamesha and hoped their son would become a CPA, to say "No, thanks" when the *Los Angeles Times* asked if he would sit for an interview and a photograph?

Today is his first day at work and his place in the comedy universe does not concern him as he drives onto the Studio City lot of Lynx TV. What Lloyd is thinking about is how is he going to possibly justify what Lynx is paying him because, along with everyone else in his incapacious little world, he, too, knows he doesn't deserve it. Turning down the radio, where a debate about the abrogation of the Bill of Rights is taking place, Lloyd gives his name to the uniformed guard at the gate, a pale Caucasian man with a comb-over, and is handed a pass to place behind his windshield. Moments later he glides into a parking space at the head of which sits a piece of concrete five inches tall and two feet long emblazoned with the stenciled letters LLOYD MELNICK.

Lloyd gets out of the car, hitches up frayed khakis, and walks into Bungalow 42, his ostensible home for the next three years. The ground floor of the two-story building contains the offices of *Men Are Tools,* a struggling sitcom about a high-powered single lawyer who returns to his hometown to run his father's hardware store and the high jinks that ensue. It is exactly the kind of tired nonsense the writers of *The Fleishman Show* looked down on from their cushy perch in the cottony white clouds of critical and ratings approbation.

Lloyd takes a brief gander around the sad-looking hallway in which he can see the doors leading to the offices of the people working on *Men Are Tools,* people who are striving to entertain America with their low-rated little show, a show they are desperately hoping won't be canceled and replaced with something from the network news or reality departments. This should be a moment of triumph for him, Queen Elizabeth at her jubilee, Sally Field at the Oscars, a moment where he could thrust his fists into the air and declare, "I am Melnick, hear me roar!" But, oddly, he finds he can't move. Literally. Lloyd looks toward the stairwell, which leads to his second-floor aerie, inside whose four walls he is expected to perform great, or at least profitable, things, and he feels as if his feet were magnetized to the floor by an unseen force. He'd like to turn around but is even unable to execute that simple maneuver. Were a pirouette within his current repertoire, he would get back in his Saab, drive home, call his manager, Marty Lavin of Invisible Entertainment, and order him to give the money back to Lynx, informing them it's all been a big misunderstanding and he's sorry for the whole thing.

Lloyd hears life proceeding around him, the quiet hum of voices, the soft tapping of fingers on a keyboard, the deferential laugh of a writer's assistant, and is overwhelmed by the simple desire to stay where he is, to not move, to root in the ground and remain there, inanimate, inviolable, forgotten and left alone. Behind him is Stacy, wielding fabrics, furniture catalogs, and squares of Tuscan marble samples for the Brentwood pleasure dome. In front of him are the expectations of a major American corporation, which have taken human form in the fast-talking men and women clad in expensive suits beckoning Lloyd to their pernicious paradise. A light-theadedness comes over him. Darkness encroaches in his peripheral vision. Lloyd, conscious of the tension across his upper back and neck, tries to relax his shoulders, but they are frozen. Then he remembers his lungs, which have not taken in oxygen for the last forty-five seconds. He tries to breathe deeply but is only able to manage a short intake of air.

★   ★   ★

Five minutes later he is still in the same position.

"Lloyd?"

Lloyd does not have to move any part of his body to see this person who has parked herself in front of him. It's Tai Chi Chang, his assistant, a petite Asian hipster in a black miniskirt, white tee, red canvas Converse high-tops, and a thin silver ring in her nose.

"Are you okay?"

"I'm terrific," he manages to croak, the presence of a familiar face serving to relax him, albeit not entirely. He had met Tai Chi a week earlier and retained her on the spot, not wanting to go through a lengthy search for someone whose primary function would consist of picking up the phone when it rang and saying, "Lloyd Melnick's office." She was twenty-five; she was cute; she was hired.

"Should I make coffee?"

"Sure."

Lloyd has already had his dose, but declining might lead to a discussion of his coffee-intake patterns, and anything that detailed and personal is unwelcome at this point given the difficulty he is experiencing simply forming words. Tai Chi turns and heads up the stairs, followed by Lloyd, who would ordinarily have admired the contours of her posterior and wondered if she'd ever slept with a Jewish guy, but not today. Sex is not on the Melnick agenda right now, focused as he is on getting himself up the stairs and into his office without announcing his presence to the staff of *Men Are Tools* by howling like a banshee.

Ten minutes later Lloyd sits in his empty office behind a large, boxy desk that seems to be swallowing him. Against one wall is a standard-issue office couch, in front of which lies an oblong coffee table. A nondescript chair is parked opposite his desk. Lloyd is as expressionless as the furniture. Tai Chi walks in holding a cup of coffee.

"I hope you like milk. I put it in. Should have asked."

"Milk's good."

She places the coffee on the desk, then hesitates. Lloyd wonders why she doesn't turn around and walk out; and can she actually see the jagged crack he feels developing in the center of his forehead?

"Need anything else?"

"I'm fine."

"Okay. I'm right out there." She points to the door. Lloyd nods. "I know."

"Okay. Cool."

Finally, she goes. Lloyd touches his forehead and is relieved to feel it is intact.

It is not the first time Lloyd's consciousness has played host to an anxiety attack. Once, while seated in an American Airlines jet next to Stacy getting ready to fly to Cancún, Lloyd had nearly been overcome by an urge to run up the aisle and leap from the door of the plane onto the tarmac. He attributed this sensation to adult-onset claustrophobia, and the Valium Stacy provided took care of it that day, allowing him to withstand the flight without incident and more or less enjoy a week of sunbathing and piña coladas. But it was not claustrophobia. Stacy was three months pregnant and Lloyd had the incipient sensation he was not married to the right woman. They'd bought the house in Mar Vista and a child was on the way, but Lloyd was beginning to question the pillars on which he was constructing a life. Outwardly, all was well. He'd been working on *The Fleishman Show* for several years, he was married to an attractive, intelligent woman (Stacy no walk in the park, to be sure, but it was generally acknowledged Lloyd had acquitted himself satisfactorily in the wife derby), and they were starting a family. Then why did he feel that day, sitting in seat 24C, his face pressed against the cool plastic of the window in a primitive attempt to calm his rampaging nervous system, the plane getting longer and narrower as if undergoing some kind of Lewis Carrollization? Claustrophobia was the easiest explanation, the one least inclined to crack his porcelain life. When they returned from the holiday in Mexico, he was referred by one of the Jews Without Jobs, the conclave of writer confrères with whom he breakfasted each Tuesday

(Tuesday is Jewsday, they'd say), to Dr. Len Tepper, a fiftyish psychiatrist well versed in the garden-variety neuroses of the local citizenry. He prescribed Paxil, the Reese's Pieces of the urban bourgeoisie, and in the ensuing years, while not entirely symptom-free (there was the time he'd been squeezing plums in the produce section of Ralph's Supermarket on Olympic Boulevard and was suddenly overcome with an ineffable sadness that nearly caused him to weep), Lloyd was able to keep these feelings under control.

Until today.

"Dr. Tepper, it's Lloyd Melnick. If you could call me back when you get a chance, I'd appreciate it. My cell phone number is 310–613–2461." Lloyd hangs up. Tepper was in session and would probably not call him back before the end of the day. How had he sounded? Did he sound too normal, too under control? Might Tepper not return his call until tomorrow, at which point he could be in a straitjacket? Should he call Tepper back? *Jesus,* he thinks, *get a grip.* Lloyd takes a breath and finds he is able to fill his lungs with air this time. Just calling the psychiatrist has clearly helped.

Now what to do? He looks at his watch: 11:07. He would have to stay at least until three his first day to put Tai Chi on notice that he intended to work something approaching real hours. Her respect could not be earned by leaving for the day before noon, and he needed her respect if having sex with her was going to be an ongoing fantasy of his because Tai Chi would never sleep with him in his fantasy if she didn't respect him. Lloyd realizes he's having a sexual thought about Tai Chi, which comes as a great relief since it indicates his brain function is returning to normal.

Lunch could be justified at twelve-thirty. That leaves an hour and twenty-three minutes to fill. But fill with what? He had read the paper over breakfast three hours earlier. There is no TV in his office yet. No Internet hookup. Lloyd glances around the room. He feels as if he were sitting in the furniture section of a Staples store.

Tai Chi enters holding a pile of legal pads.

"I thought you might want these."

Lloyd wrote on a computer until he was hired on *The Fleishman Show,* where he observed Phil Sheldon's collection of legal pads. Sheldon was a technophobe and only wrote longhand. Lloyd soon converted.

Tai Chi places the pads on his desk.

"Thanks."

"You want more coffee?"

"No thanks."

Say something clever, he's thinking. You're the high-priced Lloyd Melnick for godsakes. Look at her; she's waiting.

Nothing.

"Okay," Tai Chi says, not exactly sparkling in the conversation department herself.

As Tai Chi leaves, marveling at Lloyd's apparent absence of social skills, he reflexively picks up a legal pad. Pulling from his pocket the gravity pen he was given as a gift at the end of the fifth *Fleishman Show* season, a pen that would allow him to write lying on his back should the need arise, he moves the point slowly across the yellow tablet as if the simple act of putting ink to paper will eventually result in something useful.

An hour later he has filled the page with doodles of a doghouse, an airplane, constellations, horned beasts, and several musical instruments. Tai Chi has not reappeared, preferring instead to sit at her desk outside Lloyd's office and work on the novel for young readers she is writing.

Then, voices.

"I did the DeLorenzos' house and Abby DeLorenzo swore to me her eczema cleared up a week later," a woman says.

"I think Lloyd's gonna love it," says Stacy Melnick, who at that moment appears at the door of Lloyd's office accompanied by a stick-thin woman in her late thirties wearing black leggings and a satin smock that goes down to her knees, giving her the look of a collapsed café umbrella.

"Hi, honey. This is Cam Rousseau."

"I loved *The Fleishman Show,*" Cam exclaims.

"Thanks." Then, to his wife: "I didn't know you were coming."

"I called Tai Chi and told her not to tell you." *I've known Tai Chi three hours and already she's betrayed me,* Lloyd thinks. "I hired Cam to feng shui your office."

Lloyd notices Stacy is holding several picture frames in her hands and she begins arranging them on Lloyd's desk, saying, "I thought you needed some personal touches." He looks at the pictures and sees they're of Stacy and Dustin in different combinations with Lloyd. There they are at SeaWorld, visiting Stacy's parents in New Jersey, and at Dustin's last birthday party, which the boy demanded be held at Chuck E. Cheese's, causing Lloyd and Stacy to spend an endless afternoon somewhere deep in the San Fernando Valley in an animatronic rodent-infested Day-Glo nightmare. "In case you forget why you're doing this."

"I'm not going to forget." She either doesn't hear or chooses to ignore the slight edge with which those words are uttered.

"Did you write the episode where Charlie and the kids get stuck in the elevator? I loved that one." This from Cam.

"It's a good one. Phil wrote it."

Cam is now looking around, a painter of medieval frescoes regarding a naked church wall, trying to determine where the energy planes reside. Stacy looks at her husband and mouths, "She's good."

"Everything in the office is in the wrong place," Cam pronounces. Including me, Lloyd wants to say. "Your desk needs to be over there." She points to the opposite end of the room with the confidence of General Patton arranging a battalion placement. "The coffee table is facing the wrong way. The sofa wants to be against *that* wall." The next hour is passed moving the pieces of temporary furniture around the room in various configurations until Cam is satisfied their energy potential is being maximized.

Ordinarily, Lloyd would have wanted to pour hot lead down the throat of someone like Cam Rousseau, but today her presence is a welcome diversion that almost makes him forget Tai Chi's treachery.

Content that her labors appear to have ended, Stacy tells Lloyd she wants to give him time to get some work done on his first day. "I got a babysitter. Let's go out tonight to celebrate."

"What are we celebrating?"

"Hello! Lloyd! Your deal!" She kisses him on the mouth to assert possession, as Cam, recently divorced from an unemployed actor, watches jealously.

Lloyd spends the rest of the day with his feet on the desk, the legal pad on his knees and the pen in his hand, trying dutifully to bring forth a concept for a frothy network half hour. But what, exactly? A family show about a husband and wife and their adorable kids? Did it have to have kids? Lloyd doesn't want to do television kids, all of whom sound to him like middle-aged Jewish comedy writers stuffed like giblets into the bodies of gentile cherubs. Dustin Melnick, his own four-year-old, rarely said anything an adult would find amusing; or another four-year-old, for that matter.

As Lloyd sits in his Spartan office, ruminating on children, he continues to ponder his own son and reflects on just how unamusing the kid is. When Lloyd and Stacy learned their child was going to be a boy, Lloyd would entertain himself by fantasizing about all the dad-type things he would do with his son. They'd play catch and take walks, climb rocks and learn to swim. They'd ride roller coasters and bodysurf, go to ball games; maybe even go camping. To Lloyd's chagrin, not much of this was coming to pass. Dustin was a delicate, unathletic child who was scared of water, upset by direct sunlight, and would only eat chicken nuggets and cake. He was demanding, petulant, and given to tantrums. That Stacy viewed Dustin as her personal project, her hobby, her raison d'être, was of no small relief to Lloyd given what a handful the boy had turned out to be. They'd heard from mothers whose sons he had had play dates with that Dustin seemed to take unabashed joy in pulverizing elaborately built LEGO structures, destruction that would usually leave the host child lying on the floor gasping for breath in a paroxysm of grief and wounded feelings. The truth was Lloyd didn't really like Dustin right now. He felt guilty about it; he knew it was wrong but he couldn't help himself. His son was obnoxious and Lloyd could only hope Dustin would grow out of it and not become someone who tortured little animals.

So, no, he would not be doing kids on his show, which meant a family comedy was not in the offing. A workplace comedy, perhaps? But to set it where? A television station, a magazine, a store, a doctor's office, a radio station, a record company, congressman's office, a hair salon; it all felt so familiar and cloying. *The Fleishman Show* had been about a suburban family who ran around their suburb doing suburban things. *That worked pretty darn well for Phil*, Lloyd thinks. *Why don't I take the same idea and set it in a different suburb? I'll take characters that have new and endearing quirks and I'll . . . Oh, who am I kidding? It's so utterly transparent and lame.*

Hours later, Lloyd still has nothing. But the Tag Heuer wristwatch Stacy purchased for him upon the signing of his deal told him he had done a day's work, so Lloyd puts his pen down: 3:47. If he leaves now, he'll beat the afternoon rush hour.

"Going home?" Tai Chi asks as Lloyd walks past.

"Yeah. Don't want to shoot my wad on the first day," he says, immediately regretting his choice of words. *She'll probably file a sexual harassment suit tomorrow*, he thinks. Then, noticing a page of prose on her computer screen, he tries to move the conversation along. "What are you writing?"

"A novel for teenagers."

"A novel? Really?"

Really, indeed. Tai Chi is writing a novel? Not a spec screenplay or a sample television script like every other sentient person in the greater Los Angeles area but an actual book? Something that would appear between hardcovers to be read by more than ten development executives? This number ten, incidentally, is a fairly accurate representation of the number of individuals who will generally peruse a bought-and-paid-for script since the ratio of what is written to what is made is virtually a hundred to one, and these development executives are the collective readership of most professional writers in Hollywood.

"How's it going?" Casual, trying not to show surprise.

"I'm about halfway through. I'd love for you to read it when I'm done." She's already forgiven the unfortunate wad-shooting image, he realizes with great relief.

"I'd be happy to. Oh, Tai Chi, by the way, if my wife ever tells you to not tell me something, tell me immediately." He smiles at her, wanting to diffuse any possible tension, but letting her know not to conspire with Stacy again.

Lloyd spends the drive home to Mar Vista regretting not having taken himself more seriously as an artist back in New York before he had assumed the obligations with which he is now burdened. Had he followed his better instincts, the ones that had led him to earn a B.A. in English from SUNY at Albany where he'd pursued a sincere interest in nineteenth-century American literature, particularly the Transcendentalists (*Oh, for a beach chair on Walden Pond!* Lloyd often thought), something worthwhile might have been produced. Instead, he had become another man's water carrier. Well compensated, to be sure, but still drenched from the splashing of the pails. *Yes,* he whines internally, *I may be doing better in the crass terms that enslave everyone around me here in Los Angeles, but it is Tai Chi, my lowly assistant, who is going to be the author of a novel.*

This is the disturbing thought he focuses on as he makes love to Stacy that night after their celebratory dinner.

Lloyd is thinking about Tai Chi. *Her breasts. Her novel. Her breasts. Her novel. Her breasts. Her novel.*

Stacy is thinking about upholstery.

She comes first.

Chapter 7

The day previous to Lloyd's anxiety attack, over the hill from the San Fernando Valley office, a man visited Rosa's Florist on La Brea, produced two crisp hundreds, and left with a three-foot-high horseshoe of white carnations that appeared to have been diverted from their intended appearance at a Mafia funeral. They were not just flowers, these carnations; they were a statement, a message, an avowal of eternal devotion writ in flora.

The man with the hundreds was Frank, who had stopped on the way back from his North Hollywood acting class/tryst/animal attack to arm himself for his return to Honeyworld, and the statement he wanted to make was The Bones Digs You, Babe.

Frank pulled the Caddy back into the Cedars-Sinai parking lot. Turning off the engine, he removed the towel from under his shirt and looked at it; the blood appeared to have dried. Frank folded the evidence, hoisted the carnation horseshoe, and walked quickly back into the hospital, his back still sore from the recent feline assault.

Frank was a guilt-free cheater, a man whose personal moral code was not constrained by anything approaching the traditional view, at least when it came to his own behavior, and felt himself entitled to spread his very special Bones Love hither and yon. He wakes up and goes to sleep with Honey, he reasons, and what greater proof of true fidelity was there than that? What he does in between those two events, those twin signposts of the quotidian day, he is quite certain is no one's business but his own, least of all Honey's. In their time together, she had had suspicions, most notably during his tenure on *Hollywood Squares* when a young makeup artist took what Honey perceived to be an unusual interest in the condition of Frank's pores, but Frank was a smooth and careful liar and she had never been able to uncover any tangible evidence that would suggest he had slept with enough women during the time they had been together to field a baseball team.

With a designated hitter.

And four subs on the bench.

Which, when you thought about it, was only about two and a half extracurricular sexual partners per year, a number that allowed Frank to bask in the glow of what he considered to be his commendable self-restraint.

Entering the lobby, he deposited the bloody towel in a wastebasket and walked to the elevators.

Frank arrived at Honey's private room and gently pushed open the door. Sticking his head in, Frank saw her lying in bed looking like Billie Holiday after an opium bender, her consciousness the beam of a flickering flashlight as the batteries run down. She looked over at him. Frank clicked into Dutiful Mode.

"How're you feeling, babe?" Respectful. Quiet. Caring.

Then she focused and the ethereal swamp in which Honey appeared to be wading drained and left her wriggling her painted toenails in a moist silt of displeasure. She hadn't said a word but Frank thought, *Does she know what Daddy's been up to?*

"Babe, how're you feeling?"

Honey came at him full tilt. "How come you weren't here when they brought me up?" Was that an accusation?

"I was out getting you these." Frank presented the three-foot-high carnation horseshoe with a flourish befitting the Hope Diamond as he walked over to the bed and kissed Honey on her uncharacteristically pale lips. "If some guy named Chickie No-Neck shows up looking for 'em, don't mention my name," he said, shifting easily into performance gear. She tried to laugh. Frank noticed with no little relief the flowers had done their time-tested trick, that of mitigating female annoyance on

101

some impossible-to-understand biological level. The effort at laughter caused her to grimace in pain.

"How are you feeling?" One more time.

"Like my tits were hit by a train."

"Ouch!"

"Hand me my purse. I need to put some makeup on."

Holding a pocket mirror in front of her face, Honey restored herself to her former glory with a few simple strokes of blush and powder and was once again ready to perform unnatural acts with the ninja king in front of a movie camera. At least from the neck up.

"Did you get the scrip for the Vicodin?"

"It's in my purse."

Frank stuck his hand in the purse and rummaged around, a truffle pig on the trail. In a moment, he had the prescription in hand. Looked at it, frowned.

"Only a one-week supply?"

"I'm in the hospital getting a boob job and all you can think about is Vicodin?"

"I was thinking about you."

"Sure."

"It's just I can't usually get it legally."

"Yeah, whatever."

"I spent the whole time I wasn't getting you flowers sitting in that waiting room surrounded by other people's anxious relatives hoping you'd come out of the anesthesia alive."

"So you could cop my Vicodin."

"No. Not because of the Vicodin."

"You're such a liar."

Frank saw she was teasing him now, her personality starting to return.

A nurse came in, checked her vitals, and an hour later Honey's new breasts were pronounced ready to go home. She was sitting in the passenger seat of the Caddy appearing to listen to the Metallica CD Frank was playing when she looked over at him.

"Do you think this is going to help?"

"What?"

Honey glances down at her bandaged chest, then over at Frank, as if he were slow. "The boob job?"

"Hell, yes. Movie people love the big boobs."

"I'm not thinking about movies."

"No?"

"I'm thinking about TV."

"Oh?"

"I want to play Borak."

Borak, temptress of the tundra, was the titular Kirkuk's girlfriend.

They weren't even home from the hospital and she was starting up again. Frank tried to remain impassive.

"I told you, the Eskimo show is not happening."

"You should do it."

"Why?"

"Because I'll look totally hot in an animal skin."

"I'll buy you an animal skin."

"Don't patronize me, babe."

This from Honey? Did she just say "Don't patronize me, babe"? For a moment, Frank was too astonished to respond. Had the doctor who had enlarged her chest adjusted other aspects of Honey Call as well? Had an assertiveness chip been implanted while she was in surgery? Did the newly minted D cups portend further changes in the heretofore sweet Honey persona? Frank had never even considered this.

She had gone into the operating room with the simple goal of becoming more drool-inducing in a hormone-dominated industry, a thought bovine both in its simplicity and its result (at least in Honey's case, since she had taken it to the logical conclusion of silicone implants), but now she had emerged from the procedure physically rounder yet paradoxically more sharp. How could that be? Frank had assumed they'd go home, drink a bottle of merlot, and order some Chinese takeout; then, after some post-lo-mein cunnilingus (intercourse being out of the question given Honey's delicate state), he'd go to the Comedy Shop and let Honey spend the evening watching TV and fantasizing about her future prospects as a newly busty thespian. But she wanted to talk business. Now. On the way home from the hospital, for godsakes.

Well, if Honey could thrust, Frank could parry, because what was a tetchy girlfriend to a comic except a heckler on the local level?

"How about a Stuart Little toy? If you want to wear an animal hide, I'll get you a Stuart Little and you can skin him and make a thong," Frank suggested as E. B. White spun like a rotisserie chicken in his austere New England grave.

"You're not doing the Eskimo show because you don't want me to have a part."

Honey appeared headed into previously uncharted waters of psychological exegesis. What *had* happened during that surgery?

"That isn't true at all. If I do a show, I'll get you a part," Frank said, regretting it instantly. "It's just not going to be the Eskimo show."

"Promise?"

"Yes."

So, there it was. Frank on record as saying he would make Honey a part of whatever television context he was thrust into.

"We're coming around the bend when someone shifts their weight and the whole raft tips over. One second I'm sitting back with a Corona in my hand, floating down the river soaking up the sun, and the next second I'm in the rapids trying not to smash into a rock. So I get my bearings and swim to the shore, and the beauty part is I don't spill a drop." This is Robert Hyler talking about his recent trip down the Snake River in a raft of industry players whose collective heft could have launched a small country. Frank and he are seated in the sterile Studio City office of Pam Penner, head of comedy at the Lynx Network. It's hard to visualize Robert in a drizzle much less a river as he sits on the sofa, tasseled loafer crossed over worsted-wool knee, a picture of pampered prosperity, regaling Pam with tales of wilderness derring-do. Frank is seated near him trying not to stare out the window. He's already heard his manager perform the river story, and whatever amusing quality it once held has vanished.

They are in a pitch meeting, a gathering whose mysterious rituals are as proscribed as a Kabuki performance (only with less room for improvisation), and currently the schmooze phase is taking place, where the pitchers entertain the pitchees with something having as little as possible to do with what they are there to discuss or, rather, sell. Common subjects are home renovations, children (but only if more than one person in the room has them, otherwise their very existence suggests a superannuating that augurs the grinding end of a promising career), restaurants, and, of course, vacations. Hence Robert's seemingly relaxed recounting of the rafting anecdote. After ten minutes or so of light banter, this overture to the sales buck and wing, often with no segue more deft than a sudden "So!" from the chief pitchee, the pitchers get the signal that they have finished performing the introductory part of the show and are now expected to dim the houselights and bring on the headliner.

Pam Penner, a cherubic dumpling of a lesbian in her forties, Jurassic (though childless!) by the standards of the network television business, exudes the eager charm of a well-adjusted teenager. Her loose clothes can barely contain the vibrating energy emanating from her as she leans forward in her chair, listening to Robert, nodding, laughing, the blond tips of her dark hair jiggling attentively. Pam was a lesbian before it was a career move and spent many years hiding in the darkest reaches of the closet, up on the shelves behind the shoe boxes, certain imminent discovery of her sapphic proclivities would put an end to the dreams of industry glory she had nurtured from an early age and consign her to life with a Nissan Sentra and no expense account. But without much time to spare, given her relatively advanced age, the cultural climate in Hollywood had shifted, and just prior to AARP having found her, portly Pam Penner came rocketing out of the closet with the force of an F-16.

"How's Maria?" This from Robert, the final stroke of the fur, the acknowledgment, the I-know-you're-gay-and-I'm-down-with-it question, Maria being Pam Penner's much younger, raven-haired girlfriend, whose framed picture sat on Pam's desk near a bowl of guppies.

"She's good. We have to go out with you and Daryl."

Given the nature of the conversation that is taking place, you would be forgiven for thinking Pam was unaccompanied in her office. You would be mistaken. Network executives, like urban pigeons, never travel alone.

Pam has two young minions in the room with her, one of whom, having proven his mettle as a taker of notes, has graduated from that humble function and is now allowed to be padless, the better to participate in the conversation. The other, untried and recently out of college, is expected to take the minutes. The non-note-taker is Jason Fendi, a stripling of indeterminate sexuality whose lanky, Prada-knock-off-clad frame folded forward as he tried to look interested in Robert's river story while thinking about the restaurant he is going to dine in tonight. The note-taker is the inappropriately named Jessica Puck (her persona more Hamlet-ish than Puck-like), and she is as humorless as only someone in the network end of the comedy business can be, which is to say her demeanor is that of a North Korean bureaucrat in the Ministry of Collective Farming listening to a request for a new thresher. Yet, ironically (for where else should irony abide if not in the comedy business?), Jessica Puck's function is to record the concepts, jokes, the wit—every bon mot spritzed by the visiting shtickmeisters as it comes sailing through the ether—and then later remind Pam, whose job in this situation is to be delightful and encouraging, what she had heard and whether she had liked it.

Each hapless purveyor of light entertainment entering the Penner lair to beat the sales drum dreaded the notion of Jessica Puck being the underling designated to encapsulate what had been said, given the apparatchik-like gravity of her bearing. So they desperately hoped

Pam Penner would immediately buy whatever wares they were hawking, rendering Jessica's assuredly desiccated summaries moot.

"So." This from Pam, Segues "R" Us, right on schedule. "Frank, you've got an idea for a show?"

Robert glances over at Frank, who has been wondering when enough time will have elapsed for him to call Candi Wyatt without her thinking he's interested in a more than carnal way. "You're on."

"Thank you, Bobby." Frank leans forward in his seat and makes eye contact with Pam Penner. Jason Fendi and Jessica Puck may as well have vaporized. "This is a show about"—here he pauses and observes the looks of benign anticipation they're affecting—"me."

Tentative laughter because of the attitude with which he delivers the line, a casual arrogance that presumes complicity on the part of the listener, one that says, "What else would the show be about?" Not that he's said anything actually funny yet. But the idea of Frank, his essential Bones-ness, has prepared them to be amused. They lean forward expectantly. He hesitates for a moment.

"Okay . . . and . . ." This is Pam. Encouraging, but let's-get-on-with-it.

"My life and high times, and by the way, I think I smell a title." Saying it again: "*My Life and High Times*. I like it." Frank turns to his minder. "Bobby?"

"It's good," Robert reflexively replies. He may be a mogulossus, a giant in the industry if not in physical stature, but in this situation he's Charlie McCarthy to Frank's Edgar Bergen, or Lester to Frank's Willie Tyler, depending on your frame of reference or race.

"So I play me, you know . . . if Ralph Fiennes isn't available." The self-deprecation always works. Frank hesitates to use it since in his case it's so transparently inauthentic, but he has work to do here so the trick is dutifully hauled out of the bag.

"Do you have a job? In the show, I mean."

What fool whose name is not Pam Penner has had the impudence to ask a question? Could it be Jason, the padless underling?

Frank shoots Jason a look that could fry a duck at fifty paces, but realizing he's not in a club and can't eviscerate this wearer of pretend Prada and feed him to the guppy family silently swimming in the bowl on Pam's desk, he quickly covers it with a smile. Jason, however, does not miss the withering beam shone on him and silently, if impotently, vows to do what he can to sabotage Frank.

"I'm the Bones, babe. *That's* my job."

"So you're a comedian?" Jason innocently asks, leaning forward. Robert looks over at him, dreading what the young fashion victim is about to say. "Didn't Charlie Fleishman already do that show?" At the invoking of Charlie Fleishman's name, Frank looks toward Jason like a falcon eyeing a small rodent. Robert readies himself to pull Frank off the kid, but Frank has it under control.

"He didn't do this show because he isn't me, okay, babe? Now just listen. I'll tell you when I want to do a double act." Equally chastened and resentful, Jason eases back into his chair. Frank turns back to Pam. "So, I'm me, okay?"

"That could work, but who else is in it?" Pam keeping things on track.

"I'm just out of rehab where the court remanded me after I had a few pops one day and hit a nine iron—"

"You're a golfer?" Jason asks. Robert wishes he would dematerialize, having no idea how long Frank can keep from murdering him.

"Into a guy's windshield," Frank clarifies. "After a fender bender. The judge gives me a choice, you know, rehab or jail. So I play cards for twenty-eight days at some Lazy Acres Burnout Clinic—this is just backstory, by the way, we don't see me in rehab, been there, *boring!*—then I move back into my house and my manager moves in with me, you know, like a zookeeper. And by the way, it's a fictional one, not Robert."

"I don't get to act?" This from Robert, unable to resist an opportunity to not be amusing.

"Your job's to count the money, babe."

"I think he'd develop repetitive stress syndrome," Pam Penner weighs in, everyone a comedian, and Robert's chuckle is drowned out by Jason's obsequious braying.

Frank continues, not wanting to fall under his train of thought. "But I'm sick of comedy; I am not a happy woman in the comedy business so I start a band because I fuckin' rock. Did I mention that to you kids?"

This last fillip being rhetorical.

"I *was* a comic but now I'm rockin'. My band needs original music because the Bones can't be in a cover band, I mean, what am I gonna play, weddings? Like I'm gonna stand up there and sing 'Celebrate' while some fat chick cuts the cake?" Frank is steamrolling now, paying no attention to the possibility that the plump Penner might take exception to the fat-chick/cake allusion. "So I have to write songs. And the show, *My Life and High Times*, Tuesdays at nine on the Lynx Network, is about how I get the material that becomes the songs. I go to the store; I get a song. I buy some shoes; I get a song. I go on a date—"

"You get a song." Jason again. Frank is starting to wonder if he is baiting him.

"I saw you with that band a few years ago." Pam tells him this in a way that suggests she liked it.

"Killer Bones." Frank name-checking his tenuous place in rock 'n' roll history.

"I loved the Dylan-at-the-dentist bit."

"I was actually at a dinner party with someone who was dating Dylan's dentist," Robert says, contributing again. Frank wishes he'd shut the hell up so they could get out of there. "You would have thought he was famous, you know, the dentist! This woman was acting like she was dating a famous person."

"I did that bit for Dylan one night and he nearly swallowed his harmonica," Frank relates, easing Robert back out of the spotlight and letting the people in the room know exactly who it is he is able to hang out with. "He'd do the show if I asked him."

"What show?" The annoying Jason again.

"The one I'm pitching, babe." Trying not to stab this kid with a pen.

Pam, ever the conscientious sheepdog, keeps the herd from roaming too far afield. "So you play yourself but you're a musician, and the show's about where you get your material?"

"Basically." Frank's done.

"It's good," Pam assures them, without a great deal of enthusiasm. Clearly, she will not be buying it in the room.

"There are three places on your schedule it could work," Robert says, trying to connect the dots so a picture resembling a deal can be discerned.

"Frank, did you ever read the *Kirkuk* script?" Pam says. "We think Orson Dubinsky did a really good job and he's out of his mind, which I think you would relate to." Orson Dubinsky was the creative force behind *Kirkuk* and his whole antic arctic world, its writer/producer/auteur. No one was confusing him with Phil Sheldon, although the Lynx people were hoping his semicoherent effusions masked actual talent.

"With all due respect, I can't work with a talking walrus."

"Because . . . ?" If Jason says one more word, Frank is going to render him a stain on the fabric. Robert sees he'd better earn his fee and rushes to Jason's rescue.

"Because Frank feels his persona is better suited to other things."

"Like *My Life and High Times*." Frank reminding them.

"Okay. Good to know," Pam says as she pushes herself out of her chair and stands, indicating the supplicants are free to leave. Jason and Jessica Puck rise as one.

"Is it really the walrus?" Jason asks again, incredulous.

"Harvey likes the Walrus," Pam explains. "He thinks the merchandising potential is through the roof."

"Frank and a walrus, personally, I'm not seeing it," Robert explains, denying Frank the opportunity to further disembowel the script.

Good-to-meet-yous all around, and the pitchers jet leaving Pam and the Development Twins to ponder Frank's future in television.

★   ★   ★

110

"How'd you think it went?" Frank casually inquires as they wait for their cars at the valet stand on the Lynx lot. Robert has just closed his cell phone after calling the office to check in. "I thought she might buy it in the room."

"I was hoping that would happen," Robert says. Frank looks over as if waiting for him to explain why it didn't. "You absolutely refuse to do *Kirkuk*?"

This is not what Frank wants to hear. "Don't ask me that again."

"Okay, fine."

"I'm not kidding."

"Relax."

"I'm fuckin' relaxed, Bobby," Frank says, ignoring the current condition of his sphincter, which could crack a walnut.

"It went okay, not great. She may buy it, she may not." Robert Hyler silent for a moment, a diver standing on a high platform preparing to leap. "Listen, Frank, if they pass on *My Life and High Times,* you need to think about the other thing."

"What did I just say?"

"Not to mention it."

"And?"

"I mentioned it."

"Because . . ."

"Reality, Frank."

"Reality? You mean that thing for people who can't handle their drugs?" Frank instantly wishes he hadn't referenced the hippieish button he'd noticed in the late 1960s, but Robert is upsetting him, his normally agile mind suddenly sclerotic and cliché-plagued.

"You want a career in TV, then you have to play by a certain set of rules, which there's no getting around. These guys"—here he points in the direction of Pam's office—"right now they control the ball, the field, the whole enchilada. If you want to keep touring and playing clubs and having that kind of career, then go with God, you'll always make a living. But if you want to take a bite out of the enchilada, and I say this as your friend, you'll talk to the fuckin' walrus. And by the way, I read the script. The walrus is in what, like one scene?"

Frank hears this and almost feels his body mass decreasing. However much bluff and bluster compose the Bones public persona, the fact remains that his services are not much in demand lately, and at tax time come April this truth is going to be hard to escape. Nonetheless, he screws himself up for another sally.

"There's what, four other networks? Why don't we pitch it around town if Lynx passes?"

Robert pauses momentarily, as if weighing the potential effect of the words he is about to utter. Ready, set—

"None of them want to be in business with you."

This piece of unwelcome intelligence has the effect of a full-throttle blow to Frank's solar plexus, and he instantly has a gloomy vision of himself at sixty, squinting through bifocals as he drives a rental car between gigs in Asheville and Raleigh-Durham, *Hello, North Carolina.*

"Since Cleveland, it's been an uphill battle," Robert continues, referring to Frank's spectacularly unfortunate behavior back in Ohio. "And it's been nearly five years now. Lynx is desperate. They want edge and they know that's your stock-in-trade, so they'll take a chance on you. But right now no one else will."

The valet arrives with a red Hummer. Robert tips the former Sandinista and hoists himself into the vehicle looking as if he were about to stage an amphibious assault on the nearest Pottery Barn.

"What's with the Hummer? I thought your wife was pro-ozone-layer," Frank remarks as nonchalantly as possible, trying to show his stomach hasn't dropped six inches as a result of the bomb Robert has just detonated.

"I have it out for a test-drive. I couldn't resist. Don't tell her, she'll divorce me." Robert turns the key in the ignition, and as the motor of the massive machine roars to life, he turns back to Frank. "Think about *Kirkuk,* okay?"

Robert drives off and Frank notices his back hurts where Candi

Wyatt's cat had used it for a scratch pole; realizes over four hours have passed since he's taken a Vicodin. He quickly remedies that and makes a mental note to replace the pills he's borrowed from Honey.

A Saab comes driving past.

Behind the wheel of the Saab, Lloyd Melnick, talking on his cell phone and saying good-bye to Pam Penner, looks at Frank, briefly moves his foot from the gas to the brake, and waits to see if Frank notices him. Observing Frank looking in another direction, Lloyd does not put pressure on the brake. He doesn't want to risk Frank's opprobrium and there is nothing to be gained today by saying hello. Lloyd glances into his rearview mirror as the parking valet pulls Frank's car up and, for a moment, regrets not stopping because he thinks he could have made Frank laugh by relating the phone conversation he just had.

It had gone like this:

"Lloyd, it's Pam. I don't want to be pushy, but I'm curious if you're working on an idea you'd throw yourself in front of a herd of elephants to do."

"Maybe one or two elephants but not an entire herd."

"Okay, then listen to this. I don't need to tell you how competitive the environment in our business is right now, so we need to do television that's going to cut through the clutter, okay?"

"I was thinking the same thing."

"Good. Then we're nearly on the same page already. I want you to consider this and you don't have to answer me right away. How do you feel about doing a show set in a massage parlor?"

"A massage parlor?"

"In Las Vegas. And I already have the title—are you ready? *Happy Endings*. What do you think?"

"Happy Endings?"

"You know, when the girl finishes up—"

"No, no . . . I get it."

"Lloyd, I'm sensing some hesitancy in your voice. I want to be clear about something. We don't want to do a sleazy show. It won't be a sleazy massage parlor. It'll be a place where everyone knows your name. You know, friendly."

"A massage parlor where everyone knows my name?"

"Not *yours* as in Lloyd Melnick's, but *yours* like it's welcoming."

"A friendly massage parlor?"

"It's very cutting-edge and I know we can build it around a star. What do you think?"

"I want to get back to you."

"It'll be breakthrough television."

Until that phone conversation, the past week had gone relatively well for Lloyd. His psychiatrist, Dr. Tepper, after a brief telephone consultation, updated Lloyd's Paxil prescription, which returned him to his normal state of manageable despair. He had spent his days at the office generating hackneyed ideas for television shows, but he knew that when the time came, so strong was the *Fleishman Show* mojo, he could take whatever dross he had concocted around to the various networks and stimulate a bidding war simply by showing up. That Lloyd was sanguine regarding this complete abdication of creative responsibility was clear testament to the efficacy of the Paxil. Feeling duly under control and empowered, he had called the LAX Gun Club and booked a lesson. This is where he is now headed.

Five minutes later he's driving west on Ventura preparing to make a left on Coldwater Canyon. He had cogitated on Pam Penner's notion and quickly determined he would not allow his talent to be besmirched in so ludicrous a fashion. Now he's thinking about the meeting he has to go to after his lesson where he will listen to Stacy discuss final stage modifications on their Brentwood palazzo with the builder. The mid-afternoon traffic is moving as Lloyd eases the Saab to a stop at a red light. He glances at a copy of the *Los Angeles Times* sports section lying on his passenger seat. The Lakers defeated the Dallas Mavericks the previous evening. Before his eyes can find the score, Lloyd is thrown backward by the sudden impact of a rear-end collision, which inflates the air bag in the steering wheel, pinning him against the seat as he bounces forward. The adrenaline released by the ramming causes him to stiffen, and as soon as he realizes he isn't dead, he is seething about having to take the car to the shop and deal with the insurance company of whatever pinhead smashed into him. Were it not for the Paxil, Lloyd would be flying out of the car looking to wreak havoc on whoever had caused the accident (only to flee in the other direction if it was someone he couldn't take), but as he is under the influence of this salutary smoother-of-rough-edges, he squeezes out from behind the air bag and emerges to survey the damage loaded for squirrel rather than bear.

"Babe!" Frank stands next to the Caddy, one foot in the car, the other on the road, smiling at Lloyd as traffic glides by them in both directions. "Fancy running into you." Frank's insouciance belying their location at the nexus of this busy intersection.

"Wha—" Lloyd is not able to articulate his question as cars whiz past in both directions. He notices one of his legs has begun to shake.

"I take my eyes off the road for two seconds and I'm kissing your metallic ass. Serves me right for rolling a joint when I'm driving. If the cops stop while we're here, I'd appreciate if you wouldn't mention that." Lloyd walks to the back of the car, consciously trying to control the independent movements of his leg, and sees the Saab is unmarked. Relief. "What are you doing out in the Valley?" Frank making with the small talk.

"My office is in Studio City."

"Right, right, the Lynx deal."

"Hey, look, I'd love to stand around and get sunstroke in the middle of Ventura here, but I have to be somewhere." The leg beginning to settle down.

"Lloyd, wait a minute. I just sold a show to Pam Penner over at Lynx," Frank lies, needing to bait the hook.

"Congratulations."

"You want to write it with me?" Frank offers, thinking he could call

Pam from his cell phone and tell her he's persuaded Lloyd Melnick, whose very name sent a frisson of greed up the collective spine of every network executive in town, to cowrite *My Life and High Times*.

"You know, I'd love to but I'm working on my own stuff."

"So I should go fuck myself?"

"I'm not saying that."

"Suit yourself, babe."

Frank may need Lloyd, but begging is not going to happen, and although the conversation is clearly over, Lloyd is not sure how to get offstage.

"Where's Otto? It's a shame he didn't get this on tape."

"Fuckin' kid has no follow-through," Frank replies. "He booked."

"That's too bad."

Frank's face is back in neutral, and looking over Lloyd's shoulder, he says, "Get in your car, the light's green."

Lloyd turns and walks back to his Saab. His last two encounters with Frank, at the doughnut shop after the farcical reenactment of the Kennedy assassination and here on Ventura, have ended unhappily, and both times, Lloyd realizes with a slight rising of bile, were because Frank refused to acknowledge the shifting of Lloyd's place in their universe, his ascension to a loftier plane. He arrives back at the car and attempts to gather the air bag, but he can't get it to move. Lloyd shoves it this way and that, but the hard rubber has inflated to its limit and is not showing signs of pliancy. As things stand, he can't get into the car.

Frank, who has been watching this, approaches.

"Problem?"

Lloyd can't help reading the sentiment "Who's in control now, punk?" in Frank's seemingly innocent question.

"The air bag won't deflate."

"I should leave you here in the middle of the street until some Mexican with a tow truck comes and bails your white ass out, but I'm a gentleman, so stand back, Lloyd, Dr. Bones is in the house."

Frank reaches into his pocket, removes a gravity knife, and before

Lloyd can say "What's a Jew doing with a switchblade?" flicks it open with the ease of a *West Side Story* cast member and shanks the recalcitrant rubber, causing a stream of air to forcefully expel and the bag to deflate.

"You're good to go, babe."

Stunned once again by Frank's capacity for the sudden spasm of violence, Lloyd stares at the comic's receding form as he walks laconically to the Caddy, looking to Lloyd like the dark stranger ambling out of town after having saved the women and children from the rustlers. *What does that make me?* he wonders. *Certainly not a rustler.*

Pushing the spent air bag aside, Lloyd gets in the car and starts the engine. The light turns red before he can get away so he sits there looking at Frank in his rearview mirror.

Who carries a knife nowadays? I mean, other than Crips and Bloods? And what is Frank's pathology anyway? It can't just be that he grew up in Texas. What deep interior weirdness is manifesting in the guns, the knives; the who-knows-what-else that's lending such piquant flavor to the Bones persona?

When the light changes and Lloyd turns up Coldwater Canyon, it occurs to him that Frank slammed the Caddy into the Saab intentionally.

Lloyd makes it to the LAX Gun Club in time for his lesson, which is given to him by the same man with the wispy goatee who rented them the guns the previous week. After some perfunctory talk about gun safety, the goateed man, whose name turns out to be Zip, has Lloyd firing away with a Colt 9mm. Under Zip's expert tutelage, Lloyd is regularly hitting the target, and when his hour is up, he leaves the building feeling like a killer and wondering if he should call Frank and challenge him to a shooting match.

Chapter 8

The cell phone sitting on the passenger seat of Stacy Melnick's new Sunsation, the latest in electric-car technology, trills impatiently. Navigating down a leafy Brentwood side street, one hand on the wheel, the other holding a mocha latte with an extra shot of espresso, Stacy maneuvers the candied caffeine into a cup holder and reaches for the phone, quickly checking the caller ID and seeing the ubiquitous PRIVATE CALLER on the tiny screen.

"Hello."

"Stacy, it's Daryl Hyler."

"Daryl!" Stacy exclaims, not bothering to hide her surprise and pleasure that this paradigm of well-heeled decency has tracked her down on her cell phone. She gently presses the brakes, slowing the Sunsation to better be able to concentrate on Daryl's needs.

"How are ya, hon?" Everyone *hon* to Daryl until she needs to shove them off a cliff.

"I'm great. What's going on?"

"I'm calling you from our jet. We're about to land in Spain so I have to talk quickly. I'm putting a little dinner together for Save Our Aching Planet at the Beverly Wilshire Hotel for about a thousand people and I wanted to ask you to be on the committee."

These are magic words indeed to a social mountaineer like Stacy Melnick. It is all she can do to keep from crawling through the phone and emerging on the other end to kiss this woman on her spa-softened cheek. "And it's not until May so don't tell me you have a conflict."

"I'd love to be on the committee."

"You used to be a dietitian, right?"

"I have a degree from NYU."

"Then you can help with the menu. Just remember, Robert doesn't like squab. A lot of times people want to fancy the menu up at these things with stuff like squab, but let's stick to chicken for the poultry choice, okay? We're an egalitarian organization."

"That's fine. There's a lot you can do with chicken."

"And, hon, one more thing. Everyone on the committee is expected to contribute at least twenty-five thousand, okay? I'll have my assistant call you next week to tell you when the first planning meeting's going to be. Bye-ee."

"Bye." Stacy hangs up, flushed with a feeling of infinite possibility. Her husband has a huge television deal, their son is matriculated in the Tiny Tuna Pre-School, they are almost ready to move to their new home in Brentwood, and now Daryl Hyler, doyenne of relatively young Los Angeles, after having offered to help Dustin Melnick gain admission to the Horizon School, wants Stacy to join in her noble quest to save the planet. Life is too, too rich.

"Tell me again why the wood floor has pegs?"

Stacy and Lloyd are talking to Garrett Quickly, their laconic builder. They're standing in the entrance hallway of the new Melnick home looking into the empty living room. There is no furniture in the entire house, and with its expensive woods and moldings it has the feel of a giant plush jewel box emptied of its baubles and waiting for the duchess to return from a ball. Garrett, a slender, low-key guy in his forties accustomed to navigating the challenging personalities of his clients with the aplomb of an experienced sailor caught in a squall, looks at Stacy and scrunches his eyes up as if to imply amusement. She might have shared his amusement were he not already five months behind schedule.

"My guys ordered the wrong wood."

"Well, we can see that," Stacy retorts.

Lloyd, more concerned with the inner workings of the Mongolian yak trade than the accoutrements of their prospective living room, looks on impassively. She knows help from this quarter will not be forthcoming.

"I want it ripped out and replaced."

Stacy continues in this vein, reciting a litany of problems that must be attended to by Garrett and his subordinates before the upwardly mobile Melnicks can justifiably relocate. When she has exhausted her list of items and received assurances from the eternally patient Quickly that everything will be attended to immediately, the builder takes his leave, desperate to escape before Stacy realizes she has further demands that must be addressed.

Stacy finds Lloyd in a small room upstairs.

"What's this space going to be used for?" he asks.

"A wrapping room."

"A wrapping room?"

"For gifts."

"We need a special room to wrap gifts?"

"I thought it would be nice. I ordered a big table and this thing that lets you hang ten kinds of gift wrap." Seeing the incomprehension in his eyes, a look that seems to ask how it could be that this middle-class daughter of New Jersey now required a room whose sole purpose was the wrapping of gifts, Stacy changes her tack. "Lloyd, I just got a call from Daryl Hyler on my way over here. She was on her private jet." Said with great relish: *Lloyd, people are calling me from private jets!* "She asked me to serve on a benefit committee, hon." Pausing briefly, vainly hoping for congratulations. "We're moving in a different world now."

"Okay." Not worth the fight.

"Come on, I want to show you something."

A few moments later they are standing in the spacious bathroom of the master suite, a mélange of marble tile, high-end porcelain, brushed steel, and beveled glass with a twelve-jet shower, a raised Jacuzzi, and a crystal chandelier that appears to have been purloined from one of the grand hotels of Europe. Lloyd is thinking its intended purpose seems at odds with the museum-like sense of order and quiet when he looks at his wife's reflection in the mirror and sees tears running down her face. Turning from her image to the actual Stacy, he reaches a hand out and tenderly touches her cheek.

"Are you thinking about what all this is costing me?"

Stacy smiles and, pushing his hand away, chokes back a sob.

"No."

"What, then?"

"I just never thought I would ever have a bathroom this beautiful."

Lloyd can think of no response to this statement other than silence. Then the dam breaks and she is openly weeping, clutching Lloyd to her, wetting his frayed T-shirt with her copious tears. Not knowing what else to do, Lloyd hugs his wife, puzzled by this Ecstasy of the Fixtures he is witnessing.

"Thank you so much for giving it to me."

It occurs to Lloyd this might not be the best time to tell her he is toying with the idea of walking away from his deal and writing a book.

As Frank drove away after having rammed into Lloyd, he noticed the Vicodin borrowed from Honey was not performing its dependably pain-hammering magic, so he headed to the Beverly Hills offices of Dr. Randy Cashman, an internist whose quickness with a prescription made him a favorite of innumerable professional entertainers. Cashman was a much loved figure in the recording industry, many of whose denizens had, in appreciation of his services, gifted him with framed gold records, which now lined the doctor's office walls, gleaming reminders of a glittering clientele. Frank admired these totems of triumph as he sauntered toward the examination room to await the doctor's tender ministrations.

"Why don't I do an album?" Frank sits on the examination table in his blue bikini underwear talking to Robert on his cell phone. "I'm here in my doctor's office and the place is lined with so many gold records, I don't know whether he's going to give me a tetanus shot or a Grammy."

"Let me look into it. I'll see if there's interest."

Robert is seated at his desk in his office, having put his lawyer on hold to take Frank's call, talent always first, never mind he was in the middle of dealing with Barry Bitterman's hundred-million-dollar lawsuit.

"Can we release it ourselves?"

"What, you're gonna sell it in the back of the clubs like Girl Scout cookies? Don't think like a *pisher,* Frank. Let me see if I can get you a deal."

"Anything from Lynx yet?"

"Still waiting."

Frank snaps the phone shut just as Dr. Cashman glides in, slim, balding, all business.

"What's up, Mr. Frank? Nothing life-threatening, I hope. I got one of the surviving Bee Gees in the next room with an inflamed larynx." Doctor-patient confidentiality out the window here in Beverly Hills.

"Take a look at my back, Doc."

Cashman steps to the side of the examination table and makes a sound that indicates he does not like what he sees.

"What is that?"

"It's a cat scratch."

"You banging a lion tamer?" The doctor conversant on all levels of show business, Frank choosing to ignore the crude, if somewhat accurate, implication.

"What's going on back there? It feels like someone's doing acupuncture with a rusty nail."

"You've got a nice little infection. When did this happen?"

"Couple of days ago."

"Your own cat?"

"Don't ask."

"Fair enough. I'm going to give you an injection, and do you have a painkiller of choice or is that a stupid question?"

It was a stupid question.

Frank was duly injected and left the office with his own legitimate

122

prescription, with which he would surreptitiously replace what he'd borrowed from Honey, who had been known to count pills.

Frank drives home pondering whether he has enough good material to fill an entire CD. He knows he won't be able to get a contract by saying he'll play with an audience for an hour and hope for the best. It occurs to him he may need to freshen his set, which, other than his riffing-on-the-headlines material, has remained unchanged for ten years. That will require the laborious process of actually generating new material, which, despite his recent minting of the Kennedy-Jesus-Muhammad-looks-like-Phil-Silvers bit, has not been flowing of late.

Parking the car in front of his house, Frank reaches into the tin mailbox, removes the contents, and heads up the path to the front door. Along with three bills, a charity solicitation, and Honey's copy of the *New York Review of Books,* there is a mortgage-payment notice for his place in Playa Perdida, the out-of-the-way Mexican beach town where he had purchased a cliffside shack. This was seven years ago when, on a coke-fueled trip to Mexico with a bunch of comics looking for pure, cheap tequila and the ladies who liked it, Frank, in a drunken haze, had inadvertently stumbled into a Day of the Dead festival, which seemed to consist, at least to his inebriated eyes, of an entire town, men, women, and children, dressed as skeletons, running around, wailing, cavorting, emitting otherworldly sounds; banshees having touched down on Earth and materialized in the forms of these temporarily deranged Mexican townspeople. Their bold embracing of death and decay appealed to Frank's morbid streak. However clean American life appeared to be, however sterile and antiseptic, Frank knew it to be a shimmering illusion sold to a nation of narcotized consumers who signed on to the fantasy of eternal youth, blind to the skull lurking behind every polished face. Mexico had it right. Death was nearby; it was with us; it was inescapable. All the Botox in the world wasn't going to smooth out that wrinkle. Sometime in the middle of that night, while throwing back shots with a taxi driver who barely spoke a word of English, Frank decided he

123

possessed a deep and abiding love for Mexico's people and culture (if not it's cannabis, which he found harsh), a love he intended to consummate with the purchase of real estate.

Frank opens the envelope and pulls out the payment slip. A barely perceptible smile dances on his thin lips. When this bill is sent to the Mexican bank that floated his mortgage, he will own Casa del Bones outright. In his head he hears a mariachi band play the Clash song "I'm So Bored with the USA."

"Where the fuck is my Vicodin?"

Honey stands in the middle of the living room wearing nothing but jeans so tight they seem to have been Krylonned on. Her new grapefruit-size breasts are cantilevered over a gym-bunny stomach at a ninety-degree angle as if, having found themselves incongruously marooned on her slender torso, they are longingly looking for their place of origin. She points these distended interlopers at Frank, nipples large and angry. "My tits are killing me. The incisions are swollen or something so I open the fuckin' medicine chest because I think there might be some painkillers in there and the fuckin' Vicodin is gone! Did you take them?" *J'accuse!*

Frank reaches into his pocket and pulls out a prescription bottle, which he presents with a flourish, a pharmaceutical magician producing a narcotic rabbit.

"Give me that!"

Frank hands her the pills and gets her a glass of water. She pops the painkiller, chasing it with the water, and looks at the bottle, her mood still querulous and her breasts unmoving.

"How'd you get this?" she demands, knowing something's not kosher.

"I saw Cashman."

"Why?"

"I have a little infection, too."

Infection? That's certainly not the word she wants to hear coming from the man she has slept with exclusively for nearly five years, entirely faithful to his microbes. And he to hers, she had hoped. Infection smacks of the odious STD family and the viral mayhem inherent therein; not an area of possibility Honey, clean of body if not pure of mind, is keen to entertain.

"What kind of infection?"

Frank had taken some time to prepare this story. He had tried a few angles that incorporated a house cat, but none were remotely plausible, and the notion of a squirrel having dropped onto him from a tree would not fly in Los Angeles, where the indigenous ones move with the studied insouciance of 1950s jazz musicians, so he had had to generate a narrative that did not involve an animal. Here is what he came up with:

"I didn't want to tell you this because I thought it might upset you." Frank is slightly distracted by the sight of her breasts, clearly larger and more immobile than Dr. Nasrut Singh had advertised. "By the way, is that their final size?"

"Are they too big?" Honey asks, distractible as a puppy.

"No, but . . ." They are curiously unsexual in their current state, but he can't tell her that since it will only cause more aggro.

"Dr. Singh says the swelling goes down in a couple of weeks. You don't mind if I walk around like this for now, though, do you?"

"Just put something on when the pizza guy comes."

"You were saying about your infection . . ."

"I'm at the Comedy Shop the other night and this guy is heckling me so I do what I usually do, you know . . . I tied him in knots and I think I embarrassed him in front of his girlfriend, which, when the guy is a drunken sociopath, is not a good idea. So I'm having a drink after I do my set and all of a sudden I feel something raking down my back, tearing at my skin almost like a cat was scratching me."

"He attacked you?"

"With a fork!"

"Frank, why didn't you tell me?"

"I just told you why I didn't tell you. But I got a scrip from Cashman and I'm glad I can help." Frank always thinking of others, a regular saint.

She kisses him on the mouth, careful not to press the new additions against him for fear of aggravating her situation. They kiss for a few moments and then Honey, her suspicions allayed by the tale of the fork-wielding fan, leads Frank into the bedroom.

A few moments later, with Honey in bed on all fours and Frank distractedly humping away behind her, the phone rings. There had been a time when they had sex that a stick of dynamite could have detonated in the closet and Frank and Honey would not have stopped rutting. The building could have caved in around their entwined bodies, surrounded them in rubble and torn pipes, covered them in a cloud of dust, and still they would have kept at it like weasels, so devoted were they to the pure carnal pleasure each took from the other.

That time had passed.

Both Frank and Honey, believers in the canard that their lives could be changed with a single phone call, glanced at the caller ID: NADA.

Honey forms words first. "Are you going to get it?"

Frank answers by picking up the receiver, multitasking. "Hello."

"Frank, it's Tessa from Robert Hyler's office." Ah, the lovely Tessa, Frank almost able to smell her Pear's-soap scent as he continues to move in and out of Honey at a slightly slower pace.

"Hi, babe. How's tricks?"

"I'm good. Are you coming to the office soon?"

"If you're there." At this, Frank sees the dragon tattoo on Honey's shoulder shift position and a millisecond later Honey's one-eyed profile, hissing.

"Stop flirting with her!"

Frank covers the mouthpiece with his hand, giving Honey a hard thrust, intended to distract; instead, it has the opposite effect.

"I'm working, babe," Frank whispers. "It's part of the job." The dragon having returned to its original position, Honey staring at the pillow, not pleased. Then, back into the receiver: "Does the Hyler woman want to talk to me?"

"He's waiting," Tessa replies, not getting into the gender-shifting game Frank is playing.

At that moment, Robert gets on the line and Tessa's soothing English tone goes silent, the imagined scent of Pear's evaporating.

"Frank." Matter-of-fact. "How you doing?" Matter-of-fact never a good tone with Robert, who loves to call with glad tidings and could make a simple "Hello" sound like Christmas morning.

"I'm great, Bobby. What's shaking?" The blood in Frank's loins is starting to punch the clock and head out for the day what with all these conversations. He quickens the pace of his thrusts in an attempt to delay the exit dash.

"Lynx passed on your idea."

So much for stanching the internal flow. Frank's suddenly flaccid member forlornly flops out of the peeved Honey as he sits on the side of the bed, his free hand working his right temple where he is starting to notice a dull pain.

"What do you mean they passed? Was it a soft pass?" *Soft pass* meaning "Can we come back in and try again after making humiliating adjustments?"

"It wasn't a soft pass. It was the kind of pass where they don't want to do it."

"You're killing me, babe."

"Now listen, and let me finish before you jump down my throat. I talked to Pam Penner about *Kirkuk* and they're still interested in you, but they're about to go out to Cheetah Thayer, so if you're going to do it, you have to decide now."

"Cheetah Thayer?" This name is a cannonball fired across Frank's bow, Cheetah Thayer being a comic ten years younger than Frank whose act consists of caterwauling as if Arabs are torturing him while he works his way through a series of banal observations about politics and family life, ending with an impression of Bono from U2, to whom he bears a faint resemblance. Frank holds Cheetah in very low regard.

"They're ready to give him the show."

"Forget it, Bobby. Any interest in the record deal?"

"We first discussed it an hour ago. Give me a few minutes."

"I'd like to get something in place before we establish a Mars colony," Frank says.

Another twenty seconds of subtle digs, both Robert and Frank annoyed with the other, and the conversation is terminated. Frank is naked and motionless on the side of the bed, headache arriving, depression phoning from the Greyhound station, murmuring, "I'm in town, Frank, send a car." Honey lies on her back, looking over at Frank, whose shoulder she is seeing for the first time since his close encounter with the animal kingdom.

"A guy did that to you with a fork?"

"Yeah, that's what I said."

She sits up and runs a press-on nail along the skin next to the wound.

"Really?" Her tone suggesting something other than credulity.

"I'm lucky he didn't kill me. I could see that headline: 'Bones Assassinated with Fork.'" Frank grandiose enough to think someone murdering him would qualify as an assassination, a homicide with a larger agenda. "You don't want to get smoked in a ridiculous way," he reflects, knowing he can divert her, at least temporarily, by riffing on the subject at hand, Honey always one to stand back and watch him rip. "Like getting hit by a Good Humor truck or something. You don't want to die getting hit by some guy dressed head to toe in white with a money changer on his belt. Because that's how they're gonna remember you. He's the guy who was crushed by a truckload of toasted-almond bars."

But it doesn't work. Honey's not distracted.

"What happened to the guy? Did they arrest him?"

"He got away in the confusion."

"Really? He got away?"

Same lack of credulity; the whole absurd death-under-the-wheels-of-an-ice-cream-truck run not working at all.

"Babe, what's with the third degree? It's enough someone stabbed me with a fork, I don't need Helga, She-Devil of the SS," referring to the Aryan Honey, "beating up on me like I'm Rabbi Flakeman of Chelm."

"I'm Helga now?" Pissed. That's what Frank calls her whenever he wants to draw attention to their disparate ethnicities, Honey's being German-Irish and Frank's being obvious.

"I mean, that fat dyke Pam Penner just passed on my show, never mind she didn't stop grinning like an idiot the whole fuckin' meeting, so frankly I don't need any shit from you or your new tits right now. And, by the way, I'm paying for the procedure in installments, which means I have to do three nights in Sacramento next week so Dr. Nasrut Singh doesn't come in here and repossess them."

Frank, having worked himself into a righteous froth, goes to take a shower, his diatribe having had the effect, along with the Vicodin, just now kicking in, of momentarily silencing Honey. But after a few minutes of soaping and shampooing during which he wonders how much longer he can take having to make up ridiculous lies to cover his philandering, he squints through wet eyes and makes out her still-naked form on the other side of the shower curtain.

"I've owned cats, Frank," she informs him in an even tone. "That thing on your back looks like a cat scratch."

All is quiet as Frank works the cream rinse through his thick hair. When did Honey turn into Hercule Poirot?

"Whose cat was it, Frank?"

"I told you what happened."

He tilts his head back, letting the water run the milky dregs of the conditioner out of his hair and down the drain. Watching it swirl on the shower floor and wondering whether to unburden himself, he quickly realizes that could do no possible good, which leaves silence as the only plausible alternative for the time being. His mind goes to his soon-to-be-paid-for house in Playa Perdida and whether he might entice Candi Wyatt down there for a weekend of sodomy and burritos.

Honey abruptly pulls the curtain back and stares at Frank's damp face, red from the heat of the shower, her own determined physiognomy wrenched into place, ready to do a job. She prepares to deliver an ultimatum, one that will set the course of their relationship from this point on, her nakedness taking nothing away from her clench-jawed determination.

"You're going to do that Eskimo show."

"That is not going to happen."

"Then I'm moving out."

Five minutes later Frank gets out of the shower. He towels off and heads for the bedroom, where there is no sign of Honey. He gets dressed in silence and goes to the kitchen. No Honey. Looks out the back window toward their small pool, where he often sees her relaxing on a chaise longue with *People* or, lately, the *New York Review of Books*. Not there. Frank takes a Corona out of the refrigerator and sits at the kitchen counter. At this point, he is wondering if Dr. Nasrut Singh put some kind of time-release assertiveness-inducing chemical in Honey's implants because, narcissist that he is, Frank can see no other cause for her recent behavior.

What are his options? He can do the show without Honey, thereby saving his television career but destroying his apparently tottering relationship. He can do it with Honey and save his television career and his relationship. Or he could not do the show, thereby destroying both his career and whatever you want to call the sorry state of affairs at which he and Honey have arrived. On the other hand, if the show is, as he presumes, a stinker, his television career would tank but he would still have the increasingly enigmatic Honey at his side. None of these strike Frank as particularly pleasant alternatives as he sits in the gathering twilight drinking his beer. Frank has another beer and then another, and as he slowly becomes drunk, his feelings are increasingly scabrous. If that self-important twit Lloyd Melnick had agreed to cowrite *My Life and High Times,* I wouldn't be sitting here entertaining evil thoughts about him, went Frank's causal thinking. Somehow, his inability to recognize himself, through a long series of behaviors and decisions, as the author of what he viewed as his misfortune redounded on the balding Melnick head.

That night the Melnicks have dinner at Drago, a pricey Italian place on Wilshire Boulevard, with Marisa and Jonathan Pinsker. The Pinskers have been friends of Lloyd and Stacy's for several years, the wives having bonded during a Mommy and Me class at Temple Isaiah. Jonathan is an accountant at Paramount and Marisa spends his money. Their modest Beverly Hills–adjacent house is constantly being remodeled, but no matter what Marisa does, whether it is painting or putting in a new bathroom or kitchen countertops, she is still left with a house that is Beverly Hills–adjacent when she longs for the real thing. At dinner the Melnicks and the Pinskers discuss their children, who had been classmates at the Montessori school, upcoming vacation plans (the Pinskers are going to visit their families in New York), and whether Home Depot is a good stock to buy since everyone seems to be remodeling these days.

The Pinskers are pleasant, but it is Stacy, not Lloyd, who keeps the friendship alive. Lloyd finds Jonathan irredeemably boring. His only subject of conversation other than his daughter is business, and to Lloyd there are few duller areas. The prism through which Jonathan Pinsker sees movies, television, and music is entirely financial, and in Lloyd's mind, it is the Pinskers of the world, these bloodless human spreadsheets, that are ruining something that had once been great. They have been very deferential to Lloyd since his Lynx deal was announced, the numbers being something Jonathan can relate to.

Lloyd tries hard to focus on the conversation. Periodically he interjects a comment so it does not appear as if he's fallen asleep. He perks up when Stacy tells a story about Dustin having had a meltdown of such intensity in the women's shoe department at Saks that when he finally calmed down, shoppers actually applauded in relief and mock appreciation. Although she is clearly suffering with their son's behavior, Stacy manages to give the story an amusing spin, which Lloyd finds endearing.

"I can't believe you guys don't have any child care," Marisa remarks, stabbing a porcini mushroom and putting it in her mouth.

"The one real advantage of that is your kid speaks Spanish, which, I suppose, is good these days," Stacy replies. It is a point of pride with her that she and Lloyd have never hired a nanny to look after Dustin. Lloyd would gladly spring for one, but Stacy decided, having quit working, that she wanted to spend as much time with her son as possible. Lloyd knows, given the boy's challenging personality, this has not been the easiest task, and he has a great deal of respect for the way Stacy has stuck with her plan. Marisa Pinsker, on the other hand, is puzzled by what she perceives to be her friend's eccentricity.

"You should just hire a nanny, Stace. Your life would be soooo much easier," Marisa says as her husband nods mutely.

"Wasn't yours stealing from the medicine cabinet?" Stacy asks.

"Yeah, but then we got an honest one. From Honduras," Marisa adds, as if endorsing the nationality.

"I don't want a stranger raising my son," Stacy concludes, accidentally violating the social contract that proscribes the obvious questioning of a friend's life choices. Lloyd inwardly smiles as the table falls silent for an awkward moment. Unfortunately, when Marisa changes the subject and begins telling them what happened on her favorite reality show last week, staying awake becomes an uphill battle. That Stacy seems to be enjoying herself does not surprise him. What does surprise him, however, is what she says on the ride home.

"What do you think Jonathan makes?"

"I don't know. A hundred, a hundred and twenty-five, maybe," he says, placing them in the heart of the new Los Angeles middle class where the numbers sound large but bill paying is an E-ticket ride. Stacy always liked to talk about other people's money and often asked Lloyd what he thought this person or that one earned.

"And she can't stop remodeling that crappy little house."

"That's what they can afford."

"Jonathan's maxed out on his salary, right? How much can you make as an accountant?"

"I have no idea and to be honest, I don't really care."

Stacy thinks about this a moment, trying to answer her own question, then looks over at Lloyd. "Do you think they're losers?"

"They're *your* friends."

"I know. But they're from where we've been, you know? Not where we're going."

They ride in silence for a few moments, before Lloyd, not taking his eyes off the road, asks, "What would you think if I wrote a book?" With this non sequitur Stacy looks at him as if he had just asked what she thought of the Molotov–von Ribbentrop Pact, her eyes saying, *What could this possibly have to do with anything in our lives?* But he is her husband so this is simply a spousal peculiarity she will have to put up with, like an interest in model trains or orchid growing.

"I think it's fine. What would you do, like a Michael Crichton thing?"

"I was thinking about something more literary."

"He makes more money than God."

"Yes, he does," Lloyd says.

"If you want to write a book, you should write a book," Stacy concludes.

Slinky slivers of salmon sunlight . . .

The sun washed gently over the bumpy hills, leaving a residue of pineapple light . . .

God's fingers swept the sky . . .

Lloyd, wearing old sweatpants and a T-shirt, is seated at the computer in his home office in Mar Vista. Stacy and Dustin are asleep elsewhere in the house. It's nearly two in the morning and he has been up trying to write. On what is he laboring at this late hour? Is it the pilot idea every network in town is vying for the privilege of purchasing? No, it is nothing so mundane as a mere television script. Rather, it is what he dreams will be the beginnings of the Lloyd Melnick oeuvre, an early

133

effort at what he hopes will come to be referred to by future cultural historians as "Melnick-iana," his first novel. Or at least the notebook that will lead to the first novel. Because Lloyd does not actually have characters or a plot just yet, although he has faith those will come. In the meantime, he has set about doing a series of literary exercises: piano scales for the beginner, whereby he would attempt to render people's faces or physical landscapes in the kind of prose you might find in a literary novel, the kind reviewed in the pages of respectable newspapers. Lloyd had assigned himself the task of describing a sunset and has been trying different versions of red/orange/sienna, orb/globe/sphere, for the last several hours. He stares at the screen and reads softly to himself.

"The slinky sun sloped southerly . . ." Realizes maybe he's leaning a little heavily on the alliteration. Concerned he may lack the poetical skills necessary to render a sunset in any but the most prosaic terms. Worries Tai Chi could be another Amy Tan. Lloyd takes a deep breath. Writing was never this difficult when he was a journalist, he reflects. When he was doing a story, he would simply sit at his desk accompanied by a cup of coffee and the assembled facts and begin typing. Unconcerned with posterity, he would usually have something perfectly serviceable an hour later. But this literature business is an entirely different animal. He has been at it for weeks now, banging away with mounting frustration and increasingly tortured by the thought that everything he comes up with is crap.

The slinky sun sloped southerly?

Who am I kidding? This is bad D. H. Lawrence. No, it's not even up to that standard. It's more like bad Dr. Seuss. Where is my voice? Where is that distinct prose style that will separate me from the wannabes who can't tell a participle from a diphthong and scream LLOYD MELNICK WROTE THIS? I was good in grammar back in the seventh grade. I had a positively geometric sense of how words fit together on a page. Yes, that was just engineering, the practical skills that let me function as a journalist, but I was a happy bricklayer and I sensed the presence of a muse at the time. I remember the poems I wrote in high school, the short stories in college. All right, they weren't very good but who was writing good material at that age? And they weren't bad, exactly. Okay, the poems were bad, but not the short stories. *The creative writing professor I had in college liked them. He was a drunk, yes, but he had won some prestigious literary prizes. He would know. Certainly, I had the glimmer of a muse. Why didn't I keep writing back then? Why did I stop? How did I allow myself to get sidetracked by the mundane day to day of existence—career, marriage, parenthood, mortgage, car payments; the pinched life of a middle-aged man? Oh, for a muse of fire!*

Fire? I'd settle for a matchstick at this point.

How did Homer get away with "rosy-fingered dawn"? What, exactly, is so great about that?

Lloyd has finessed his way to a career as a successful television writer, but in the years since he'd left New York behind he had lost touch with an animating insight he'd had in his youth—if the whole world is filled with mediocrity, then to be a little more than adequate is to excel. While this philosophy works should you find yourself on the staff of a sitcom, it is less dependable if you are trying to create literature.

Tired and knowing he has to show up at the office the next day or risk being underestimated by his industrious assistant, Lloyd hits the SAVE key and consigns the evening's output to the hard drive, pleased to have at least taken another step, however minuscule, in this new direction. He turns off the light in his office and walks quietly to his bedroom. Tiptoeing on the soft carpet so as not to awaken Stacy, Lloyd enters the bathroom, and closing the door behind him before turning on the light, he opens the medicine chest and removes a bottle of NyQuil. Lloyd doesn't have a cold, not even the hint of a sniffle, but he finds a belt of the green liquid serves the same function as a nightcap did for his parents with the added benefit of not requiring mixers and ice. He removes the plastic shot glass that covers the cap, unscrews the cap, and pours himself a fix. Tossing it back, he grimaces as the medicinal liquid coats his throat. He rinses the shot glass with water before capping the bottle. Then, placing his drug of choice back in the immaculate medicine chest, he turns the light off before opening the bathroom door and quietly walks over to the bed, where he lies down next to his sleeping wife. Getting under the covers without disturbing her, Lloyd turns his back and goes to sleep, wondering exactly how far Tai Chi has gotten in her novel and what was the likelihood he could persuade her to have sex with him.

The following day Frank is at a table in Duke's desultorily picking at his matzo Brie. It's the time between breakfast and lunch and the place is empty save for a few sleepy-eyed layabouts with their noses buried in newspapers, several strivers with laptops, and two waitresses who are rearranging the condiment displays on the tables. Across from Frank, working his way through a plate of eggs, sausages, and hash browns, is Orson Dubinsky, auteur of *Kirkuk*.

While most sitcom writers affect an entirely unthreatening, domesticated façade, the kind of face that says you can leave your car/baby/bank balance with me and it will be washed/educated/wisely invested when you get back, Orson Dubinsky opts for another mode of presentation: he looks like Rasputin, the mad monk of czarist Russia. His long, dark hair is parted in the middle and falls nearly to the bottom of his back. Thick, black-framed glasses cover the upper reaches of his face while the lower forty is foliated by tendrils of beard growing in multi-directional clumps out of his pale cheeks and neck. His skin bears the telltale pockmarks of teenaged acne, and as he speaks, he massages his jaw with his fingers to ease the pain caused by the braces he has recently installed in his mouth. Frank can't help but wonder why someone who resembles Czarina Alexandra's personal trainer is worried about crooked teeth, given his serial-killer-like appearance, but there it is.

The man's grooming would lead you to think he lived in a refrigerator carton under a bridge when in fact he makes his home in the hills above Los Feliz with a wife and three kids who go to private school, thank you very much; Orson floating the house, the pool, and the matching SUVs with a large development deal he had been given (though not as large as Lloyd's) after tilling the comedy-writing fields for lo these many years.

Kirkuk is his chance, his shot, the brass ring he's been reaching for his entire career.

"I was rocked when Pam Penner called and said you wanted to do the show, man," Orson enthuses, citing the perfidious lesbian as he attempts to dislodge a piece of potato from his braces with his little finger.

"Hey," Frank replies, all fake bonhomie, still annoyed he couldn't sell his own pilot. "It's a great script."

"Dude, you are going to take it to a whole nother level." Orson impales a piece of sausage with his fork and, stuffing it in his mouth, continues, "Pam Penner said she wanted to do breakthrough television, dude. What we're gonna do, is an apocalyptic-spaghetti-noir, half-hour Eskimo thing that is going to reveal the future of broadcast television. When you ride into the village on the walrus, it's going to be like Alan Ladd in *Shane,* only funnier. See, it may be comedy but it's got a dark edge to it, which is why we need someone like you," and here Orson stops once again to attend to an errant piece of toast lodged in his braces. "So it's really not a straight comedy exactly, it's more of a spaghetti-noir-edy," the *spaghetti* here referring not to the popular pasta but to a series of westerns filmed in Italy in the 1960s and beloved by discerning cinéastes.

Frank nods as he takes in this ridiculous conflation of sitcom, western, and film noir that in the peculiar madness induced by too much television, Orson is able to envision taking place in the environs of the arctic circle. In spite of himself, he finds it weirdly appealing.

"There's something we need to talk about. I have to bring it up and I hope you can go with it because it could be a deal breaker," Frank says, looking Orson in the eye in an attempt to convey seriousness of purpose.

"Frank, man, I've wanted to work with you since I saw Killer Bones do a gig at the Bottom Line in New York."

"You saw my band?" Here Frank brightens from gray to slightly less gray. He's warming up to Orson.

"I loved the Dylan-at-the-dentist bit. So, you know, whatever you need."

"Who's playing Borak?"

"We're looking for an Eskimo actress."

"An Eskimo, really?" Frank nods thoughtfully.

"Keepin' it real, you know."

137

"I hear you."

"Do you know any?"

"Not off the top of my head."

"Yeah, it's been a problem. There aren't a lot of them."

Frank looks into the middle distance, as if cogitating on Orson's inability to find an actual Inuit actress, appearing to rack his brain; perhaps trying to remember a poster he'd noticed in his more northerly travels for an all-Eskimo dinner-theater production of *Barefoot in the Park* that might have featured a girl whose talents would lend themselves to the role of Borak.

"Do you know the name Honey Call?"

"She's your girlfriend, isn't she?"

"And a very talented actress."

"Dude, don't take this wrong, okay? I hope you're not offended . . . I have *Hot Ninja Bounty Hunters* on DVD. My wife loves that movie."

"Mrs. Dubinsky is a man of wealth and taste," Frank comments, noticing Mrs. Dubinsky's husband has a piece of egg half an inch long hanging from his beard.

Mr. Dubinsky ignores Frank having referred to his wife as a man and plows ahead. "Does Honey want to do the show?"

"I could talk to her. But she's not an Eskimo."

"To tell you the truth, that idea was coming more from the network than me, and honestly, I think it's a losing proposition." Orson reflects for a moment on the vision of Honey swathed in animal pelts and likes what he sees. "To get Honey in the show with you . . ." Here Orson Dubinsky squeezes his eyes shut, envisioning the heights of artistic accomplishment that could be scaled with such a team at his side, internally rhapsodizing about the possibilities, the encomiums, the quintessential sense of attainment that would be his. "That's the kind of message I want to send the network. *Kirkuk*"—Orson pauses to gather his thoughts—"it isn't just some workplace comedy about a recovering alcoholic Eskimo trying to run scams out of his uncle's casino. It's a little guy fighting the machine, trying to grab a crumb from the capitalist pie.

It's about nonconformity, man," asserts this dues-paying member of the Los Feliz Neighborhood Watch. "Putting Honey in it is so . . . so . . ." Here Orson searches for the mot juste that will describe his vision in the most unique, unclichéd way and arrives with "Edgy! Lynx needs that kind of statement to cut through the clutter."

"Oh, she'll cut through the clutter."

"Let me tell you something, Frank," Orson Dubinsky says, leaning toward his new collaborator. "If I'm sitting on the couch channel surfing after a hard day at work and I see Honey standing on an ice floe in a bikini . . . dude, I'm throwing out the remote."

Frank is thinking this could work.

Chapter 9

Lloyd sits across town in a Euro-Laotian restaurant with fish tanks embedded in the floor and koi swimming beneath Plexiglas at his feet. He is meeting with Bart Pimento, a preternaturally handsome movie star whose career had recently run aground after he capped a string of flops with some dubious professional behavior involving creative differences and facial hair. Lloyd stares at Bart, a specimen on a slide, as the actor prattles on about himself and his many concerns including animal rights, Wicca, and what he believed to be the criminally underappreciated societal value of the hemp plant. Bart's blond mane, which is usually pulled back into a ponytail between gigs, hangs loosely and frames a traditionally handsome, unlined face. His cobalt blue eyes are set apart at the perfect distance, his nose the gold standard for plastic surgeons everywhere. The lips are full and slightly bowed, lending them an almost feminine quality that makes him nonthreatening yet desirable to women and gay men, for whom he has become something of a poster boy.

As Lloyd gazes at Bart, he is feeling the elaborate façade all not particularly handsome men construct, the one that allows them to peer in the mirror each morning and think, *I look good,* begin to crumble. He senses his eyes moving closer as his nose, already generously proportioned, expands and his lips begin to flap clownishly. And what's that? Hair growing out of his ears? Right now?

Bart Pimento possessed the kind of looks that could make ninety-eight percent of male humanity gaze in the mirror and see the reflection of a warthog, and Lloyd is a member in good standing of that ninety-eight percent. He takes some comfort in the realization that although Bart may be fine looking, his own SATs were way higher—if the actor even took them, since he probably didn't go to college. At least Lloyd fervently hoped he hadn't. The thought that someone as beautiful as Bart could also be intelligent was simply unbearable.

He needn't worry.

Bart has recently returned from the northern-Canadian set of a big-budget movie where he had been let go the day before shooting was to commence for refusing to shave the mustache he had grown for the role, the aforementioned creative differences and facial hair. Normally, if the star is important enough, and certainly there had been a time when Bart was important, a mustache would not be a problem. Doctors might have mustaches, scientists, teachers; they could all be hirsute. But Bart had been hired to play a monk, specifically, an American monk adept at the various martial arts. Despite the director explaining to Bart that the highly paid consultant-monk, flown in from Tibet at great cost specifically to advise on this movie, had informed him his brethren did not sport mustaches, the actor, who believed this particular character, this multilayered violent holy man, must have a mustache, could not be persuaded to shave it off.

There was a time when Bart floated above ordinary life, when his name, always in boldface, had been romantically linked to myriad movie stars and supermodels and his gorgeous visage graced the cover of every glossy magazine. During those charmed days that had drifted by in a haze of photo shoots, publicity junkets, and cocaine snorted off the bare bottoms of young actresses in bathroom stalls of trendy nightclubs, Bart had existed in the exalted hothouse of pop cultural approbation; it was then he could have gotten away with the prima donna act. But that ship has sailed.

He was the star of three consecutive flops.

He was a pain in the ass.

He was fired.

Having made his point, that he is nobody's fool (!), the mustache came off in the bathroom of the first-class cabin on the flight from Saskatch-ewan to Los Angeles. Bart relates this story to Lloyd while absentmind-edly twiddling the strings on his hemp sweatshirt.

"At the end of the day," Bart says, employing a verbal construct that makes Lloyd wince, "that putz," meaning the director, whose last film had won the Palm d'Or at the Cannes Film Festival, "wasn't going to tell me what to do. But it's all good." Lloyd winces again. "I wasn't crazy about the role."

A quick aside about why Lloyd is having lunch with a fading movie star.

Due to the collective inferiority complex of most television execu-tives, which cause them to erroneously believe movies are better than TV, the various network brain trusts are always ready to be persuaded that movie star A, whose career is on life support, will be able to find a huge audience in television. Never mind people have stopped going to their movies. The collective wisdom holds that movie stars are good for networks because that gives them known quantities to promote to a cretinous public, who, it is assumed, are not interested in mere stories but are easily seduced by stars, however unpopular they have become in movies.

This phenomenon had led Pam Penner to take überagent Yuri Klipstein's call the previous week:

"Pam, Yuri Klipstein."

"The well-known flesh peddler? Who are you selling?"

"Oh, fuck you, you big dyke. Don't pretend I don't care about you as a person."

"I love it when you talk dirty."

"How's tricks?"

"I could use more pussy."

"That's two of us."

"Your wife not putting out?"

"This conversation just got way too personal."

"I show you mine but you don't show me yours?"

"Okay, enough with the schmoozle. I don't want this getting around town."

"My lips are sealed."

"You're the first person I'm calling because I think I can blow your mind."

"You're gonna get me a lunch date with Uma Thurman?"

"Let me make a phone call."

"Yuri, I'm all ears."

"Bart Pimento *may* be—and let me stress I'm emphasizing the word *may*—he *may* be willing to do television."

That was all it took. Bart's agent runs the flag of his possible availability up the pole and the Lynx Network instantly salutes with a deal guaranteeing him a show within a year and awarding him a big payday whether or not he gets one. After the signing, Pam Penner went to see Harvey Gornish to discuss the best possible way to deploy this new hunk of potential ratings muscle, and after kicking around several ideas including having Bart play a doctor, a lawyer, and a navy SEAL, Pam phoned Yuri Klipstein to gauge Bart's level of interest in them.

That conversation was brief.

"Harvey would like to see Bart in a franchise show," Pam says. "Does he want to play a cop or a lawyer?"

"He wants to do an edgy comedy" was Yuri's reply.

"He's never done comedy," Pam pointed out.

"He wants to do an edgy comedy," Yuri repeated, concluding the exchange.

This mandate was obediently delivered to Harvey, and after mulling over the Lynx development slate with Pam, who was feeling less jolly than usual now that she was to be part of the Bart Pimento comedy trial balloon, and weeding out the obvious mismatches (all of them requiring Bart to play a parent, something he categorically refused to do, believing it to be the kiss of career death for a sex god), it was decided that Pam's idea for a show set in a Las Vegas massage parlor could provide Bart with the perfect television vehicle. Pam called Yuri to run it by him and Yuri called his client to gauge his interest in the concept. Bart was thrilled at the prospect of playing what was going to be America's first prime-time pimp, and when this was relayed to the people at Lynx, they did everything but go up on the roof and set off fireworks.

Harvey believed the extremely overpaid Lloyd Melnick was the perfect man to write it, and Pam was summarily dispatched to discuss this with Lynx's favorite new employee. As for Lloyd, he was expected to accept this managerial fiat with the equanimity of a five-thousand-dollar hooker staring down at a foot-long dildo and being asked to turn around.

"Bart Pimento?"

Lloyd could not keep the sense of distress out of his voice. Indeed, it had caused his inflection to rise as he hit the second syllable of Bart's last name, causing him to instantly regret having spoken. Pam Penner and Jason Fendi had dropped into his office on the lot the afternoon previous to his lunch with the youthful flickering star. Lloyd's laptop lay open on his desk where he had been working on a description of a mountain lake, having just written the sentence *The blue faraway of the sky reflected fetchingly in the trembling water,* when Tai Chi, who had been interrupted at her own literary labors, buzzed him on the intercom and said, "Uh, Lloyd, you have some visitors."

A moment later Lloyd had looked up expecting to see Stacy and Cam Rousseau arriving to once again rearrange his office furniture for maximum energy flow, and was quite taken aback when instead of his wife and her feng shui consultant, Pam and Jason crossed the threshold. After a short exchange of pleasantries Lloyd was apprised of the situation and you are familiar with his response.

"You don't like him?" Pam asked, chagrined but not surprised. "We just signed him to a huge holding deal. Harvey is beside himself."

"It's not that I don't like him. He's fine. But do you go to his movies?"

"Lloyd, no one goes to his movies. That's why we could sign him," Pam explained, being no dummy. "If anyone went to his movies, he wouldn't be doing TV."

"But I don't have anything I'm ready to pitch."

Now came the part of the conversation Pam was dreading, the part where she was going to have to inform Lloyd that a power higher than the two of them was controlling this particular situation.

"Harvey really wants you to write *Happy Endings*."

"The massage parlor show?" Lloyd responded. He had assumed that idea had slinked back to the swamp from which it emerged. Now he was wondering if the horror he was feeling had been sufficiently concealed.

"And he wants it for Bart."

Lloyd looked at Pam as she said this and knew she was simply doing what she was programmed to do. He couldn't fault her personally because she has car payments, a mortgage, and a cute young girlfriend whose career in origami she is subsidizing with her Lynx salary. But he had the dawning sense that this could be the exact moment his career goes into the tank.

"Why does Harvey think I'm the guy to write this?"

"You're his favorite!" This from the ever-annoying Jason.

"Wasn't Bart Pimento arrested for throwing fake blood on some old lady's fur coat at a PETA protest?" Lloyd said, trying to change the subject.

"He's entitled to his opinions," Pam assured Lloyd. "We're in America."

"I defer to no man when it comes to the First Amendment, but I'd like to point out that it seems like the act of an overly earnest guy, and earnestness, as we know, is the enemy of comedy."

"Have lunch with him."

"Could we just share a bag of Doritos outside the commissary for five minutes?"

"Lloyd, look, no one's going to ram him down your throat, but it's Harvey's idea so you kind of have to take the meeting. And then you have to write the script," she added, laughing uncomfortably, as if she were joking.

Lloyd closed his eyes and ruminated on how he could have sold his soul for a house in Brentwood.

"I think it's a really good suggestion," Jason offered.

"I know he's not a laugh riot," Pam sympathized. "But, hey, if you have a better idea, pitch it to him. Then you won't have to write the massage parlor thing. Do it for Mama."

This was a reasonable request given Lloyd actually likes Pam, not perceiving her as adversarial, but rather as a high-level functionary who hasn't become completely inured to the absurdity of her job, a kindred spirit to some degree, capable of regarding her surroundings and the duties she performs within them with a certain degree of wry detachment. Nonetheless, he put his head in his hands and emitted a loud moan. He knew he was being overdramatic, but he had once seen Bart Pimento on a talk show discuss how he prepared for a role by employing the techniques of Sun Tzu. And he wasn't kidding. Lloyd, having conveyed his thoughts, looked up at Pam and Jason. But Lloyd says nothing further on the topic, and after another minute of small talk during which he wonders if stress can cause internal bleeding, they leave.

After the executives packed up their meat grinder and departed, Lloyd found himself too distracted by the unanticipated politics of his job to pursue further work on the description of the mountain lake. Unable to get beyond *the trembling water*, and knowing it was chaff anyway, he turned off his computer and called his manager, Marty Lavin. When Lloyd explained the nature of his dilemma, Marty reminded him that his three-year deal was at the studio's option, which meant they could dump out of it at the end of the first year, and economics what they were, the people at Lynx would prefer if he just played ball with them. Miserable, he hung up and went for a walk around the lot to clear his mind and ponder how he could foil Harvey Gornish's extraordinarily misguided notion. As Lloyd walked out of his office, he noticed Tai Chi leaning over her printer, the top of a purple thong peeking out invitingly from her jeans.

"What are you printing?"

"My novel."

"You're done?"

"One chapter to go."

Lloyd sucked in his cheeks, swallowed, and nodded in a way intended to convey encouragement but only succeeded in looking vaguely nauseous.

"Are you okay?" Tai Chi inquired.

"Terrific," Lloyd assured her, making for the exit. "One chapter to go. That's great. Weren't you, what, like halfway through about a month ago?"

"I write every night."

Lloyd absorbed this unintended dart as he walked down the stairs and through the offices of *Men Are Tools,* speculating on what strange god creates a world where he, this poetic author manqué trapped in the life of a sitcom writer, was now dealing with the odious task of extracting a pompous clod of a movie star from his maiden project, while Tai Chi, a mere support person, had nearly finished a novel.

That evening, after reading *Goodnight Moon* to Dustin five times before the kid would even agree to lie down, Lloyd forced himself to kiss his son good-night and went downstairs to brew some chamomile tea, thinking it might calm his nerves, which had been jangling like wind chimes in a monsoon since Bart Pimento was decreed an integral part of his life. Stacy was in the kitchen poring over a recipe book.

"You're cooking?"

"I'm designing the menu for that benefit dinner for Save Our Aching Planet," she replied, burrowing back into the book. Then, after a few more seconds of intense concentration: "Hon, for the appetizer course, lemon kelp or sesame seaweed salad?"

Lloyd, who was standing at the sink filling the teakettle, wondered whether she'd ever called him *hon* before. It's usually *Lloyd* or, if she's feeling particularly affectionate, *sweetie. Hon* is a new thing. Where did she get it?

"Is this a theme night?"

"Save the Sea."

"Did I tell you who they're making me have lunch with?" he said, not really interested in edible sea vegetation.

"Who?" Stacy asked, chewing on a pencil, trying to arrive at an informed decision.

"Bart Pimento."

"You're kidding." That got her attention. "He's, like, the sexiest man alive."

"You never want to see his movies."

"I don't like all that thriller/action junk but, hon, don't take this the wrong way, I'd leave you for him." She smiled as Lloyd looked at her quizzically. "I'm kidding."

Lloyd was now able to add this to the list of his wife's unforgivable sins. Not that she'd joke about leaving him, but that she'd joke about leaving him for Bart Pimento.

"You really like him?"

"He's totally hot."

A few days earlier, Stacy had reminded Lloyd that if he intended to pack his own books, something he'd told her he wanted to do, not trusting the movers with a personal library that featured at least a hundred mint-condition pulp-fiction paperback originals from the 1940s and '50s obtained over the years in various local flea markets, he needed to do it soon since the move to Brentwood was imminent. Feeling pushed from her orbit by the pulsing force field of her attraction to Bart Pimento, Lloyd decided now would be a good time to start packing up his library and excused himself.

Lloyd wandered into the family room and began pulling books out of shelves and placing them in corrugated boxes he'd found in the garage. The Melnick collection was a good one since both Lloyd and Stacy read avidly, and a wide variety of areas were represented. There was modern fiction, mostly in hardback, and at least fifty paperback Penguin Classics from college days, their familiar orange spines frayed from use. There was history, sports, film, women's fiction—whose exemplars Stacy regarded with great seriousness and could never get Lloyd to read—and there was

Lloyd's crime fiction and its subgenre, detective fiction, a genus for which he held a particular affection.

This style of writing in the hands of its more deft practitioners had long provided Lloyd with shocking tours of worlds he would occasionally think about visiting in real life, if only he had the courage; places populated by grifters and prostitutes, crooked cops and sadistic criminals, people for whom the world was a steel-cage death match, trust a chimera, and life itself nasty, brutish, and short. Lloyd knew no one like this in Mar Vista. He'd known no one like this growing up in the Riverdale section of the Bronx or while he was in college or in his years in a bubble-like Manhattan its residents often mistook for the larger New York City, which was another concept altogether.

Lloyd would read these books and lower himself into their murky depths, Orpheus vicariously descending, to peer around, titillated at the crazy quilt of pathology swirling about him. The very darkness of these worlds was a tantalizing opiate, beckoning him to leave behind the cozy confines of his dull suburban existence and venture forth to lose himself in their stygian mysteries. Then, finishing a chapter, he would close the book, turn off the light, and nestle into his comfortable bed.

After lovingly packing his vintage paperbacks, Lloyd turned his attention to the film section. There were books on Billy Wilder and Italian neorealist cinema, books that purport to teach someone how to write a screenplay, and one small red paperback by Rudolf Arnheim called *Film as Art* (a touchingly quaint title), which had been given to him by a college girlfriend twenty years earlier after he had taken her to see a Jean-Pierre Melville double feature at the Bleecker Street Cinema (which had since become a shop selling tchotchkes to tourists, he recalled with no little distress). He almost laughed at the naïve aspirations he had held so long ago as he stood alone in the family room in his Mar Vista house listening to Stacy puttering in the kitchen. Lloyd pulled the Arnheim book off the shelf and opened it. On the title page was written simply:

Dear Lloyd,
    May you get all you deserve.
    Love, Kim

What was Kim doing now? She was a clever girl from Connecticut who wore Laura Ashley dresses and talked about becoming an architect and moving to Italy, a country she'd fallen in love with during a junior year abroad. Lloyd had heard some years ago Kim was working for a hospital in Maryland. *Probably married a doctor and lives in Bethesda, couple of kids, car pools, IRAs, the golden cage.*

Lloyd felt a brief tightening in his throat. He swallowed and breathed deeply, looking at the book, which, he realized, he'd never actually read.

"Lloyd?" He glanced up and saw Stacy standing in the door. Guiltily, he let the book drop to his side as if it were incriminating evidence. "I found renters. Older couple, no kids."

"Great." Lloyd and Stacy had decided to hold on to the Mar Vista house as an investment property, and there was some concern that it would be hard to find people who wouldn't trash the place.

She walked toward him, smiling. "I am so excited. Are you excited?"

"I'm excited, too," he said.

"What are you reading?"

"Nothing." And he stuffed the book into a box.

Three hours later, somewhere between midnight and one o'clock, Lloyd was flopping around the mattress like a hooked trout desperately wishing some fisherman would materialize out of the darkness to whack him on the head and put him out of his misery. He had taken two shots of NyQuil, but that had done no good, and his febrile mind, which was leaping from subject to subject like a monkey in a tree, had landed on the problem of devising a way to frame the Pimento situation to the Jews Without Jobs. Bart Pimento was the kind of celebrity he and his cronies would regularly eviscerate: dim, humorless, and impossibly good-looking.

But Bart was a name of sizable dimensions, even if his image had taken a beating lately, so that would be good for something. And his presence in the project, barring a disaster of truly Chernobyl-sized proportions, guaranteed the show would get on the air. That, too, certainly counted for something, as the various Jews would be clamoring for jobs and those jobs would be Lloyd's to bestow. But something chipped away at Lloyd, cutting inward toward his core until it broke through to the hidden chamber where his self-image was kept inside a fortress of willful delusion, protected and safe. And there it was, superhuman, awesome, like a face in the sky: Phil Sheldon. Phil Sheldon's white-hot righteous glare burned through the protective layer and left Lloyd defenseless, vulnerable, and ready to fire his manager for getting him into this situation.

Phil Sheldon would not let the network push him around on a casting decision. Phil Sheldon would not be having lunch with Bart Pimento tomorrow.

Phil Sheldon would . . .

He'd . . .

Okay, so what exactly would Phil Sheldon do? For starters, he would have come up with his own idea already so he wouldn't be in the position of having to write something like *Happy Endings*.

The NyQuil had dehydrated Lloyd, and as he lay there, he could almost see the tiny green NyQuil men chasing down the ornery sleep-inhibitors in his brain like characters in a Tex Avery cartoon. The NyQuil forces were firing their six-shooters, but those wily sleep-inhibiting varmints kept dodging the bullets in a Technicolor extravaganza of slapstick violence and near death. Lloyd had a whole Saturday-morning animation festival going on in his head.

After another half hour of this shoot-out at the Cerebral Cortex Corral, he got out of bed without disturbing Stacy and downed two more shots of the sticky, viscous liquid. He went downstairs, removed the copy of *Film as Art* from the box, sat on the sofa, and began to read. After a few pages, the NyQuil deputies, now reinforced to posse size, were able to obliterate their crafty adversaries and Lloyd fell into an uneasy slumber.

He dreamed he was driving a Mini Cooper east on the 101 toward Burbank. Although the tires of the tiny car hugged the freeway, its body was suspended one hundred feet in the air on a loosely mounted hydraulic pole, so as the Mini careened down the asphalt, Lloyd swung wildly north, south, east, and west, dangling over roads, houses, and antlike pedestrians, futilely attempting to restrain the out-of-control machine, constantly on the verge of crashing to the pavement, where his smashed body seemed destined to lie, a limp sack of blood, organs, bones, and excrement.

And so Lloyd is seated across from Bart eating Euro-Laotian cuisine as the koi swim beneath their feet.

"I really relate to the concept, Lloyd. But I have some ideas . . ." And Bart goes on to give Lloyd the benefit of the deep thinking he has done regarding his character, a wacky Las Vegas pimp who runs the massage parlor. That his character is not a character in the traditional sense but rather a vaporous construct Pam Penner had pitched over the phone to his agent does not register with Bart, who approaches the nonexistent material as if it were *Long Day's Journey into Night.* Lloyd listens dutifully as he picks at his sea bass on a bed of Asian radishes, wondering (a) how is he going to maneuver Bart away from his show since he knows the actor's participation will spell doom for the project, and (b) what exactly *is* his show? Because if Lloyd doesn't come up with his own notion of a hit network comedy pretty quickly, he is going to plight his creative troth to both Bart Pimento and *Happy Endings,* which explains the speed with which the bile in his stomach is churning.

"You know what's funny, Lloyd? Comedy-wise, I mean?" Bart asks, breaking into Lloyd's reverie. Lloyd looks at Bart wondering if he's expecting an answer. Then Bart provides it. "Jell-O. Jell-O is funny. Fill a hot tub with Jell-O, put me in it, and people will laugh their assess off. Am I right?"

As Lloyd ponders this follow-up question, another thought announces itself: whether or not *Happy Endings* ever gets on the air, Lloyd's weekly checks will continue to arrive with the predictability of swallows to Capistrano. His ego would be vested in its success to some degree, but as we have seen from his recent literary exertions, he wants to turn his creative attention in a more emotionally satisfying direction, one where the inner Melnick will be allowed to flower. It isn't as if he is going to replicate the success of *The Fleishman Show* whatever he does, he reasons, so perhaps it is best to remove the ego and find another field on which to play. These disjointed thoughts combine to create a moment of stunning clarity for Lloyd, one that allows him to vent the long-submerged subversive streak that usually, and blandly, only manifests in his wardrobe—

It does not matter if my show fails. Then, further: *Maybe it will be good if it fails.*

Maybe it will be good? If the show fails?

Lloyd Melnick, overpaid envy of every comedy writer in town, is pondering failing on purpose. Not by subverting his project himself, for that would be too obvious, but by engaging in the far more subtle sabotage of not standing up to protest a powerful executive's idiotic idea. This is radical behavior for a television writer, a breed known for, perhaps more than anything else, the intensity with which they will rail, always in private, against the perceived nincompoopery of the decision-makers with whom they work. And then do absolutely nothing about it. Yet, in the mind of the television writer, no obscenity is too strong, no feeling too deep, when it comes to describing these whoring, arrogant malefactors with their expense accounts and their charts and their focus groups whose uninformed regurgitations they regard as holy writ to wave in the faces of the poor schnooks who have given their life's blood to get their work produced only to be told, "It didn't test well."

DIDN'T TEST WELL??!!

Because eleven fat-assed submorons who had been found perambulating on the Universal City Walk were wired up to some gizmo created to record their effusions as they watched a new show and suddenly considered themselves cultural critics with whom to be reckoned? When half an hour earlier their bulbous noses had been buried in chili dogs as they were deciding whether to see the third sequel of a banal action movie or a ninety-minute comedy whose gags, if spliced together, would provide thirty seconds of feeble laughs? "Well, fuck that" went the general reasoning.

Lloyd knows he has to escape the creative strictures of Television World while still maintaining his cash flow and realizes this is perhaps his ticket.

Yes, sign off on Bart and Happy Endings. *The guy's a movie star. He's promotable. Harvey Gornish loves him. What could be bad? The show will be an abortion and Lynx won't expect anything from me until the next development period, which is a year away. It's the perfect crime. Not only will there be no suspects, no one will realize what I've done. It's revolutionary. I'm revolutionary. I'm Che Guevara, only without the beard, the beret, and the followers. No, wait! I'm not just Che Guevara. I'm Max Bialystock! I'm Che Guevara and Max Bialystock. This is brilliant . . . brilliant! Hold it. Didn't Che get killed and Bialystock go to jail? Yes, but they weren't Hollywood comedy writers. We just get old and bitter. At forty. But now . . .*

Seated in this Beverly Hills restaurant, Lloyd reasons that if the show goes forward, he will be tied to it like an indentured servant for years, lashed to the mast and whipped with rolled-up copies of the Nielsen ratings as the *Happy Endings* schooner sails toward Syndication Bay. Whereas, if it sinks like the shipwreck he knows it could become with the comedically impaired Pimento in the wheelhouse, he will be free to surreptitiously advance his other, higher agenda.

Welcome aboard, Bart!

"Lloyd . . . dude?"

"I'm sorry. What?" Lloyd asks as he wrenches himself back into the present moment.

"About Jell-O and hot tubs. Am I right?"

"Absolutely."

The bill comes and Lloyd reaches for it, Bart still as statuary, having not picked up a check since . . . well, ever. The two of them walk the Plexiglas path over the koi stream and out the door, Lloyd noticing that even a movie star on a downward trajectory attracts eyeballs the way a diamond attracts light. As they're standing in front of the restaurant waiting for their cars, Lloyd says, "I have to ask you, what's with the fur attack?"

Bart's laugh is a big, simple guffaw that almost makes Lloyd like him. But he really still has no idea how an adult can throw paint on another adult for wearing a particular garment, unless it was made from the skins of humans.

"Dude, that was a trip! But, hey"—now the laughter mysteriously disappears and is replaced by the sincere tone of the failed autodidact whose small mind can brook no contradiction—"I believe animals have souls and shouldn't be used for fur coats. Simple as that."

"So you actually threw paint on some lady?"

"I sent her a check to pay for the cleaning. I'm not a complete dick."

Lloyd, cell phone pressed to his ear, heads through the Cahuenga pass on his way back to the lot after his lunch with Bart.

"Pam, it's Lloyd."

"How was lunch?"

"He'll be perfect."

"He will?"

"He's a very funny guy."

"Bart Pimento?"

"Tell Harvey I think we have a winner."

"Lloyd, what are you smoking?"

"Dust off your dress, dollface, we're going to the Emmys."

"What show did you talk about?"

"Happy Endings."

"You're going to write it?"

"I can't wait to get started."

155

Lloyd clicks the phone shut before the conversation can go any further, smiling to himself as the San Fernando Valley spreads out before him beneath a sallow sky. It's a beautiful plan. Unfortunately, he can't share the idea with anyone since its ultimate success lies in its insidiousness.

Frank drives home from his meeting with Orson Dubinsky like a man with an entirely new lease on life. It seems increasingly likely that he will be playing an Eskimo on network television, and although this is not where he had seen his career heading just a few weeks earlier, Orson Dubinsky appeared to be some kind of twisted visionary.

As the Caddy rolls down La Cienega toward his West Hollywood home, he tries to concentrate on generating material for the CD he wants to record and makes a mental inventory of areas he could reasonably mine for comedy. Concepts arrive and depart like cumulonimbus clouds on a windy day: travel, drugs, Melnick, rave culture, suicide, Melnick, why black people shouldn't get tattoos, birthdays, the failure of the public education system, Melnick? Why does Melnick's condescending face keep appearing in Frank's mind's eye, popping up like a demonic sprite, taunting, razzing, throwing spitballs?

Back to the concepts: the mainstreaming of homosexuality, why white people shouldn't get nose rings, Melnick . . . Melnick again? Christ! UFOs, pets, Civil War reenactors in Van Nuys, and none of it really sticking except Lloyd Melnick, whom Frank is thinking about with a degree of antipathy he normally reserves for Nazi war criminals and comics who work with props. Had Lloyd not spurned his entreaties to cowrite the Bones project, Frank is concluding, he'd be doing his own show rather than appearing in the Dubinsky opus, not that the Dubinsky opus isn't good. It's just that Frank's ego requires he have his own show based on his own life and that America love a character based specifically on him.

But Frank has rent to pay on the bungalow, the mortgage payment on Casa del Bones, and now there are Honey's new hood ornaments, which cost a lot more at Cedars-Sinai than they would have at the Bodacious

Body Plastic Surgery Clinic he had located in the pages of the *L.A. Reader* when she first expressed an interest in breast augmentation.

Viewing himself as an artiste, Frank has always taken great pride in almost never having booked a gig purely for financial reasons. Even when he's appeared on game shows, he would always be sure another comic more important than him had done the show already, thereby allowing Frank to point to that guy and say, "Well, if he can do it . . ." But that is not the case with *Kirkuk*, and in his view it is clearly Lloyd's fault he is in this situation. That it isn't entirely a bad situation does not register, the ego being what it is.

Who does Melnick think he is, that second-rate little pissant of a Phil Sheldon wannabe, to turn down an opportunity to write with Frank Bones? goes Frank's thinking. *When Lloyd was a grubby little pauper of an ink-stained nobody and I was the cheese, I granted the little twerp hours, days in my presence to talk to me, to write about me, to publish my desires and fears under his byline: my unique reflections on existence. Who, exactly, does he think he is? When I'm poised to finally elevate, to get my shot (maybe my last one, I'm not going to kid myself), Frank's Big Score, and collect at last? This Melnick, this worthless nonentity of a no-talent sycophant who is too fuckin' happy to write for an American cheesedick like Charlie Fleishman but won't write for the Bones? Who, exactly, does this cocksucking, motherfucking son-of-a-whore think he is?*

Frank has worked himself into a righteous froth regarding Lloyd's disloyalty, and by the time he opens the door of the bungalow and walks in, he is pondering sending him a live tarantula via UPS. If he can figure out a way to keep the hairy arachnid alive while in transit, he schemes, Lloyd will open the package and the spider, driven mad by the darkness and confinement, can be counted on to sink his poisonous pincers into him with great enthusiasm. *Yes,* Frank thinks as he opens the door, his mind clouded by purple thoughts of revenge, *that is what Melnick deserves.*

"Who is Candi?"

Uh-oh.

This from Honey, now seated calmly on the living room sofa, dressed in black leggings and a belly shirt, glowering at a bouquet of flowers arranged in a ceramic vase on the coffee table in front of her. The anti-inflammatory administered by Dr. Nasrut Singh has done its job and she has descended a full cup size since last seen, but her anger, rather than waning with the dimension of her chest, is clearly moving in the opposite direction. With a rapid motion, Honey rips the flowers out of the vase, choking the stems with her hand, and brandishes them at Frank, as if it were they who had been caught in flagrante.

"She sent you these."

"Yeah?"

"Yeah? That's all you're gonna say? Yeah? The flower guy arrives with them and I think they're from you so I take them inside and I open the card and I see this." Here she picks the guilty envelope off the coffee table, removing the card and holding it with the tips of her fingers as if the very pulp of the paper is poisoned, and reads:

Dear Frank,
   Thanks very much for the coaching session. It must have really helped because I got a callback. Let's do it again soon.
   Hugs, Candi

"Hugs? Who signs a letter 'hugs'? How old is this one, Frank? Fifteen?"

Frank, who, mere moments before, was fantasizing about ways he could surreptitiously murder Lloyd, quickly has to refocus on the more immediate problem.

"She's a grown-up," Frank lamely offers, a name, rank, and serial number answer.

"And what part, Frank? How were you coaching her? She got a callback?"

"This chick is a waitress at the Comedy Shop who was auditioning for a commercial and I gave her some acting tips," Frank explains perfectly reasonably.

"Acting tips? Like what? 'Suck harder'?"

"Oh, please."

"All of a sudden you're Lee Strasberg?"

"It might be a surprise to you but there are people who value my advice in that area."

"Slutty young waitresses," Honey petulantly sniffs, looking away. When she realizes Frank isn't going to answer, but has walked into the kitchen, she calls out to him, "What was she auditioning for anyway?"

"A douche commercial."

"Do you mean a feminine hygiene product?" Honey could be unpredictably prim for someone who had appeared unclothed in front of a film crew.

"Yeah, exactly," Frank says as he emerges with a bottle of beer in his hand.

"Did you fuck her?" Ah, the old Honey is back. "I bet you fucked her, Frank, and I bet she has a cat, doesn't she? And it was her fuckin' cat that scratched you, you fuckin' . . ." Here, after having unwittingly cracked the Case of the Concupiscent Comedian, she loses her powers of articulation and finds herself at the departure gate boarding a flight to Illogic, staring out the large terminal windows watching airborne fragments of lucid thought repeatedly circle the runway only to be denied permission to land by the wild hormones who have taken over the control tower. Frank watches her silently, secretly impressed with her powers of deduction and relieved that her emotions, which have bubbled completely out of control, will not allow her to press her case to a conclusive end.

Having exhausted her verbal options, Honey reaches to the coffee table, picks up the vase the flowers had been in. Frank cringes in anticipation, preparing to ward off the airborne pottery attack, but Honey heaves it against the wall, where, rather than shattering into a million shards, it incongruously bounces off the Sheetrock and rolls to the middle of the floor, coming to a stop on the shag carpet.

"It's not enough some crazy-ass fan attacks me with a fork, but now I have to come home and watch you play dodgeball with a vase? I don't need this shit," Frank says, a lifelong believer in the principle that the best defense is a good offense. "And by the way, babe, Dr. Singh said no physical exertion or you'll rip out your stitches." As he moves easily from reinforcing the mendacity of the fork story to professing genuine apprehension about Honey's postoperative condition, there is a pause in battle.

Throwing the vase seems to have had a calming effect on Honey, and breathing deeply, lucid thought having landed and now taxiing toward the terminal, it occurs to her a recalibrating of perceptions might be in order. She collects herself and asks, "If you knew she was auditioning for a commercial, don't you think you maybe could have gotten me an audition?"

"You've got bigger fish to fry than an audition for a fresh-coochie commercial." This was a statement that implied the dawning of an entirely new and possibly glorious era for Honey, since an audition for a gig like the one Candi Wyatt was up for would have been the highlight of Honey's month, necessitating much additional taking of acting classes, experiments with new hair colors, and reshooting of head shots, all on Frank's dime.

"I do?" Honey grabs on to Frank's implied encouragement like a dangling climber who is being offered a foothold in the rock face.

"Way bigger fish." Frank making her wait.

"Really?"

"Orson Dubinsky wants to talk to you about being in *Kirkuk*."

"Oh my god!" Frank nods in response, realizing with no little relief the immediate danger has passed. "As Borak?" she squeals, instantly forgetting Frank's suspected betrayal.

"No, babe. As a seal."

"Frank!" Utter disbelief.

"Yes, as Borak. He's a fan of yours."

"He's seen my movie?"

"Seen it, has the DVD, the whole family watches it on Friday night . . ."

"He watches with his kids?"

"I don't know if he has kids, babe. I'm just making the point that Honey Call is a name to reckon with at Chez Dubinsky."

"Oh, baby," Honey purrs, putting her arms around his waist and hugging his hips tightly to her but leaning back to avoid pressure on her breasts, which still hurt from the incisions. "I love you!"

We needn't go into what Honey means by "love" in this context, her behavior upon learning of her new career prospects making that implicit. Suffice it to say she was willing to overlook certain behavior on Frank's part at this juncture in their relationship if it meant she was going to be on television.

The cat scratch became a fork wound, Candi Wyatt simply a struggling, chaste young woman in need of some guidance from an experienced member of the Screen Actors Guild, and Frank, well, he was just a wonderful guy, and talented, too, respected by others who sought his wise counsel and then thoughtfully sent flowers in gratitude.

That night, Honey cooks dinner, an unusual event since they almost always ordered in from one of the myriad take-out joints in the neighborhood. She makes a meat loaf with rice pilaf and cleans up the kitchen herself. Later, they sit in the living room reading magazines, and when Frank goes off after ten o'clock to do a set at the Comedy Shop, she simply says, "Enjoy yourself," and seems to mean it, not bothering to request he come home at a reasonable hour.

"Babe," Frank says to Candi as she walks past him with a tray of drinks. He's standing in the back of the Comedy Shop, the area between the main room and the bar, where the comics hang out nervously awaiting the MC's summons to the stage. She stops and smiles.

"How's your back?" Candi inquires with real concern.

"It's fine. Listen, I appreciate the thought but don't send anything else to my house, okay?"

"Are you busy later? Maybe I can take you out and thank you more, you know, personally," she says, trying seductiveness on for size and sounding like a high school girl in the senior class play.

From the stage comes the booming voice of Benny Ripps, the comic working the emcee slot tonight. An overweight man in a loud sports coat and a bow tie who everyone assumes is gay although he will never acknowledge it, Benny is saying, "Ladies and gentleman, one of the best acts in the business—he just signed to do a pilot for the Lynx Network, so if it gets picked up, he better let me do a guest shot—please put your hands together for Frank Bones."

An electrical charge passes through Frank at the sound of his name. Turning quickly to Candi, he says, "Let's do it another night," and bounds toward the front of the room to the drunken applause of a roomful of tourists. Frank climbs to the stage, shakes Benny's hand without looking at him, and steps to the microphone.

If you don't applaud any louder than that, I'll be so depressed I'm gonna go out later and smoke crack.

A little before one in the morning Frank is parked in front of a modest house in Sherman Oaks with a cell phone pressed to his ear and the motor running.

"Sparky, it's Bones. I'm in front of your house. Get out here."

Frank closes the cell phone and waits, twiddling the knobs on the Caddy's radio. The station Frank is listening to is playing some kind of techno music he can't stand. After breezing down the dial he lands on Al Green's voice and, satisfied, puts his head back and lets the velvet tones fill the car. In less than two minutes there is movement on the lawn and Frank sees a short figure dressed in jeans and a plaid shirt heading toward him. Sparky has a big Fu Manchu mustache, the kind that has been out of style for about thirty years everywhere but motorcycle gangs, falling off his sad drinker's face. He arrives at the Caddy and leans against the door, lowering his head so it is inches from Frank's face.

"What're you doing still driving this shitbox, Bones? Aren't you some big important guy?" Sparky asks in the flat tones of his native Kansas.

"Christ, Sparky, pop a fuckin' Tic Tac," Frank says, recoiling at his friend's breath.

"Dude, you woke me up. Am I supposed to brush my teeth before coming out here?"

"It wouldn't kill you."

"Let me hook you up with a new car."

"I can't drive a hot car, Sparky. What're you, nuts?"

"They're not hot and I'm ticked off at the implication." Sparky's dignity wounded. "I'm selling to a guy who deals Ferraris. I'll hook you up with a very favorable lease."

"Not tonight. You got Daddy's Christmas present?"

"Ho ho ho," Sparky says, handing Frank a vial. Frank peels off a hundred-dollar bill for his dealer and places the vial in his shirt pocket.

"You know, Sparky, you ought to think about shaving that mustache."

"My thigh tickler?" he replies, stroking it gently. "In your motherfuckin' dreams."

Frank drives home, where he climbs into bed with Honey, who has been asleep for hours after having made a list of things she is going to do the next day that include getting new head shots, having her hair color adjusted, and making inquiries about hiring a publicist. She briefly awakens when Frank arrives between the sheets but, not wanting to talk to him, pretends to be asleep.

Chapter 10

Several months go by during which Lloyd writes a draft of *Happy Endings*. He endures the task by telling himself he is following in the footsteps of Plautus, an ancient Roman writer of phallocentric comedy, a satirist who took a great interest in the sexual misbehavior of his contemporaries. The pilot story concerns a new girl accidentally putting nail polish remover in her massage oil and an important customer getting a skin rash. It's garbage and Lloyd knows it, but that doesn't matter. He put in some good jokes to throw the network off the scent and a Saul Bellow reference to gild it with an intellectual patina. Then he made sure to give Bart a big scene with two naked girls in a hot tub filled with Jell-O. Bart read it and called Lloyd to tell him he was gifted.

Mission accomplished.

Lloyd is drinking coffee in his kitchen one February morning trying to coax his daily NyQuil hangover into dissipating. He's cursorily looking at the *Los Angeles Times* sports section, more out of habit than interest, and watching his son work his way through a bowl of cereal that has been laced by the manufacturer with enough sugar to induce a diabetic coma. Today is what's known as the table read of *Happy Endings,* the day the cast sits around a table and reads the script to a privileged assemblage that includes production company executives, people from the network, and assorted friends of the writer, all of whom are hoping for jobs on the show should it test well and the powers that be decide to put it on their broadcast schedule.

Given what is happening later, Lloyd appears calm, even serene. But that is not to last.

"Lloyd!" Stacy shrilly calls out from upstairs.

"What?"

"Can you come up here, please?"

Whenever Stacy called Lloyd from another room and further communication between them was deemed impossible after initial contact had been made, it was always he who moved into her territory for the exchange to continue. She would never come to him. He used to argue with her about it ("Can you come in here for chrissakes, I can't hear you!") but now just accepted it as another in a long line of issues he had given up contesting, marriage in Lloyd's mind having become a series of small surrenders. Putting the newspaper down, he sluggishly trudges upstairs, the coffee not quite victorious yet in its battle with the rear guard of the NyQuil.

He crankily barks, "What?" as he ascends the stairs.

Stacy is in their bedroom standing in front of a dresser holding one of his favorite T-shirts, an old, gray rag with the word IDAHO emblazoned in block letters across the front. He'd been a camp counselor one long-ago summer and had traded one of his own college T-shirts with another counselor who attended, not coincidentally, the University of Idaho. Since it had started to fray, he's only worn it sparingly, but it held great sentimental value for Lloyd, the way cheap things can when they remind us of simpler times.

"Do you mind if I throw this out?" she asks him when he appears at the door.

"Are you kidding? Yes, I mind."

"Lloyd, it's in tatters," Stacy says, holding it between two fingers at arm's length.

"I like it, okay?"

"Fine. Wear it as a pajama top. But I'm going through our stuff and I want to get rid of some things before we move, which is in a couple of days, I know I don't have to remind you." In one of the few indulgences he's allowed himself since his newfound riches have materialized, he has opted out of their moving process and told Stacy to hire elves to pack up the family possessions and unpack them once they are ensconced in stately Melnick Manor, as he has taken to referring to their new home in a satiric tone that flies beneath Stacy's radar. "I want you to think about a new wardrobe, Lloyd."

"Me? A new wardrobe?"

Stacy inhales, the look on her face the same one she gets when her son is being particularly uncooperative and she needs to restrain her desire to smack him.

"We're living in a new house, you're working at a new place . . ." As if that's reason enough and she needn't continue. But it's not reason enough for Lloyd.

"Yeah?"

"So you need to look the part."

"I do look the part."

"Lloyd," she whines. "When we went to that party at the Hylers' house, you were the only guy there who was dressed like a homeless person, okay?"

"Where do the homeless dress like me?" he asks, looking down at the cargo shorts and University of Arizona Wildcats T-shirt he's wearing. "Bermuda?"

"I'm not saying this to be mean, but come on, you're a grown man, you're successful, you're my husband"—here she tries a different approach, letting a hint of flirtatiousness creep into her tone—"and I want you to look good." Lloyd just shakes his head as if he can't believe he's actually having this conversation.

"Robert Hyler has a personal shopper. He gets all his clothes and never has to leave his office," Stacy informs Lloyd, attempting to make the notion easier for him to swallow.

"Who told you that?"

"His wife told me when we were hiking."

"Since when do you hike?"

"Since Daryl asked me to."

"You're hiking?" This is too hard for Lloyd to believe. The Stacy he knew would pack Dustin into the car to drive the boy to a play date five houses away.

"If I asked you to hike . . ." Lloyd can only finish the thought by once again shaking his head in disbelief.

"Oh, Lloyd, get real, I'm not going to pretend I like hiking. She dragged me up some mountain trail . . . I thought I was going to step on a rattlesnake. But I'm doing it for us!"

"What has running up a mountain with Daryl Hyler got to do with us?"

"She's very connected in a world I admire."

Well, there it is, Lloyd's thinking. Just coming right out with it, as if it weren't something to be embarrassed by, this desire to ape the life of a nouveau riche poseur whose alleged social conscience mostly served to create a stage on which to parade her own bountiful ego. When did this happen to Stacy? he wonders. When was the precise moment this former New York City dietitian with the NYU degree, this child of middle-class New Jersey, became so anxious about her place in the social firmament that she would walk up the side of a snake-infested mountain with someone like Daryl Hyler? Because Lloyd certainly didn't share her concern, and as he looks at his wife, now holding another of his T-shirts she has marked for destruction, he senses one more chink appearing in the façade. How much abuse can the structure take before it collapses in a heap of rusty memories, battered hopes, and worn-out recriminations?

"Would you like a personal shopper?" Stacy asks.

"I'll see you later."

Lloyd turns around and walks out, the exchange with his wife having done what the caffeine was not able to do. When she calls after him and says, "Will you at least think about it?" he pretends he doesn't hear her.

Lloyd guides his car into the parking space in front of his office and heads into the building. He has banished from memory the conversation with Stacy, and there has been a bounce in his step since he agreed to write

Pam's idea, then took the network casting note and hired Bart Pimento. The fate of the show is now out of his hands. If the impossible happens and it works, he will receive the plaudits and subsequent attention, and if it craters, as he knows it will, people will say the network made Lloyd work on an awful idea, then compounded it with an unfortunate casting choice, and there was nothing Lloyd could do. As for those big, fat checks? They'll keep right on coming.

He takes the stairs two at a time, and as he approaches Tai Chi's desk, where she has been seated forlornly for the past week unable to devise an ending to her novel, his assistant looks up and tells him, "Frank Bones is in your office."

What could Bones possibly want? Lloyd had read in the trades Frank was doing *Kirkuk,* so it couldn't be about that semiautobiographical piece of self-aggrandizement he had been pitching. What then?

Lloyd goes into his office and sees Frank seated behind his desk smoking a joint. The comedian is dressed in his familiar black pants and a loose black shirt.

"Babe."

"Bones."

While Frank's manner gives no hint that he'd recently been fantasizing about secretly engineering Lloyd's death by arachnid, Lloyd's attempt at conveying neutrality stalls out somewhere between impatience and irritation. He tries to cover it with a tight smile. When Lloyd follows with "What's going on?" he manages to suggest the dispassionate tone he was attempting in the first place.

"I'm doing a show on the lot."

"Yeah, I heard. The Eskimo thing. Listen, Frank, I'm doing a table read today so I'd love to kick back and get arrested for smoking dope but . . ." Here he trails off, letting Frank draw his own conclusion.

Frank takes a long hit from the joint and exhales, filling the office with a cloud of sweet smoke. "Lloyd, what happened to you, man? You were a fun kid when we used to hang back in the city." No other city but New York to the people who had lived there.

"Could you at least put the joint out? Harvey's on the President's Counsel to Kill All Drug Users and he's got spies."

"Workin' for the man!" Frank says, affecting a blaccent, something he would do when he got high and lapsed into Ebonics, *man* coming out "maayy-un." "Okay, fine," he says in standard English, wetting the tips of his thumb and forefinger with his tongue and then pinching out the burning joint and putting it in his wallet. "So I'm doing this show . . ."

"You told me."

"And Honey's in it."

"Always good to keep it in the family."

"She's surprising a lot of people."

"God bless."

"I'm sure it's not as good as your thing . . ."

Frank leans back, deciding whether to come to the point or massage Lloyd for a few more moments. Despite the cannabis currently clouding his cognitive capabilities, it is finally dawning on him exactly where Lloyd is in terms of their relative positions in the industry firmament, and right now he occupies a far more exalted position than the one occupied by Frank; Lloyd, no matter what becomes of *Happy Endings,* is financially set for life if he shows up at the office for the next three years and does crossword puzzles, but Frank . . . that was an entirely different and less predictable story. Although his agent had negotiated a payday that would make him a well compensated man, at least as far as the current fiscal year is concerned, it is a one-shot deal. If *Kirkuk* arrives with a toe tag, Frank will be back on the road once the money runs out, doing four shows a weekend and all the waitresses he can eat.

"Lloyd, the script's a train wreck. And I'm here asking the guy who one day long ago I put up on my couch, ladies and gentlemen, to take a pass at it with me." The script was anything but a train wreck. In fact, the tonsorially challenged Dubinsky had concocted something quite entertaining and original. But Frank, correctly fearing this could be his last shot at a starring role in a network project, has become consumed by the idea it is not all it can be. In Frank's mind *Kirkuk* needs to be some kind of amalgamation of the Marx Brothers, Monty Python, and Richard Pryor before all the freebasing. Hence, his painful pilgrimage to Lloyd's office.

"When?"

"Now."

"Frank . . ."

"I'm not gonna beg, but I'll buy you a car."

"I told you I have a table read today. I'd like to help you but . . ." And here Lloyd changes tactics and decides to lapse into complete honesty. "Bones, listen . . . I don't want to be here. I don't want to be doing *Happy Endings* or any other show, okay? I'm clocking for the paycheck because I have a huge nut and I have to feed the beast," he explains in a riot of metaphor. "Don't want to do my show, don't want to do your show. I can't sleep at night, okay? I drink so much goddamn NyQuil I'm personally causing their stock to spike. Most nights I come downstairs and sit on my living room couch, which by the way cost more than most people in Bakersfield are going to make this year, and I read."

"Scripts?"

"No. Books, okay? I don't want to be writing television anymore. I want to write a book, so I'd really like to help you but I'm barely holding on doing this piece of crap they're making me do. I don't mean to unload all this on you, but I don't want you to take it personally when I say I'm not going to look at your script. Actually, I heard it was good."

Frank chews his lip and ponders his situation, Lloyd's confessional monologue not having registered. *How prepared am I to completely debase myself at this moment?* "I'm not going to get another chance if this one goes in the tank," Frank tells Lloyd, trying to plead without sounding pleading, a nearly impossible trick that he does not entirely pull off. "I'm almost forty-five years old." Even under these circumstances he couldn't completely stop lying. Lloyd knew Frank had turned forty-eight that year. "We start shooting tonight."

"I told you I can't do it."

"Okay, then. I'll beg," Frank says, despising Lloyd for his success, his luck, his seeming control. Then, dropping all pretense. "Please do this for me."

"I'd love to but—"

"How could you write for someone like Charlie Fleishman and not write for me? He's vanilla pudding, man, mayo on white toast." Then, what is intended to be the coup de grâce lands: "I thought you were cooler."

Lloyd ignores the dig and says, "I took that gig a long time ago." This is a neutral statement by which he intends to imply three things: that he is older and wiser, that he is beyond writing for Charlie Fleishman now, and that this entire discussion is the bailiwick of someone far less successful than he.

None of this is lost on Frank, who looks up at the ceiling. Inhales through his nostrils. Tilts his head to look out the window. Lloyd watching him the whole time. Then removes a gun, a Walther 9mm, from his waistband and places it on Lloyd's desk. Lloyd, already emotionally shaky, tries to look at it impassively but his eyes involuntarily widen. Frank rubs his chin with the back of his hand and shakes his head, looking down. Raising his eyes, he stares directly at Lloyd and says, "Don't make me." Lloyd is feeling his body do involuntary things. His foot twitches. His heart starts to pound. Strangely, he feels blood rush to his penis. The seconds tick by, five, ten, a minute? Lloyd losing all sense of time. Then Frank smiles tightly, picks up the gun, points the barrel at his temple . . .

"Frank, no!"

"Don't worry, babe. I'm not going to shoot myself. I'm just fuckin' with you." Without another word, Frank gets up from behind the desk and walks out of the office, his Capezio shoes not making a sound on the soft carpet, thinking of tarantulas and how well they withstand travel in confined spaces. Lloyd presses the tips of his fingers against his temples and begins massaging. He wonders if Frank could have shot him and doesn't reach a clear conclusion. After a few moments Tai Chi appears at the door.

"It smells like an opium den in here."

"It's Frank's scent," Lloyd replies with fake calm.

"Evening in Shanghai," Tai Chi remarks. Lloyd has the quick thought that if he'd said that she could file a suit claiming racial harassment and a hostile work environment. As he's smarting from this PC curtailment of the comedy impulse, she hands Lloyd a gift-wrapped rectangular box about eight inches long saying, "This came for you."

Accepting the package, Lloyd says, "Would you mind opening all the windows?" He takes the little card attached to the gift and opens it, seeing a handwritten note.

Dear Lloyd,

   Thanks for a wonderful script. You da bomb!

   From,

   Pam, Jason, Jessica, and all your fans at Lynx

Lloyd removes the wrapping paper and ruminates on the phenomenon of white executives who will roll up the windows of their BMWs when they see a black person on the sidewalk casually dropping phrases like *you da bomb* on company stationery. Inside the box is a solid-gold pen, which he looks at with a combination of amazement and guilt; amazement that they would send him such a generous gift after having already paid a king's ransom for his presence and guilt since he will be using it to stab them in their collective back. But he comforts himself with the thought that the backstabbing he has planned is not just with their acquiescence; they've actually instigated it. Then his leg begins to shake again as he remembers Frank just pulled a gun on him. A series of breathing exercises brings things back under control.

Lloyd is feeling sanguine about his situation a few hours later as he walks from his office to Stage 23 where the set of *Happy Endings* has been built. Opening a side door, he enters the cavernous space and lets his eyes adjust to the shadowy light. In the distance he sees people seated at a table set up between the bleachers where the audience will sit when the show is taped and the set itself, the gaudy Las Vegas home of Lee Roman, the character to be assayed by Bart Pimento. As Lloyd approaches the table, he hears a loud cry of "Author, author" delivered in the booming tones of the aforementioned Pimento, followed by respectful applause, all of which makes him want to beat an immediate retreat.

Advancing while trying not to look skittish, Lloyd sees the cast seated around the table along with the sleekly dressed director, Andy Stanley, who appears to have stepped out of the pages of *In Style,* Pam Penner, Jason Fendi, Jessica Puck (with her ever present pad), and various underlings, all of whom are desperately hoping Lloyd can deliver some much needed boffo-ness for Lynx, which is currently mired in a ratings miasma.

Lloyd smiles abashedly, gives a little wave, and sits, wondering whether Andy Stanley's wife makes him dress that way or if he does it on his own. Tai Chi is seated to his left and she has had the foresight to have a cup of coffee and a legal pad prepared for him, should inspiration arrive during the proceedings. Lloyd takes a sip of the coffee and looks up. For the first time since his wedding, he senses everyone in the room staring at him, and it is not a sensation he enjoys. That their faces evince a mixture of worship and respect does nothing to mitigate what he is feeling.

Why are they looking at Lloyd this way? Because he is no longer a humble scribe, a pasty-faced, late-night denizen of the writers' room, released from confinement only to attend table reads and tapings, before having to slink back to his moldy lair and work on next week's episode. No, now he is the creator and producer of the network television pilot all of them desperately hope will become a show and as such is their fearless leader, their father, *el jefe!* Traditionally, writers in Hollywood have been viewed as well-remunerated doormats to whom absolutely no one has to kiss up. Everyone knows the joke about the Polish actress who tried to get ahead by sleeping with the writer. What people don't realize is that joke is about the movie business. The television business is something else entirely, because in the television business, successful writers automatically ascend to loftier levels, and if they create a show, they become what is known as an executive producer, and royal powers come with that exalted title. So if this Polish actress had been in television, the writer/creator is *exactly* with whom she would have career-advancing sex, for these men and women are the new power centers of the TV world and careers are often forged in the smithy of their whims.

Now Lloyd has joined these ranks.

Pam Penner shatters the nervous silence, calling out, "Thanks for coming," to Lloyd, causing everyone to erupt in forced laughter. Lloyd surveys his cast. The bouncer is to be played by Kurt Umoja, a black New York stage actor with a shaved head and a bad attitude about television, doing his best to make others realize he's here under duress. When Lloyd met with him, Umoja said he intended to use the money he'd make from the TV gig to float his Brooklyn-based theater company, which was currently working on a ten-hour, multimedia version of *The Upanishads,* to be performed entirely in Hindi.

Then there is Teddy Gilliland, a little person, whom Lloyd had cast as the towel boy. Teddy had gotten very hot off a series of action movies where he played the funny pint-size sidekick to a much larger, steroid-engorged star. Lloyd felt he needed a dwarf to fully execute his vision, and Teddy is happy to have a job.

The distaff side comprises Dede Green, a thirtyish actress who years ago had starred in a successful teen-angst picture as the not-so-pretty girl who finds love, then promptly got a nose job, making herself both unrecognizable and uncastable, since her offbeat charm had rested in her asymmetrical, slightly cubist features. Lloyd's conceit, of which he was proud, was that she play herself, Dede Green, an actress who had destroyed her career by getting a nose job, then put a nightclub act together and moved to Las Vegas, where she is now the wacky next-door neighbor of Lee Roman, Bart Pimento's character. Finally, there is Jacy Pingree, a twenty-one-year-old, blue-eyed blonde from Virginia whose lack of acting experience is redeemed by perfect features, unblemished skin, and an ability to recite dialogue in an almost indiscernible Southern accent without bumping into the furniture. She boasts the added feature of being able to effortlessly make every married male in the room want to leave his wife, a quality never lost on network casting departments. Barely dressed in tight, pink linen shorts and a tighter white T-shirt that exposes several inches of flawless belly, Jacy is there to fulfill the Lynx mandate for maximum jiggle, a function she performs ably whenever she moves. Jacy is to play the chief masseuse. Dede already hates her and they met five minutes ago.

The actor playing the client who gets the skin rash, a guest-starring role, is Rob Lowe. Lloyd had met him during the run of *The Fleishman Show* and he had kindly consented to be here today.

Lloyd looks them over. *All this effort*, he thinks, with no little amusement. *All these people, all this time. Such a shame. Ah, well, not my fault.*

A sharply dressed man in a dark suit, silk tie, and Oliver Peeples glasses takes a seat at the far end of the table. He looks familiar but Lloyd can't place him. Then, he realizes—Yuri Klipstein! Clearly, his agency, a Mafia-like monster feared by its own clients, has big hopes for *Happy Endings*.

Lloyd says, "Okay, let's get started," and the revels commence.

Scripts like the one for *Happy Endings,* a show meant to be shot on tape in front of a live audience, are composed with the rigor of haikus. There are usually three jokes per page and usually two setup lines before the joke is delivered, creating an unbreakable rhythm of line-line-joke, line-line-joke, ad infinitum. This rule can change only after a show has been on the air for several years if the producers decide they need to spice things up and stretch their own creative muscles, an unfortunate impulse that can wreak havoc on the lives of the main characters, usually in the form of a divorce or a cancer diagnosis. "A very special episode" often results, containing slightly fewer jokes and significantly more hugs than usual. But generally speaking, the line-line-joke rhythm is as inviolable to a television comedy writer as waltz time is to a boring pianist.

A viewer exposed to this form of entertainment over long periods will develop an internal cognitive signal that is trained to respond to the rhythm of a joke much the way someone listening to a "shave and a haircut" knock on a door will stand there, ear cocked, waiting for the "two bits" that will complete the aural equation and resolve the tension created by the rhythm of the setup. This leads to laughs where the audience is not laughing because something is necessarily amusing, but because someone just said the third line and hit it with special emphasis, indicating a joke has arrived. The laughter, as anyone versed in psychological theory and remotely familiar with the American sitcom realizes, becomes Pavlovian. In the room at a table reading, this involuntary response can often lead to a collective delusion regarding the quality of the project or the actors therein.

Bart Pimento barges through his lines with the same brio that led him to throw paint on the lady with the fur coat at the PETA demonstration, and the various executives around the table laugh uproariously whenever he hits a punch line, Pam Penner leading the chorus and occasionally guffawing at the setups for good measure. The rest of the cast follows Bart's lead, and by the end of the nearly half hour it takes them to work their way through the material, you would think the script had been written by Feydeau and performed by the Comédie-Française in front of an audience of nineteenth-century Parisians who had been fed pot brownies an hour earlier, such was the hilarity on display.

When the cast breathlessly crosses the finish line, everyone in the room looks at Lloyd, newly minted master of the comedy cosmos, waiting for his verdict. He purses his lips and sucks in his cheeks, nodding slowly in the manner of Phil Sheldon.

"Not bad. Needs a little work, but overall . . . not bad." Oz has spoken, Lloyd notices from the collective reaction, the group rendering of respect something he is still not accustomed to. He wishes it were more welcome. Or deserved. "Cast, take a five."

While the actors all produce cell phones and call their agents, Lloyd meets with Pam, Jason, Jessica, and network spy Nick Newborn—who will immediately report everything back to Harvey Gornish—to be given their notes on what he'd wrought. Everyone is in agreement that Bart Pimento is a future television star (Pavlov!), so the postreading creative input being served up to Lloyd involves how to make everyone else more likable, likability being perceived as the key to television success.

Teddy Gilliland's character, despite his diminutive stature, is a womanizer, but it is decreed he should not have sex with one of the masseuses on a pool table in the first episode because it will make him less likable. Dede Green's character shouldn't call Jacy's character "bimbotic" (*that* is unlikable behavior), and it is further determined Jacy's character wouldn't refer to Dede's character as "desiccated," not because it will make her unlikable, but because she wouldn't know what it means; instead she should call her "prune face," the thinking being Jacy is so darn cute, she could perform an on-camera vivisection of a live baby goat and the audience will still love her. Lloyd nods as he listens to this, his insincerity completely undetectable, telling the helpful executives he will take it all under advisement.

As Lloyd is walking back toward the door, he is approached by Yuri Klipstein, who, hand extended, introduces himself, saying, "I represent Bart. The show's brilliant."

"Thanks," Lloyd says, polite, noncommittal, as he shakes hands with the agent.

"Are you happy with your representation?"

In a drafty studio on another part of the lot, Frank finds himself standing next to a Styrofoam igloo dressed in the polyester animal skins of his character, Kirkuk the Eskimo, his mind drifting toward Russia as a result of Dubinsky's Rasputin-like visage and the artificial tundra with which

177

he is currently surrounded. Having exhausted all means of getting the script rewritten by an expensive jokemeister of his choosing, he is scanning the Dubinsky-penned pages pencil in hand, outwardly unruffled despite the Battle of Borodino raging behind his eyes, replete with galloping horses, flashing sabers, and the harsh clap of gunfire as the Napoléon's Army of Frank's Need to Make a Living invades the vast Russian Motherland of His Self-Respect. He calmly alters the rhythm of a joke by crossing out an offending word while cannons only he can hear roar in his ears. Looking up, he checks on the progress of several technicians who have been trying to unravel the mystery of why the animatronic walrus is malfunctioning at this critical juncture.

"Do you want to run lines?" Honey asks, appearing in front of him in her faux-wolverine anorak.

"Not right now, babe. I'm tinkering," he calmly responds, as a hundred of Napoléon's soldiers are slaughtered in a Slavic countercharge.

They have been rehearsing for the past three days and are scheduled to tape the show in front of an audience tonight. Honey is so juiced she can barely stand still, bouncing on the balls of her mukluked feet, fingering the imitation-whale-tooth jewelry around her neck and wrists, and popping sunflower seeds to keep from smoking, a habit she has fallen back on as a result of the tension that is so often the handmaiden of opportunity. Somewhat to Frank's surprise, her performance has been quite good. Her years with him appear to have paid off in an unanticipated ability to time a joke, and the voluble reaction of the crew to her mimetic interpretation of a female walrus taking liberties with her husband's tusk revealed a heretofore unknown rapport with a live audience.

"How're my two stars doing?" says Orson Dubinsky, arriving from the craft services table with a dripping taco (traces of which can be seen in his voluminous beard) in one hand and a prop harpoon in the other. Orson has unsuccessfully been trying to forge a bond with Frank since the start of rehearsals and has availed himself of his company at every opportunity, something that has led Frank to install a lock on his dressing room door.

"We're great," Honey tells Orson, whom she regards with respect born of deep gratitude.

"Frank? Feeling good?" Orson asks, laying an unwelcome paw on Frank's shoulder.

"The world's my oyster, babe," Franks says. "Cold, slimy, and oozing botulism."

"Okay," Orson replies, laughing and trying to sound engaged. He had attempted to banter for the first couple of days but after failing to get any reaction quickly gave up, consigning Frank to the tortured-artist category of performers who did not put a premium on interhuman communication.

At this moment the tortured artist shifts his attention from Orson's harpoon to his metallic mouth, where Frank briefly pictures an assortment of brightly colored fishing lures hanging from the orthodonture, to Pam Penner, who is heading toward them, her squat body angled forward on high-heeled boots.

"Got frostbite?" she asks by way of an entrance line. Then, turning to Honey: "After I watched you during rehearsals yesterday, I went back to my office and called Harvey and I told him I think you're going to pop." Before Honey can respond to this extraordinary piece of intelligence, Pam asks Orson, "So, Dubinksy, what's with the walrus?"

"Performance anxiety."

"I hope he can get it up for the show," Pam says, showing no fear of repartee in Frank's presence. "So, Mr. Bones, are you ready for your close-up?"

"You gotta trust the material," Frank responds.

"We love the script," Honey assures Pam. At that moment, the costume design person approaches, a pale young woman with blue hair and a lip ring.

"Honey, we need to make an adjustment on some of the jewelry. It's reflecting the light." Honey excuses herself to go look at some new pieces as Frank turns his attention back to the script, hoping Pam will take Orson and his taco elsewhere. After a few seconds of silence Pam speaks.

"Frank, we're a little concerned."

Frank looks up, as if surprised to find them still there. "Everything all right?" he asks, trying not to sound patronizing.

"We're worried you're not committing completely to the character," Orson tells him.

"Really?" Frank looks away from Orson toward Honey, who is now happily autographing a DVD of *Hot Ninja Bounty Hunters* that had been handed to her by a crew member, as the costume woman looks on, impatiently tugging her lip ring.

"You're the star," Pam reminds him. "We want you to be into it. When the audience is here tonight, you need to take it up a level."

"When the lights come on," Frank says, "the Bones delivers."

After assuring them at great length that he can be counted on, Frank retreats to his dressing room and locks the door, reaches into the pocket of the jacket he has hung on the back of a chair, and removes a vial of rock cocaine and a pipe. Frank unscrews the cap from the vial and taps a crystal into the stained silver bowl. Producing a Zippo from his pocket, he flicks the lighter on, places the pipe to his lips, and ignites the crack, which goes from an opaque, grayish white to burning orange-blue. As Frank inhales deeply, filling his lungs with smoke, and feeling the almost instantaneous rush from the drug, his cell phone rings. Holding the smoke in, he picks up the phone and checks the caller ID: Nada. Frank exhales slowly and presses the phone to his ear.

"So, Tessa," Frank croaks, his voice scratchy from the smoke, "when are we flying to Hawaii?"

Laughing, Tessa replies, "What are you smoking, Frank?" After the briefest of paranoid flashes, Frank realizes she is playing with him. "Hold for Robert."

Robert gets on and says, "How's it going over there?"

"I can't believe you couldn't get me Lloyd Melnick."

"Hey, I tried, but the guy doesn't need the work. Nothing I could do. Meanwhile you're starring in your own pilot so stop bitching."

"I'll never stop."

"I have a favor to ask."

"Sorry, babe. I'm incurably hetero," Frank says, looking at the ember of crack smoldering in the bowl and wondering if it will stay lit until the end of the conversation.

"Listen, my wife is doing a benefit for Save Our Aching Planet and they'd like you to emcee."

"Yeah, sure. Happy to. Maybe there'll be someone there who can put me on a real show," he says, tossing a spear in the direction of his manager's heart.

"I'm sure there will be. Are you behaving yourself?"

"No, I'm sitting in my dressing room smoking crack. Of course I'm behaving," Frank says, surreptitiously sucking in a tiny hit. "Why wouldn't I be?" The smoke causes a contraction of his throat muscles.

"You sound like you're choking."

"Because I have Orson Dubinsky's cock in my mouth. That's what a good boy I'm being."

Frank hangs up and takes a couple of more tokes on the pipe before exhausting its supply of fuel. He glances at the script. With a brain swimming in crack, suddenly the travails of a middle-aged comedian having to play an Eskimo in *Kirkuk* take on a new perspective. Frank begins to laugh, softly at first, more of a chortle, but then louder and full-throated, increasing in intensity until it becomes almost hysterical, a paroxysm of uncontrollable laughter emanating from Frank's dressing room where he is doubled over nearly in tears. If the show clicks, he will forever be known as someone who had a first-rate future but somehow wound up in an Eskimo suit, a puppet dancing to the mad rhythms of Orson Dubinsky. If it flops, he's back on the road looking at an endless stretch of one-nighters, hotel rooms, and highways crisscrossed by a world of performers who don't make enough money to spend more than a few nights a month at home. As the drug saturates his brain cells, taking them on the Space Mountain ride of a crack high, Frank laughs until his throat starts to hurt, shoulders heaving, doubled over, gasping, the drug momentarily shielding him from clear contemplation of a potentially baleful future. He's laughing at the thought of doing gigs at seventy with shortness of breath and a balky prostate; laughing at the thought of his health insurance expiring and the benefit that would be staged in his name in the event some disaster befell him; laughing at the realization that this is where it could all finally implode, under the hot lights of a soundstage in Studio City, with him dressed as an Eskimo.

Slowly, Frank begins to discern a percussive sound emanating from the inky corners of his frayed consciousness. *Thump, thump, thump.* Is it inside his head? He glances around the room. There it is again. *Thump, thump, thump.* Of course! Someone's knocking at the door. "Frank, open up, it's me. What's so funny?" Honey asks. Frank instinctively looks around for a window to climb out of but the room is without one. He swallows and clears his throat, doing everything he can to make sure that when he opens his mouth normal human sounds emerge. "Frank . . . ?" No answer. "Frank?"

"Go away, I'm rewriting."

"Open up. I know what you're doing in there. I've got my cell phone and I'm calling Robert."

Shit!

Frank doesn't need a don't-do-drugs lecture from Robert. After a moment, the door opens a few inches and Honey slides in, takes a whiff, Ms. Buzzkill.

"How could you do this to us?"

"To us? And by the way, I have to tell you, the northern look, the bulky-animal-skin thing? I like it on you. If you just let me—" Frank reaches for her coat to make an adjustment and she swipes his hand away.

"Don't touch me!" She takes a moment to gather her thoughts and then launches a gale force onslaught. "Do you know how long I've been waiting for something like this to happen? My whole life! Frank, they're handing us a network show on a platter! Don't screw it up by acting like a drug-addicted tweaker asshole!" He remains silent, unmoving. She's not done. "Give me whatever you have!"

Frank has never seen Honey like this. Certainly, he's seen her angry before; just never with this kind of laser focus. "Give it to me," she repeats in a low growl that penetrates the crack fog and actually scares him. Thrusting her hand into his pockets while he stares at her, she roots around and produces the vial and the pipe, shaking her head in disgust. Frank muffles a laugh.

"You think this is funny?" As he looks away, she smashes her fist into the side of his head, causing him to fall to the floor. His sniggers begin to sound more like whimpering. "Because it's not funny," she says, staring down at his prostrate form with a primal glare that calls to mind the young Cassius Clay and shaking her hand, which is beginning to hurt. "Not after what I already put up with. Now get up off the floor."

She watches as Frank rises up on all fours, then puts one foot on the floor and pushes himself into an upright position. He looks into the mirror as Honey watches him. "Don't do this to me, Frank," she says, walking out. Frank stares after her, rubbing his throbbing cheek and marveling at her bravado.

A few minutes later, a calmer Honey stands outside the studio smoking a cigarette and trying not to feel guilty about it. She huddles inside her costume, shifting her weight back and forth for warmth as she exhales a cloud of smoke. It had been a good week for her until a few minutes ago. Right now she's doing a cost-benefit analysis regarding the value of remaining with someone as unreliable and self-involved as Frank. She knew he'd had other lovers even if he wouldn't admit it; he was self-centered enough to go on a drug binge the day their show was taping; but he was semifamous and proximity to him could help her career as long as she could keep him from flaming out completely. It was a no-brainer, really. Certainly, Honey would have liked a man in her life who could provide stability, money, and glamour, but those guys usually had wives *and* girlfriends and she is ready for a less complicated situation. For someone like Honey, who longs to be taken seriously as an actress and regrets her extensive on-camera nudity in the ninja movie (while retaining a sense of humor about it), a man like Frank is about as good as it gets.

As she contemplates this conundrum, she hears a familiar voice behind her saying, "I hope that's not real fur." Honey turns around and nearly gasps as she gazes into the familiar visage of Bart Pimento. "Because if it is, I may have to throw paint on you."

"It's a costume," Honey manages to squeak, trying not to giggle.

"That's no excuse," Bart replies, clearly taken with Honey, who looks vaguely familiar to him. "Have we met?"

"I don't think so. I'm Honey Call." She notices a female figure hovering twenty feet away, looking at them. Is she with Bart?

"Bart Pimento," he says, nodding his head and trying to place her.

"I know," she manages to stammer. "We're doing a pilot on the lot, my boyfriend and I."

"Sorry to hear about the boyfriend," Bart says in a confidential tone, fingering her faux-wolverine pelt. "Are you sure this thing is fake?"

"It looks really real, doesn't it?"

"It certainly does. I should have my people test it. What is it?"

"Wolverine."

"Poor little bastard probably died a painful and terrifying death locked in the jaws of some rusty trap as the lifeblood drained from his mangled leg," he says to the horrified Honey.

"I swear it's real!"

"It's real?"

"I mean, it's *fake*, it's fake. Fakefakefake!!!" she says, unnerved by her proximity to Bart and laughing anxiously. "Woooooo!" she says, for no particular reason.

Bart says, "I was joking!" in that way he has of switching tones without warning.

Greatly relieved and suddenly serious, Honey asks, "What are you doing on the lot?"

"This completely brilliant pilot called *Happy Endings*. The guy who created it is a mastermind. At least that's what they tell me. So," Bart says conspiratorially, petting the wolverine as if to confirm it is indeed not genuine, "how serious are you and the boyfriend?"

"I think that depends on how well the pilot goes."

"I'll check the trades to see what happens."

Jacy Pingree, ingénue du jour, moves out of the shadows and takes a few steps toward them, wielding a cell phone.

"Bart, the reservation at the restaurant was for five minutes ago. Should I call them?"

"I'm coming, I'm coming." Then, to Honey he says softly, "I hope your show goes great tonight and all your hopes and dreams come true, pretty lady."

Hopes and dreams, Honey thinks. Did he just say "hopes and dreams"? Could it be possible Bart Pimento speaks her language? Frank couldn't utter words like *hopes and dreams* without making it clear he was micturating on the very concept. Her insides swooned just a little more. Did Bart really call her "pretty lady"?

Bart turns and walks a few paces before turning back to face Honey, who averts her gaze so he won't think she was looking at him. "Are you sure we haven't met?"

Twenty minutes later, Frank has mustered the courage to leave his dressing room and is back on the set trying to work the cappuccino machine at the craft services table. The problems with the walrus have been solved and the *Kirkuk* family is poised to make television history.

"Frank! How are ya?"

Frank, who is watching his latte drip from the machine's metal udder into a cup and trying to will the crack to last a little longer, glances over and sees the lizardlike visage of Harvey Gornish, president of Lynx television. Harvey's presence on the set of a pilot is the equivalent of a papal visit to a local parish. With his slicked-back hair and unnatural tan that ceased an inch above his eyebrows where it became a strip of perpetually flaking skin whose effusions would reliably find their way to the shoulders of his Italian suits, he looks like an aging gigolo disintegrating from the head down.

"I just talked to Robert," Harvey tells him in the raspy tones of his native Newark, N. J., whose gray streets he abandoned for sunnier climes during the Johnson presidency. "He says you're gonna be great. Hey, you better be." Harvey follows this statement with a nervous laugh intended to show he is only kidding but has the opposite effect of revealing the truth, that he isn't kidding at all.

"Everything's going to be terrible, Harvey. Right before we shoot, I'm going to get so high that I'll come out and bone the walrus. It'll be breakthrough television. That's what Pam Penner said you wanted."

Harvey smiles indulgently, picturing Frank carnally engaged with the creature the Lynx Network intends to market to the families of America via a lucrative deal with a world-famous hamburger chain. "We just want the Bones to be as good as the Bones can be."

"I'm with you, Harvey. It's all about the Bones."

"Frank, I need to talk to you," Harvey says casually, trying to imitate the subtly threatening tone he's seen in so many Mafia movies. "Over there"—motioning to the empty bleachers that will be bursting with giddy anticipation in a few hours.

Harvey walks behind the bleachers followed by Frank, who is wondering whether he still looks high. Reaching a spot sufficiently private, Harvey stops and turns to the jittery comedian.

"I don't usually come to tapings, much less to rehearsals, so you're probably wondering what the hell I'm doing here."

"Who can resist free food?"

Not bothering to laugh, Harvey locks eyes with Frank.

"I know you haven't exactly been Mr. Clean in the past. I've seen your act with the drug references and all that shit, and, hey, Bones, let me tell you, I'm no puritan myself, okay? I'm not preaching here. Back in the day I did so much blow I had to get my left nostril cauterized, all right? So I'm not coming at you all high and mighty, Mr. Network Heavy Guy, who's laying some kind of morality thing on you because

186

this is not about morality, Frank. Let me be very clear, okay? It's not about morality. It's about money. Lynx has a lot of dough riding on this project. We think the show could be very successful, and with this *facockta* walrus, who knows? The sky's the limit! You see where I'm going with this?"

"Is it some kind of pep talk?"

"Sort of, but not exactly. What I'm asking, Frank, is for you to give me your word that you're gonna stay clean through this process. Let's get the show on, let's get the good numbers, and when the whole thing is over, you can buy a house in Colombia and snort up the whole fuckin' country for all I care, okay? When we're in syndication, you can take the city of Bogotá and shove it up your fuckin' nose. But right now, you gotta be a good boy." Harvey stops and once again looks into Frank's eyes, attempting to discern if any of this has registered. "Will you give me your word?"

"You really had your nostril cauterized?"

"It was very hush-hush. No one knew I had a problem except my second wife, who, God bless her, waited until I straightened out before she divorced me. Can I have your word?"

"And you've been a good boy?"

"Sober almost sixteen years, *kineahora*. Frank, I want you to promise you won't screw me, okay, because I take this kind of thing personally. You come through for me and I'll come through for you," Harvey says with the assurance of a man who can change the lives of others with the stroke of a computer key. "You don't come through, you'll wake up with a horse's head in your bed." Here he laughs hollowly. "I'm kidding!"

"I promise."

"Alright," Harvey growls, smiling like an alligator. Then he subtly brushes some of the flakes from his disintegrating forehead off his shoulder and walks away.

Lloyd sits in his office, looking at his watch. It's almost six in the afternoon and he has spent the last few hours with a legal pad on his lap making the characters who populate *Happy Endings* more likable, per the instructions he's been given. It is busywork in the truest sense since he knows no matter what he does, the television audience is not going to embrace Bart Pimento as a transplanted New Yorker, operating a Las Vegas massage parlor serving bons mots and hand jobs to the locals, for more than a few episodes, at which point the network will mercifully yank the show, letting Lloyd off the hook. He gathers himself up, walks out of the office, and sees Tai Chi seated at her computer desolately staring into space.

"How's the book coming?" Lloyd asks, schadenfreude leaking out of his ears.

"I'm completely stuck."

"Could you put these changes in?" he asks, handing her the legal pad. "Pam wants to see them tonight."

Tai Chi accepts the pages with a sigh and places them on her desk. "Lloyd, would you mind if I ask you a career question?"

Well, he thinks, *I'm totally unqualified to answer one given my own has been a combination of luck and ass-kissing,* but he says, "Sure, go ahead."

"If the show gets picked up, do you think maybe I could write a script? I know it's presumptuous and everything but . . ."

"I thought you wanted to be a novelist."

"I read my book from beginning to end last night except for the last chapter, the one I haven't been able to write? And I think I know why I've been stuck."

"Why?"

"Because it sucks big, fat moose cock."

"Really?" This is good news.

"I may not be cut out to write fiction."

"Not everyone is, Tai Chi."

"But I know I can write TV."

"Talk to me when the show gets picked up."

Lloyd leaves the office with a spring in his step, there being nothing like someone else's failure to buoy the secretly unconfident disposition.

While Lloyd may be enjoying Tai Chi's difficulties, he knows they are not enough. In fact, they are completely irrelevant unless he can begin his own long-planned opus soon. If only he could arrive at a subject, something he can hold to the light and render in prose that will ring, pop, fizz; coalesce into a shimmering, sparkling new music guaranteed to render the author's previous forty-odd years a dim memory; a bog from which he will burst forth, born anew, and into the consciousness of all who cherish the literary arts.

As he walks out of the building into the soft, chemical San Fernando Valley twilight, he remembers *Kirkuk* is due to start shooting in about half an hour. Were he to go over there now, he could probably find Frank in his dressing room. Lloyd had felt guilty about not helping out when Frank came to him in his hour of need, concerned perhaps he was making excuses and really only wanted to lord over Frank that he, Lloyd, was no longer beneath him on the tree; was holding his own in the jungle very successfully; could say, simply, no. Lloyd understands there is some truth in this, but still a lingering remorse tugs, compelling him, if not to apologize, then to show the flag on the set, letting Frank know he is concerned with his welfare and wishes him all good things. Not concerned enough to actually do anything, but concerned nonetheless. Yet what would that accomplish, going over there for a schmooze fest as if nothing has passed between them? Frank had all but pulled a gun on him this morning. He hadn't pointed it at Lloyd exactly, but the effect had been the same. It was not an act that boded well for future intercourse.

Perhaps Frank has spent the day brooding about the unsatisfying trajectory of his career. Maybe he was going through a lifelong catalog of indignities that had culminated in his having to sign on to *Kirkuk* and the failure of one Lloyd Melnick to help him elevate the quality of the endeavor. He could shoot Lloyd in his surgically reconstructed knee, Irish Republican Army–style, effectively ending Frank's own eccentric career, or he could put a bullet right through Lloyd's envious heart, thereby ending both their careers. Neither possibility was good for Lloyd.

Frank is a live wire, no doubt about that; unpredictable, evanescent, and not a little dangerous.

Maybe I shouldn't go over there and wish him good luck. Maybe I should just wish him well from a distance.

Lloyd gets in his Saab, turns on the engine, and drives off the lot, leaving Frank to sink or swim without the Melnick imprimatur.

Later that evening, *Kirkuk* is committed to tape in front of a live audience thrilled to be in a television studio. Frank, effectively chastened by Harvey Gornish, withstands the pull of the crack pipe and makes it through the evening without succumbing to its smoldering song. Unleashed before a crowd of spectators hungering to be entertained, Honey blossoms in new and charming ways, a bright jonquil peeking through a dusting of snow on a spring morning. The audience adores her sexy, vulnerable, slightly distracted take on Borak and laughs merrily whenever she hits a punch line. Her new breasts, encased in a plunging fake-sealskin halter top personally selected by Harvey Gornish, have the precise effect Honey had prayed for when she'd submitted herself to the artful scalpel of Dr. Nasrut Singh. And the walrus performs with nary a malfunction. The crowd laughs with the rhythm of the script and applauds heartily even when the APPLAUSE sign isn't flashing, so thrilled are they to be in the presence of television actors. Robert, effusive in his praise to Frank, assures him the role of Kirkuk is going to add years to his professional life.

Honey returns to her dressing room after the late-night party on the set where, as her new colleagues looked on, she listened to toasts from Orson Dubinsky, Pam Penner, and Harvey Gornish, lauding her untapped talents as a comedienne and welcoming her into the big tent of mainstream show business. It would have been pleasing if Frank had made a toast as well, but perhaps that was too much to ask. Now she closes the door behind her, shrugs off the faux-wolverine coat, letting it drop to the floor, and slumps in a chair in front of the mirror. Then she notices an envelope sitting on the counter in front of her. Curious, she picks it up and opens it, removing a note.

Dear Wolverine Lady,

I hope your taping went well. When can I see your fake fur again? Call me on my cell phone, 310–769–4329.

Yours, Bart

To say Honey feels a frisson run through her entire body would be understating the matter considerably, so thrilled is she to be the recipient of this missive and the object of what it implies. A movie star, albeit one who hasn't had a hit lately, is taking an interest in her at a time when she and Frank are in flux, their relationship reordering itself in the wake of *Kirkuk,* swaying, tilting, and settling in the manner of a house after an earthquake, looking the same on the surface but with an invisible adjustment having occurred in the foundation.

If the show were to go, Honey could well become a star, the subject of magazine articles and puff pieces on television entertainment shows, invited to premieres and awards extravaganzas as a person in her own right rather than as an accoutrement, a glittering bauble on the arm of someone more successful. Certainly, Honey would owe her ascent to Frank, but once she had arrived in the popular consciousness, her course would be irreversible since fame, like time, cannot be undone. Were the show to flatline, she would return to her status as Frank's concubine, someone who couldn't navigate the tortured path to Parnassus. With her future in abeyance, Honey reads the note again, smiling, then neatly folds it and gently places it in a side pocket of her purse.

Frank is quiet on the ride home from the taping. He watches Honey out of the corner of his eye, sees her looking out the window as they come over Laurel Canyon and head down Crescent Heights. Since the incident in Cleveland, Frank has enjoyed performing less each passing year. Audiences would respond to drug jokes or dick jokes; anything slightly more esoteric flying directly over their heads, and the process of making this mass of human Wheatena react has begun to alternately bore and enrage him, depending on his energy level.

But tonight felt good. Not because of the material, obviously, although the material was excellent, or even because of the laughs it generated. What was buoying him was something implied by the presence of cameras, network executives, and a bleacherful of mall-walking tourists who had been given the opportunity to be present at the creation of what they were told could be a piece of broadcast history—refuge. Insecurity was the coin of the realm in Frank's world, and if by some miracle *Kirkuk* actually worked, Frank could banish it to the furthest reaches of memory, a deposed tyrant never to be feared again. He had resisted the idea of this show for all the reasons you have seen, but when he was actually on the set in front of the crowd, saying the lines without his head exploding, he realized, yes, he could be an Eskimo on a television show, yes, he could show up and do it again, and, yes, he could cash the checks they would send him again and again and again. As Frank made a right onto Beverly Boulevard, he felt a level of comfort both surprising and palliative.

He could compromise.

Chapter 11

Lloyd awakens the next morning feeling more chipper than usual, probably because it only took one shot of NyQuil to get him to sleep the previous evening. He looks at the bedside clock—6:37, somewhere in the neighborhood of half an hour before Dustin would awaken and begin to recite his litany of post-toddler demands. Stacy is still sleeping, the copy of *Architectural Digest* she was reading last night resting on the bedspread. Today is moving day and Lloyd wants to get out of there quickly, but as long as Stacy is not yet awake and giving orders, he knows he can relax for a few minutes.

Although Lloyd had been pleased to hear of Tai Chi's troubles with her book, his own inability to seize on a topic was beginning to disturb him. He was aware of the pitfall of first-time novelists writing auto-biographically, how that was a ripe cliché, and while forgivable in someone with no life experience, it would not be looked upon indulgently in a man of Lloyd's mileage. But how, exactly, were those miles accrued? Down what colorful highways and byways had the Melnick caravan motored? On what medians and exit ramps had the seeds for his nascent fictional universe been planted? Lloyd had a theory that while half the world was recovering from unhappy childhoods, the other half was recovering from happy ones since, having been raised in functional homes, they were less able to cope with the disappointments, betrayals, and regrets of the typical adult existence. Since Lloyd claimed membership in the second group, that eliminated his prosaic childhood as a subject. He did have an aunt in Queens who had been plagued by psychotic episodes and spent time in an institution, but Lloyd had no interest in writing about how a Forest Hills housewife negotiated the descent from neurosis into psychosis and didn't want his cousins angry with him for revealing family secrets about their mother.

His college years were the typical smorgasbord of movies, television, and attempted sex leavened with the occasional class or term paper, all of which led to a degree of no particular distinction. His addiction to newsprint had delivered him to the world of journalism, and although he had written pieces on subjects as diverse as television psychics, the scenery you could see from the trains of the New York subway system, and fetish clubs, none of them called out to him as a subject for a book he wanted to write. When he met his future wife, he found himself easing into the rhythms of a bourgeois relationship, and feeling like a private in an army where Stacy held the rank of general, he knew he had no fresh insights in that area.

Almost twenty-five minutes pass before Lloyd realizes if he wants to leave before the movers get there, he'd better get going. Rising from the bed as quietly as possible so as not to wake Stacy, he heads into the bathroom and silently brushes his teeth. Padding back into the bedroom, he opens the top drawer of his dresser to pull out his clothes for the day. It's empty. *That's strange,* he thinks. *Maybe Stacy already did some packing.* Pulls open the next drawer. Empty. Then the next one. Same thing.

"Stacy, honey?" Lloyd says, trying not to let the strain show in his voice.

"Hmm?" Stacy rolls over on her side and opens her eyes. "What?" Groggily.

"Where are my clothes?"

"I was going to tell you last night but I forgot," she says, the sleep working its way out of her voice.

"Going to tell me what?" Now the strain has arrived at the station.

"I took them all down to Goodwill and gave them away."

"All of my clothes?"

"Pretty much."

"You gave them away?"

"To the Goodwill. They're a charity. We get a tax deduction."

"I don't care if we get a tax deduction, Stacy!" Lloyd says, a vein in his forehead beginning to bulge. He's trying not to scream. "How could you give my clothes away?"

"You weren't going to do it."

Lloyd stands there in his IDAHO shirt and sweatpants, both of which Stacy would have tossed out had Lloyd not had the unintentional foresight to fold them neatly and tuck them under his pillow where she didn't think to look, glaring at her with the stupefied yet impotent rage familiar to all men who know that beating their wife is not a viable option.

"I bought you some stuff to wear today. It's hanging in the closet," she informs him as she throws off the covers and gets out of bed, heading to the bathroom, where she closes the door behind her in a way intended to bring the exchange to an end. But Lloyd's not done. After fuming alone in the room for a moment, he pounds on the bathroom door.

"What?" Muffled, from within.

"Open the door!"

Stacy dutifully complies, and as the door swings open, Lloyd sees her energetically brushing her teeth.

"How the fuck could you throw out my clothes?" Lloyd rarely uses profanity with Stacy and her shock seems genuine.

"Let's talk about this tonight," she says, rinsing. "The movers are going to be here any minute. And watch your language, Mr. Salty Sailor. Dustin could walk in."

Without saying another word, Lloyd turns around and goes into his closet, where he sees a new pair of Banana Republic khakis and a Polo golf shirt. He angrily pulls them on and walks out of the room while Stacy is still performing her morning ablutions. In the hallway outside the bedroom he passes the sleepy Dustin, who is on his way to his parents' room.

"I want breakfast," he announces, a miniature advertisement for mandatory charm school.

"Mommy's going to fix your breakfast today, pal. Go ask her," Lloyd tells his son as he walks down the stairs. "And check your drawers. Make sure she didn't throw out all your favorite clothes."

Less than thirty seconds later, Lloyd is in the car and out of the driveway. It's not even 7:20 and he is almost trembling with rage. Doing some breathing exercises he remembers from a Lamaze class, he manages to de-intensify the internal burner to the point where he no longer feels like letting loose an earsplitting shriek. Having accomplished that, he briefly thinks about checking into a hotel, before realizing he hasn't bothered to pack any clothes. Then he remembers he has no clothes to pack since the ones he had are now at Goodwill, and unbridled rage consumes him once again. His anger continues to ebb and flow as he drives to Farmer's Market to have breakfast. He knows eggs, coffee, and the *Los Angeles Times* sports section will be a balm to his tortured soul.

Lloyd is seated in a booth in DuPar's a little later dipping a piece of rye bread in an egg yolk and considering his options. Clearly, what Stacy has done is beyond the pale. Yes, she's a runaway train, as evidenced by the house they are about to occupy, a move she has engineered against Lloyd's feeble protestations. Like the stock market, his wife was not something he was going to control. That much was clear. But until now, she has let Lloyd be Lloyd. Apparently, that approach is no longer operative.

Stacy wants to sculpt him, mold the clay of Melnick into something more to her liking. Lloyd had noticed that same quality in many of his friends' wives, but none has taken it so far as giving their husband's entire wardrobe away to Goodwill. He wonders if he can live with her under these circumstances. Was he willing to face a divorce? Certainly, he can afford one at this point. Write a big check, give the Brentwood château to her (after never even having lived in it!), and that would be that. Yes, she would get custody of Dustin, but Lloyd could see the boy on Wednesdays and alternate weekends, which wouldn't be much of a hardship since he hadn't noticed they had much in common at this point anyway.

That left dating. Did Lloyd want to be out there as a guy in his forties with a little paunch and a receding hairline in a world full of younger women whose beau ideal was not Melnickian? The fatness of his wallet with its excrescence of cash and the myriad life choices it made possible would certainly smooth his way in that area, but the prospect was nonetheless unsettling. Lloyd in a bar? Lloyd in a club? Lloyd holding a bottle of beer in a sweaty hand as he attempts to chat up a woman who wasn't born when the Beatles broke up? It was not a happy image, but at least it didn't include Stacy.

Lloyd is turning this over in his mind as he drives from Farmer's Market over Laurel Canyon and down into the Valley toward his office. He realizes he has never ascertained the status of Tai Chi's personal life. He hadn't noticed a ring, other than the one in her nose. Was there a Mr. Tai Chi? If there was, she was certainly discreet about it. He makes a mental note to subtly determine where and with whom she slept. *Oh, yes,* he thinks, walking past her empty desk since, even with his breakfast stop, he was getting in early, *this new life could be a good life.*

Glancing at his watch, Lloyd sees it's only 9:37. The day's rehearsal doesn't begin until one o'clock so he plans to spend the morning alternately tinkering with the script and trolling his memory bank for something that will inspire him to put pen to paper other than the gentle curve of Tai Chi's bottom in the miniskirt she was wearing yesterday.

Walking into his office, Lloyd is greeted by the sight of a young man seated on his couch with skin so shiny Lloyd suspects he could see himself in the man's cheeks, which, upon closer examination, reveal a restrained use of blush. He has dyed-blond hair, cut in the mod style popular in England circa 1964, and wears a tightly fitting pale green suit with an open-collared mauve shirt and little black boots. The legs are crossed thigh over knee and the torso leans forward in happy anticipation. The general effect is one of fabulousness.

"Lloyd Melnick?" The voice is breathy, a little high.

"Yeah?"

"I'm your personal shopper!" He says this with a brio you would associate with an announcement like "You're our one millionth customer" or "You've just won the lottery," something to be prefaced by "Congratulations!" Lloyd's mouth must have dropped open because a moment later the man says, "Don't worry. We'll have fun! My name's Kevin."

"I don't need a personal shopper," Lloyd assures him with understandable pique, given recent events.

"That isn't what Stacy said," the personal shopper tells him, invoking Stacy's name in a way that suggests to Lloyd she confided in this guy in a wholly inappropriate way. And how did he get on the lot? Stacy and Tai Chi must be in cahoots again. Lloyd resolves to fire his conniving assistant this afternoon, never mind that it will end all possibility of his ever seeing her naked.

"Look, my wife threw out all my clothes yesterday without asking me so I'm not inclined to get involved in anything she set up right now, okay? Don't take it personally." Lloyd sits down at his desk and pretends to busy himself while he waits for Kevin to leave. Two minutes later, Kevin is still standing there.

"I can wait," the shiny-faced personal shopper says.

"Kevin, really, no offense, but I'm not going shopping with a guy."

"Too gay?" Kevin asks campily.

"Something like that."

"I've already been paid."

"Then have a party," Lloyd says with finality, going back to trying to appear occupied.

After several more minutes of this to and fro, during which Kevin earns Lloyd's trust by laughingly referring to Stacy as a "controlling bitch," it is decided that since Lloyd's clothes are probably on their way to some place like Burundi by now and he must eventually buy replacements, the two of them will spend the morning trying to rebuild the wardrobe Stacy so heartlessly discarded. Lloyd further concludes that because he may be dating in the near future, perhaps a subtle refurbishing of the exterior with an eye toward attracting the young and the willing wouldn't be a bad thing.

So this odd pairing gets in Lloyd's car and drives back over the hill to Melrose Avenue, where an effort will be made to render Lloyd's presentation more contemporary. But after half an hour of Lloyd telling Kevin every item he's suggesting will make him feel like a male version of Cher, the personal shopper throws his hands up and capitulates. The two of them spend the next couple of hours and several thousand dollars walking up and down Melrose, assembling the equivalent of Lloyd's former wardrobe, only in far more expensive fabrics. Freshly, if self-consciously, togged, he returns to his office with shopping bags full of silk T-shirts and baggy linen pants, comforted by the knowledge that after this stuff is given a few cycles through the washing machine he'll look his old shabby self.

At one o'clock he heads to the stage, where he spends the remainder of the day alternately watching Andy Stanley (who Lloyd now realizes buys his clothes in many of the same places he himself was shopping this morning) put the cast through their paces and brooding over the best course of action to take regarding his duplicitous wife. Now that he has replenished his wardrobe, a supply trip to Rite Aid will render him hotel-ready should he decide to make that statement, the one saying, "Stacy, you may have done some things to piss me off in the past, but this time you crossed the line."

After Andy tells the adequate cast they've been brilliant and he'll see them in the morning, he and Lloyd confer for a few moments going over whether Lloyd's changes have sufficiently addressed the likability issue. Andy informs Lloyd he finds everyone satisfactorily likable now, and so work for the day is declared done.

"By the way," Andy says as they're walking out of the studio, "I like what you're wearing."

Lloyd gets in his Saab and wheels off the lot without a specific plan. He could go to the Château Marmont and watch the Eurotrash drift in and out, or he could head to the Four Seasons and hang out by the pool gazing at the out-of-town actresses visiting Los Angeles to promote their projects. Or he could drive to the desert and get a bungalow at La Quinta, maybe play a little tennis under the desert sky. Anything to make Stacy feel a fraction of the powerlessness he suffered upon realizing the contents of his drawers and closet had been preemptively retired.

But he does none of these things. Instead, he drives to Brentwood. Pulling into the driveway of his new house, he gets out of the car and walks through the front door, where he gazes into the formal dining room and sees a meticulously arranged display of furniture that looks as if it had been relocated from the palace of a Viennese archduke. He immediately wonders at the number of zeros he is going to see on his Visa bill as a result of Stacy's newly high-end taste in interiors, but then realizes this is not a thought that will bring anything positive into his life right now, so he goes into the kitchen, where he finds his wife making rigatoni for Dustin, who is sitting on the marble countertop near the double-wide Sub-Zero refrigerator watching cartoons on the plasma TV screen mounted in the corner.

When Stacy hears Lloyd enter, she looks up, and in that instant that takes place when two spouses have had a fight and then not seen each other for the day while they both decide whether to pursue their respective grievances, she notices what he's wearing and squeals with delight.

"Lloyd! You look amazing! Doesn't Daddy look amazing?" she asks Dustin, who is too enthralled by the antics of an animated rat to look up. Then, to Lloyd: "Thank you *so much* for going shopping with Kevin. I know you were really mad and, okay, I don't blame you, I think maybe, you know . . ." Here she looks at Lloyd with a crinkly smile of relief. (Relief he hasn't left? Relief he hasn't killed her?) But she doesn't finish her thought. Was she going to apologize? Lloyd wonders. That would call for a national holiday, Stacy never being one for apologies, full speed ahead. As she kisses him on the mouth, then takes his hands and places them on the denim stretched tight across her gym-built ass, Lloyd has the thought that it is not easy being Stacy, to live a life where everything must be designed, lit, and stage-managed, where the opinions of others matter so much more than your own and where perception trumps reality; the show that is Stacy must go on, ticket sales must be maintained, despite the flagging energy of the one-woman cast for whom each performance is increasingly like a Wednesday matinee on a snowy February day. The concentration it takes to maintain the presentation that is her existence produces waves of stress that come and go, flitting through her nervous system, a continual thrum of low-level anxiety. The genuine joy Lloyd sees in Stacy's face as she looks at his new clothes almost makes him feel for her.

"What do you think of the dining room?" Stacy asks. "Cam Rousseau was here this afternoon and she had the movers help her with the feng shui. Don't you love it? I wanted to surprise you."

"You bought some nice stuff," Lloyd says in a manner that could be interpreted any number of ways.

"So did you from the looks of things."

A sheepish smile that Lloyd cannot restrain crosses his lips, despite his best efforts, since he doesn't want to provide her with the least bit of satisfaction. He quickly gets it back under control. Stacy isn't looking at his face, however. She's still looking at his clothes, which she regards as nothing less than a complete capitulation to her worldview.

"Hon, tell me, did you like Kevin?"

"Where did you find that guy?" Lloyd asks.

"Daryl recommended him. He buys all of Robert's clothes."

"He was a real character."

"I knew you'd like him."

"I didn't say I liked him." Then, to his son: "Hey, bud, what are you watching?"

"TV," Dustin replies, unwilling to shift his attention from the screen. And with that the Melnicks are back on track, their marital train roaring toward a new and radiant future redolent of promise and possibility, the declared cargo of joy and forgiveness camouflaging the shipment of resentment being furtively transported to a place where the erstwhile combatants would warehouse it for future use.

★   ★   ★

From her own days as a user, Honey learned never to throw drugs out, since in her experience there may come a time when you need them again. Frank was aware of this philosophy, having watched her try to straighten out many times but never actually discarding a stash since, she explained, she wanted to keep it handy for when they entertained. So in the hours after the *Kirkuk* taping Frank had staged a daring search-and-rescue operation in Honey's purse and heroically liberated both his crack pipe and dwindling supply of rock. When they arrived home and Honey collapsed into the exhausted sleep of a five-year-old who has spent a day having her circuits overloaded at Six Flags, Frank put *Sketches of Spain* by Miles Davis on the CD player in the living room and smoked up the rest of the crack. He got so high he had to drink the better part of a bottle of Courvoisier to come down and passed out before he had the chance to return the evidence to Honey's purse.

The next morning finds Frank sprawled across the floor of the living room, his right cheek pressed hotly against the shag carpet. The left side of his head, starting at the orb of his eye and continuing in a throbbing arc to the area just above his ear, feels as if it has been crushed by the kick of an irate mule, his mouth like it has been used as a bedouin encampment replete with tents and camels, and his tongue sports a viscous coating that will need to be removed with sandpaper and turpentine. He attempts to open his eyes and finds this simple action impeded by the dried gloop that has sutured his eyelids shut. Exerting monumental effort, Frank is able to will enough strength into his right eyelid to overpower the gluelike excretion and open it infinitesimally, but the ruthless morning light causes it to snap shut with the velocity of a mousetrap. The tentative equanimity with which he had grown to accept recent events has vanished, and Frank lies in this position for the next several minutes wishing his whole absurd life would be over.

"Good morning, Frankie Bad Boy," Honey chirps.

The sound of Honey's voice causes such an aural assault on the inner precincts of Frank's delicate eardrums his entire body seems to wince, and the wincing sets off a further chain reaction, making it seem as if every one of his cells were nefariously conspiring to cause him eternal and irreversible pain. He tries to lie as still as he can.

Frankie Bad Boy was what Honey called him when she was in an extremely good mood, and the sort of behavior on Frank's part that would ordinarily render her hysterical is by virtue of her temporarily buoyant disposition transformed into something she finds forgivable if not endearing. "How are you feeling?" This is said in a chipper tone laced with a subtext of awareness, letting him know she's up on his shenanigans but will not be affected by them today. Honey is still so energized by her adventures of the previous evening that if she walked into the room and discovered Frank lighting his hair on fire, she would ask him if he wanted to toast marshmallows. That she physically assaulted him in his dressing room is clearly not something she's thinking about. "Frank?" she repeats sweetly, her previous queries having gone unanswered.

He manages a gentle groan that is nonetheless strong enough to register as an earthquake in his delicate brain. Gathering every fraction of faded strength still lingering in his body, he manages to croak, "What?" Actually, it sounds more like "Wha . . ." since hitting the consonant at the end of the word requires more vigor than Frank can muster.

"I'm going out to pick up some things for the house. I'll make you a pot of coffee before I leave," she pipes.

Honey gets into her car and instantly fishes out Bart's note. The second she pulls away from the curb, she starts dialing, her fingers nearly trembling in anticipation of beginning a flirtation with a movie star. On the third ring she hears a recorded voice—*This number is no longer in service. If you think you have reached a wrong number, please try again.* Honey tries two more times and gets the same recording. She can't believe Bart would give her the wrong number on purpose. *Well,* she charitably thinks, *he must have a lot on his mind,* and she begins her round of errands, still hopeful. It's going to take a lot more than Bart Pimento's screwup to excise the spring from Honey's step today.

By the time Frank is able to remove his cheek from the carpet, rise first on an elbow and then to one knee, before, in a superhuman effort, finally reasserting his status as a biped and staggering toward the kitchen, where he intends to unleash the coffee on his damaged system, Honey has been gone for an hour. Frank manages to pour himself a cup and make it to the kitchen table without toppling over, a small victory under the circumstances.

He has been sitting there for fifteen minutes with one hand supporting his head letting the bitter black liquid massage his battered brain cells and, like thousands of tiny loofah-wielding Ukrainian immigrant masseurs, beat them back to life. Suddenly, the deafening blare of a fire engine siren shrieking two feet from his ear startles him. It takes Frank a pained moment to register this as the ringing of his telephone. With an effort, he moves his eyeballs in the direction of the caller ID: Nada. He answers it.

"Yeah," Frank says, his voice emanating as if from someone lying deep in a cave.

"Frank Bones please," says an unidentified male. Clearly, this is not Tessa, Frank realizes, relieved he will not have to engage in his usual coy badinage.

"You got him, babe."

"Hold for Robert Hyler."

A moment later Robert comes on the line. He skips the schtummy and pops the champagne. "Harvey Gornish called and he loves the show. He thinks Dubinsky is a visionary."

"Really?" At this news Frank's hangover evaporates like morning mist on a warm June day.

"I just got off the phone with him. And listen to this: he loves Honey!"

"I knew she'd kill," Frank lies.

"But just 'cause Harvey likes something doesn't mean they're gonna pick it up. They have to test it. But it can't hurt."

"What did he say about me?"

"He loves the show!"

"Does he love the Bones?" Frank asks; let's get to what matters here, please.

"Yeah, yeah, yeah—you, the show, Honey, Dubinsky, the whole nine yards!"

Frank gets off the phone thirty seconds later, his headache having returned (the effect of good news on the human system sadly temporary); but despite the throbbing pain that was clearly not leaving town without a fight, he feels much better about the universe and the benighted, wind-blasted rock face he occupies in it; the approbation of the Harvey Gornishes of the world something he requires to solidify the tenuous hold he maintains; without it he knows he will lose his grip and tumble to oblivion.

Several cups of coffee later, Frank manages to get into the shower, where the warm water edges him ever closer to temporary sobriety. He gets dressed without trying to pull his pants on over his head and soon finds himself sitting alone in the living room, where after a few minutes of staring into space he picks up the phone and dials.

"Sparky, it's Bones. You want to shoot some pistols?"

Sparky is seated in the passenger seat of Frank's Caddy as the two of them cruise down the 405 toward the LAX Gun Club. The diminutive dealer is looking at Frank and shaking his head, not saying anything. Sensing his friend's opprobrium, Frank glances over at him, eyes still bloodshot behind his shades.

"What?"

"Bones, you mind if I ask you a personal question?"

"Does it have to do with Honey? Because I'm not answering those."

"I want to know something about Honey, I'll ask Honey. Here's what . . . and I don't mean any disrespect."

"Ask the fuckin' question, Sparky. You're getting on my nerves."

"You're a famous comic, right? You just did a pilot for Lynx, you're gonna be a TV star . . ."

"Yeah, so?"

"So what the fuck are you doing driving this shit-ass spookmobile?"

"Spookmobile?" Frank repeats, laughing. "You're calling my ride a spookmobile?"

"Don't get me wrong, Bones. I love my black brothers. But listen, you are what you drive in this town. And you're trying to make some kind of oblique cultural statement with this piece of shit we're riding in, some seventies superfly, pimp-by-association thing, right?"

Frank thinks about this for a moment. "Fuck you," he responds halfheartedly.

"Yeah, fuck me," Sparky says. "But I'm your friend so keep listening. The Caucasians who run the world see you and they're shaking their heads saying poor Frank Bones can't afford a white man's car."

"You're a fuckin' racist."

"I'm no fuckin' racist, man. I got every CD Prince ever released including the ones that were only sold on the net. What I am is an astute observer of social mores."

"Social mores?"

"I observe them and then I interpret them for my obtuse friends, such as yourself. Anyway, I looked under your hood the other day, Frank. This car don't have long to live."

The two spend a few carefree hours at the Gun Club happily shredding paper targets with Sparky's new Ruger. When they are nearly out of ammunition, Sparky turns to Frank and says, "You're getting a good paycheck on this pilot thing?"

"It's alright."

"So you can actually afford a new car?"

"Don't patronize me when I'm holding a loaded firearm, babe."

"I got a proposition. Let's have a little competition, and if I win, we're going car shopping for you and you're gonna retire the Caddy."

"And what do I get if I win?"

"Oh, don't worry about that, Frank. You ain't gonna win."

A little over an hour later, Frank and Sparky walk into the Hummer dealership of Beverly Hills, where they are attended to by a former U.S. marine who introduces himself as Mike and looks uncomfortable in his sports jacket.

The purchase of a particular car always reveals much about the purchaser. A middle-aged man in a Porsche is generally assumed to be compensating for declining virility. A young mother in a Volvo wagon is saying: Style? Phooey! The safety of my children is paramount. Someone in a PT Cruiser is implying: I may not have much money but I'm cooler than you. As for the Hummer, the message sent out for the world to hear is: Get the fuck out of my way or I will crush you like a bug. This makes it the perfect vehicle for someone who can afford the steep price tag but still feels impotent in subtle ways. It's not a coincidence that Robert Hyler, a man all-powerful in his professional life, wanted to test-drive one given his relationship with his wife. In the case of Frank, someone with precious little control over the circumstances of his life and whose whole professional career rests in the hands of others, a Hummer is an obvious fit.

After persuading Mike they'd be more comfortable if he didn't come along for the ride, the salesman, who recognizes Frank from *Hollywood Squares,* gives him the celebrity pass, and Frank and Sparky roll off the lot for a test-drive. They smoke a joint heading east on Wilshire, making sure not to dirty the ashtray, then head south on La Brea to Olympic, east on Olympic, up Robertson, and then back to Mike and the lease documents. Frank leaves the Caddy with Mike, who informs him he can get him a good deal on storage since Frank can't bring himself to permanently part with it. Then the great comedy hope of the Lynx Network drives home in a bright yellow marvel of military engineering. He wants to take Honey for a ride but she's not there.

*   *   *

207

Happy Endings was shot later that week, and all concerned professed great happiness with the results. Lloyd spent the ensuing days in the editing suite choosing the best takes, laying in music, and generally buffing the piece to a fine sheen. He delivered it to the network confident in its mediocrity but secretly concerned he had not done an effective enough job of sabotage. Bart Pimento was famous, Jacy Pingree was sexy, Lynx could confound him by picking the thing up.

While Lloyd was torturing himself with these worries, Stacy supervised the ongoing furnishing of Château Melnick. More plasma televisions were loaded in and wired with TiVo. Chaises and chairs and sofas covered in damask and silk were arrayed around the airy house. Precious antiques purchased at full retail from auction houses in Beverly Hills strategically accented various corners, lending the new home a burnished sophistication.

But Stacy's pièce de résistance was the living room, or "great room" as she had taken to calling it—somewhat pretentiously, Lloyd thought. He insisted on referring to it as the living-great room, and Stacy, who scented satiric intent, couldn't get him to stop. The house faced west and in the late afternoon of a cloudless Southern California day shafts of rich butterscotch sunlight poured through French windows, creating shimmering squares of shadows that played gently over exquisitely woven Persian rugs purchased at great cost from the Mardosian Brothers Emporium on La Cienega Boulevard. Two Italian leather sofas whose supple surfaces were a murmured invitation to sensual abandon had been arranged in an L-shape and separated by a marble-topped side table. Arrayed opposite were wing chairs embroidered in swirling floral patterns of softest Thai silk. In the middle of the sofas and chairs was a sleek circular, silver coffee table, six feet across, which looked like a huge, smooth-surfaced Eisenhower dollar. A large hearth crowned with an oak mantel piece shipped from southern England anchored one side of the room. At the opposite end stood a new baby grand piano patiently waiting for young Dustin's lessons to begin, since neither of the senior Melnicks was musically inclined.

Months earlier Stacy had decreed they must adorn the walls with art, and after carefully perusing the works of a group of local artists introduced to her by a toadying dealer who treated her royally from the moment he learned the Mar Vista address was temporary, she had chosen several large abstract canvases whose colors matched those of her decorating scheme. And all of it had been feng shuied to perfection by Cam Rousseau, who assured Stacy the energy flow of her great room could not be improved upon.

In the first few days they occupied the new house, after putting Dustin to bed, Stacy would often sit alone in the great room in one of the Thai silk chairs and sip decaf, looking out the window and reflecting on the joyful abundance that had come to be hers.

While Stacy was reflecting on her joyful abundance, Lloyd was in the guesthouse, a freestanding structure out back that he had claimed for his home office, a place he had come to refer to internally as the Bitter Barn. Ensconced there in the evenings, he would stare out the window at the rock-bordered swimming pool with its raised Jacuzzi and gurgling waterfalls, watching as the lights from the house projected shifting patterns on the dark water and wondering how he could possibly escape. You can only guess at the inner turbulence Lloyd was suffering, given the inability of his plush surroundings to ameliorate it. Kitted out to his exact specifications, his personal environment was a high-end adult playpen. The distressed-wood flooring lent it a country ambience (the country of which Ralph Lauren was president), accentuated by an oak credenza that had cost Lloyd's entire income for 1983. There was a plasma television set, a pinball machine, and several original vintage movie posters on the wall (including one for *Double Indemnity,* whose spouse-murdering plot was not without a certain wish-fulfillment angle for Lloyd), and a small refrigerator kept stocked with low-calorie snacks. Lloyd's books had been unpacked in here and filled the new shelves, warmly welcoming him whenever he sought sanctuary, which was increasingly often as he grew less and less interested in engaging with Stacy, who didn't seem to notice or care.

The next few months crawl by for both Lloyd and Frank as they wait for the people at the Lynx Network to determine their respective fates. Lloyd splits his time between his office on the lot and the Bitter Barn in the backyard. In the Barn he would eat sushi, listen to alt rock music by bands far younger than he, and ruminate on various ideas for his book, none of which gained traction in his increasingly febrile mind for more than a few minutes at a time. In his office on the lot he would read the trades, drink coffee, and talk to Tai Chi, who, it turned out, had been cohabitating with a stuntman for the past year.

One day, when Tai Chi wore something particularly provocative, he locked the door to his office and masturbated, but when he had finished and cleaned himself up, he was so repulsed by his behavior he waited a full twenty-four hours before doing it again.

Frank was at the Comedy Shop every night working on new material for his CD. The surprisingly positive *Kirkuk* experience seemed to revivify him, and the news passed along by Robert that the show had "heat" at the network further boosted his creative metabolism, resulting in several new bits that he was pleased with, including one about former members of the Taliban opening a strip club in Kabul called the Satanic Pussycat where burka-clad women would show their toes. Near the time the network was getting ready for their "upfronts," when they all fly to New York to announce their fall schedules to the cash-fat advertising community, Frank did a gig at the Sun Theater in Ventura that was recorded for release on CD by Razor Records, a division of a huge German conglomerate that owned everything from amusement parks to publishing houses to movie studios. During this time he carried on a desultory affair with Candi Wyatt, usually having sex in the back of the Hummer since going to his place was not a viable option and he didn't want to risk being attacked by one of her cats again.

★   ★   ★

The electric effect the *Kirkuk* pilot had on Honey seemed to build with each passing day. She got her hair tint redone to make the blond a little less brassy for the new head shots she ordered, which she now took to calling "publicity photos," because she assumed her auditioning days were over. She didn't hear from Bart again, which saddened her, and she sensed Frank was engaged in his usual infelicitous behavior; he seemed in need of far less sex than usual. But the renaissance of her career prospects clouded her vision, and a combination of willful delusion and optimism conspired in Honey to assure life on the home front remained peaceful.

Stacy occupied her time putting the finishing touches on their new home and helping Daryl Hyler with the benefit for Save Our Aching Planet. The aquatically themed menu, which featured six different varieties of edible seaweed alone, bore the unmistakable mark of Stacy's professional handiwork, and she and Daryl would discuss future projects on the weekly hikes they were taking on the fire roads in the Santa Monica Mountains. Daryl even hinted that Stacy and Lloyd might be invited to spend precious vacation time at the Hyler beach house on Ibiza, where they were currently engaged in suing the zoning board to be allowed to tear down three one-hundred-year-old homes so they could build the Spanish equivalent of Mar-A-Lago on the windswept island dunes. The day after Stacy heard this, she sent Daryl a gift of beach towels with a note reading, *Buena suerte.*

This brief period during which Lloyd and Stacy and Frank and Honey went about their lives as if in suspended animation while awaiting the phone calls that would tell them whether the gods were going to program warm, golden sunshine or cold, driving rain came to an end one morning in early May. The panjandrums at Lynx had been deliberating the last several weeks in the secretive mode of the College of Cardinals choosing a new pope. Lloyd received a call from his agent on a Friday telling him Lynx was dragging it out to the last moment, try to stay optimistic. Over dinner, Lloyd relates this to Stacy, who needed a cup of chamomile tea to go to sleep that night (the equivalent of three Ativan for her), such was her anxiety.

Saturday morning finds the normally chatty Stacy unusually quiet. It as almost as if she believes her voice might drown out the ringing of the telephone, causing them to miss the call that will change their lives forever. The Melnicks are in their kitchen and she is putting peanut butter on wheat toast for Dustin while Lloyd stands in front of the pantry, squinting at the back of a box of oatmeal, trying to locate the caloric content and wondering if he needs reading glasses. They've been up for an hour and hardly exchanged a word, which Lloyd does not mind. Then it happens. The phone rings. Stacy tenses like a penurious immigrant hearing a landlord's knock, knowing something momentous is going to happen in the next minute. Whether she will be allowed to stay in the tenement apartment for another month or be tossed on the sidewalk with her family and possessions, she doesn't know. She knows only that her immediate future rests in the long-fingered hands of the powerful person on the other side of the door, for although Stacy is three generations removed from the Lower East Side of Manhattan, her DNA is wired directly to Rivington Street.

She doesn't move.

The order to do a network series is double-edged, because while a creator craves the approbation the pickup reflects, the price he pays is the sacrifice of his life for the foreseeable future, since the shows usually require eighteen-hour working days for the better part of a year. And Lloyd, as we have seen, is already more than ambivalent about the prospect of devoting himself to these endeavors. Having learned long ago never to answer the phone before the third ring, since it implies an unseemly eagerness, he waits two rings. As the third one begins, he lifts the receiver.

"Hello?" He frowns, then says "Uh-huh. No," as he looks over at Stacy, who is trying to keep from levitating. She's mouthing, *Who is it?*

"This isn't a good time right now. Thanks for calling." He hangs up. "Sales call," he says to Stacy, who almost visibly deflates as she refocuses on feeding her son. Having accomplished this, she turns to Lloyd and asks him if he wants pancakes. This comes as something of a surprise to Lloyd, since Stacy has shown little interest in carbohydrates since she has crossed the threshold of forty, but sensing her need to occupy herself, he answers in the affirmative.

She gets out the batter and a one-quart Pyrex measuring cup and begins breaking eggs. One, two, three eggs. She wills the phone to sing to her, a ringing song of possibility and hope, of swollen investment portfolios and vacation homes, of private jets and famous friends, of . . .

Nothing.

Four, five, six eggs. Now she's really concentrating. *Ring, dammit!* Still nothing. She looks over at Lloyd reading the paper. *How can he be so cool?*

After breaking six eggs and stirring them together in the Pyrex measuring cup, she pours them into a metal mixing bowl. Now she's stirring the viscous goo with a wooden spoon in a hard, clockwise motion, completely unaware that she is gripping the utensil with a force that would choke a snake.

Then it happens again. The *riiiinnngg* cleaves the air like a hatchet. Stacy looks up from the pancake batter she is wrestling with at Lloyd, who is waiting the requisite two rings before answering. On the third ring he lifts the receiver.

"Hello?"

"Lloyd?"

"Yeah?"

"It's Harvey Gornish. How are ya?"

All right, Lloyd thinks. *Game over. The head guy doesn't call to tell you you're a loser.*

"Fine, thanks," he says wearily.

"You're flying to New York for the upfronts tomorrow." Harvey pauses here, awaiting the anticipated whoop of surprised enthusiasm or the obsequious whimpering of thanks everyone who receives these calls

213

immediately performs. When neither is forthcoming, Harvey continues, slightly confused. *Is this Melnick hard of hearing or something?* "Congratulations, you're on the schedule." Lloyd feels as if he were a giant coffee press and someone were pushing down from the top, causing all his energy to be forced from his head, shoulders, torso, arms, stomach, groin, thighs, calves, and out through his toes, where it puddles on the floor around him. "Lloyd? You there?"

"Yeah, I'm here."

"I'm here?" Clearly this is not the reaction Harvey expects from the supplicants he deigns to personally call and apprise of their ascension above the striving hordes who have spent years crawling blindly on top of each other like frightened mice in a shoe box awaiting the wide gullet of a pet iguana. Lloyd was being removed from the mouse house, his life spared, Harvey's thinking, and all he can say is "Yeah, I'm here"?

Stacy, meanwhile, in barely controlled hysteria, is looking at Lloyd's torpid expression and mouthing, *What? What?*

"Are you available to go to New York?" Harvey asks in a tone intended to be chaffing but that actually says, if you're not available, don't bother coming to the office on Monday since I'll have had the locks on your office door changed.

"I'll be there," Lloyd says in the same voice he uses when his dentist's assistant calls to remind him of an appointment. Lloyd hangs up the phone with a resigned air. He looks at Stacy, whose face is hovering somewhere in agitated, nervous anticipation slung like a hammock between the twin poles of sorrow and joy.

"So?"

"They picked up the show."

A look of fevered rapture shimmers over Stacy's features, the kind of shining-eyed expression common in portraits of medieval saints in the throes of religious ecstasy. The last thirty seconds spent watching her apathetic husband's dilatory telephone conversation has been a tortured eternity, and her constrained emotions find release in a shriek of such volume her son begins to cry. She runs to the boy, lifting him from his chair and covering him with kisses, saying, "Mommy loves you, Mommy loves you, Mommy loves you," all the while looking gratefully at Lloyd. Having calmed the frightened child, Stacy turns toward her husband, who has risen inestimably in her eyes. "Lloyd," she says in a voice that implies if he wants to step into the bedroom and lock the door, she will be happy to spend the next several hours fellating him, "Congratulations!"

"Thanks."

Stacy is entirely too concerned with her own internal drama to bother reading the tea leaves of Lloyd's glum expression, so she hugs him and immediately calls Daryl to share the good news. Daryl, for her part, is thrilled since she knows Stacy can be counted on to tithe a significant part of Lloyd's income to SOAP.

Swept away on the warm wave of approval, Lloyd retreats to the sanctuary of his backyard bell tower to ponder his options. How could this disaster possibly have occurred? The second Bart Pimento was cast, he'd known the show was doomed. When they'd shot the thing, the dandy Andy Stanley had managed to raise the level to mediocre, but still, it was not good. How was it possible that Harvey Gornish and his minions at Lynx did not have anything better to put on their schedule? Didn't they have another piece of cloying crap featuring a desperate movie star whose career was in free fall? Why couldn't they just leave him alone?

Lloyd puts his head back and looks up at the distressed beams, meant to evoke a Vermont barn, running across his ceiling. He supposes he can always hang himself, but the thought of dangling neck-snapped from a piece of wood slowly choking to death doesn't have much appeal. That leaves the less radical options of either doing the show and maintaining the status quo, or not doing it and so ending his career, since he would surely be found in breach of contract. The checks would stop arriving and his days as a lottery winner would come to a fast and unceremonious close, resulting in a humiliation that would only be exceeded in scale by the ensuing garage sale. Lloyd simply needs to picture an apoplectic Stacy standing on the Brentwood lawn surrounded by price-tagged Persian rugs and damask sofas to arrive at the third option: to become a secret agent, a traitor, a fifth column in the *Happy Endings* comedy nation, working surreptitiously toward its defeat. Should he tread this path, he would retain his perks, memberships, and general equilibrium. The choice was obvious.

"It didn't test well?"

In a kitchen across town Frank slumps against the green Formica counter in a near swoon, the blood rushing from his head with the alacrity of passengers on a sinking ocean liner heading for the lifeboats. He is talking to Robert, who has called to tell him the network was less enamored of an Eskimo on their prime-time schedule than they had initially indicated.

"There's nothing we can do, believe me, I tried."

"They don't even want it as a midseason replacement?"

"It's dead, Frank. Say kaddish."

"Bobby, I don't even know what to think." A monumental admission for Frank, who is never at a loss for subjects on which to masticate.

"I'm sorry."

"Thanks."

"It was a nice payday," Robert tries.

"Don't patronize me, babe," Frank says, knowing Robert's income will be roughly fifty times his own this year.

"I don't mean to. If it's any consolation, and I know it's not, I feel terrible, too. Harvey Gornish basically told me they were picking it up, so we both got gut shot here." Robert waits for Frank to respond to this attempt at empathy. When there is only a burning silence, he continues, "But they liked what you did, so I'm going to work on Harvey to get you written into one of the series they already have on. He mentioned they're firing an actor in Lloyd Melnick's show, so let me get going on that."

"Great," Frank says blankly.

"I'll see you at the benefit tonight, right?"

"Yeah."

"Sorry about the timing. Oh, Frank, one more thing, is Honey there?"

"She's getting her legs waxed."

"Have her call me."

A sense of desolation that seems to have brought with it a different weather pattern pervades the West Hollywood bungalow when Frank hangs up the phone. He looks out the kitchen window and sees clouds scudding in from the north, collecting over the hills above Sunset Boulevard and forming into threatening shapes. Walking into the living room, Frank collapses on the couch. Ten minutes go by during which he meditates on what he perceives to be the exquisite futility of his life. Here he is punching fifty in the mouth looking at a failed pilot and a bunch of road dates in cities you can't even fly to without making a connection in some place like Minneapolis or Atlanta. Having reached the painful decision to sell out, he is astounded that no one is buying. And what did Bobby want to talk to Honey about?

The one thing that illuminates Frank's dark moment, that shines soft light in the gloomy shadows, is the realization that tonight he will get the chance to face an audience of industry players in a ballroom at the Beverly Wilshire Hotel and tell them exactly what is on his mind. Imagining the expressions on their pampered faces as he uncorks twenty-five years of pent-up aggravation is almost enough to make him smile.

Two dresses are being held up for Lloyd's inspection, and he looks from one to the other marveling that what appears to be less than three yards of material could have resulted in such a vast sum on his Visa card.

"The Anna Sui or the Balenciaga?" Stacy asks, standing in their bedroom clad in a lavender silk thong-and-bra combination she wears when she wants to send Lloyd the message that if he behaves himself, the night's menu will be spicy.

Not knowing one from the other, Lloyd says, "The one in your left hand."

"The Anna Sui," Stacy replies indulgently, smiling at Lloyd as he struggles into the tuxedo he wore to the Emmys every year as a staff writer on *The Fleishman Show.* "Did I tell you Daryl asked us to visit them on Ibiza this summer?"

This was not good news. "No. You didn't mention it."

"We won't be able to go for more than a weekend since you'll be in town doing the show, but she said she'd send their jet for us."

"They have a jet?"

"I've never been in a private jet."

Lloyd looks over from the mirror where he's been thrashing around with his bow tie and says, "Doesn't it seem weird to you that Madame Save Our Aching Planet flies around in a private jet? Tell me, what's the point of having that fleet of electric cars if she uses more jet fuel during one trip to the East Coast than ten SUVs would use in a year? I mean, isn't she actually making the planet ache *more*?"

"Lloyd, for godsakes! Don't be so judgmental. She's serving a higher good."

The gray light of the late afternoon filters through the French windows and falls on the golden cellophane wrapped around the huge gift basket Lloyd received from Lynx earlier in the day. Overflowing with cheeses, gourmet salami, Cristal Champagne and two flutes, biscuits, pâtés, sweetmeats, utensils, and a cutting board, it is a sign of corporate gratitude indicative of the high hopes they have for *Happy Endings.* Recognizing this, Stacy has chosen to place it on the circular metallic coffee table in the middle of the living room, where she intends it to serve as a trophy of sorts, much as she would have mounted the head of an elk Lloyd had bagged were he the hunter/gatherer type.

Lloyd sits in his scratchy tuxedo on the chair upholstered with Thai silk and stares at the gift basket miserably. How could his nefarious sabotage have backfired so completely? he wonders, as his eyes bore into the cellophane. Images begin to take shape on its crinkly surface, ghostly human faces emerging from within its overstuffed depths, Pam Penner laughing, supercilious Jason Fendi, the silent Jessica Puck, sanguine Andy Stanley, their features separating and then merging into a single icon of want and need and desire and . . .

"Lloyd?"

Lloyd turns around to see Stacy standing at the threshold of the room ready to go out. The cocktail dress she has chosen to wear shows off her gym-toned body, and her makeup has been perfectly applied. In the gloomy half-light she looks beautiful, Lloyd's news having had a restorative effect a year at a spa could not accomplish. For a moment Lloyd sees the face she had before the climb began. She's holding a wrapped gift.

"You look nice," he tells her.

"Thanks," she says, giggling a little. They look into each other's eyes from across the room and nearly share a human moment. "The babysitter's here. Are you ready?" Nodding, he rises. "Oh, and I got you something. To celebrate." Lloyd takes the oblong object, looks at it phlegmatically. He doesn't recognize the wrapping paper. What could this be? An item of clothing? A watch? Surely something he didn't need and would want to return. "Open it," she tells him, smiling. Lloyd tears at the wrapping paper. Pulling it off, he sees a white box, which he opens, revealing a hardback copy of *The Long Goodbye* in mint condition. "It's a first edition. I bought it this afternoon because I thought you deserved a congratulations gift. You like Raymond Chandler, don't you?" Lloyd is stunned. He kisses her on the mouth.

"Yeah, I do. Thanks."

"I read about him on the Internet. You know he didn't publish his first novel until he was fifty?"

"I know." What amazes him is that Stacy knows.

For Lloyd the conundrum regarding his marriage was this: just when he thought he was living on his own planet, she would beam in and join him. It hadn't happened much lately, but when it did, it was something that touched him somewhere he had forgotten existed.

219

"You can still write a book, if you want. Just don't give up your day job," Stacy says, smiling, a few flecks of iron in her voice, just enough to let him know that if he is thinking of pursuing an actual career as an author, he'd better think again.

A light rain beats against the windshield of Stacy's Sunsation as Lloyd drives the two of them toward the Beverly Wilshire Hotel. Surrounded by much larger vehicles, he frets about the slipperiness of the Los Angeles roads, which upon becoming rain-slicked often cause cars to hydroplane in unforeseen directions, and Lloyd has a vision of a head-on collision with a West Side mother driving her kids home from a rain-shortened baseball practice in a sturdy Volvo. He had wanted to take his Saab to the benefit—compared to the Sunsation it was like driving a semi—but Stacy wouldn't hear of it, the Sunsation a reverse status symbol in her new world.

The choice of transportation is the only area in which she has not deferred to Lloyd since he received the phone call from Harvey Gornish that morning. From that fateful moment, Stacy has been treating her husband like a returning war hero who has arrived at the door of his beloved with a chest full of medals and an officer's commission. She places her hand on his tuxedoed knee and rubs it.

Lloyd waits. He prays something unbearably trite is not about to come out of her mouth.

"I'm so happy!" Stacy says, flashing her beautiful caps.

His hopes are dashed.

Before Frank went out that day, he left a note for Honey in which he told her if he wasn't back in time to accompany her to the event, she should meet him there. He also informed her in the same note, which had thoughtfully been Scotch-taped to the refrigerator, that Bobby wanted her to call him. Frank didn't mention the show hadn't been picked up, wishing to tell her in person. Honey wanted to hold off calling Frank's manager back at least for a while so she could tell herself her eagerness and anxiety were under control. Now she needs to kill a few minutes.

Honey stands at the refrigerator leafing through the mail. She wears a miniskirt, tight T-shirt, and fuck-me pumps; her newly waxed legs shiny in the kitchen light. The mail today is the usual assortment of bills, catalogs, and solicitations. As she prepares to dump the entire pile into the trash, the return address on a thick envelope catches her eye: People for the Ethical Treatment of Animals. She drops the other envelopes into the bin, placing the one from PETA on the counter, where it awaits her perusal. Picking up the phone, she calls Robert, consumed with curiosity. Robert had never asked her to call him before. He'd barely noticed Honey, preferring to parcel out his limited attention to Frank when they were together. And then there was Daryl, whom she found insufferable. Every time the four of them had dinner, Robert's wife would pretend Honey wasn't there, only condescending to speak to her about items on the menu or how much traffic there had been on the way to the restaurant. What could this possibly be about?

"Is Robert Hyler there, please?"

"I'm sorry," Tessa says in her dulcet tones, "he's out. May I take a message?"

Honey leaves word and then calls Frank on his cell phone to determine if he knows anything, but he doesn't pick up. Blissfully unaware that her future has been hijacked by the network research department (which had handed Harvey Gornish all the ammunition he needed to disembowel the entire *Kirkuk* world), Honey takes the PETA envelope and heads into the living room, where she sits in a chair and inspects its contents. And what are its contents? Along with the mailing is a note reading:

Dear Sweet Honeylicious,
   If the pix of these poor critters don't break your heart, you don't have one.
But I know you do. Send a check, come to a meeting, get involved!
   Love, Bart

221

Honeylicious? Love, Bart?

Clearly this is not a form note. She has seen those. They appear in fund-raising mailings aping real handwritten notes, truly personal pleas, but never fooling anyone. Honey examines the ink closely to be sure it isn't one of these misleading missives. A cursory look confirms that Bart Pimento himself has indeed written her. Flipping it over, Honey looks for a phone number, an addendum, some kind of RSVP that will allow her to take this flirtation to the next level, but finds nothing. Bart Pimento, apparently, works slowly. Honey ignores her disappointment. Instead she smiles to herself (after all, he had taken the time to write her a note after having given her the wrong phone number) and braces for the grim task—the actual perusal of the solicitation.

Within sixty seconds of looking at the photographs of cruel mink farms and entire cities of caged chickens who never see sunlight and reading about a pig who was taught to play checkers, Honey is so appalled she has almost forgotten where she is going tonight. Normally, when she is affected by a PETA-style plea, she asks Frank to send a check. Iraqi orphans, African AIDS sufferers, and Nicaraguan earthquake victims had all been recipients of Honey's financial largesse. But the enclosed form letter (the one everyone got, the one that was not addressed to *Dear Sweet Honeylicious* and did not conclude with *Love, Bart*) signed by Bart Pimento detailing the hellish cruelties endured by the innocent animal community at the hands of devious humans makes her think perhaps she needs to take more of an interest.

The PETA mailing actually made her nauseous, so after downing an Alka-Seltzer, Honey goes about getting ready for the benefit as if it were her professional debut, which, in a sense, it is for she will not be attending this event as a Bones moon late of the cheapie naked-action-flick universe but as a legitimate planet in her own right, about to launch into a radiant orbit all her own. At least that's what she thinks as she bustles about the modest bungalow dreaming of more square footage, a larger pool, and what she can possibly do to help those unfortunate minks and chickens.

* * *

Having waited for Frank for the better part of the increasingly soggy afternoon and early evening, Honey puts the finishing touches on her toilette, anoints herself with Fixation, a new perfume she'd seen advertised in *W,* slips into a black sheath dress that barely contains her subtly undulating flesh, and totters on new Jimmy Choo shoes out to her Honda Accord. Sliding behind the wheel of this quaint illustration of what she considers her soon-to-be-former life, she silently curses Frank for making her arrive at the ball in a metal pumpkin when she had planned on descending from her carriage, a Beverly Boulevard Botticelli, Venus Alighting from a Hummer. *Well*, she thinks, putting her Honda into gear, *there's going to be plenty of time for that.*

The Hummer weaves between lanes on the 405 freeway headed south. Frank has decided he doesn't like his large new toy after all. The torque of the suspension makes it ride with the all the smoothness of a tractor plowing a field, and given Frank's slender physique and resulting lack of natural buttocks padding, the vehicle gives him what amounts to a continuous Swedish massage. Then there is the placement of the front seat, which feels as if it is ten inches from the windshield, good for its original intention of spotting land mines in the road but not much else. The noise emitted by the powerful engine is too much for any muffler to stifle, which leaves Frank cranking the CD player to untenable levels to hear Sinatra's crooning on *Songs for Swinging Lovers*. Unfortunately, he reflects, driving in the increasing precipitation, the Hummer is the least of his problems.

After going on a shopping spree at Sparky's house, Frank has spent the past five hours driving the freeways under darkening skies. He started out going east on the 10 past the forest of glass buildings that comprised downtown Los Angles, finding his way to Fontana, a redneck town on the edge of the Mojave, before cutting north on the 15, where he connected with the Foothill Freeway and then headed back in a westerly direction through Pasadena, merging into the 170 south aiming for the Studio City hills, today a fulcrum of swollen thunderclouds, and then to the 101 west, from which he was able to connect to the 405, rolling south in the shadow of the looming white Getty Center, citadel of lost worlds, and toward Los Angeles International Airport, with the idea that perhaps he will get on a plane and fly somewhere.

He's pleased the rock he's smoking helps him concentrate on his driving, while the whiskey chasers balance the drug and ease him toward what he considers a mellow equilibrium. Gliding off the 405 at the La Tijera exit, Frank ruminates on the remarks he will make at the benefit this evening but struggles to get them to gel into something coherent, something he can perform, something with which he can kill, since, given his current situation, tonight's event is going to serve as a massive audition. Robert has told him Harvey Gornish will be there, and Frank ponders tweaking the executive for passing on his show, wondering how far he can go in making the reptilian Gornish squirm without scaring off potential employers. He supposes he can fillet Daryl Hyler, but his lack of strong feelings for her one way or the other does not bode well for comedy. As he considers his options in the liquid twilight, he senses the evening slipping out of his control like a wet glass from the hand of an inebriated reveler making a drunken attempt to clean the kitchen after a party and regrets having agreed to perform tonight.

Lloyd pulls the Sunsation up to the valet station at the Beverly Wilshire Hotel, gets out, and waits for Stacy to circumnavigate the tiny automobile and join him. In the roughly two seconds it takes for her to arrive by his side, he looks around at the other vehicles driving up and notices most of them are also tiny and electric. When he points this out to Stacy, she tells him Daryl has arranged for everyone who didn't already own an electric car to have use of one for the evening. Did this woman's goodness know no bounds? The Melnicks walk into the hotel behind the host of a politically themed talk show and his date, a well-dressed hooker.

The anteroom of the ballroom has been set up for cocktails, and Lloyd and Stacy linger in a corner over glasses of chilled chardonnay watching the heaving mass of people. There's a movie star talking to a senator near a studio head having a pleasant discussion with a lawyer suing the studio for a nine-figure sum. An exercise guru is having an animated exchange with an attractive young woman who has been convicted of running a prostitution ring and is now marketing a successful line of lingerie from a store on Rodeo Drive in Beverly Hills. And there is Daryl, who, upon seeing Robert (he had arrived separately, having flown to Las Vegas that day to play a round of golf with a potential client who was shooting a movie there), tears herself away from the real estate developer promising her a huge contribution tonight.

Grabbing her husband, she says, "Where's Frank?"

"Don't worry, he'll be here," Robert answers reassuringly, wondering where exactly the hell *is* Frank. Temporarily mollified, Daryl goes back to find her contributor as Robert spots Honey standing alone sipping from a wineglass, her steel-eyed gaze sweeping the room like a search-light. Seeing Robert walking toward her, she brightens and waves. Robert chastely kisses her hello, compliments the way she looks, and upon learning Frank has not informed her of the fate of *Kirkuk* tells her he has good news and bad news. The bad news is obvious and her face falls along with her stomach, which feels to her as if it dropped six inches. Robert quickly says, "But the good news could be very good."

"What is it?" Honey asks, seeming as if she might actually start to cry. From her expression anyone watching the two of them could be forgiven for thinking Robert is ending an affair with her.

"Harvey told me he wants to do a show with you."

Honey's face and stomach instantly reverse their course and an incredulous smile bursts forth.

"Are you kidding?"

"He wants to make a holding deal."

"With me?"

"Next week."

"Robert . . . I'm . . . I'm . . ." Honey is so overwhelmed that this could be happening her power of speech deserts her momentarily. It

225

returns when she realizes she doesn't actually understand her good fortune. "What's a holding deal?"

"They want to pay you not to take a job somewhere else while they try to find a show for you."

"They want to give me a show?"

"You tested very well. Particularly with males between the ages of fourteen and thirty-five."

At this news, Honey actually feels faint. Eventually she recovers, and when Robert asks where Frank is, she tells him she doesn't know before happily going to get her glass refilled.

"Schmelnick!"

Lloyd looks up from his conversation with Stacy to see Phil Sheldon approaching him, hand outstretched. This middle-aged comedy deity has remarkable posture, which brings him to just over six feet tall. His features are highlighted by a prominent nose and widely spaced green eyes. A thatch of dark brown hair creates a nimbus effect around his head. "What are you doing here?" Phil nods to Stacy. "Mrs. Schmelnick."

"Hello, Phil," she says, smiling. She hadn't seen him since Lloyd signed his deal and swears not to feel belittled by his presence.

"Same as you," Lloyd says. "My wife dragged me."

"I can't stand these things. I don't know why I can't just write the check. Why do they have to give you dinner? What's the point of dinner?"

"I chose the menu," Stacy says, slightly offended.

"Excuse me!" Phil says, chaffing his own apology. "I'll make sure I take home what I don't eat and have it for breakfast. So, Schmelnick . . ." Stacy takes this opportunity to excuse herself. Phil always ignores her after saying hello and she wants to talk to Daryl anyway. "I heard about your megadeal. Very nice."

"I feel like I should give you a percentage," Lloyd says.

"Nah, forget it." Phil waves his hand, dismissing what is actually a perfectly reasonable notion. "Schmelnick, let me tell you something," he says in a mock-stentorian tone. "It's all a shiny penny, my friend. A very shiny penny." Phil looks out over the room of well-heeled Angelenos, and before Lloyd can ask what this Zen pronouncement means—and didn't he say the same thing the night they met?—Phil mumbles, "Okay, bye. I need to keep moving or my wife'll find me."

The ballroom being used for the Save Our Aching Planet dinner is set up to accommodate a thousand people, testimony to the prodigious arm-twisting ability of Daryl Hyler. The tables are filled, and although many of the attendees are slightly puzzled by Stacy's menu, which is deemed perhaps too heavy on the sea vegetation, the evening proceeds smoothly with only one slight problem: after a determined and increasingly agitated hunt it is concluded the master of ceremonies is AWOL.

But Phil Sheldon, after being aggressively beseeched by Daryl in a display that verges on groveling, agrees to step into the breach. His curmudgeonly persona and hostile self-deprecation go over well with the crowd, most of whom do not appreciate his subtle drollery but are most respectful of anyone who can generate a billion dollars with one television show, and as they drift out of the hotel casually examining the contents of their bulging goody bags (chocolate truffles, DVDs, perfumes, skin cream, CDs), the evening is pronounced a grand success.

The steady rain joins with a violent wind blowing from the Pacific Ocean, both increasing in intensity until a drenching downpour lashes against the windows of the Hummer. Frank has parked on Sepulveda Boulevard near the airport and has sat for several hours watching the planes take off and land beneath the wet, moonless sky. Looking at his cell phone, he checks the messages. There are twelve of them, probably all about the fund-raiser, wanting to know where he is and why he's not there and how he could possibly be such a self-destructive fuckup.

Bobby is not going to be happy, Frank thinks, feeling slightly guilty. Bobby, after all, has treated him well.

It's over, he realizes; not just the evening, but also any chance Frank has at getting off the road. All he has to look forward to now is two nights at a club in Phoenix next week and a college booking up in Santa Cruz.

He wonders what his father was thinking about the day he topped himself. He was beset by the financial problems that dog the middle class, certainly, but his difficulties in that area were nothing out of the ordinary. There was always enough to eat; their lights were never turned off. He and Frank's mother, a bitter woman who dreamed of a singing career, would have voluble fights, but those, too, seemed commonplace. Frank knew they were still having sex because he could hear them when they retreated to their bedroom every week after Sunday lunch for a one-hour "nap."

Frank's father was forty-nine, the same age Frank is now, when he put the gun to his head and foreclosed his future, and Frank has never been able to pinpoint a single overriding reason for the act of self-nullification that took place in their basement that day. Perhaps it was simply the realization that he had already seen all he needed to see, done all he could do, and the limited pleasures life afforded him were not going to be enough to sustain his interest.

He and Frank had not been close, but still Frank was deeply affected by his death. Frank was only fourteen, a callow and unformed age, and a parent's suicide, devastating at any time, is particularly difficult for an adolescent to understand. Frank carried a simmering antagonism toward his father from that day forward, a burning sense of rage at the abandonment that had occurred, for how is a boy to regard it when his guide, his role model, his shining example, decides he doesn't want the job?

Despite intermittent bouts of therapy taking place over years and years, Frank has never been able to forgive his father. Until tonight. He has spent the last five years rebuilding his career from the ashes of that catastrophic gig in Cleveland. A major network finally decided he had redeemed himself and determined he could be trusted with a lead role in a prime-time show. But it has all come to naught and the feeling of futility is utterly overwhelming.

Putting the Hummer in gear, he pulls out of his parking space and heads north on Sepulveda back toward town. As Frank passes through Culver City, he gets the idea that maybe he won't go home because other than Honey, who is not going to be pleased about his absence this evening, what is there for him other than a reminder that his little bungalow is the only local real estate he can afford in a neighborhood that isn't gang-infested?

He is clearheaded enough to realize lying down and trying to sleep only to be overtaken by a restless, dehydrated slumber that will result in another paralyzing hangover is a bad idea, a whimpering abdication of his self-appointed role as prankster and provocateur. If it really was over for Frank and he had missed the opportunity for a grand-exit gesture at the SOAP dinner, what is left for him in the way of making an impression, some last bit of sparkling, pointless Dada by which to be remembered?

As he drives north across Santa Monica Boulevard ruminating on the nihilistic possibilities available to him, he passes through a red light. A police cruiser heading in the opposite direction does a U-turn and puts the siren on. Lost in his darkest thoughts, Frank hears through a loudspeaker, "YOU IN THE HUMMER! PULL OVER!" His response, to the great aggravation of the officers in the car, is to keep driving, making a left on Wilshire as the rain continues to flood from the sky, forming slick, greasy puddles on the hard asphalt. "YOU IN THE HUMMER!" Again, angrier. "PULL OVER NOW!"

When Frank disobeys the third time, the cops send out a radio alert and another cruiser heads north on Twenty-sixth Street to join the pursuit. Frank is now speeding west on San Vincente Boulevard, the first cruiser tailgating him, the cops cursing the arrogance of the people who buy these military assault vehicles. The second cruiser is now heading east on the same road barreling past the Brentwood Golf Club. In the distance the cop at the wheel of the second car sees the first cruiser right behind the Hummer. Slowing down to make the turn that will enable him to join the chase, the cop in the second car then floors it across the median divider just as Frank pulls a hard right onto Carmelina. *Carmeliiina!* Frank watches in his rearview mirror as the second patrol car smashes bang into the first one as if they were a couple of good old boys in a Burt Reynolds movie.

Not bad, he thinks.

Frank slows down now, getting his bearings. This neighborhood between Sunset and San Vincente is a magnificent effusion of abundant flora, which creates an awning that slows the rain on the side of the roads, allowing Frank to better read the house numbers.

This is it, the climax, the finale, the end in one incandescently stupid, futile gesture.

The hard rain beats a bleak tattoo against the bedroom window as Stacy pulls the comforter up to her chin. Having lain in bed in lace panties and a teddy for the last twenty minutes, her hopes that Lloyd would take the hint are vanishing. Lloyd, meanwhile, has been reading *The Great Gatsby* (the well-known novel in which a circumspect man attempts to plumb the depths of an audacious one) and making notes in the margins with the gold pen given by his friends at Lynx. When he closes the book, turns off the bedside lamp, and says good-night, her hopes rally, but are again dashed when moments later nothing unto-ward has occurred. Lloyd, for his part, has been staring at the ceiling wondering what Phil Sheldon had meant when he told him it was all a shiny penny.

"Lloyd?"

"Hmm?"

"Did you enjoy yourself tonight?"

"I don't like those kind of things."

"It was important to me."

"Fine. I hope you had a good time."

"I did."

"Good."

Silence ensues. Stacy searches for a conversational topic that Lloyd will warm to while he closes his eyes and hopes she will go to sleep.

A violent shuddering of the house shaking the struts and beams to their very foundations causes Stacy to yelp in fright, suddenly interrupting this moment of marital bedtime banality. They feel the bed move and hear the sound of glass breaking. Then a second impact jolts the house.

"It's an earthquake!" Stacy exclaims, when her breath returns. "Go get Dustin!"

The two of them leap out of bed and, terrified, head for their son's room. Arriving in that incongruously peaceful precinct, they see the sleeping boy and heave a sigh of great relief. Stroking Dustin's hot cheek, Stacy turns to Lloyd and says, "Go downstairs and make sure everything's all right."

Lloyd crosses the airy second-floor hallway, heads for the stairs, and quickly descends to the marble foyer, which is surprisingly drafty. The marble feels cool beneath his bare feet as he crosses to the living room, where he sees a yellow Hummer that destroyed a hedge, drove over the well-tended front lawn, burst through the French windows launching shards of glass in all directions, muddied a Persian rug before crushing the coffee table and the huge cellophane-wrapped gift basket sitting on it, obliterated a damask sofa, and then crashed into a wall, sending its occupant through the windshield and leaving him lying on the hood, bleeding from the head. When Lloyd recovers from his initial shock, he walks over to the man whose identity he quickly grasps.

"Frank . . . Jesus, are you okay?"

Frank moves his lips but nothing audible is emitted other than the popping of a pink bubble of blood, indicating internal bleeding. Lloyd leans closer, realizing he could be listening to the last words of Frank Bones. Frank's cheeks billow slightly and his head has a tremor. Air comes up through his throat and his mouth moves, trying to form a word through the blood.

"P-patronize m-me . . . ," he says, exhausted at the struggle, putting his lips together for one last try. "M-more . . ." Here he looks up at

Lloyd, the light and the life leaving his eyes, and with one final effort manages to say, "Babe," before losing consciousness.

Thus does the story for which Lloyd has been so assiduously searching begin to present itself.

Book Two

Killer Bones

Chapter 12

In the early 1980s, after having graduated from college with a degree in English and a desire to direct films, I found myself writing for a downtown rag called the SoHo Weekly News. *I was living in a roach-infested basement apartment equipped with a shower in the kitchen and a depressed girlfriend in the bedroom. Her name was Sonia and she was constantly threatening to kill herself, which kept me continually generating reasons to leave the apartment so I wouldn't have to be there should she actually follow through. It was on one of those excursions that I encountered Frank Bones for the first time. In desperate need of laughs, which were in very short supply where I was living, I and a friend went to a comedy club on the Upper East Side of Manhattan. Frank was working as the emcee and he was . . .*

"Lloyd, they need you on the set."

Lloyd sees Tai Chi standing at the door to his office. It is the middle of August and Lloyd has been working on *Happy Endings,* which Lynx intends to display to the American public with much promotional fanfare at the end of September. Returning to his computer screen, he considers words like *revelatory, amazing, extraordinary,* and is unable to come up with something that doesn't sound like a hackneyed encomium lifted whole from a newspaper ad for a movie.

"Lloyd?" Tai Chi again.

"Yeah, yeah, yeah," he says impatiently, hitting the SAVE key and committing his labors to the hard drive. After much internal struggle, Lloyd has reluctantly abandoned the idea of writing a novel and concluded perhaps his literary talents are better suited to nonfiction. With this in mind, he has, for the past several weeks, been trying to find a way into Frank's story and had lit upon the idea of a memoir. What

Lloyd thought he could do was a kind of *Frank and Me* book, only with a more felicitous title, which he promised himself he would come up with before submitting his effort to a publisher.

The geometric manner in which Frank's life intersected with Lloyd's provided a natural architecture for ruminations on the subjects of envy, success, and money, key themes identified by the hopeful author in the tale he intended to tell. The reversal of their positions had a symmetrical aspect to it that lent a tidy structure to the story, and Frank's decline and fall provided a sordid touch that did nothing to lessen the project's appeal in a society ravenous for factual elucidations of bad behavior engaged in by the famous and near-famous. If by some chance Lloyd could not elevate his prose above the commonplace, he believed people would still clamor to read the story of how a well-known comedian smoked a bonfire of crack and then drove a military assault vehicle over a well-tended suburban hedge, through a set of French windows, and into a media hailstorm. Told with the right flair, Lloyd believed, there would always be a market for that kind of thing.

As for the a forementioned media hailstorm, anyone expecting a squalid carnival of cheap moralizing within the extensive coverage by cable news channels and supermarket tabloids was not disappointed. Since there were no international crises that week and no attractive white women had been mislaid by their families, the lurid saga of the Frank Bones meltdown was given far larger play than it deserved. Pundits on the shouting shows railed about the immorality of an entertainment world that allowed a decadent creature like Frank to exist in its dim corners. Frank's picture graced the covers of sleek magazines and pulpish newspapers, his unsmiling visage hinting at an unspoken and terrifying inner darkness, the kind that makes people plunk down several dollars so they can read about it. Honey gave dozens of interviews and sold pictures of Frank and her to a tabloid that usually trafficked in aliens and fad diets, for enough money to lease a starter Mercedes, which she promptly did.

Lloyd was the subject of much speculation in the mainstream media and was quoted cryptically in an Associated Press story saying, "We've known each other for a long time but I had never had him over to the house." The lack of ire in his tone was notable perhaps because he already knew he was going to be writing about Frank's life and didn't want to carelessly feed valuable material into the bottomless maw of the daily press as if it were simply tawdry gossip and sentimental reminiscence rather than the raw material for the spun gold he hoped it to be.

The fountain of vituperation in the Melnick household was Stacy, who was so incensed at what the Hummer had done to her meticulously designed home environment that much of what she had to say on the subject was unprintable in family newspapers, thereby rendering her role in the voluminous press coverage minimal.

And then there was the larger question, which was never satisfactorily answered in any of the thousands of words expended in the exploitation of the episode by the journalists whose job it was to explicate these things: Was it an accident? We know the answer, of course. But as it was masticated over in the diners and four-star restaurants of the town, opinion was divided.

During their weekly lunch at the famous Nate & Al's deli in Beverly Hills, Robert Hyler and Jolly De Meo discussed the question over bowls of beet soup. "Accident-schmaccident," Jolly said. He was of the opinion that good riddance was the order of the day. "I feel terrible about what happened but not terrible-terrible. He doesn't bring in enough commissions to feel terrible-terrible, and he was a pain in the ass, to boot."

Robert took a more emotional point of view saying, "A man so talented, it shouldn't have come to this," but he was pretty angry about what had occurred that evening, too, and relatively certain Frank had been using the Hummer as a weapon.

Somewhere high in the Santa Monica Mountains, several days after the event, Daryl Hyler, who shared her husband's suspicions, was saying, "If the legislation I'm busting my ass to get enacted, where everyone's gonna have to drive electric cars no matter what, if that becomes law, there's no way Frank commits this act. You can't drive through someone's house in a Sunsation." Then she looked over at the panting Stacy,

237

with whom she was hiking, and said, "Anyway, I'm never gonna forgive him for blowing off the SOAP benefit. I don't care that my husband's been carrying him for nearly twenty years. Frank Bones"—here she made a face and a gesture that were so infernally dismissive the crow gliding above her changed its flight pattern in fright—"is a man I have absolutely no use for, hon. You accumulate people as you move along in this town," Daryl lectured her disciple as the crow flew away, its tiny adrenal glands surging. "The ones that can help you, you hang on to them with your life, but the others . . . that's when the red pen comes out. You take out the red pen"—she made a sweeping motion with her hand—"and you get rid of 'em." Stacy was familiar with the red-pen concept, having exercised it with Marisa and Jonathan Pinsker, whom she hadn't spoken to in several months. Now she wanted to talk about getting Dustin into the Horizon School, something with which Daryl had promised to help, but Stacy knew it was useless to interject when her mentor was on a roll. "Robert is too nice sometimes. He doesn't understand the red pen."

This was the background against which Lloyd had commenced his literary labors in earnest. He would work late in the evenings at home and during the moments between crises while at the studio. In three months he had produced roughly thirty double-spaced pages, which he found meager if not pathetic. He had given up the legal pads for this project since he associated them with his television work, and this tome about Frank and him, this labor of love, *Dem Bones* or whatever its title would be, was meant to transcend that meretricious world. He wanted to believe the paucity of his output could be ascribed to the mode with which he was writing, that he would be cranking out the pages if he would go back to the legal pads.

But Lloyd knew this to be a self-serving canard. The reason he had only produced thirty pages, he realized, had much more to do with an absence of things to say that did not sound either like a quickie down-market paperback biography of Frank or a pretentious rumination on the state of the entertainment business. This usually left him with his head in his hands staring into the soft glow of the computer screen, rousing himself only long enough to check his e-mail eight times an hour.

Lloyd's frustration was kept moderately in check by the whirlwind of responsibilities distracting him during the days and leaving him exhausted in the evenings. He would routinely find himself driving the freeways at four A.M. turbulently digesting pizza and M&M's after late-night, fluorescent-lit sessions with the writing staff, where forty-five minutes could be expended debating whether Bart Pimento's character would, when referring to a jockstrap, use a word like *carapace* or simply say *jockstrap*.

As he lay tossing in bed, trying to settle down so he could gain a few hours of precious slumber before fighting through the traffic back to the studio to do it all again, he would try to work through the book in his head. Would he be served by alternating chapters, one about Frank followed by one about himself, or was it an act of inestimable hubris to think anyone would remotely care about the pampered, yet tortured and indescribably small life of Lloyd Melnick? If that were true, and who could doubt but it was, he considered the possibility of simply and poetically reflecting on Frank's existence, its meaning within the larger context of American life and its metaphoric resonance for true artists in a mercantile society. But Lloyd knew himself to be no poet, and certainly his ruminations on the artist's role in anything would be of no use to anyone.

One late-summer night, in a rare moment of clarity that descended upon him as he was drifting into a disturbed sleep, Lloyd realized his nascent book lacked a defining event, at least an event that he could use as a defining event, given what he was beginning to suspect were his limited descriptive capabilities. Whereas others of a more literary bent could perhaps tease two hundred and fifty or three hundred pages from a story of parallel lives culminating in a dramatic car wreck, examine the depths of the characters in forensic detail, seek telling psychological tidbits to be gathered and stitched together to form a pleasing and satisfying whole, it was becoming increasingly clear Lloyd was not up to the task.

He had tried to describe Frank's shattered face, the red blood blending with the bright yellow of the Hummer to create some kind of horrifying tequila sunrise on his Persian rug, but after several false starts, he knew he couldn't do it for the simple reason that it made no sense to him; he just was not able to put the pieces together, to structure them into a coherent pattern. He tried to comfort himself with the notion that this could change with time, and as the events themselves receded, a deeper understanding might begin to form and resolve into something clearer and more comprehensible, much as a photograph comes into focus in the developing bath.

But it was a sad realization nevertheless and made all the more enervating with the approach of first light and the anticipation of the constant demands that would be made upon him from the moment he arrived at the studio. This grim awakening arrived around four-thirty A.M. and caused Lloyd to leave his bed and retrieve his slender manuscript from his office, take it back into the house, place it in the fireplace, and put a match to it. Then he sat on the damask sofa, which Stacy had had reconstructed at great expense, and gloomily watched the pages burn as the first rays of depressing dawn asserted themselves in the sullen sky.

What had happened the night Frank Bones paid a call on the Melnicks?

Lloyd was standing at the linen closet grabbing a towel when Stacy let out a screech that made the hair on his neck stand up. He knew instantly that was the moment when she beheld her ruined living room, and whether her shock was motivated by the sight of a prostrate bloody man who appeared to be negotiating the transition from breathing human being to corpse under her roof or by the great gash his vehicle had torn in her perfect house, Lloyd would never know. The wound on the crown of Frank's head was leaking blood, and the glass from the windshield of the Hummer had carved his face like a Thanksgiving turkey, leaving it a suppurating pulp. Lloyd had run upstairs to get towels to stanch the bleeding, praying Frank would at least hold on until he got to the hospital, where he could expire under the watchful eye of an ER doctor.

Stacy came to her senses as soon as Lloyd reappeared laden with thick towels in a shade of cerulean she had painstakingly matched with the Italian tiles of the master bathroom. She ordered him to the kitchen to get the dish towels instead. This he dutifully did, quickly returning to Frank and gently tamping their less luxurious but still one hundred percent cotton terry-cloth softness over the terrible wounds and looking for signs of life in Frank's motionless features.

Lloyd tried to take Frank's pulse but had no idea what he was doing and then absurdly flashed on Groucho Marx, who, finding himself in a similar situation, had so famously said, "Either this man is dead or my watch has stopped." Stacy cowered in the corner, alternately poleaxed by the thought of death's chilly presence making a surprise visitation to her wonderful world and trying to remember whether she had removed the name of Garrett Quickly, her builder, from the speed dial and how late was too late to call him.

The grip of terror Lloyd had felt at the sight of Frank's bloody body had begun to ease because the second thought he had, the one arriving immediately on the heels of *Christ! Someone's driven a truck into my living room,* was *He came here to kill me.*

Lloyd knew Frank to have violent proclivities; he'd been with him on a gun range and seen Frank handle pistols with the airy casualness of an NRA member. And there was the little matter of Frank having pulled the gun in Lloyd's office. He was familiar with the rage that underpinned much of Frank's comedy, the deep well of brooding acrimony from which he drank and the long-term ramifications of those feelings. Frank had needed Lloyd to do him a favor, Lloyd had not heeded the call, the situation had imploded; a more stable mind than Frank's could draw a line between these events allowing blame to be apportioned accordingly.

Lloyd casually patted Frank down to see if he was packing, then looked in the Hummer's glove compartment and backseat. He was somewhat surprised to find nothing to indicate murderous intent. Still, Lloyd realized Frank's means of entry certainly displayed an unacceptable level of hostility. There was always the possibility Frank was parking and simply lost control of the car, but Lloyd could not take that seriously. No one was that bad a driver. And even if Frank's driving skills were so pitiful that a disaster of these proportions was not incomprehensible, what was he doing dropping by the Melnicks' house in the middle of the night?

Stillness descended on Frank, blood and the life it carried seeping out of him, running through his hair and down his face as Lloyd watched helplessly. When the ambulance arrived, Frank appeared to have drifted off to the obituaries.

It occurred to Lloyd as he watched the paramedics, a Mexican and an Anglo who talked quietly to each other as they gently packed Frank on a stretcher and loaded him into the meat wagon, that if Frank had wanted to kill him, he would not have driven the Hummer into his spacious living room in the yawning middle of the night unless he remembered that Lloyd had told him he often sat there reading a book at that hour. Would he have remembered that detail? Unlikely, given the amount of pot he had consumed that day in Lloyd's office.

Rather than wanting to kill Lloyd, did Frank want to kill himself in Lloyd's home? Lloyd could not at first imagine that his refusal to either cowrite *My Life and High Times* with Frank or to punch up *Kirkuk* when he'd been asked would provoke this kind of baroque reaction. But it struck him as he watched the red taillights of the ambulance disappear into the misty night that Frank's moment, his shot at the main chance, had passed, and clearly he was having some difficulty assimilating that information. While hardly excusing his behavior, Lloyd understood it was nonetheless the kind of thing that might cause a person to do something extreme. Or perhaps he had intended to kill himself *and* Lloyd. That was certainly a vexing thought.

As Lloyd cogitated on this, a disturbing sound reached his ears, wavering between a low guttural moan and a high-pitched but still soft keen. He looked over to see Stacy sitting on the love seat in the foyer, her knees pulled tightly to her chest as she rocked back and forth.

Lloyd walked over, careful not to step on any of the plentiful broken glass that glistened on the floor, the anarchy of its arrangement a sharp rebuke to the classical lines of the room, and sat next to his sobbing spouse. He put his arm around her heaving shoulders and squeezed her to him. After a moment she caught her breath and her crying slowed.

"L-Lloyd . . . ," she said. "Oh, God . . . oh, God . . ."

Stacy usually pulled her thick hair into a ponytail when she slept, and in this light it accentuated the bareness of her face, which was entirely without makeup. Lloyd noticed the vein sticking out in her neck, trembling. Finally, through sheer force of will, she stopped crying and her sobs petered into nothing more than a quivering lip.

"It's going to be okay" was the best he could do under the circumstances, as he removed his arm from her shoulders and rubbed her back with the palm of his hand.

"Is he going to be alright?"

"I don't know."

"His poor wife."

"Yeah, it's tough. Although I don't think they're actually married," he adds unnecessarily, needing to fill the air. Then Stacy resumed crying. Softly at first, then a fit of jagged sobs that died away again. She looked at Lloyd, a flicker of discomfiture in her expression. "What?" he asked gently.

"Honey, I'm embarrassed."

"You can tell me."

"No."

"The place was a mess when the paramedics got here?"

"*A-A-Architectural Digest* is coming to take p-pictures tomorrow!"

"They are?"

"I w-wanted it to be a s-surprise! I feel terrible even mentioning it because of Frank but still . . ."

Having articulated that piece of information, hysteria returned with startling speed, and Lloyd was left holding his grieving wife, staring into the wreckage and wondering if AAA is the group to call when you want a vehicle removed from your living room.

★　　★　　★

243

Frank lay unconscious in the back of the ambulance while the two paramedics, Miguel and Freddie, carried on a curious debate. Los Angeles had more celebrities per square foot than any other place on earth. From gangsta Long Beach to the deep North Valley, from the parched San Gabriel Mountains to the wide beaches of Malibu, celebrities almost literally fell from trees. A trip to the gas station, the dry cleaner, a restaurant, a dojo, or a bookstore could result in a sighting of the famous and near-famous, whose visits to these establishments were often immortalized in framed autographed photos proudly mounted on the walls, announcing in cheap black and white, CHEVY CHASE GETS HIS SUITS CLEANED HERE! This proliferation of stars, all of whom, despite their fame, were treading the same high wire as the rest of us, meant that when the life's breath left them and their souls journeyed toward whatever heaven they believed in, their earthly remains stayed put, resulting in the Corpse of the Dead Celebrity. Given the rapacious hunger for visual aids on the part of the less scrupulous members of the journalistic community who were serving a market that could only euphemistically be called readers, it didn't take much to imagine the financial opportunities available when it came to photographs of famous cadavers.

For the past year or so Freddie had brought a camera to work in the event of just such a golden opportunity, and while Frank Bones may not have been the jackpot, his death mask would bring in a nice piece of change from some unscrupulous publishing outfit in Florida.

The camera was loaded with film, and as Miguel sped along the tree-lined Brentwood lanes, past darkened homes whose sleeping occupants had accumulated large fortunes feeding the fancier relatives of the same beast Freddie was looking to nourish, the enterprising shutterbug scrambled into the rear of the ambulance and tried to calculate how much light he needed to get an image. He wanted to do this back at the house, but that guy and his crazy wife wouldn't leave the room so he had to shoot on the fly, before they arrived at UCLA Medical Center at Wilshire and Fifteenth and unloaded the cargo.

"Slow down, man," Freddie ordered Miguel. "I need a smooth ride for this." Miguel obediently pressed his foot to the brake.

"Fifty-fifty, right?"

"Are you crazy? It's my camera!"

"You said fifty-fifty."

"No way. Seventy-thirty."

With this, Miguel began to swerve the ambulance, hitting the brakes hard, then speeding up.

"What are you doing?" Freddie asked reasonably as he tried to keep from lurching into the front seat.

"Negotiating." Miguel almost sideswiped a Lincoln Town Car doing a middle-of-the-night pickup. "Fifty-fifty, you greedy bastard."

"I'm greedy?"

"We're partners in this, man. Where your ethics and shit?"

Their argument was interrupted by a soft sound, and it presaged a rather larger problem for Freddie and Miguel.

"My f-fuckin' head" was all Frank managed to mumble, but it was enough to encourage the aspiring death paparazzo to lay his camera down and attend to Frank's needs, which were manifold.

Frank's disappointed escorts unloaded him in the emergency room, where he was instantly set upon by a trauma team, which began the laborious process of putting him back together. He had multiple contusions and several broken bones, including his jaw, along with lacerations of his face and head, which took more than a hundred stitches to close. His blood loss required a transfusion and he was supplied with intravenous antibiotics to keep an infection from setting in.

As Frank lay on his back, enduring the well-meant medical attention, his body felt pain in every corner. He drifted in and out of consciousness and reflected on his behavior in the intermittent moments of lucidity that arrived and departed, floating like soft dirigibles over a blasted landscape. By the time the doctors stabilized him and administered an anesthetic that was going to deposit him in the easy arms of Morpheus for the foreseeable future, he had cobbled together enough coherent bits of thought to acknowledge the incontrovertible truth he was going to have to face when he awoke: things were worse now than they were yesterday.

His first visitors upon returning to consciousness in the late afternoon are two dour members of the Los Angeles Police Department, who inform Frank he is in a lot of trouble. Lloyd, over Stacy's strenuous objections, had refused to press charges, but the combination of not stopping for a police officer when ordered to do so and crashing into someone's house was a toxic cocktail that only became more hangover-inducing when the amount of illegal things in his system was revealed. Frank is issued a summons and is told he does not have to be present to be arraigned. He says nothing to the cops the entire five minutes they are there.

His first unofficial visitor is Honey, who learned of the accident on the local Lynx morning show, which she watches each day while doing yoga. In the middle of a downward-facing dog she heard Frank's name and looked up to see a reporter standing in front of Lloyd's home, recounting last night's events. Honey ran to the phone and dialed the police, who, given she was not a relative and didn't think quickly enough to lie, suggested she call around to the various area hospitals. It took her a few minutes to locate him, and not bothering to change out of her workout clothes, she immediately drove out to Santa Monica and parked herself in the lounge area down the hall from his room, awaiting an explanation, which she intended to get the moment he returned to waking life.

Honey is curled up in a chair reading an eleven-month-old copy of *People* when Robert arrives in the late afternoon.

"I'm getting him into rehab" are the first words out of his mouth after the full-body hug and cheek kiss he gives Honey. Frank may have been recovering from a near-death experience down the hall, but an opportunity to pull Honey's surgically enhanced form to his and luxuriate in her comfortable sexuality, if only for a fleeting moment, was something the husband of Daryl Hyler was not going to miss. "I've already called

Four Winds up in Malibu, and the second he gets out of here, he's checking in, assuming he's okay."

But what if he isn't okay? That is something neither of them wants to contemplate. What if he has lost brain function, distressingly common in these situations, and is facing life as a vegetable? For a man who made a living in Frank's line of work, that would cause insurmountable problems. Then there was the vexing question of insurance. In the tradition of artists everywhere, the subject of disability coverage did not come up in the rare moments Frank entertained the hopelessly middle-class habit of estate planning, which, given the life he led, he considered a whimsical concept anyway.

Honey and Robert are thinking about all of these disturbing possibilities, but neither wants to alarm the other so they just smile wanly at one another as they settle into chairs where they wait for permission to see the patient. After a few more minutes of discussing Frank's future (assuming he had one), which, it was clear to the two of them, he was not capable of managing without a great deal of help, Robert, casually and with a little reluctance, hands Honey a script, saying, "Look at this when you get a chance. Lynx is giving it a midseason pickup and there may be something for you." Honey grasps it in her warm hands and immediately begins reading, grateful for any distraction, particularly one such as this. She has read it three times and made copious notes in the margins when the nurse appears and says they can see Frank.

It is never easy to see someone you love lying in a hospital bed, but it is particularly difficult when that someone looks as ghastly as Frank. His head and face are wrapped in thick gauze, giving him an ancient-Egyptian aura. One arm is in a cast and a bulky bandage, which straps his forearm to his chest and immobilizes his clavicle. He looks as if he has been hit by a truck, which, in a sense, he has. Honey and Robert enter silently, the way you do in the presence of the dead or the grievously injured, and shuffle respectfully to the bed, where they stand over the broken Bones.

You can never say "How are you?" in this situation since the answer is painfully obvious, so Honey and Robert quietly say, "Hi," to which Frank, having had his fractured jaw wired shut and barely able to move his lips, responds, "I look like Claude Rains."

Frank's *Invisible Man* reference comes as a great relief to his visitors since it indicates, however battered he may be, however many bones have fractured and however much blood has been lost, his sense of humor remains intact; he is still the Bones. When Honey realizes Frank is not headed for life as an asparagus stalk, she has to control the impulse to begin yelling at him, much in the manner of a mother who has anxiously been waiting for a wandering child to come home, only to feel, after the initial overwhelming relief at the kid's safe return, a desire to brain him for putting her through this trauma. The more circumspect Robert, curious to know exactly what has transpired, murmurs soothing bromides to his friend before telling him he has contacted a lawyer and arrangements are being made for Frank to formally detox in lieu of more draconian punishment. Frank appears to take this news stoically, although you couldn't really tell, since the morphine trickling into his willing veins has relaxed his facial muscles to the point where they can form only the mere suggestion of an expression.

"And Melnick's not pressing charges, Frank," Robert tells the battered comic.

"That's awfully white of him," Frank says before drifting off.

Frank spent two weeks in the hospital, during which he requested no visitors other than Honey, who would arrive promptly at ten in the morning and leave at four to beat the afternoon traffic. Since Frank was not very communicative, she would quietly read gossipy magazines and periodically hold a straw to his wired mouth so he could suck his food. Interviews, Robert had advised him, were not to be given now, so what was written and said about Frank did not have the benefit of his unique perspective. Ever the loyal manager, Robert had issued the standard statement calling it "a terrible accident" and let it be known Frank was seeking treatment. Honey briefed Frank on the press coverage, and he was amused by its usual scolding moralistic tone, only wishing it were tied to a project he could promote.

She enjoyed the role reversal since rarely did Frank's deep neediness assume such literal shape, and although one wouldn't associate the maternal instinct with Honey's résumé, the simple act of taking care of Frank in his hour of vulnerability, of doting on and nourishing him, made her feel as if she had a role to play beyond that of the striving doxy.

Frank's experience led to the traditional series of usually short-lived vows taken by people who have, by some dire circumstance, been rendered painfully aware their time on the planet may be more brief than they had initially realized and perhaps their behavior needed to be reexamined. These included, along with the court-mandated drying out, resuming psychotherapy and being more solicitous of Honey, who, in his helpless eyes, was doing the Florence Nightingale routine rather touchingly.

Ordinarily a man with Frank's extensive injuries would be sent home to recuperate, but given his special circumstances, it was determined, rather than going where he would be prey to temptation and the depravity to which it invariably led, it was best for him to head directly from the hospital to the Four Winds Clinic in Malibu and do his convalescing under their rigorous supervision. So when the doctors pronounced him ready to leave, Honey and Robert bundled him into Robert's Sunsation and deposited him on the clinic doorstep. After completing some cursory paperwork, Frank was admitted to the community of accountants, lifeguards, chefs, housewives, doctors, office workers, rich kids, actors, salesmen, bankers, and Indian chiefs within.

Frank was placed in a Spartan room with Barney Coughlin, a middle-aged Century City lawyer who had been reduced to eating out of Dumpsters after his alcoholism had caused him to mislay his wife, kids, house, and law practice. Barney had been a taciturn guy who drank to allow himself to access the inner sexy dragon that, at the ingestion of the third highball, would reliably burst forth, flames shooting from each orifice, and dive headfirst into the nearest punch bowl. At a loss without a

Scotch and soda in his hand, Barney was learning how to communicate while sober, which, for a boozehound, is like learning to speak after a massive stroke, and his counselor had told him that to begin healing he must acknowledge the destructiveness of his actions by verbalizing them. Barney took this to mean verbalizing them to whoever happened to be nearby. It was the beginning of Frank's punishment to be a captive audience for Barney's endless mea culpas about how his terrible behavior had prompted his Dumpster-diving descent.

After ten minutes in the room with the now pathologically apologetic Barney, Frank had an overwhelming desire to fire up a joint. But he had nowhere to go so he sat on his cot, stripped of his everyday wardrobe (they all wore blue jumpsuits), his professional role, his dignity, everything other than his identity as a drug addict/alcoholic (he had been informed he was both), and took the logorrheic medicine Barney administered.

Like virtually every other clinic whose mission was to treat addiction, Four Winds embraced the twelve steps much in the way the medieval church embraced the Eucharist; that is to say, questioning it was frowned upon. After Frank had been given the Big Book, the Bible of AA, and told to commit its precepts to memory, the first task he was charged with was writing an autobiography of his addiction. He was issued a Bic pen and a writing tablet and put to the grim task. Writing didn't come easily to Frank (the detective novel he had told Lloyd about those many years ago had been chimerical), so while the prospect of telling his story appealed to his narcissism, the actual writing of it was a colossal struggle made more difficult by the fact that he would rather walk barefoot on broken glass than be at Four Winds in the first place. Frank's normal tendency in this situation would have been to have Robert find him a ghostwriter, but alas, that is not how rehab works.

Left to his own desperate devices, stripped to his bare, humbling essence as a man of nearly fifty whose life has veered completely out of control, Frank sits at the cheap pressed-wood desk in his room (mercifully, Barney is at one of the endless meetings) and tries to think where to begin. Enough of Frank's brain cells are functioning coherently to let him know if his performance in rehab is less than tip-top, the court will not look kindly when it comes time to recommend punishment, so he grudgingly forces himself to put pen to paper and eventually manages to fill enough pages to convince the people who are running the program that he has the requisite sunny attitude.

It is the standard litany of substance abuse that has now become so worn-out you can watch it on the Recovery Channel, and its clichéd aspect does not escape Frank, who has always fancied himself a pedigreed descendant of renowned artistic toasters like Thomas De Quincey, Arthur Rimbaud, and Lester Young, all of whom believed copious intake of intoxicants lit their creative fires and led them to heights unimaginable had they twelve-stepped their way to dull sobriety. But as Frank reflects on this, it dawns on him that addiction, once the exclusive purview of the explorer, the outlaw, the artist/deviant who lived a heightened, poetic existence on the twilit edges of polite society, had now become about as freaky-deaky as Cheez Whiz. It reminds him of the time he had first seen a cop with long hair. If cops had long hair, it was no longer the signifier it had been. It had lost its meaning so what was the point? Ergo drugs and alcohol; at least on an intellectual level. The physical level, the lewd tango they reliably performed with the pleasure center of the brain, was something else altogether, something more difficult to dismiss.

But as Frank sits in his chair and stares at the wall, a perception he had held from his teenaged years, when he had discovered sex and jazz and Zap Comix, begins slowly to change. And it leaves him depressed. Because if he is not a hipster, a flipster, a chemically enhanced finger-popping daddy who lives a blessed outsider's existence passing merry judgment on the burghers of America, then what, exactly, is he?

Willpower is not something people usually associate with Frank Bones since his life is hardly a paragon of self-restraint, but spending over twenty years, as he has done, in the trenches of a brutal, thankless business without once wavering in his determination to succeed, while perhaps not on the order of Mao Tse-tung driving the Kuomintang off the mainland, certainly required a great deal of focus and perseverance, and he draws on these qualities as he sits through interminable meetings where all the attendees have been indoctrinated in the same gospel that has transformed Barney Coughlin into a Twelve Stepford Wife and listens to the alternately pathetic, lugubrious, only fitfully amusing stories that collectively form a road map of how everyone had wound up in Loserville-by-the-Sea spilling their guts out to a group of pasty-faced, coffee-swilling strangers.

"Hello, my name is Frank and I need a fuckin' drink." Still working the room. "But seriously, I'm a joker and a soaker and a midnight toker . . ." Here he sees the group leader, Donny Sober Fifteen Years, a burly man in his fifties with thinning hair pulled into a ponytail and wall-to-wall tattoos, shoot him a look to curdle milk. In his newly oversensitive state Frank instantly changes course, saying, "Alright, alright, I'm an alcoholic and a drug addict and . . ." Blahbity, codependent, blahbity abusive childhood, blah blah blah. It would not be exaggerating to say after a few days of struggle (starting with the seven A.M. wake-ups, the middle of the night for a user) Frank got into the swing of the rehab thing, and ninety days later he is pronounced ready for another try at life in the so-called real world.

Honey picks him up and they ride down the Pacific Coast Highway with the California sun glinting off the early-autumn ocean. She smiles when she sees a dolphin leaping in the blue distance. Looking straight ahead, Frank raises his right hand like the Boy Scout he'd been in Texas nearly forty years earlier and swears to try harder.

When he returns to the stage the following night, three and a half months after his nocturnal visit to the Melnick home, he looks at the audience, primed for some kind of reference to his recent misadventures, and says:

This is the first time in more than three months I'm talking to a group of people who can handle their liquor.

It is good to be back onstage because the stage is his clean, well-lighted place, an area of roughly eighty square feet in which he is the undisputed potentate and from which he can rule unchallenged with all the dramatic bravado of Vlad the Impaler, the Romanian monarch/psychopath who meted out justice by literally skewering people. To leave the charmed space, this enchanted area of laughter and applause, is to experience disappointment, contradiction, and complication, in short, the inherent vicissitudes of daily life that mortals must endure. But to remain in its spotlighted confines is to cling to the idea that some kind of control is achievable.

The first few nights he's back at the Comedy Shop, Frank breezes through his allotted twenty minutes, the pace of his set picking up steam as he feels himself hurtling toward the moment he will have to descend from the stage and into the debauched miasma of the bar area, where he is invariably made the center of attention by its comedian habitués, most of whom are not on a wagon of any sort, much less one that doesn't serve booze or pot. They jokingly tempt him by waving drinks or joints in front of his face as they say things like "You don't have a drug problem as long as you can afford drugs."

Frank appreciates these transgressive efforts with the eye of someone for whom transgression is a way of life, but he is resolute in his desire to at least try to stay clean. He doesn't want to repeat the experience he has just had because, however much it may have added to his legend, what he will never admit to anyone is how embarrassing it was.

Sparky has gone back to Kansas after having heard his activities had come to the attention of local law enforcement, and his absence is well-timed given Frank's attempt at reformation. But when Candi Wyatt approaches him on his second night back, pushing her breasts into his arm as she leans in for a kiss in a dark corner of the club, he is faced with another level of enticement. She suggests repairing to the Hummer later for some reunion sex, not having heard it had been returned to the dealer, and Frank is faced with a question as important as whether to continue as a substance abuser: Is it still open season on pussy? Honey, after all, had more than come through when he was in the hospital recovering from the grievous bodily harm he had done himself. She had been there every day, never judging, and provided him with a loving kindness in short supply in other areas of his life. He believes he should at least attempt to reward this behavior with a stab at fidelity, if for no other reason than to see if he is capable of doing it. So it is with an exceedingly heavy heart and an effort bordering on heroic that he looks down at Candi's eager, unlined face, sees the contours of her nipples pressing against her tight Comedy Shop T-shirt, and says, "I'd love to, babe, but when I was in rehab, I took a vow of chastity." And then his head bursts like a honeydew melon hit by a shell from a .357, sending shards of skull and brain bits in all directions as horrified onlookers dive for cover.

No, not really. It just feels that way.

When Candi asks if they can at least go for a drive later he imparts the deeply unfortunate news that his license has been revoked.

At this point Frank is not suited for a life without access to either a well-stocked bar or stash. Users usually have no hobbies, since being a user, more or less, *is* their hobby. Anticipating scoring, scoring, using, coming down, and then repeating the cycle take up a lot of time, and other than his interest in guns, which he felt he should steer clear of at this point for self-evident reasons, he didn't have a lot of outside interests with which he could easily distract himself. It isn't as if he is going to learn Chinese or study art history or take up photography. That perhaps he should, that it might actually not be a terrible idea to develop an interest in an area where he could apply his considerable intellect, hasn't yet occurred to him. So on a typical day, he would rise around noon, go somewhere walking distance for breakfast where he would linger over coffee and the papers for two hours, then trudge home and watch television or casually read about UFOs or politics or nuclear proliferation until it was time to go to the club, where for twenty minutes he wouldn't feel like a corpse.

As anyone with substance issues will tell you, being around friends who are still using is not conducive to staying clean, so, other than at the

Comedy Shop where he would be with his comic compatriots in a public setting that served as a cap on their more depraved tendencies, the only person Frank saw with any regularity was Honey. Although she was simpatico, her skills as a psychologist were limited, which left them without much to discuss that was any help to Frank, who was not primed for their maundering exchanges.

The script Robert had given Honey at the hospital hadn't turned into a job, but he called regularly and was confident he could get her cast in another pilot since everyone to whom he had shown *Kirkuk* had responded favorably to her work. This kept her as bubbly as could be expected given Frank's deteriorating mental condition, which bore an inverse relationship to his improving physical one. When Robert got her a guest shot on a new sitcom that required her to be out of the house for three days, for Honey it was as if Lincoln had freed the slaves.

Frank is seeing a court-mandated therapist in Westwood, an Israeli woman called Naomi Glass. She is a former Mossad officer in her late fifties whose stylish jet-black hair and formfitting suits make her look twenty years younger, and the result-oriented approach she practices is precisely what you would expect from someone whose curriculum vitae included targeted assassinations.

She is not a priestess in the Church of Psychology who holds that her parishioners must occupy their pews for life. On the contrary, she wants to give them the good news and send them on their way. Naomi Glass believes that if you are having a crap day but have the wherewithal to physically smile for a time, to stretch your mouth into a gaping grin, no matter how ridiculous you feel doing so, some kind of interoffice memo will be sent from the muscles in your face to the receptors in your brain reminding them that when the face acts in this way, the happy synapses should fire, and fooled by the face's muscular duplicity, the brain will respond, causing your inner mood to mirror your cheerful expression.

When Frank first heard this, he actually laughed out loud at what he took to be the utter silliness of it. To which Naomi Glass responded in her Israeli accent, "See? It's already having an effect." Frank demurred and told her, no, he simply found it absurd, but she got him to promise to try the technique, which he dutifully did on the cab ride home, stuck in traffic on Santa Monica Boulevard. He was amazed to find that, for a few minutes, it actually seemed to work. But then his face started to hurt. He stopped smiling and quickly tumbled once again into the Slough of Despond. By the time he got back to his house, crawling into bed seemed the most logical response to the universe.

Frank is making an honest effort to stay clean, and as a result his life has become increasingly circumscribed. Performing was not a panacea after the initial pleasure of being back on familiar ground wore off, so his visits to the Comedy Shop are less frequent. His CD came out but it was hard to get Frank booked on TV to promote it; in the months since the crash the all-seeing media eye has moved elsewhere, and currently the interest isn't there. Robert managed to get the record company to buy a billboard, but it was on a lightly traveled road in the San Fernando Valley and did no good at all.

Predictably, no one bought the CD. Frank refused to go out on the road because he didn't want to be away from home, but he didn't particularly want to be home either, which left him in an uncomfortably existential position where all choices were wrong.

Honey couldn't take his behavior. She was gone for longer and longer during the day, and when she returned, he wouldn't ask where she'd been. Bills were piling up, but still Frank wouldn't work. He'd sleep, watch TV, and if he could bestir himself, float in the small backyard pool after the peak melanoma hours because however much he may have wanted to die, skin cancer was not the way he wanted to go.

Frank lies in his underwear on a cheap blow-up raft in the pool (which has become increasingly brackish since he decided to stop paying the pool man) staring at the dwindling sun one afternoon in late October. Flying saucers are migrating across his line of vision from one side of the pool to the other, small silver disks that look as if they've beamed in whole from a 1950s sci-fi movie, little creatures with big heads at the wheel. Only Honey's agitated voice lets him know he is in the presence of the familiar.

"There goes the *Atlantic Rhythm and Blues Collection,* Frank, the one with Aretha singing 'Respect.' R-E-S-P-E-C-T, that's what you don't give to me!" Honey yells in juvenile doggerel, mangling the lyric. Frank realizes the flying saucers are his shrinking CD collection, which thanks to their sleek aerodynamics are beginning to collect on the surface of the pool. "There goes Bernard Herrmann's sound track for *Taxi Driver.* Oooo, there goes the John Coltrane you were always playing. Hello, Frank! You haven't moved in nearly six weeks!" That cheerless fact does not change as the number of CDs on his shelves continues to decrease. Honey, energy spent, drops to her knees, beseeching, "Frank, baby, please . . . I've been praying for you so hard, but I don't think it's working." Frank continues to bob in silence. What's left of the afternoon sun glints wildly off the floating silver CDs, sending shafts of jagged light in all directions. Honey watches him for a few moments, then turns, walks off the patio, and out of the house.

A pale sun floods the late-autumn sky, but the Bones household is lit for permanent twilight. Frank is in the middle of the living room at an imaginary mic stand looking out over an imaginary crowd. He has been up nearly twenty-four hours, his blue funk having worked its way toward vexation.

I'm driving to work today, he begins, immediately deciding to change course and going to *Gangs have taken over our cities,* then veering back to *and this cop pulls me over . . . Arab guerrillas are shelling each other . . . so the cop says to me . . . Christian values in the White House . . . do you know how fast you were going . . . then the president fucked a kosher chicken . . . and I said, "I certainly do, Officer" . . . he was courting the Jewish farm vote . . . immigrants are pouring over our borders . . . but here's the kicker . . . heavily armed white people are planning a revolution in the Pacific Northwest . . . after he gave me a ticket . . . ladies and gentlemen, the chicken wrote a book! And that chicken is our guest today.*

Then he collapses on the couch and begins weeping, remaining there for an hour before crawling back to bed.

In the middle of the following day, Frank is still indisposed. "How are you going to make a living if you don't get out of bed?" Honey reasonably asks. Frank, as has become his habit, does not respond. Then, Honey produces a Zippo lighter from the pocket of her jeans and with a flick of her finger a tiny flame springs to life. This she places to the bedsheet on which Frank reclines. The sheet, after initially only managing to smolder, finally catches fire and a small flame begins to eat away at the weave. When the fire approaches Frank's leg, he silently rises, fills a bucket with water, and douses the bed as Honey looks on. Then he goes to the couch and lies down there. He says nothing to her about lighting the sheet on fire. Angered beyond articulation, Honey smashes a plate against a wall and leaves the house. She doesn't come home that night.

The next afternoon Frank lies on the couch in the living room, gazing at the slit of sunlight visible under the drawn shades. The phone rings insistently. Frank doesn't move. After the fourth ring the answering machine picks up and Robert's voice can be heard, the voice of mission control in the space capsule. "Frank, it's Robert, your manager, remember? Believe it or not there are people who want to hire you. Go figure. Call me." Frank may as well be dead.

Midafternoon the following day and Frank is floating on the raft in the middle of the pool.
"Frank?" He looks up and sees Honey standing at the side of the pool, a suitcase next to her. "I'm moving out." No argument from Frank, who wants her to go. In his deteriorated psychological condition he cannot bring himself to ask her to leave, but his actions are intended to produce that result. It was one thing to fail. He can almost begin to process that. But to fail and then have to watch as Honey begins to

succeed is entirely too much to bear because it is a rule carved in Hollywood stone that when two performers are romantically involved and the one in the subservient position begins to surpass the dominant one, the entire house of cards collapses. Honey has to go and both of them know it.

"By the way, Frank," she says after loading her effects into her newly leased Mercedes. "I know you were banging that waitress."

And then he is alone.

During the following week Frank eats nothing but Campbell's chunky beef soup directly from the can. He leaves the television tuned to the Shopping Channel twenty-four hours a day to ensure a secondary human presence in the house while making sure he won't see or hear anyone whose career is in a better place than his.

One morning, as Frank sits on the couch in the filthy living room watching a thirty-year-old former child star selling cubic zirconium jewelry, the doorbell rings. He makes no move to answer it. In a moment, it rings again, more insistently this time. Then the door, which Frank doesn't bother to lock when he's at home, opens, and a male figure is silhouetted in the doorframe, haloed by the morning light.

"Why aren't you answering my calls, you asshole? I'm the only one in this business who cares about you."

"Bobby?"

Closing the door behind him, Robert Hyler, nattily attired in a two-thousand-dollar worsted-wool suit, steps gingerly into the house and picks his way across the room holding a rolled-up magazine in his hand. He looks at Frank and shakes his head in disgust.

"You fuckin' pig. Pull yourself together." Robert glances at the TV, sees the child star pitching the cubic zirconium. "You know why that chick wound up on the Shopping Channel flogging fake jewelry to fat housewives? Bad management. Unlike you, my friend. You have a manager who cares." Robert sits next to Frank on the couch, gazes around the room. "You kill your cleaning lady?"

259

"Honey left."

"I know. She told me."

"She told you?"

"We're managing her now."

"You're managing Honey?"

"She's a piece of talent, Frank."

"Why don't you just take a cocktail fork and stick it through my heart?"

"You gotta grow up, kid."

"Then you can carve it up, put it on crackers, and serve it for hors d'oeuvres at your Christmas party." This image is enough to make Robert pause for a moment, which allows Frank to ask, "What are you doing here?"

"I'm enough of a putz to care about you. Arrest me and put me in manager jail. Herman Melville and Vincent van Gogh? They died in obscurity and now everyone thinks they're the greatest, you know? But it doesn't work that way for comics. You die now? In six months, no one outside the business is gonna remember you. Don't give up, man." Frank looks at Robert, sees the sincerity in his eyes. And what about those references? Van Gogh and Melville? Robert's not just a loyal manager; he's a renaissance guy. "I booked you some dates in the Southwest. Texas, Oklahoma, Arizona. You can do a little work, pay some bills, get back to L.A. and we'll make a plan."

Frank doesn't respond to Robert for a moment, so moved is he by this grace note, this simple act of faith. Robert may be a shark capable of devouring entire schools of smaller fish, but however successful he has become in a business that offers no reward for basic human decency, he has retained a touch of kindness that will occasionally reveal itself, and Frank is dumbstruck for a moment at having seen it.

"You want some Campbell's chunky beef?"

"No, thanks. The first date is next weekend in Tulsa."

"I can't go to Tulsa alone."

"I'll find someone to go with you."

"I may not make you another nickel. You know that, right?"

"Some things you don't do for money."

Robert stays for a few more minutes during which he tries to restore Frank's belief in anything other than an endless unadorned present. He senses he can go when Frank assures him he will be on a plane to Oklahoma the following week. As Robert's leaving, he says, "Oh, I almost forgot," and he hands Frank the magazine he's been holding. "It's the new *Rolling Stone*. Turn to page ninety-four." Frank obliges and smiles when he sees a review of his CD. "Look at the part I underlined."

Frank Bones's new CD is a blast of comic semtex. When is America going to get wise to the fact that one of our best comedians is still working in small clubs because no television network has the balls to give him his own show? Catch him live before he explodes, but if you can't, this CD is the next best thing.

"How about that?" Robert says, smiling sardonically as he steps out the door. "You're not the only one who thinks you're a genius. Some jerk-off critic agrees with you."

Before leaving town, the sole place Frank goes is the office of Naomi Glass. It is his seventh session with her since being discharged from Four Winds.

"Honey lit the bed on fire?"

"She thinks I need to get out more. Why would anyone want to leave the house? I used to watch CNN before I switched to the Shopping Channel exclusively. I know what goes on out there. Too many crazy people."

"You've told me you thought you were crazy."

"I was crazy when crazy meant something. Now the whole world's insane. There's no money in it anymore."

"But if that's the case, perhaps you're less alienated than you realize."

Frank considers this a moment, then suddenly leaps to his feet, shouting, "I'm cured!"

Naomi Glass regards him placidly. "Do you really feel that?"

Frank sits back down dejectedly. "I was having a Prozac moment." Prozac is a delicate subject between the two of them. He had resisted any kind of psychopharmaceutical intervention, believing antidepressants nothing more than crack for the melancholy and they did not fit in with his new drug-free lifestyle, Frank only able to deal in extremes. But once the long blue tentacles of depression had entwined themselves around his body and squeezed for nearly two months, he finally gave in. He'd been taking Prozac for a couple of weeks now and, to his amazement, was starting to sense something beginning to stir within his frozen breast. Feeling progressively better since Robert's visit, he believed he'd soon be able to think more clearly about his future.

"Are you sure now is the best time to go on tour?" Naomi Glass is not entirely certain Frank has achieved the level of psychological stability necessary to sustain two weeks on the road.

"I have to spread laughter and cheer."

"Frank . . ."

"There are a few things I need to say before I shuffle off this mortal coil."

"Do you feel your death is imminent?"

"My work here is done. How can I be a legend if I don't die young?"

As a means of coping with the difficult reality of not having achieved his professional goals, Frank has recently begun to focus on the van Goghs and the Melvilles, the non-show-business artistic giants recently referenced by Robert, men who died in penury, unappreciated in their own lives yet lionized by subsequent generations, legendary in death; at this point, an option that is once again sounding pretty good. He jokes about his own death, predicting future fans of comedy will be perceptive enough to assure his rightful place in the starry heavens. As long as he seems to be joking, the comedy impulse is alive and Naomi Glass believes him to be getting better.

He leaves the office in Westwood and tells her he will see her when he returns.

Chapter 13

It's an early-November afternoon and Frank sits on a Southwest Airlines jet to Phoenix next to Milo Baylis, his temporary babysitter. Milo is a twentysomething employee of Nada whose jurisdiction is normally the mailroom. This week Robert has assigned him the task of helping Frank stay clean and sober during his time on the road. In Phoenix they will change planes and get on a flight to Tulsa, where Frank has been booked to play two nights in a place called Club Louie.

Since they met at LAX, Milo has been sneezing uncontrollably every few minutes. Frank turns from looking at the pad of clouds beneath them, saying, "Milo, babe, do me a favor, don't breathe on me." He waves the copy of *Billboard* he's been reading in the air to move the airborne stream of Milo's germs in another direction.

"Sorry," the kid says adenoidally. Frank likes Milo; he is eager and appropriately deferential. Now placing the magazine on his lap, Frank opens it to the charts, his face darkening.

"Look at this. The CD's been out for a month and it's at ninety-eight."

"Someone's buying it."

"Percy Sledge reissues are outselling me. The record company's not going to let me live off good reviews." Milo leans toward Frank to look at the pages Frank is examining, gulping air through his mouth. Frank glances at the poor sick kid, asking, "Milo, could you breathe in another direction, please? I don't want to get plague or whatever the fuck it is you have, and I say that with genuine concern for your health."

The plan called for the two of them to arrive in Tulsa the day before the first show, get a night's sleep, relax, and then go to the gig, the whole thing designed to be as low pressure as possible.

"I don't trust a city you can't fly to direct," Frank says, looking at the *Los Angeles Times* Calendar section where a small item catches his eye.

"Happy Endings" May Be Yanked

Highly touted "Fleishman Show" scribe Lloyd Melnick's much ballyhooed series about a Las Vegas massage parlor may be facing cancellation after a mere two outings. Ratings have been anemic despite heavy promotion by the Lynx Network. The show received a 2.8 share in its second airing, which represents a drop-off of more than three ratings points from its lead-in, the similarly ratings-challenged "Men Are Tools." "We believe in Lloyd Melnick," said Lynx prexy Harvey Gornish. "And we still believe in the show. Every opportunity will be given for it to succeed."

Frank puts the paper down and smiles. He recognizes the kiss of death when he sees it and inside he leaps with joy.

"We arranged for me to be paid in cash, right?" he asks Milo. In what is perhaps an unacknowledged reflection of his own inner turmoil, Frank has become convinced during the past few months that the American republic is becoming somewhat less stable than it has been at any time during the past 230 years. As a result, he has developed a suspicion of checks and checking accounts, preferring to deal in cash for the foreseeable future, knowing it to be a more dependable means of payment should some kind of international disaster lead to a meltdown of the banking system.

"It's been taken care of," Milo assures him.

A large, gaudy neon sign consisting of a palm tree and tropical-hued lettering spelling out TRADE WINDS MOTEL lights up the Tulsa night, warm for November. The Polynesian-themed, two-story motel is completely congruent with a multicultural highway landscape that is also home to a Pollo Loco, a Buca di Beppo, and an International House of Pancakes. Frank stands next to his suitcase in the parking lot, wishing he were back in Los Angeles. He found the Trade Winds by calling the owner of Club Louie since he no longer has the stomach for Hyatts or Radissons, and this was what he recommended. Frank's taste in accommodations is puzzling to Milo, for whom a bed is a bed, but Frank patiently explains he is trying to do what little he can to keep the entire United States of America from being subsumed by one giant corporation. Milo, looking worse than he did on the plane, appears from the motel office and hands Frank a key, saying, "I'm going to find a doctor. I think this is a sinus infection."

Ten minutes later Frank lies on his bed in Room 21 on the second floor of the Trade Winds with the television tuned to the Shopping Channel. An actress from a seventies cop show is selling her own line of intimate wear specially designed for plus-size women. Through the cheaply constructed drywall Frank can hear the primal thump of sex in the next room. He debates whether to bang on the wall to get them to rein in their fervor or, in an if-you-can't-beat-'em gesture, simply buy one of the pornographic movies available to all Trade Winds guests, providing himself with a visual accompaniment to the jungle sound track pulsing through the wall. Instead, he does neither, preferring to lie penitently on his bed suffering the torments of a saint. "Who are these people?" he wonders, despising them.

Overcome with a road sadness familiar to anyone who reluctantly spends time away from his day-to-day life, Frank rises from the bed and walks to the window where he looks into the moonlit Oklahoma night. Cars speed by on the highway, their headlights slicing the darkness. The lights of the fast-food restaurants, filling stations, and motels combine with the gaseous streetlamps to create a glowing canopy over the asphalt world that makes it difficult to see whatever stars are out tonight. Fifteen hundred miles to the west is Los Angles. New York is the same distance to the northeast. In between is a vast country of mountains, prairies, towns, and cities that doesn't care about Frank Bones tonight. He thinks about why he's in Tulsa and whether he even wants to perform anymore, but he already knows the answer. Even if it goes well and he can continue making a living as a comic, it's no longer a life he can comfortably live; the indistinguishable clubs with their drinks and bad food; the shifting mosaic of faces belonging to people who represent a world from which he feels himself further and further removed. But what else is there? The endless road may be over for him but right now there's nowhere to pull off, no oasis at which to rest and get his bearings. He considers the lessons of rehab; just get through the day, the night. Then go to sleep, wake up, and do it again.

The noise in the next room has subsided. It isn't midnight yet but Frank, who has been staring out the window for the last hour, has to be up early to do a radio interview to promote the show. He goes back to bed and falls into an anxious asleep.

Wilson "Wildman" Simms, a shaggy-haired young man wearing thick prescription sunglasses and a satin baseball jacket with TULSA TRIPLE A TIGERS spelled out in cursive lettering on the back, hunches over a microphone in the studios of WHTZ, a local rock 'n' roll radio station. He is on probation with the station's owners for falsely reporting someone had attached a dachshund to a helium balloon and floated it over the city, then giving updates on the dog's fate every ten minutes, until finally reporting a hunter had brought the balloon down with a blast from a high-powered rifle, leaving the nonexistent dog an imaginary blot on Highway 44. Some listeners were upset, which led to Simms being disciplined by an ownership that was secretly quite pleased with the attention he had brought to the station, however grotesquely. Frank is seated next to him at the console enduring Wilson Simms's attempts to live up to his tired nickname.

"When was the last time you were out on the road, Frank? You were opening for Glenn Miller, right?"

Ignoring the age-related dig from the younger schlock jock, Frank says, "I am the road, Mildman, if I can call you by your real name. I've got tar in my veins."

"That's not all you got in there from what we hear!" Wildman ripostes. Frank does not bother to respond. "Okay, you've just released a CD—I listened to it on the way to work this morning, and I just want my listeners to know Frank Bones is a very funny older guy. The critics love you apparently."

"What do they know?" Frank asks, falsely modest.

"So you had some pretty well-publicized problems. Any truth to the rumor you're doing an ad for Hummer?"

"That's funny," Frank observes. "In Tulsa."

"So what's in the future? More crack?"

"I want to achieve mythic stature. Like Bigfoot."

"Don't you have to be dead for the mythic business to kick in?"

"Yeah. And you have to go out spectacularly. I want to die in a flaming car wreck while I'm having unprotected sex with J.Lo. That's how legends are made. That is what you call a career move."

Their forced banter continues in this vein for another ten minutes, and then it is time for Wildman to begin shilling for the sponsors, at which point he thanks Frank and starts to read ad copy for a fertilizer store. Frank leaves, relieved at having done his promotional duty, and wondering how, exactly, is he going to kill a day in Tulsa?

That afternoon, Mercy Madrid stands behind the bar in Club Louie rinsing glasses. She's somewhere short of thirty, and experience has already begun to chisel away at her lovely features, on which a summer tan has faded. Ripped jeans over black cowboy boots and a clingy, ribbed V-neck T-shirt that shows off full breasts. Large green eyes and a mouth you want to bite into a peeled grapefruit, just to watch the juice run down her chin. Perfection, however, is avoided by her nose, which has a little bump just below the bridge (broken at some point?). Her shoulder-length hair is a honey-brown mop; she has to shake it out of her eyes when she looks up to see Tino Suarez walking in. As soon as she realizes who it is, she goes back to rinsing the glasses.

Tino is a feral-looking man hovering somewhere in his forties. Dressed pimp casual today, silk shirt open one button too far, gold bracelet, several rings on his fingers, and a gold chain around his neck. He's the kind of guy who moves when he sees opportunity, nothing more than money motivating him. He opened Club Louie during the comedy boom of the eighties and has ridden it to its conclusion, Tino having no love for comedy or comedians. If magicians had been the happening thing, he would have been in the magic business, every entertainment trend just a way to sell drinks. As the comedy boom waned, Tino's fortunes waned with it. Not many acts could fill his room anymore, and no new genre of live entertainment had appeared to supersede comedians, so he was left nursing a faltering business as it reeled into the sunset. Recently, other ways of making money had begun to present themselves.

He sits at the twenty-foot-long bar, placing a package in front of him. "Put this thing under the floorboard."

"Sure," she says, accustomed to enigmatic orders.

"I don't want my wife to see it."

Mercy takes the package. Knowing Tino is waiting for her to bend over so he can stare at her ass, she squats on her haunches to remove the floorboard, taking great satisfaction in disappointing him. She lifts it, places the package in the space, then replaces the board.

"Give me a Jack and Coke, baby," he says in a way she doesn't like. Turning around, no way to keep him from staring now, she pulls a bottle of Jack Daniel's off the shelf and begins to mix her boss a drink. Finishing, she hands it to him, still holding the bottle. Tino tastes it. He tells her, "You mix a weak drink, Mercy. That's good for the customers, but bad for me." Mercy makes to top up the drink but Tino stops her, placing his hand on hers, which causes her to recoil slightly. He says, "That's alright. I'll get it." And he does, pouring another jigger's worth of whiskey into the glass. Mercy returns to her work, hoping Tino will take his drink to his office as he sometimes does. Instead, he stands up and walks to the waitress station at the end of the bar, lifts it, and walks toward her saying, "Mercy, how you doing?"

"Just fine."

"Haven't seen you in a while." He's fifteen feet away.

"You see me five nights a week."

"That's not what I mean. Do I have to spell it out?" Starting to move.

"Spell what out, Tino?"

"I got a cabin up on Cherokee Lake . . ." Slowly. Sliding.

"You told me that, like, fifty times."

"We could go up there." Smiling. Slick.

"I don't think so."

"Mercy, Mercy . . . I got a thing for you." Ten feet.

"You got a thing for what's in my panties, man. Don't get confused."

"That's not true." Five feet away.

"Get offa my cloud, Tino."

"Come on, sugar, we married a couple of lowlifes. Vida's cheating on me."

"Call a lawyer." He's close enough now to reach out and touch her. As his hand comes up to stroke her face, she pulls a switchblade out of her pocket, flicks it open, and holds it up. "I hear Otis Cain's a good one but I don't know if he does divorces." Otis Cain is a guy much in the local news lately because of a high-profile lawsuit he's filed against the police. The ceiling light glints off the blade, which has momentarily arrested Tino's forward motion. Mercy looks at him with eyes that say, *I will drive this knife into you and the judge is gonna let me walk.*

"What's this, *Blackboard Jungle?*" Frank asks, backlit in the doorway, the guy knowing how to make an entrance.

Tino tells him, "We're just fooling around," as he backs away from Mercy. "What are you doing here? Show doesn't start for a few hours."

Frank walks into the half-light of the bar, saying, "I don't have a life. My road manager, who's supposed to be driving me around, is such a wussy he's in bed with a sinus infection, I drove the rental car over here myself without a driver's license, ladies and gentlemen . . . don't tell anyone . . . I'm in a town I've always flown over and I've got no one to bitch to. That's what I'm doing here. I didn't catch your name."

"Tino Suarez. You want a drink or something?"

"You're the owner?"

Tino nods as Frank looks around the room. God, this place is depressing with its neon beer signs and retro jukebox and fuggy air, as if it were all expectorated by a computer program designed to produce the standard-issue American bar for the new century, the bar with no regional signifiers, the place you could just walk in and feel as if you were in the Minneapolis airport; or the one in Pittsburgh; or Orlando. He wonders how it has come to this, how he, His Royal Bonesness, has descended from the lofty perch of a personal HBO special, as if he were nothing more than a playing piece in some diabolical game of Chutes and Ladders, and landed in this sticky-floored, beer-reeking circle of hell. It's all he can do to keep from collapsing into a grand mal, but instead he says, "No thanks," to the proffered libation.

"Mercy, give him a drink," Tino orders, walking toward his office in the back, to Frank's relief. As soon as his eyes adjust to the light, he notices how attractive Mercy is, and Tino's retreat opens the playing field. Willing his incipient depression into retreat, he sits at the bar and immediately looks for a wedding band.

On happy inspection, he sees only two silver rings with turquoise stones and says, "Frank Bones."

"I know who you are, Mr. Bad. Tino probably thought you were gonna shoot him."

Frank smiles at this acknowledgment of his status (thank you, cable television). "Jeez, what a reputation. Could I get a beer?"

He has recently decided the culture of recovery is not for him and so developed a drinking strategy that eschews hard liquor and calls for a two-beer limit. So far it is working.

"I read in the *Star* you were in detox."

"To help me cut down."

"Funny." Not laughing, but it's an effort.

"So, Mercy . . . Are you free later?"

"I don't date comedians. They're as sleazy as rock stars but not as good-lookin'."

Frank is beginning to sense the frisson of repartee for which he is a sucker. As much as he enjoyed Honey's physical gifts, he was always a little disappointed that she couldn't do the verbal razzmatazz. And now here he is in some Tulsa dive jazzing with a girl bartender on whom he wants to trace figure eights with his tongue. Things are looking up.

"Thank you," he says, appreciating her attitude. "A guy can't be friendly anymore."

"All the desperadoes try and flirt with the lady bartender."

"But I love you."

"Nothing comes with the drink but the pretzels, babe."

"Did you just call me babe?" This is taking it to a new level. Mercy's subtle yet pervasive aura of sexuality conflating with the verbal confidence she displays is combining to make Frank temporarily stop hating his life.

"Isn't that what you call everyone? I've seen you on the talk shows. Not recently, but I've seen you."

"So nothing comes with the pretzels?"

"That's right."

"And they say romance is dead." As if hearing her cue, Vida Suarez strides through the front door, her hard features burning a hole in the shadows. Somewhere in her thirties, but she's trying to turn back the odometer. Vida wears a tight white blouse buttoned down the front, and a miniskirt reveals cut legs working high-heeled pumps that click off the floor of the bar like castanets.

"Where's Tino?" she demands.

Mercy tells her, "In back," with no inflection. Vida marches through the bar and toward her husband.

"Who's the Lizard Queen?" Frank wonders.

"Vida, Tino's loving wife. If you're still lookin' for a date, I bet she's gonna be free later." Frank can't keep from laughing at Mercy's deadpan delivery.

"Let me see that knife," he says.

Mercy smiles at him, her kind of guy. She takes the weapon out of her pocket, flips it open, and lays it on the bar. The steel blade is seven inches long and the handle is onyx, inlaid with pearl. Frank picks it up and runs his finger along the blade, nearly drawing blood. He whistles in appreciation.

"Where'd you get this?"

"The Internet. Get anything you want these days."

"Pretty fancy for a deadly weapon."

"I thought I deserved a treat when I turned thirty . . . but I didn't want to wait." Frank takes his knife out and places it on the bar. Mercy picks it up, looks at it, Frank waiting for her reaction. She flicks it open, feels the blade. "This thing's junk." He starts to laugh, loose, relaxed. "That's funny?"

"You and me already have more in common than I did with both my ex-wives."

Vida Stice met Tino when she worked for the beer distributorship he bought from. They struck up a phone relationship, and when he asked her out, she was only too happy to see what the man who owned a popular local nightclub looked like. When they began dating, Vida was in her early thirties and had recently left her first husband, a cop who beat her, but never around the face. Tino had a big condo in a nice part of Tulsa and a second home on a lake. He told her he was doing better than he really was and she bought his line, accepting his marriage proposal after knowing him six months and wanting to quit working anyway. That he didn't seem violent was an added incentive, given her marital history. They'd been married almost five years now and Tino's deteriorating financial situation had recently become apparent when he had to trade in her Corvette and lease her a RAV4.

Outside the bar, Tino and Vida face each other in front of a Dumpster. The muscles in their faces are taut. It's no picture for the family album. "I can't give you a thousand bucks," he tells her.

"You better if you want any more customized amateur home video," she says, referring to the previous evening's escapade when she'd finally consented to his repeated requests to videotape the two of them having sex.

"Go home."

"Let me see your wallet."

"I said go home, if you didn't hear me."

"Let me see your damn wallet."

"Would you get out of here, please?" he says, rediscovering his good manners.

"Afraid to show me what's in there? What is it, a condom so you can pump your little bartender?" The contempt with which she regards him is mirrored in his own face. Physical violence would be the next step but she just did her makeup in the car and he's wearing a new shirt, so the situation resolves when Vida walks away, leaving Tino with murderous thoughts.

A young blonde with country-singer big hair stands at the door of Club Louie with a rubber stamp of a duck, inking patrons' hands as they go in, saying, "Quack, quack," as she does it. This is Bobbie Jo Horton, and her tight stonewashed jeans, belly shirt, and navel ring all say she wants to have fun. Right now. The bar area is filling up behind her with guys drinking longnecks and girls sipping cosmopolitans, thinking they're still trendy. It's a Friday night and Club Louie is buzzing with the anticipatory energy people who work regular jobs bring when they're ready to get their groove on at the end of the week.

Frank sits in a small dressing room just off the stage checking himself out in the mirror. A wall-mounted speaker in the tiny space receives a feed from the house PA. On the counter in front of him is a table with several tapes next to it, one of which he is going to use to record his act tonight. Rising from his chair, he feints and jabs at his reflection, two lefts, a right, then shakes his shoulders loose. Mercy appears at the door with a beer on a tray.

"Tino thought you might want this." Placing the beer down on the counter. "Such a thoughtful guy." She turns to leave, choosing not to see Frank's smile.

"Wait a minute."

Mercy stops in her tracks and without turning says, "You think I was too rough on you before?"

"When someone looks beneath my suave veneer and sees I'm horny and desperate . . . well, I don't have to tell you . . . my heart goes pitty-pat. I just want to share the warmth."

"Save the love for a sucker, dollface." She leaves, and Frank wants her even more than he did before.

Half an hour later, Tino stands on the small stage of Club Louie squinting into the lights of the three-quarters-full house and trying to hide his disappointment at Frank not selling out. "How's everybody doing tonight?" he asks, feigning enthusiasm. He gets the kind of tepid response that indicates the audience could be at a ball game, a bowling alley, or a racetrack, any place that serves alcohol. Tino forges ahead, "We got a great show for you. Before I bring up our headliner I want to remind you we're doing dwarf tossing on Tuesday nights now, so be sure to come around for that." Tino waits a moment for this intelligence to sink in, then proceeds. "Alright. This is a big thrill for us tonight."

In the dressing room, Frank hits the RECORD button on his tape player, checking his hair as Tino's voice pours out of the wall-mounted speaker. "You've seen him on TV. You've read about him in the papers. Give it up for the bad boy of comedy, Mr. Frank Bones!"

Frank bounds out to the stage, passing Tino on the way, shaking his hand without looking at him. Tino continues backstage, where he sees a man wearing gold-tipped cowboy boots standing in the hallway. Tino tells him, "Let's talk in here," indicating the dressing room.

In the background Frank's saying, "Hello, Tulsa."

In Frank's dressing room there's tension between Tino and the man with the gold-tipped boots. Tino says, "I need to see the money before you get the tape."

The guy reassures him in a flinty tone, "You'll get it later tonight."

While Frank is trying to amuse the Tulsans who have come to be entertained, and Tino and the man with the gold-tipped boots engage in their nefarious two-step, a Harley-Davidson 1250 comes roaring up to the front of the club. The rider is Creed Baru, a muscular man in his thirties wearing a T-shirt, jeans, and cowboy boots. He's good-looking but his features have a fierce quality. Creed sees the ferret-faced kid who has taken Bobbie Jo's place at the door. The kid says, "Twenty dollars, please."

"Just here to see my wife," Creed says, breezing past him. Mercy looks up from the bar where she is mixing four Southern Comfort and Sprites for a table of sorority sisters. She does not appear happy to see him.

Taking no notice of this, Creed sits at the bar and stares at her for a full minute before she says, "What are you doing here, Creed?"

"I'm movin' back in."

"I'll tell you right now, I won't be cohabitating with a man who shovels bullshit for a living."

Just then the kid from the door arrives, having gathered enough courage to do his job. "I said twenty dollars, please."

Creed just laughs in the kid's face in a way that says, *I'm gonna blink now and if you're here when my eyes open, I will kill you.* Mercy tells the kid, "I'll take care of it," letting the eager beaver save face and walk away, flexing his skinny shoulders as he does, ready to kick some ass.

"Bourbon," Creed says to his wife. Mercy pours the drink. As Creed looks toward the main room, she spits in his glass. Frank's voice is hard to hear above the babble of the bar area, but Mercy manages to make out something Frank's saying about why don't all black people hate Elvis since he's a fat cracker who stole rock 'n' roll from the brothers.

She wishes she could hear the rest as she places the drink in front of her future ex-husband. Turning his attention back to the bar, Creed sips the bourbon while Mercy does her best to ignore him. "The deal came through," he tells her, as if he had just swung a leveraged buyout on Wall Street.

"What deal?" Puncturing his little balloon.

276

"The one with that old boy in Okmulgee? For the Ford truck? The one I bought for five hundred bucks less than I'm about to sell it for?" He waits for her reaction, and when there is none, he continues, "And I don't appreciate the lack of encouragement I'm hearin' in your tone of voice. I'm workin' the angles, girl. I'm talkin' to people, lookin' to expand my horizons." Mercy regards him skeptically, Creed's speech a rerun. "Meantime, I got you a gold necklace." He pulls a thin gold chain out of his pocket and lays it on the bar with a flourish befitting a far more impressive piece of jewelry.

"You're makin deals like I'm layin' eggs. Where'd you steal it from?"

While Creed ponders how to answer this affront to his abilities as a provider, Bobbie Jo approaches the bar with an empty tray saying, "Two tequila shots, a banana daiquiri, a crème de menthe, and four longnecks."

"I'm out of crème de menthe," Mercy tells her. "Let me check the back."

When Mercy leaves, Creed gets off his barstool and sidles up to the waitress. He says, "Hey, Bobbie Jo. How you doin'?" She answers by rubbing her slender leg against his thigh.

"How come I ain't seen you lately, Creed?"

"I'm a busy man."

While Creed and Bobbie Jo are engaged in the early stages of their adulterous assignation, Mercy finds herself in the back of the main room, listening to Frank, who is saying:

I love being back on the road because it's a great opportunity to meet new women. Comedians do great with women. We're as sleazy as rock stars but not as good-looking, which means we get an even lower level of groupie.

Mercy is surprised and a little flattered to hear her words repeated by a professional performer and doesn't mind the implied knock, knowing he's embellishing for comic effect.

And there is nothing more attractive than a horny road comic. I had a romantic interlude with a lady bartender today. And when I told her I wanted to be her Yoko Ono, she said, "Nothing comes with the drinks but the pretzels." Then we exchanged bodily fluids.

277

Mercy's outraged for a split second but then laughs with the rest of the crowd when Frank informs them:

She spat in my beer.

A few hours later, just short of midnight, and the place is mostly emptied out. What passes for country music now but is really just mediocre rock with a cowboy hat plays on the stereo behind the bar. Vida, who saw the second half of Frank's show, sits at the end of the bar sipping a drink while Mercy talks to Frank, seated at the opposite end nursing a beer.

"You gotta pay me if you're gonna use my material," she tells him.

"You can have my child."

"How about a house?"

"I've got a house but it's in Mexico."

Creed has been talking to Bobbie Jo in the back of the room but now he's walking toward Frank and Mercy. He's heard the tail end of their conversation. "You know the problem with Mexico?" Creed asks, preparing to weigh in with his anthropological observations. "Too many Mexicans."

Frank does not respond. Turning away from Creed, he smiles at Mercy. "Can I get a beer?"

Creed places his hand on Frank's shoulder a little too heavily. "Frank, lemme ask you somethin'. I'm thinkin' 'bout headin' out to Hollywood, maybe try to catch on as a stuntman. You got any contacts in the movie business?"

"Creed, why don't you drift?" Mercy says with no love.

"Shut up, alright? I'm askin' you nicely." Then, turning to Frank and trying to ramp the menace in his eyes: "Stay away from my wife, dude. I know what you're thinking."

"Take it easy, babe. We're having a conversation."

Creed looks at Mercy and says, "Let's go home."

"I'm not goin' anywhere with you."

He reaches over the bar, grabs her arm. "Don't show me up, Mercy."

"Let go of her." Frank all chivalrous.

"Frank, stay out of this," Mercy tells him.

"You're comin' with me," Creed says, tightening his grip.

"When dogs talk," she says, and he slaps her hard in the face. The slap came so fast Creed surprised himself, but his shock was nothing compared to what Mercy was feeling, which is shock, too; and also deep embarrassment at being humiliated in front of Frank.

But before she can say or do anything, Frank draws on the vast storehouse of hostility he's accumulated in a lifetime of disappointment, rejection, frustration, and regret and punches Creed so hard in the jaw he loosens two of the man's teeth and sends him sprawling. Recovering with the nimbleness of the ex-athlete, Creed quickly rises, rubbing his face, and starts to circle Frank.

"You're gonna be sorry for that, you little peckerwood."

"Alright, that's enough," Mercy says, her hand to her own face. "Creed, go home. I just finished cleanin' the place up." Then, turning to Vida: "You wanna help me out here?"

Smiling, Vida says, "This is Tino's place. I don't care what happens." She settles in to watch the show.

Frank reaches into his pocket and produces his gravity knife, which he flicks open, once again startling Okie-bred Creed, who did not anticipate this urban pansy would be armed with a shiv.

"Go on outside and practice bleeding. I'll be there in a minute."

"I don't think so," Creed says. Knowing his way around a bar fight, he quickly grabs a bottle off the bar and smashes it, brandishing the jagged business end at Frank, who responds by picking up a barstool and swinging it at Creed, knocking the bottle from his hand. Creed steps out of Frank's range and picks up a table, which he tosses at the middle-aged comic. He then leaps over the bar, shoving Mercy out of his way, taking two liquor bottles and smashing both of them, only to be rocked by the table, which Frank has picked up and heaved back at him. Frank then picks up another table and pitches it at Creed, who ducks this time, the table sailing over him and crashing into the mirror behind the bar, shattering it and hundreds of dollars' worth of liquor bottles with it.

279

Covered in broken glass and spilled liquor, Creed leaps back over the bar, and Frank's waiting, thinking, *If I have to die, this isn't the worst way*.

Frank's got his knife, Creed's got two broken bottles, and they circle each other feinting and lunging but no one able to cut, until Tino barks, "Enough!" and the two of them look over and see a revolver pointing at them.

The gun has a dampening effect on the enthusiasm of the combatants, Creed saying, "How ya doin', Tino? I gotta go," and scuttling out of the club, no one saying good-bye or even looking at him.

Tino stares at Frank, an engine straining to not overheat. "I knew I shouldn't have booked you, you fuckin' lowlife. You come in here, you wreck the place . . ." Then he shakes his head in disgust at the level to which humans are capable of sinking, the thought of the insurance policy he held on the club having lapsed eating at his gut. "Now get outta my place."

"What?" Frank, incredulous, the victim here.

"This was Creed's fault," Mercy says, trying to be helpful.

"I want your opinion, I'll ask." Then, to Frank: "Get out."

"I haven't been paid."

"You destroyed the bar. You think I'm payin' you? Get outta here before I call the cops."

Frank doesn't move. Tino cocks the hammer on his gun, which, in the silence of the bar, is an impressive sound.

"Hey, I'm not unreasonable," Frank says as he turns to go.

Stepping into the parking lot, Frank looks around to make sure Creed has taken his act on the road. Satisfied further violence is not imminent, he crosses the highway to the 7-Eleven, where he finds a pay phone and calls a cab. When Frank is told it will take fifteen minutes for a car to get there, he decides to pick up a six-pack of beer. He pays the pimply kid behind the counter, who squints at Frank—he recognizes him but doesn't know from where—and drinks three Budweisers before remembering he's got the rental car.

Frank enters his room at the Trade Winds just after one A.M. and sees a red message light flashing on the phone. He picks up the receiver, presses the code on the keypad, and waits. In a moment he hears Milo's sick voice saying, "Frank, sorry I had to bail but I need to see my own doctor, so I took a plane back to L.A. tonight. I told Robert and he said he's going to try and find someone else to send out. I hope the show went okay. Sorry again, man." Frank places the phone back on the cradle and sits on the bed. Looks at the illuminated numbers on the bedside digital clock and knows he will have to wait until the morning to call Robert and tell him he's ready to eighty-six the comeback tour. Frank stays up for another hour drinking beer. The television is on but he isn't really watching. He's thinking about his father again and what was the tipping point for him, the moment he knew he couldn't do it any longer, that he lacked the will to face another morning, another day of life on this happy planet. When did he know it was pointless to continue? Then he blacks out.

Just before eleven o'clock the following morning there is a loud knock on the door of Frank's room. Fast asleep, Frank doesn't stir at the sound. There is another knock but still Frank doesn't move. After a moment, the door opens and the hulking figure of a man dressed in chinos and a shapeless light blue sports jacket appears. As the large man pushes the door in, the room floods with light and Frank's eyes open a crack and register his size; the guy is at least six-eight. Frank sees the figure of a female motel employee skittering out of sight behind this leviathan.

"Frank Bones?" the man says with the local twang in a resonant bass.

"Yeah?" He's groggy but his tone says this better be good.

"I'm Detective Faron Pike, Tulsa PD. I work robbery and homicide." At the word *homicide* Frank's ears fine-tune. *What's this?* Suddenly he's a lot more awake. "How'd the show go last night?" The big man making small talk.

"Fine." Frank struggles to sit up, the lying-down conversation too redolent of therapy.

"It's a nice club. Shania Twain's sister sang there last month," Pike says, throwing him off, Frank thinking, *If there was trouble, this wouldn't be the lead. Maybe the guy's a fan.*

"Can this wait?"

"Not really."

"Let me get dressed, okay?"

"Please," Pike says, turning around and noticing three empty beer bottles.

Frank quickly pulls on a pair of black pants and a T-shirt. Fastening his belt, he says, "So what do you want to talk about?"

"The murder of Tino Suarez." Faron looks at Frank, trying to read his reaction and sees only what appears to be genuine shock. *This guy's a good actor,* he's thinking.

"Someone killed him?"

"Last night. We heard you two had a beef."

"From who?"

"His grieving widow."

"Tino's dead?"

"I'm afraid so, Frank."

Frank thinks about this a moment, wondering at the appropriate response. He didn't like Tino and Frank isn't one of those guys who's sentimental about death, doing an about-face on some guy just because he turned toes up, particularly a guy who was pointing a gun at him at the end of their last encounter. Still, he's never had his sleep interrupted by a murder investigation. It's a disorienting feeling.

"How'd he die?" Frank asks, genuinely curious and stalling. *Jesus, does this anthropoid think I did it?*

"Two bullets. What was going on with you two?" Faron says, trying to come off friendly, maybe catch Frank off-guard. Frank needs coffee right now; his mind is too woolly, trying to focus.

"He owes me some money." Frank turns his own words over in his mind. It's more of a problem now, this owed money, than it was twelve hours ago.

"How bad did you want to collect the debt?"

Frank instantly knows where this is going. "Not bad enough to kill him."

"We'd like you to come down to the station and talk about what happened."

The interrogation room is bare except for a table and four chairs, two of which are occupied by Frank and Faron, who is still working the friendly act. He has driven Frank down here, not wanting to give him the opportunity of changing his mind, and talked sports the whole ride, thinking it was the shared language of all heterosexual men. Frank was unresponsive and now Faron is wondering if, along with being a habitual criminal, Frank is gay, too. Turning on the video camera that sits unobtrusively at the side of the room, Faron settles his bulk into his chair and says, "Why don't you tell us about last night?"

"I'll talk when I have a lawyer," Frank says, having seen enough cop movies to know to keep his mouth shut. Faron eyes Frank in a way that barely masks his suspicions. He thinks he has his man and Frank knows it. "I want to make a phone call. Can I do that?"

Just after two o'clock that afternoon Frank stands in the hallway outside the interrogation room, his cell phone pressed to his ear. A Chicano cop working at a desk nearby is watching him. Frank sees this and says to the guy, "I could be on the way to the gas chamber and my manager would put me on hold." The cop stays with the poker face.

Robert gets on the phone. "Hey, I'm heading into a meeting. What's going on?"

"There may be a little trouble here in Tulsa."

"The show tanked?"

"I might be a suspect in a murder case."

"Murder?" Frank can feel Robert's anxiety spike over the phone lines. "What do you mean murder?"

"Murder, Bobby. As in someone got killed."

"And you might be a suspect? Why are you a suspect? Who got killed?"

"The club owner."

"Tell me this is a joke!"

"He stiffed me and wound up dead. The cops brought me down to the station to talk to me. I haven't been charged yet but . . ."

"Fucking hell."

"Bobby, get me out of here."

"Sit tight. I'll get you a lawyer."

Two hours later, a brand-new Lincoln Navigator pulls into the parking lot in front of the police station and an imposing black man in his early forties wearing a cream-colored Western-cut suit and a black cowboy hat gets out. He carries a tan leather briefcase and holds a rolled-up newspaper as he strides purposefully toward the building. Nods to the sergeant at the front desk in the manner of a fighter before the bell, and the officer acknowledges him in kind. He marches through the double doors leading to the heart of the operation, sees Frank seated on a chair outside an office, and quickens his pace. A young white cop with a crew cut is walking in the opposite direction and the two men bump shoulders. The black man in the cream-colored Western-cut suit stops in his tracks, saying, "Whoa. Did you do that on purpose? Like we're in high school and you're gonna play fuck-with-the-nigger? Because we ain't in high school now and we're gonna play sue-the-damn-cop till they throw his white ass off the force and he loses his retirement benefits. What's your name?" Whoever the black man is, he knows how to mau-mau Mr. Charlie.

"Clanton," the stunned cop replies in the face of this four-hundred-years-of-pain hurricane.

Then the black man tips his cowboy hat, smiles, and says, "I'm just playing with you," sending the cop reeling on his way, wondering what hit him. The black man turns his attention to Frank, who has witnessed this exchange, and shows him the newspaper. "This is the *Tulsa World*. How do you like the way it looks?"

"It's a fish wrapper."

"Well, you're gonna be on the front page of this one tomorrow and that is some damn fine publicity!"

"Who are you?"

"Otis Cain, J.D. I'm gonna be your lawyer."

Frank looks Otis over, not sure how to take this Afro-Western apparition, but impressed with Robert that this is the guy he called. He was expecting someone more traditional. "Nice lid."

"This?" Otis says, caressing his hat brim. "My great-great-granddaddy was a buffalo soldier, rode out to Oklahoma after the Civil War and worked as a cowboy. I like to keep the legacy alive." Faron appears as Otis is informing Frank of his distinguished heritage and barely conceals a groan.

"This your counsel?" the detective says to Frank.

"Sure," Frank says, partial to black people, the white-guilt thing going strong.

Faron indicates the two of them should follow him back into the interrogation room. Watching Faron disappear into the room, Frank turns to Otis, awaiting instructions. Otis says, "Come on, let's go deal with these rednecks." Impressed with the bellicose funk Otis exudes, Frank follows him and takes a seat next to his new counsel across the table from Faron, who is not pleased at having to deal with Otis Cain. Otis, meanwhile, has opened his briefcase and removed a kitchen timer, which he places on the table. He sets the timer, looks at the big detective, and says, "You got one hour."

"Mr. Cain—"

"My client's a busy man, Detective. If you're not gonna charge him, he's got places to go."

Faron's exasperated with Otis but knows he has to deal with him. Making an effort to stay cool, he says, "Frank, why don't you start by telling us what happened between you and Mr. Suarez?"

Frank glances at Otis, who nods, indicating this question is acceptable. "I do my set. I get offstage and hang around the bar. Some mutt tries to perpetrate domestic violence in the bar area."

"Who?"

"Breed or Reed. Something like that. So I defend his wife. Tino pulls a gun and throws the guy out. I ask to get paid and he tells me he's not gonna pay me so I leave. Peacefully. Imagine my chagrin when I learned someone smoked him since now I have to collect from a dead guy."

Clay Porter, another detective, sticks his crew-cut head in the door. "Faron, can I see you?" he asks, not looking at anyone else in the room but especially not looking at Otis.

"Ticktock," Otis says to Faron, pointing at his watch. Faron leaves them alone and Otis takes a candy tin from one of his pockets, holds it open for Frank to peruse its contents. "Care for a mint? Myself, I like to feel fresh when I tangle with the po-lice."

Frank, letting his nervousness show for the first time as he takes a piece of candy, asks Otis, "Aren't you worried about pissing these guys off?"

"You want a lawyer who's going to win the good sport award or one who's going to keep you out of the joint?" Frank nods, getting Otis's point. He looks at the lawyer rolling the mint around in his mouth, cool as a meat locker. "I saw your act last night, man. I was there. That was some funny shit about Elvis and black people."

Faron steps back into the room. "Did a little search on you, Frank. I see you're from Los Angeles." It's not an observation that demands a response and he sits back down. "Let me tell you something, boy. This sort of thing might go down in L.A. but you're in Tulsa now."

"Detective Pike's seen too many bad movies," Otis tells Frank, eliciting a grin. Then, turning to Faron: "Drop the hard-ass act, Pike. This ain't Wayman French you're talking to."

"Who?" Frank asks.

Otis tells him, "These boys had a talk with old Wayman, next thing you know the minister's saying, 'What a shame, what a shame,' the choir's singing 'Swing Low, Sweet Chariot.'" Frank immediately gets the drift. Clay Porter has come in on the tail end of the conversation, leaving the door open behind him. He's holding a computer printout.

"Ol' Wayman had a heart attack, Otis. You know that," Clay says.

"Was in the papers." Then, turning his attention to Frank, Clay observes, "You were busted in Cleveland five years ago for discharging a firearm in a theater," which comes out *thee-ater.*

"I believe that case has been adjudicated," Otis informs him as Frank nods in assent, impressed that Otis has done his homework.

"Like to play with guns?" Clay asks, taking a seat next to Faron.

"You don't have to answer that," Otis tells Frank. Then, to the cops: "Would you two confine yourselves to serious questions, please?"

Frank is wondering if the cops know who he is, where he stands professionally. He can't help thinking that if this unfortunate business had occurred around the time his HBO special was on, they would be more deferential. He decides to try a little tactical reconnaissance.

"You guys get cable?"

"Too expensive," Faron says.

"How about you, babe?" Frank asks Clay, who is not accustomed to being addressed as "babe" by a man.

"Yeah, I get it," Clay says, not looking up from the computer printout he's reading.

"What do you watch?"

"Porn, mostly. So, Frank . . ." Now Clay is running his index finger down the printout. "Reckless endangerment and carrying an unlicensed weapon. What about that high-speed chase in Los Angeles where two officers got hurt? What was that about?"

"I was late for an appointment."

"Says here there was a crash."

"It's my business they can't drive?"

Trying to regain control of the situation, Otis says, "Could we stick to the events of last night, please?"

Frank is relieved when Faron and Clay exchange a look and abruptly get up to leave, saying they'll be back in a minute. When they're out of the room, Otis reassures Frank, "They ain't got shit, their mamas ain't got shit, and their daddies ain't got shit." As Otis is saying this, someone walking past the open door draws Frank's glance. It's Mercy, who meets

287

his eyes but keeps moving, her expression giving no indication of what she's thinking. Frank wonders if she knows who killed Tino and whether she had anything to do with it. As he is cogitating on this, the detectives reenter. Faron is carrying a shoe box, which he places on the table as he and Clay sit back down. Clay holds another computer printout.

"You ready to sign a confession?" Faron asks with a confidence that surprises Frank, not sure if the detective is joking.

"Sure," he says. "I was the one who pushed Humpty Dumpty."

Faron opens the box and removes a gun. "Recognize this?"

"No."

"It was found in the glove compartment of a car."

Clay, reading from the printout, says, "The vehicle was rented by Milo Baylis. He's an associate of yours?"

"My road manager," Frank replies, dreading where this is going.

"Seems ol' Milo was on Southwest Airlines Flight 29 outta here last night. That flight left at eight P.M. and the coroner says Suarez was killed after midnight, so we don't think Milo Baylis did it, is what we're sayin' here, Frank. Detective Pike and me, we're thinkin' you were driving that car illegally, which is not good either . . . but that's the least of your troubles right now. Anyway, what it is we're thinkin' is this: you shot Tino and stashed the gun in the glove compartment."

Frank feels as if he's been punched, but Otis doesn't skip a beat. "Did you have a search warrant for that vehicle?" he asks. Faron and Clay remain silent. "You boys think you can get away with anything. This time I'm gonna put your asses on trial."

"We'll see you in court, Mr. Cain," Clay says, trying not to smile. "Put out your hands, Frank."

"Why?"

"Because you're under arrest for the murder of Tino Suarez."

Truly, when Frank was suffering through his court-mandated ninety days at Four Winds, he didn't think he could sink any lower. How could life become more unbearable than being locked up with a bunch of substance abusers who had taken it to such an art form they now required round-the-clock supervision as adults? Yet that kind of thinking, the kind that allows someone to believe things can't get worse, is, in this indifferent universe, always a trap. Because no matter how awful things are, how out of control it all seems, make no mistake, bullet wounds can become gangrenous, tumors declared inoperable; any given situation can indeed get worse; and right now no amount of smile therapy courtesy of Naomi Glass is going to make the feeling Frank has of utter existential helplessness go away. Frank's forehead gently descends to his upturned palm.

It starts as a flicker, but it quickly builds in intensity until the light bursts, fragments, and becomes a series of fission-generated sparks, growing, building in intensity until they coalesce into a pounding strobelike hammer against the inside of Frank's skull, waking the slumbering beast which then lurches from the cool darkness of its resting place at the base of the neck and, thrusting its thick limbs against the side of Frank's head, fights its way through the constricting cells and crashes into the ocular nerve, creating such a vicious internal compression that Frank nearly collapses onto the table. It is with a superhuman effort that he remains erect and able to hear the simple piece of information that Detective Pike imparts.

"Officer Melendez is going to book you."

Frank's thinking, *Where'd that gun come from? Could Milo have left it there? What was Milo doing with a gun? Was the gun even Milo's? Maybe it was mine. Did I bring it and not remember? Did I use a gun last night? All I remember was drinking and passing out and then that family-size SOB showed up at my door . . .*

Moments later Frank, wearing handcuffs, is standing in the hallway of the police station with Otis, who is telling him, "We got this beat." Inside of Frank's head, meanwhile, things have quieted down as the initial shock of the circumstance has been absorbed. The beast, such as it is, has lain back down where it warily awaits further provocation. A slightly overweight white guy, wearing a fine charcoal suit with a red, white, and blue tie and wing tips, comes scurrying up with his hand extended.

"Mr. Bones!" Patriotic Wing Tips says. "Roscoe Barnwell." Seeing Frank is handcuffed, he lowers his own paw, saying, "What's going on?"

"What does it look like is going on?" Otis says in a tone he reserves for annoying white men.

Ignoring Otis, Roscoe asks Frank, "Did you talk to the police?"

"Who are you?" Frank inquires, the man's name not ringing any bells, thinking, *Maybe he's a reporter.*

The Latino uniform who had been watching Frank from the desk earlier, Melendez presumably, approaches and takes Frank by the elbow. "Let's get you booked," he says, using the word in a context Frank had hoped to never hear again.

"Hold, hold, hold," Otis says, jumping in.

"I'm your attorney," Roscoe tells Frank. "Your manager called me. Robert Hyler."

Frank, slightly puzzled at this, turns from Roscoe to Otis and asks his aspiring representative, "He did?"

"Excuse us," Otis says quickly, yanking his client aside and whispering, "Who do you want defending you? Some wing-tip-wearing motherfucker in a red, white, and blue tie who's gonna blush when he sees your act or a black man who feels what you got to say in his gut?"

"Are you really an attorney?"

"What kind of condescending question is that?" Otis barks in a whisper, his face inches from Frank, who smells his minty breath.

"Excuse me," Frank says to Otis, turning to Roscoe and telling him, "I already have an attorney." Then, to Otis: "If I get the chair, you're fired."

Chapter 14

Lloyd is in shock. Numb, jaw-dropping, thunderstruck shock. It's the next morning in Los Angeles, around ten o'clock, and he sits in his office staring at his computer screen, his mind pinwheeling with the velocity of a turboprop. *Happy Endings* is not shooting today, and there are a few minutes to kill between meeting with the costume designer about the padded bra Dede Green has requested in order to compete with the bustier and hence more popular Jacy Pingree (request gladly granted) and a weekly nonerotic massage he has scheduled to keep himself from imploding with stress. He is using this stolen moment for an Internet surf, and as he logs on to the news site he visits daily to remind himself that a world exists outside the little comedy bunker in which he's marooned, he is gobsmacked with the news Frank could be facing the gas chamber, the headline as simple and devastating as an old western death ballad: COMEDIAN FRANK BONES TO BE CHARGED WITH MURDER.

Lloyd reads the accompanying article, which contains a sketchy version of Frank's sordid story, and is filled with a mixture of wonderment and revulsion. Lloyd has been of the opinion Frank couldn't outdo himself, and here, not even four months later, he has already surpassed his standard for excess. While Lloyd is dealing with interfering network executives, egotistical actors, and no-talent directors, all of whom are laboring mightily to turn out forgettable pabulum designed to do nothing more ambitious than sell a wide array of consumer goods and services to a benumbed public, what is Frank doing? Frank is creating a desperate American flameout of truly epic proportions, a

Roman candle of a life shooting hot colors, bright and lurid, into the infinite night sky; a life that would be dissected for years to come by those fascinated with the feverish, dark corners occupied by doomed men and women whose troubles are too large and talents too vast for one being to contain; tinseled names writ large in blazing letters and etched into the vast pop unconscious forever. You know them all, our dream repositories: lovers and killers and junkies and boozers, rockers and actors and writers and poets, all of whom run faster and leap higher and live harder, until finally they burst like supernovas, exploding in billions of fiery traces that light the dark like tiny suns shining down on our upturned faces, bathing in their distant glow. *That* is what Frank is doing.

None of this is lost on Lloyd, who has yet to take a moment to consider whether Frank is guilty. That can be sorted out later. When Ulrike, his cheerful German masseuse who pulps him like an orange once a week, arrives and sets up her table, Lloyd submits to her physical abuse distractedly, his mind exploring the opportunity afforded to him by Frank's predicament. In doing so, he experiences a moment of unavoidable truth. If he is unable to conjure a book out of the current situation, where a celebrity he knows personally is accused of committing a capital crime, he should give up whatever self-aggrandizing authorial fantasy he's been indulging in and accept his gilded, if troubled, life as a television hack.

As Ulrike thumps his taut muscles, Lloyd begins to formulate a plan. He will fly to Tulsa and present himself to Frank, apologize for not helping him out when asked, and offer his services in getting Frank's side of the story out to the American public and potential jury pool before the trial. He has read the papers and knows *Happy Endings* is hanging by a slender thread. Some serious free time lies ahead, and this is going to be the perfect way to fill it.

Ten minutes after Ulrike finishes plucking the taut tendons in his neck like a cellist working her way through a particularly intricate Stravinsky passage to leave Lloyd a heap of quivering flesh lying on the office sofa, Tai Chi's voice is heard over the intercom saying, "Lloyd, Harvey

Gornish's office called while you were having a massage. He wants you to come to a meeting."

"When?" Lloyd manages to croak.

"Now."

Lloyd is walking across the lot to Harvey's office feeling like a newly liberated prisoner. He has to strain to keep from smiling lest someone see him and ask what miracle has occurred to deliver him from the perpetual tension, anxiety, and trauma common in all those who had been granted the privilege of running television shows. Truly, the happy chappie struggling not to mambo his way across the lot bears no resemblance to the stressed-out Lloyd of the past several months.

Lloyd arrives in the waiting room of Harvey Gornish's office and is waved right in by the young male assistant, a recent M.B.A. who is formulating a five-year plan to take his boss's job.

Harvey's Southwestern-style office is the size of a jai alai court. At one end is a huge desk that appears to have been crafted out of polished driftwood. The two distinct seating areas opposite the desk are furnished with soft, brown cowhide chairs and coffee tables that look as if they were lifted from the Ponderosa, if the Ponderosa had furniture built with Burmese teak. Harvey is talking to Pam Penner, who sits in the chair across from his desk. Both of them smile at Lloyd as he enters.

"Lloyd," Harvey says tanly, rising from behind his desk and coming to shake Lloyd's hand, a few stray skin flakes dropping from his forehead. "How are ya?"

"Tip-top," Lloyd responds, "considering the horrible ratings we're getting."

"Lloyd!" Pam says, laughing.

"Pam!" Lloyd responds.

She's amazing, he's thinking. *This woman could laugh at a war-crimes trial.* But he's happy to see her there since her presence indicates bad news is imminent, Harvey completely capable of delivering good news on his own.

Harvey gestures that Lloyd should sit down, and all three of them flop into chairs in the remote seating area of Harvey's airy office.

"That is exactly what I want to talk to you about," Harvey tells him. Lloyd waits, knowing that saying anything will simply prolong the process and keep him here longer than necessary. "How do you feel the show's been going?"

"Obviously, it's a disaster," Lloyd says, figuring he'll make Harvey's job less complicated. "I mean, creatively it's been great but everybody hates us."

"I disagree," Harvey declares with all the moral authority he believes his job as network programmer has granted him.

"Harvey, America flushed and we're circling the bowl."

"Hey, Melnick, let me tell you something," Harvey growls, anger flashing. "I control the handle. Nothing goes down the bowl at Lynx until I flush it." He's trying not to sound peeved at Lloyd for having the audacity to suggest the audience is more important than the executives.

"He's the flusher!" Pam assures Lloyd, gesturing toward Harvey and smiling.

Lloyd says, "Well, I'm glad to hear that," still expecting to be canceled any second.

"We need to make some changes," Harvey says. Lloyd nods, thinking, *Finally. Here it comes.* "Lynx has a lot invested in your show, and, well, the fact is, it's not really working."

"But there's a lot of good stuff there," Pam interjects.

"Believe me," Lloyd says, "you don't have to sugarcoat it. I'm a big boy."

"So regarding these changes and the way your show figures in . . ." Lloyd strains to keep from hugging Harvey in anticipation. "We want you to fire Dede Green."

Excuse me?

"What's that going to do?" asks Lloyd, his stomach sinking at the prospect of having to continue when he had so recently been planning the rest of his life. Apparently Harvey is going to implement the death-by-a-thousand-cuts management theory whereby Lloyd would be bled from successive body parts until, finally, when the pain could be stretched out no longer, Harvey would apply the coup de grâce of cancellation.

"It's going to let us recast the part," Pam informs him.

"With who?"

"Honey Call," Harvey says, nearly licking his lips at the prospect.

"Honey Call?" This news stuns Lloyd. "Frank Bones's girlfriend?"

"Ex-girlfriend, but, yeah, that's the one. She tested very well in that *facockta* Eskimo thing we did. And let me say this, Lloyd. Not many funny women come with a body that can cause a traffic accident. Pam, you wanna back me up here?"

"Harvey's right," Pam quickly assents, knowing who butters her toast.

"You see the news this morning?" Harvey asks Lloyd. Lloyd informs him that he has, and all three agree Frank is a crazy, unpredictable guy. But Harvey wants to keep the conversation on track, whether Frank Bones did or didn't kill someone not being of much concern to him when Frank is no longer under contract to Lynx and there are ratings points to chase. "Anyway, we all love Honey and we're looking for something to stick her in. What do you think?"

"What do I think?" were the only words Lloyd's suddenly throbbing brain could formulate. "What do I think?" he repeats, still trying to articulate a cogent response and stalling for time. "I think . . . " He's planning now. "I think . . . " Here it comes: "I think I'm outta here if you do that."

In the thirty seconds that have elapsed between Harvey's question and Lloyd's response, Lloyd has devised the following plan: he will play the prima donna card; that is to say, he will couch his keen desire to quit in the self-righteous language of artistic differences, thereby freeing himself from his obligation to do the show while simultaneously asserting his creative independence.

"Then you're gonna be in breach," Harvey says levelly, no emotion other than a slight don't-fuck-with-me pursing of the lips.

"Meaning?"

"Meaning we can abrogate your entire contract, my friend."

Lloyd hadn't considered that. He thought he'd be able to skulk away with a little dignity, the victim of a common ratings shortfall, and still cash those big Lynx checks every two weeks. Harvey was threatening him with, if not penury, than at least the need to actually have to go out and make a living again, something he'd never have to do if he made it to the end of his current contract. This complicated his calculations.

Harvey sighs and runs his hand through his thick hair, looking at Lloyd as if to say, *Melnick, don't be a schmuck.* Then he says, "Melnick, don't be a schmuck."

"Think about it, Lloyd," Pam offers.

"We can take care of Dede Green for you," Harvey tells him.

Lloyd's mind is thrumming as he walks back to his office. Not since his wedding has he been faced with a decision that will affect his life so profoundly. He could stay with the show. It would hardly be out of character; the path of least resistance had always been where Lloyd found himself treading. He could accept the casting of Honey and watch the reconfigured show limp along until the inevitable cancellation mercifully came, thereby ensuring his prosperity and social position.

Abandoning *Happy Endings,* however, is going to have serious ramifications. Besides the financial hit, he will immediately be tagged "difficult," a bad label to have unless your talent is so vast, your gift so great, people will abase themselves to gain from it. Further, jumping ship from your own show does not send an encouraging message to potential employers, a group whose numbers were getting smaller every day as the television business continued to consolidate at a hectic pace. It's one thing to be thought of as an inducer of massive neck pain when there is a shelf full of awards you can point to and say, "I may be an egotistical, self-aggrandizing lunatic, but I deliver the goods." An illuminating illustration of this rule is Marlon Brando, who once appeared on the set of a western he was making clad in a gingham dress. He was in a dress that day for no reason any rational person could discern, yet whatever the mania that manifested itself in transvestism, it had led to Stanley Kowalski, Terry Malloy, and Vito Corleone. Lloyd could point to no such accomplishments. Frankly, he couldn't point to any accomplishments save avoiding Phil Sheldon's attention long enough to have never been fired from *The Fleishman Show*.

An additional aspect to pulling an artistic hissy fit and resigning was not lost on Lloyd; its anticipated effect on his marriage. Since the Morning of the Disappeared Clothes, Lloyd had been harboring a simmering, silent resentment toward his wife. Actually, it had started when she insisted on building the new house. He had tamped it down because it was hard not to enjoy the more luxurious surroundings, but when his mind quieted at night, in those moments before the NyQuil kicked in and he drifted off, he wondered what exactly he was doing living like some kind of Anatolian pasha. The incident with the clothes had heightened what he was feeling, but his natural tendency to submit, to bob like a cork, to flow, kept him from acting.

From that morning on, they had existed in a state of cold peace, much like the Israelis and Egyptians have done since the Camp David accords of 1978, when Menachem Begin and Anwar Sadat famously clasped hands with Jimmy Carter at Camp David and agreed to stand down. Yes, there was a peace treaty, no rattling of sabers in the capitals, no exchanges of gunfire along the border, no open hostilities; but neither was anyone getting together to share falafel. Such was the current State of the Melnick Union, which, to Stacy, seemed quite unremarkable. If anyone had asked, she would have said the marriage was absolutely fine. Lloyd's lack of interest in sex she would have ascribed to the onset of middle age, and as for his increasing uncommunicativeness, well, men just weren't great talkers, were they? He certainly had become a high-end provider, and when you get down to it, what else is there, really?

Although the two of them lived in the same house, Lloyd occupied an entirely different reality. To Lloyd, the high-handed, preemptive manner in which Stacy had dispatched his wardrobe was an egregious violation of a tacit noninterference pact and clearly deserving of retribution. He had

297

been biding his time, waiting for an opportunity, and now it seemed gloriously at hand. If Lloyd bailed on Lynx, the money supply would be choked off, and they would be forced to sell the house he never wanted to move into anyway. It was a passive-aggressive fantasia. By doing nothing, worlds would collide! The resulting marital earthquake would set off a chain of events that would quite possibly lead to divorce, which Lloyd regarded with the hopeful ardor of a farmer in the dry season contemplating an approaching bank of rain clouds.

Stacy was going to be entitled to half of his Lynx money, but that number would shrivel like a garden slug in a salt bath if Lloyd could bring himself to go through with this plan. But could he do it? Did he have the internal strength to break out of his marital constraints, leaving his wife of ten years and his son, not to mention a comfortable home, familiarity itself, for a seat in the theater of the mysterious? Could Lloyd Melnick, who, despite his pretensions to the contrary, has led a remarkably placid life, depart from the known world and sail toward the shimmering horizon?

Lloyd walks past Jacy Pingree, who is on the lot for a costume fitting.

"Hey, Lloyd!" she chirps.

"Hey," he responds distractedly, barely looking at her.

I'm going to quit. Now is the time to take a stand. Harvey is handing me a perfect opportunity. But what'll Stacy say? She'll have a stroke. She won't accept the price for marrying an artist. Wait a minute. I'm not an artist. I've been trying to write that book for months now and nothing's coming. Nothing's coming because I've been working on this ridiculous show. With the show out of the way I'm going to get into a groove. I can see the groove and I can see me in it. Can I tell Stacy I'm writing a book? Why am I so worried what she thinks? I should just move out. I can't move out. What about Dustin? He may be a pain now but that's because he spends too much time with his mother. She's ruining him. He's going to improve, I'm going to make sure of it, and I need to be there when that happens. That's why they have visitation. Am I going to be one of those divorced dads? Those guys are so pathetic. But, Jesus, once they stop being depressed, they have much more sex. Stacy doesn't support my goals. Hemingway was married four times. What am I so afraid of? I have the talent. No, I don't. It's time to stop kidding myself. I have to have faith.

When Lloyd gets back to the office, he tells Tai Chi he is taking the rest of the day off. She asks him if he's feeling alright and he duly lies that he's never felt better.

On the ride home Lloyd is too distracted to turn the radio on. Instead, he thinks about Phil Sheldon and what he would do in this situation. He would certainly not accept this degree of interference. He would yell and scream and threaten and maybe punch his hand through a wall for good measure, all of which contributed to his mystique. That Phil Sheldon had precious little mystique prior to being party to the accumulation of a billion dollars in syndication profits is of little concern to Lloyd right now because these days Phil had mystique to burn.

Then he thought about Frank and the Zapruder-film screen saver on his computer. Frank had mystique, too, and his was increasing by the minute. A man with the Zapruder film as his screen saver would not roll over for Harvey Gornish, Lloyd forgetting Frank had done exactly that when he'd signed on to *Kirkuk*. If Lloyd aspired to a better place ("Than Brentwood?" Stacy would say, eyebrows lifted), if he thought he was a man whose ragged dreams could be taken and, like scrap metal, heated and pushed and tugged and coaxed into something finer than base elements late of the earth's heart, now was the time.

Stacy looks as if she might be having a heart attack. She has stopped breathing. A spoonful of minestrone is frozen halfway to her gaping mouth. Lloyd has taken her to dinner at Del Olio, an Italian restaurant in Venice where a bowl of linguine costs twenty-five dollars.

"I didn't say I was doing it," Lloyd nervously reassures her, concerned she might keel over right there. "I said I'm thinking about it." Already he's backpedaling, his resolve starting to wither in the gathering storm of her disapproval.

Stacy takes a couple of deep breaths to restore her equilibrium, her eyes staring straight ahead. When she returns her gaze to Lloyd, it is with the intensity of a lion tamer. "Under no circumstances can you quit. So they want you to use another actress. What's the big deal?"

"Honey Call?"

"What wrong with her?"

"Well, for starters, you can't stand her. You said so. After you met her you said she was disgusting and she made you want to take a shower."

"I don't have to hang out with her, and if I see her at the wrap party, I'll be nice."

He thought Stacy's disapproval of Honey might work on his behalf, but clearly, the prospective proximity of an actress whose sexual availability to a likely employer was something Stacy took for granted is easily trumped in her cunning mind by the economics of the situation. To Stacy's thinking, as long as he was discreet about it and her life remained unchanged, Lloyd could go to Sea World and take up with a porpoise.

"I don't think I can do it," he says without much conviction. "It completely goes against my vision of the show."

"Your *vision*?" Stacy snorts with amusement at his highfalutin word choice and the arty-fartiness it implies. "What vision? You're a television comedy writer, Lloyd. And you're a really a good one so don't worry about visions."

"You don't think I have a vision?" he says, feeling idiotic as the words come tumbling out of his mouth, in some ridiculous cross between Willam Blake and Ralph Kramden, *You don't think I have a vision, Alice? Well, let me tell you something, I have a vision! Bang! Zoom! O Jerusalem!*

She interrupts his reverie saying, "Are you Phil Sheldon all of a sudden with the vision?" This lands like an ax and cleaves him in two. His fear of her response to his plan turns slowly into antipathy toward her, mixed with the insecurity he perpetually cultivates with respect to his creative powers. "Since when are you such a sensitive flower, Lloyd? They put your show on the air, and if they're not canceling it, you're, like, I don't know, obligated? You have to make it work." She lowers her eyes, boring in. "Don't even think about quitting."

"Or what?" he asks, correctly perceiving he's being threatened, although with what he's not exactly sure. When Stacy does not respond to his question, the toxicity of his mental state begins to assert itself and he repeats, "Or what?" with more of an edge than last time.

"Do you really need me to explain?"

Money in a marriage plays the role of armaments in a war. Whoever is in possession of the better-stocked armory controls the battlefield and usually wins the war. A sound marriage is a peacetime army, whose soldiers, lazy and oblivious, are smoking pot and playing video games. But when the foundations of a marriage start to shake, the drums of war begin to sound and the army veers from unconscious to Defcon 4 in a blink. Stacy is now on high alert.

"Because I will explain if you want me to," she says in a way intended to imply he should know better than to ask.

A person does not stay married to someone for ten years without some kind of strong feeling underpinning the edifice, especially if there was no money evident when the vows were taken. However much Lloyd had not enjoyed being married to his wife recently, they had a shared history, a child, and in theory a future, and although she had transmogrified into a plucked and polished West Side, social-climbing gorgon, she was still the woman who had driven out to Coney Island to ride the Cyclone roller coaster with him, taking his penis in her mouth as they crossed the Brooklyn Bridge. And why had she engaged in this kind of salacious behavior? Because she believed in him. She knew his talent, his enthusiasm, his youthful slap and tickle, would lead somewhere she wanted to follow. Lloyd understood this, could see it in her eyes, and loved her for it. But that was a long time ago.

Reining in the ire he feels at Stacy's invidious comparison of him to Phil Sheldon, he asks her, "Remember when we sat on that beach in Jamaica, what, ten years ago?" Jamaica had been another point of contention. She had wanted to go to the Bahamas, a place where the natives were not known to hack tourists to pieces on the golf course, something Stacy heard happened in Jamaica with alarming regularity. In her mind Jamaica was terra incognita, two steps from Africa, and who went there? Lloyd had persuaded her to visit the more flavorful reggae-soaked island by promising to book them into a high-rise hotel in Montego Bay, a Miami Beach–style resort area. He had wanted to go to Negril, a tattered town of jerk-chicken shacks and funky beachfront hotels, but that was the deal: Montego Bay or nothing. "And you asked me how I wanted my life to go and I said I wanted to be taken seriously? Do you remember?"

"Sure, I remember. And now you're taken seriously."

"In a ridiculous business."

"Ridiculous to who?"

"To me! I want to write a book."

"So who's stopping you?"

"About Frank Bones."

"Why?"

"Because I know him and he's a great subject."

"He kills someone and all of a sudden he's a great subject?"

"First of all, you have no idea whether or not he's guilty. If he's not, maybe I can help him prove it."

"What are you, a detective? Lloyd, if you want to be taken seriously, this isn't the way to do it."

"I'm flying to Tulsa tomorrow."

"No, you're not. You're going back to the office and you're going to work on the show."

The ride home from dinner is very quiet.

Lloyd is in his office watching the eleven-o'clock news when Stacy bursts through the door, grabs the remote control off his desk, and wordlessly clicks over to *E! Entertainment!* Lloyd is shocked to see a handheld video image of Frank and himself at Duke's Coffee Shop. Frank is saying, "Marriage itself is a point of contention, babe," to which Lloyd responds, "I could live in a refrigerator carton, but my wife, she thinks she's Charles Foster Kane." Lloyd can feel Stacy's eyes piercing his head like drill bits as he continues to watch himself slowly die. "We're building Xanadu over on the West Side. I want to get a dog just so I can name him Rosebud. She's out of control. Whenever I leave the house, I have to remember to ask for my balls back." Before the tape ends and the host returns to the screen, Stacy leaves the office. Lloyd does not bother going after her but instead stays and watches footage of Frank and himself firing pistols. Otto has wasted no time cashing in. As for Lloyd, he can't decide whether he's more disturbed by having inadvertently aired his marital laundry on national television or by having looked so uncomfortable handling a gun.

That night they sleep in separate bedrooms. Rather, Stacy sleeps. Lloyd just stares at the ceiling. In the middle of the night, he gets up to e-mail his agent, his manager, and his lawyer, informing them he will be leaving *Happy Endings*. Lloyd loves e-mail since it means you never have to talk to anyone. He knows they'll be phoning, aggrieved at their loss of commissions, but his cell phone has caller ID and he doesn't have to return their calls.

Dustin is asleep when Lloyd goes into his room to kiss him good-bye. He stands over his son's bed, hesitating for a moment. Lloyd was never around when he was working on *The Fleishman Show*, which is probably one of the reasons the boy is so much closer to Stacy, and he has been preoccupied during the past months at Lynx. As he looks at Dustin's sleeping face, he thinks, *It's better to be going now. When I can stand to be in the same room with myself, that's when we should get to know each other. I'll spend some time with him away from Stacy, and the two of us will be like a real father and son. I worry she may have turned the boy against me.*

"Daddy?" Groggily, the kid awake.

"Go back to sleep."

"Where's Mommy?"

"She's sleeping."

"Can I ask you a question?"

Now Lloyd is resigned to the conversation taking place and uses a quiet tone, hoping to ease his son back to sleep.

"Sure, Pal. What is it?"

"Have you ever done anything for DreamWorks?"

"What?" *Where the hell did that come from?*

"Have you ever done anything for DreamWorks?"

"Do you even know what DreamWorks is?"

"Sophia's father works there." Sophia was a schoolmate of Dustin's at Tiny Tuna. "He's a producer."

"No," Lloyd says, watching Dustin's view of him plummet. "I haven't done anything for them. Now go back to sleep."

Dustin closes his eyes and Lloyd kisses the boy's forehead, eliciting a sleepy "Don't kiss me." Lloyd quietly tiptoes out of the room. Then he turns off the burglar alarm and leaves the house.

Chapter 15

At dawn Frank awakens in the Tulsa County Jail. He has had a bad night's sleep on the metal bunk. A young guard brings him an individual box of generic cornflakes for breakfast and asks for an autograph before he leaves, a request Frank politely obliges, asking the guard if he can bring him a cake with a file in it later. The guard looks at him, puzzled for a moment, then laughs as he gets the old joke. Left alone, he eats one flake at a time to make them last, Frank no stranger to incarceration, having been tossed in jail overnight for the gun incident. But he has never looked at serious time before, and right now what he is faced with feels like eternity, only without the cottony clouds and the harps.

He stares around the tiny cinder-block cell. Otis has parlayed his client's status as a man who has been on national television into a private cell, so he is being kept from the common criminals, who might amuse themselves at his expense, something for which Frank is extremely thankful, because whatever his transgressions, however much of an outsider he perceives himself to be, he was never one of those hipsters who identified with convicts. Prisoners to Frank are losers with primitive tattoos and hairnets who smelled bad and buggered each other, end of story. The Alexandre Dumas–Jean Genet–Jack Henry Abbott literary tradition leaves him cold. A mass of sociopaths divided into homicidal gangs of blacks, Latinos, and white supremacists eating dreadful food in a confined space for years on end; Frank just can't see the appeal. A concert, perhaps. Get some more street cred and maybe a CD out of it. But an extended holiday in the pen? That is not going to work.

How does anyone ever manage to break out of jail? he wonders. He's heard the stories of guys digging their way out with spoons. How long would it take to go anywhere with a spoon? More time than Frank has. And those were rural prisons anyway, Frank likely headed to some high-tech concrete nightmare that will require a Ph.D. in engineering just to open a door. The escapes he's heard about that didn't involve flatware usually required teamwork. A bunch of cons would formulate a plan and act in concert. The drawback here is it requires friends, and Frank does not anticipate making any once he's incarcerated, busy as he'll be sliding along with his back to the wall in the theory that it is harder to sodomize a moving target. Thus, in his brief consideration of the matter, escape does not present itself as a realistic possibility, so he'll just rot and either die in prison or get released at an age when he won't be able to remember why he was there in the first place.

These prison vignettes he is formulating are all predicated on a supposition so disturbing he couldn't consider it for the moment, and that is this: his winding up serving a prison sentence and not getting the death penalty. He had joked about it to Otis, but it hangs there in the air around him, grinning madly, like a skeleton's head singing, *So long, it's been good to know ya, so long* . . .

They have taken away his belt and shoelaces and his wallet. He would have loved a magazine, a trade paper (it didn't matter what trade, *Plumber's Monthly* would do), anything to distract himself, to keep him from focusing on where he is, on who he is.

As he lies on his back, staring at the ceiling, he enumerates the arguments the prosecution will lavish upon the court if the case goes to trial. The Cleveland gun incident would combine with the Los Angeles high-speed chase to create a neat criminal pattern that fit nicely with the profile of someone who would kill a club owner for money. The DA's office could send a rookie in and get a conviction. Unless Otis has talent to match his bluster, Frank is looking at a long-term problem. He runs the titles of all the prison movies he can remember through his head: *I Am a Fugitive from a Chain Gang, Riot in Cell Block 11, Birdman of Alcatraz, Jailhouse Rock, Cool Hand Luke, Brubaker, The Shawshank Redemption, The*

Green Mile, Fortune and Men's Eyes, Chicago. Then there are the movies that aren't prison movies but have memorable prison sequences: *Sullivan's Travels,* with its message that comedy is a worthwhile thing to devote one's life to, *Midnight Express,* with its message that Turkish prison guards should be avoided; *GoodFellas,* with its message that a quality marinara sauce is not beyond the reach of the connected guy behind bars. And those are just the men's prison movies. He doesn't want to start thinking about all the grade-Z prison chick flicks he's seen on cable at three A.M., with their nubile prisonerettes in clingy jumpsuits that appeared to be on loan from a Helmut Newton shoot, and their cheap but effective lesbians-for-straight-guys eroticism, for fear it will lead him in a masturbatory direction, which somehow doesn't feel appropriate right now.

Frank is fighting off a vision of a voluptuous inmate being approached in the prison showers by a lascivious, bikini-clad warden when the guard reappears at his cell door holding a pair of handcuffs. "Sorry, Frank, I have to cuff you before we leave."

"Babe, can I get my sunglasses back?"

He imagined a couple of local television crews might be there for his moment of glory, since it wasn't every day a celebrity was accused of killing someone in Tulsa, but when Frank, dressed once again in street clothes, emerges from the police van for the perp walk to the courthouse and squints into the sun (his request to have his shades returned had been denied), he is surprised to see the crews from *Entertainment Tonight* and *E! Entertainment!* pointing their cameras at him. As a guard emerges from the van to lead Frank inside, a male reporter whose dyed-blond hair tips mark him as having flown in from Los Angeles for the occasion yells, "Frank, did you shoot Tino Suarez?"

Frank, never at a loss when a camera is on, replies, "I'm a patsy! I wasn't even in Dallas on November twenty-second!" After a slight delay, the crews laugh, which causes the cameras to jiggle slightly as Frank continues to be hustled away amid cries of "Frank, Frank!" and "Over here!"

Another reporter, a local woman with hard-looking blond hair asks, "Who do you think shot Suarez?"

"Anti-Castro Cubans acting with the acquiescence of the CIA!"

Someone else shouts, "How are you going to plead?"

The last words the media hears Frank speak before his arraignment are "I'm calling Jim Garrison!" an obscure reference to the Kennedy-assassination prosecutor that no one in the media horde gets.

Frank is seated in a penned-off area at the side of the courtroom waiting for his case to be called. Several other miscreants are with him. As far as he can tell, they are mostly street criminals who were picked up the previous evening and, having all slept badly in jail, are thankfully ignoring him. But every file clerk, lawyer, guard, secretary, computer technician, and janitor who works in the building appears to be taking a simultaneous coffee break because the room is packed. It's clearly not every day a man of Frank's magnitude is arraigned on their premises.

The opening act is a fraternity boy, an undergraduate at the University of Tulsa, charged with drunk driving. He stands before Judge Marston, a large black woman glowering at him. When she inquires why he was driving after he had consumed two six-packs of beer, he replies, " 'Cause I was too drunk to walk," eliciting titters from the packed gallery. Judge Marston sets bail and waves him away as if he were a cloud of methane. When Frank looks at the crowd, he sees Mercy has taken a seat in the back. She meets his glance and smiles. Frank shakes his head wearily and tries to look amused instead of doomed.

At the front of the room the judge consults her notes. "Frank Bones?"

"Yes" comes Frank's answer from the penalty box.

The bailiff says, "Step to the judge's bench, please." Frank moves from the wings to the stage with as much dignity as he can muster and tries to ignore the eyes of the mob.

"Do you have a lawyer, Mr. Bones?" the judge asks.

Frank turns away from the judge, his eyes panning the room before turning back to her and saying, "I did."

"And where is your alleged lawyer?"

At this moment the double doors leading to the courtroom burst open and Otis Cain makes his entrance.

"Your Honor!" Otis says, hurrying to the front of the room.

From Judge Marston's expression you can see that she does not cut Otis Cain any slack simply because their mutual ancestors came over here on slave ships. "Yes, Mr. Cain?" she says with infinite patience.

"If it pleases the court, I am this man's lawyer."

"May I have a word with my attorney?" Frank inquires.

"Quickly," Marston says, having a fat docket to get through.

Frank leans into Otis and hisses, "Where the hell were you?"

"Talking to a reporter."

"About what?"

"About you! We show you in a sympathetic light in the press and no jury's gonna convict."

"I don't want any more publicity. I'm sick of being famous."

Judge Marston has already had enough of these two and brings their kaffeeklatsch to a close, demanding, "Mr. Bones, how do you plead?"

"Very not guilty," Frank says.

Judge Marston writes this down. "So noted. Bail will be set at two hundred and fifty thousand dollars." At these words Frank feels the floor open and swallow him whole.

The next morning, after another sleepless jailhouse night, Frank sits with Otis in a bare room set aside for prisoner/attorney encounters. With them is a tough-looking, fiftyish Latino whose paunch, visible under his unbuttoned brown sports coat, is a palimpsest laid over the younger, rangier version of himself. This is Manny Escobar and he is a bail bondsman.

"How much money you got?" Manny asks Frank by way of introduction.

Frank, who has thought about this, says, "I can have my bank wire twenty-five K."

Manny nods, the amount being sufficient, and writes the information down on a legal pad, saying, "I'm only doing this because my kid likes you. If you jump, there's a skip tracer on your ass in five seconds and he carries a very big gun. He brought a guy back from Texas for me with so many shotgun pellets in his ass he nearly bled to death during the ride." Then he smiles at the memory, as if it's funny.

"I'll be a good boy," Frank assures him.

Manny slides the legal pad toward Frank. "Can I have your autograph? It's for my kid."

Frank dutifully signs.

Otis makes a couple of calls to speed the process and an hour later he and Frank are back in front of Judge Marston. "Mr. Escobar has agreed to post bail for my client," Otis tells her.

"The defendant is freed and ordered to reappear to stand trial on"—she checks the calendar—"December seventeenth. That's five weeks. Mr. Bones, the court would appreciate it if you didn't leave town before then, all right?"

Frank nods in assent and is pronounced a free man.

Frank is walking Otis to his car in the empty parking lot of the courthouse. The media swarm have returned to their nests and are filing their reports.

"What am I supposed to do for money?" Franks asks.

"You need ten bucks for dinner or something?"

"I don't have a cent, Otis. Manny cleaned me out."

"Tell some jokes."

"What?"

"You're a comedian, right? I'll call Mrs. Suarez for you."

"Tino's wife is going to let me play Club Louie?"

"Why not? It's business. I'll call and tell you what she says." Otis gets

310

into his car, starts the engine. He waves distractedly and drives off, leaving Frank to contemplate his advice.

"Frank?" Frank looks over and sees Mercy standing there. He smiles, pleased to see her.

"Need a lift?"

"I need a Thorazine IV. What are you doing here?"

"I called Otis. He said this is where I'd find you."

A few minutes later, Frank sits in the passenger seat of Mercy's beat-up Camaro as they drive out of the parking lot past a gaggle of demonstrators holding placards that read JUSTICE FOR WAYMAN FRENCH. Turning to Mercy, Frank says, "This Wayman French, the cops killed him?"

"That's the rumor," Mercy says, twiddling the knobs on the radio. In a moment, a woman's voice can be heard saying, "He didn't do it. No way someone with those eyes killed anyone. They're not killer's eyes."

Then the voice of Wildman Simms, the shock jock: "First of all, he always wears sunglasses so you don't know what you're talking about."

"I've seen pictures!" the woman says.

Wildman interrupts her, "Okay, we're running four to one not guilty."

"Do you mind if we turn this off?" Frank asks, turning it off.

"I don't think you killed anyone," Mercy says, not taking her gaze off the road. Frank doesn't respond. He's staring at the pile of parking tickets stuffed between the passenger seat and the gearshift, held together with a rubber band. Frank picks them up and takes a look. There are at least twenty.

"Unpaid?"

"I got a lot on my plate lately."

"You're more guilty than me."

She laughs and says, "Probably am."

Frank is getting out of the Camaro in the parking lot of the Trade Winds. Mercy watches him from the driver's seat. "You gonna be all right?" she asks.

Frank leans on the car door, looking in. "Yeah, terrific. Think they have Court TV on cable here?"

"Want me to come up and watch with you?"

"I'm not into the groupie thing right now," Frank says, turning away from the car.

"Whoa, pardner!" Mercy throws open the car door, explodes out of her seat, and faces Frank over the roof, telling him, "I am not a goddamn groupie, okay? I am not one of those short-skirted, leather-jacket-wearin', spike-heeled chicks who live to sleep with stars. Is that registerin' on your radar, jokeboy?"

"Okay," Frank says, trying to keep from being sucked in by the backdraft. "I apologize."

"I don't even think you're so funny."

"That hurt."

Mercy slides back into the car without saying anything else, jams it into gear, and peels out. Frank stares after her, impressed by the show of force.

"Babe!" Frank says, shocked.

"Hi, Frank," Lloyd says, seated in a chair and grinning. Frank has just walked into his room after having been excoriated by Mercy, and Lloyd's presence interrupts his self-recriminations.

"What are you doing here?"

"I came to help you," Lloyd informs him. Frank doesn't respond for a moment as he weighs the depth of his quickly recalled anger toward Lloyd. Yes, Lloyd had punted when Frank asked for his help, but, then, he was a familiar and sympathetic face and those have been in short supply recently. He could throw Lloyd out but that would be little more than petty revenge for something that had occurred in what at this point was another life. Meanwhile, Lloyd sits there awaiting a response. He's self-conscious and silently beseeching Frank not to eject him.

"Who let you in?"

"The maid. I told her I was a writer on *The Fleishman Show* and the doors flew open. Who knew the Jewish thing played in Tulsa?"

"Where you staying?"

"Room twenty-eight."

"Here?"

"I checked in half an hour ago."

Frank looks at Lloyd seated in the chair, one leg crossed over the other, smiling as if in anticipation of a great adventure, and suddenly feels a bone-deep weariness overtaking him. The cumulative effect of the events of the last few days begins to press on him with the inexorable force of gravity. Frank sits on the bed. "Welcome to Tulsa," he says in a tone the Chamber of Commerce would not appreciate, and lies down. Even if he wanted to throw Lloyd out, he doesn't have the energy.

"I went back to the LAX Gun Club," Lloyd tells him. When there is no response, he continues, "Learned how to handle a weapon. Zip taught me."

Frank stares at the ceiling, watching a spider spin a web. "So how are you going to help?"

"No comedian is going to shoot anyone, Frank. Forget Cleveland, what happened there. Your mouth's a safety valve. Steam builds up, it gets released."

"Your point being . . . ?"

"You're innocent. I thought maybe I could help get you off."

"Now you want to lend a hand, Lloyd? Not when we were in L.A. but now?"

"I feel bad about what I did back there. I should have helped you out."

"Yeah, you should have."

"I was having my own problems, but never mind. I want to make it up to you."

"Babe, this conversation is exhausting me. I don't know what you think you can do, so do me a favor and leave. I need to get some sleep."

Dismissed, Lloyd rises from the chair and walks to the door. Before he opens it, he turns to Frank, saying, "I want to write a book about you."

Even in his battered state, Frank's self-promotional sensors are on alert. "What kind of book?" he murmurs from the depths of his fatigue.

"I don't know exactly. I'm thinking it'll take shape as I start to write it. I just know it's a good story."

"Fuck off, Lloyd."

"Frank . . ."

"I said fuck off."

Lloyd hesitates a moment, deciding whether to press his case. Then, realizing Frank won't be going anywhere and they will be able to resume this conversation later, Lloyd opens the door and walks out of the room, leaving Frank to drift off to a hard, dreamless sleep.

Returning to Room 28, Lloyd turns on his laptop and begins to write—about New York in the early days, about Los Angeles, and about the encounter that just took place in the motel room. Two hours later he has written fifteen pages and he's feeling good.

Frank is awakened out of a deep sleep by the persistent ringing of the telephone. It's Otis calling to say Vida Suarez has agreed to book him into Club Louie the following night, the American desire to make a buck trumping the potentially awkward situation of hiring her husband's accused killer to perform in the nightclub she inherited at his death. Frank hangs up wondering what the comedy etiquette is for appearing onstage while under indictment for murder. Robert calls a few minutes later wanting to know why Frank had not retained Roscoe Barnwell as his counsel. After Frank tells him about Otis Cain, Robert says, "I've gotten some interesting calls today. A couple of very big players are talking about acquiring your life rights for a movie."

A week ago, Frank might have cared.

Mercy pulls into the driveway of her small rented house and sees Clay Porter sitting on the front steps, the gold toes of his cowboy boots glinting in the sun. He rises as she gets out of the car, saying, "Can I talk to you for a minute, girl?"

"What about?" Suspicious. She doesn't like Clay Porter.

"Tino had something he shouldn't have had. He was going to give it to me the night he was killed."

"And?"

"Did he do anything peculiar that day?"

"He was his charmin' self. Are we done?"

"What's with you and Frank Bones?"

"He's nothin' to me."

From a window she watches Clay drive away. The phone rings as he disappears from sight. She lets the machine pick it up.

It says, *I'm not in right now. Please leave a message at the beep.*

"Mercy, it's your husband, baby. I just want you to know I'm watching you."

Not only did I marry an asshole, she's thinking, *he talks like a cheesy stalker.*

Mercy bought a gun when she and Creed started having problems, and she hid it in her closet. Now she goes to check if it's loaded.

At eight o'clock the next evening the parking lot of Club Louie is packed. The sign in front of the club reads TONITE—FRANK BONES—SOLD OUT. Groups of guys, groups of girls, and couples stream through the cars toward the club, where a long line of people is filing in, notoriety a great selling tool. The air in the club is electric with dark anticipation, the kind seen at a witch burning or a public duel, rituals where malign forces compel human eyes to focus on a morbid spectacle in which the only end is death. To watch a man twirl on the edge of an abyss by the simple act of paying a cover charge and agreeing to a two-drink minimum, to see him walk and talk and tell jokes, twisting, writhing while impaled on a large pin, is an opportunity some people cannot resist.

Frank comes onstage a few minutes after nine and surveys the packed room for a few moments, letting the tension build. The beginning of a smirk plays on his face. At this sign, there are titters in the audience. Now Frank smiles, releasing the valve, and a few of the more relaxed audience members laugh.

315

I want to thank the management for booking me when Charles Manson canceled.

The place erupts in laughter as the crowd releases their jumpy energy. Frank shakes his head, gives a short, disbelieving laugh himself. Bobbie Jo is serving drinks to a table where Faron Pike and Clay Porter are seated, two cops not enjoying a night on the town. Otis and Manny Escobar sit together at another table. Lloyd stands in the back, taking notes. Out of the corner of his eyes, Frank sees the bartender leave her post and come into the room. No one's in the bar so Mercy figures she can watch Frank.

I really killed the other night. That's the point of this comedy thing . . . to kill. I slayed 'em. I knocked 'em dead. I destroyed 'em. I killed. That's the whole idea. To kill. I kill and you die. On a good night that's what happens. Sometimes I only maim, but when I'm really good . . . I kill. Where's the comic nuance if I pull a Glock out of my pants and blow some guy's dick off? Not that anyone's dick was blown off in the situation we're all thinking about, but it's a funny body part and always good for a cheap laugh. But I won't pander. I can tell you're a discerning bunch of sophisticates. I see we have some police out there tonight. These guys love me. Come on, stand up and take a bow!

Faron and Clay are not amused at being brought into the act and remain stone-faced, riveted to their chairs.

Okay, they're being modest. Well, they have a lot to be modest about. How many people think I'm innocent? Let's have a show of hands.

Half the hands in the place go up and an audience member shouts, "You didn't do it!"

Thanks, pal. Last week I couldn't get arrested. But now, not only can I get arrested, I can get charged with murder and a guy can write a book about me. They'll make the book into a movie. Only in America—the response to someone charged with a capital crime—"We think you killed someone! Let's do a movie!" I can't get a fuckin' sitcom on the air but now they want to do a movie about me. Frank Bones, Wanted Comic. At a theater near you. It'll be classy, too. I'll go on Barbara Walters and make her cry. I'll be in all the tabloids again but I'll get much bigger play this time. I'll get billing above the two-headed boy from

Mississippi who was abducted by aliens and made to have sex with Monica Lewinsky while the ghost of JFK Jr. watched. I'll get a show on Nickelodeon because we're all cartoon characters now. Tabloid freaks in America, man. I'll get a penile implant and go on Jerry Springer. I'll go on Oprah and talk about recovered memory. I'll remember I was a black woman, and that black woman— me, ladies and gentlemen—will have lunch with Geraldo. No, I'll have Geraldo for lunch. I'll eat Geraldo. "Today on our show, killer cannibal comics." I'll have a charity. Frank's Kids. They'll have a disease that makes them act like Jerry Lewis. They'll all be on my telethon and I'll be famous for being famous. And you can all be on the show with me! Who wants to be on the show?

Two young female fans fawn over Frank in the bar later. The tube dresses they're both wearing encase their fleshy bodies like sausages. Large hoop earrings hang below their big hair. Frank is signing the breast of one with a felt-tipped pen as her friend looks on, giggling. He got offstage an hour ago, and after doing two quick interviews with stringers from *Variety* and the *Los Angeles Times*, he has been greeting admirers who have been vocal both in their appreciation of the show and in their faith in his innocence. These two have hung around, hoping to participate in some of the Bones madness, swooping and diving, moths to the fame.

"Wanna party later?" repeats the one whose flesh has just been autographed. The ignoring of her two previous entreaties has not dampened her ardor. She's had four mai tais and is in danger of throwing up on Frank's shoes, but this does not dissuade her from trying to appear seductive.

"We were with Cheetah Thayer last month," the other says by way of inducement.

"Maybe tomorrow," Frank tells her, turning away, indicating the exchange has ended. After some inebriated grumbling, the girls totter off, disappointed they won't have his pelt to hang on their wall.

At the end of the bar, Otis Cain looks up from the beer Lloyd has bought him and says, "You can't just write an unauthorized book," friendly but firm.

Lloyd says, "It's the public domain, isn't it?"

"You need life rights. You're from Hollywood, Lloyd. You oughtta know that."

"It's about Frank and me."

"You gonna write about the trial?"

"Sure, that's a part of it."

"You're thinking maybe it's a movie?"

"Maybe, yeah."

"Then you gotta get my rights and I'm not selling tonight."

Lloyd looks into Otis's face for an indication that he's not really going to play this card, but none is forthcoming.

Frank is talking to Mercy at the opposite end of the bar. "You still mad at me?"

"You're damn right I am. You know that girl whose implant you just signed? *That* is a groupie."

"Cut me some slack, okay? This indictment is playing with my stress level."

"Try and do right by someone and they cast aspersions on your character."

"Aspersions?"

"Hey, I do the *TV Guide* crossword, okay?"

Now Vida approaches, brandishing a wad of cash. Otis, having seen the money, abandons Lloyd and drifts over as Vida says, "You want to count it?" Frank takes the money and shoots the bills off his fingers onto the bar. All there.

"Thanks," he says, and Vida walks away from the man accused of killing her husband, smiling.

Otis says to Frank, "You know that guy over there wants to write a book about you?" as Mercy excuses herself and walks out from behind the bar.

"Mind if I talk to you later?" Lloyd asks her. "I'm not trying to pick you up. It's for something I'm writing."

"Sure thing." Mercy moves across the room and down a short hall with a pay phone to a door marked FILLIES. Pushing open the door, she's greeted by the sight of Bobbie Jo standing with her back to the sink, skirt hiked above her hips and her legs wrapped around Creed. As soon as they see her, they disengage. Mercy notices her husband is holding a handkerchief in his hand, then realizes it's Bobbie Jo's panties.

"Excuse me, Creed," Mercy says, dead calm. When you're done snakin' Bobbie Jo, I'd like to use the ladies' room."

Bobbie Jo slides off the sink and smoothes her skirt down. "He told me you were gettin' divorced."

Lloyd looks up from his beer to see Mercy striding across the bar toward the door. "Miss?" he says, holding his hand up, but she doesn't even see him. Lloyd throws some money on the bar, slides off the stool, and follows her out.

In the nearly deserted parking lot of Club Louie, Otis is telling Frank, "Don't be talking to nobody unless I check 'em out for you. That writer in there? He's looking for the main chance, Frank. All kinds of people looking for the main chance."

"And you're in it because of the inner goodness you have?"

"I didn't say Otis Cain ain't gonna get a taste, but that's 'cause we're a team. You scratch my ass and I keep yours outta the fryin' pan."

Mercy yells, "Goddammit," and walks quickly toward the men. "You wanna make it up to me for insultin' my womanly virtue?"

"What's the catch?" Frank wants to know.

"The cops just put a boot on my car for unpaid parkin' tickets. How about a lift?"

"My driver's license was revoked, babe. Otis?"

Lloyd watches from the door of the club as Frank and Mercy climb into Otis's Lincoln Navigator. Lloyd gets into his rented Cadillac and starts to follow them, thinking, *This is what I came for. Following a car filled with trouble on a neon highway shooting through a strange, dark city where I know no one and no one knows me. Finally, I'm doing what I'm meant to be doing. Unscripted, real. A world with no commercials, no tidy endings, just life on the fly.*

The beers he drank slosh around in his stomach and he wonders if he could pass a sobriety test if he's pulled over. Then he remembers he only had two. The Navigator weaves through the light traffic and Lloyd stares at the red taillights, gripping the wheel of the Cadillac and trying to hang back, like in the movies. He's feeling as if he were on-screen now, forty feet high and doing something cool.

A big, bleached-blond middle-aged waitress is talking quietly to a rodentlike short-order cook at the service station between the kitchen and the counter area of Critter's, a greasy spoon on Highway 44 with laminated menus featuring pictures of ribs and fried chicken. The two of them are sneaking glances at Frank, who sits next to Mercy and across from Otis in a booth where they are drinking coffee and eating pie. The waitress moves away from the cook and walks toward Frank, faking confidence as she goes.

"You're him, aren't you?"

"I just look like him," Frank tells her.

Turning to Otis, the waitress, who wears a nametag that reads LIANNE, says, "I saw your picture in the paper today."

Otis beams. He's bathing in warm milk now. "My public!"

"Good luck," she tells Frank, and goes back to be debriefed by the short-order cook.

Taking a bite of his pie, Frank says, "You like being recognized?" then shakes his head, indicating he's had enough of it for now.

"This is America, man," Otis says, somewhat unnecessarily. "That's what it's all about. Now I'm like a singer or a ballplayer. Once I win this case, I'm gonna be *Johnnie Cochran: The Sequel—Bigger and Blacker!* I got the rays, brother."

"Being famous used to mean something but now . . ."

"The shit you talk!" Otis tells him.

"Who was famous back in the Middle Ages?" Frank says, gaining steam. "If you were a great painter, you were famous. If you were a king or a playwright, you were famous. These days, you screw a teenager and she shoots your wife, hey! You're famous! Your wife takes a Ginsu knife and cuts off your manhandle, whaddya know? You're famous. Today, you get caught blowing the president and Jenny Craig makes you their spokeschick. This is where the culture is, man." As Frank is rolling along, he notices Lloyd walking toward them, but it doesn't slow him down. "Hester Prynne wouldn't just wear a scarlet letter today; she'd have a fuckin' Web site and she'd be selling Scarlet Letter lingerie," Frank concludes as Lloyd arrives at the table.

"How's everybody?" Lloyd says, sitting next to Otis.

"Who asked you to sit down?" Otis demands.

"Lloyd," Frank says. "Why are you gumshoeing me?"

"I figured you'd know the best places to hang." Then, realizing: "Whoa, bad choice of words." Mercy and Otis look at Lloyd—who is this guy?—but Frank bails him out by laughing.

"Yeah, I do."

At that moment the waitress arrives with the check. Lloyd grabs it and hands her a credit card. She takes it and departs. Otis excuses himself and Lloyd stands to let him out. Frank and Mercy get up as well, and the three of them head for the door, leaving Lloyd to await the return of his plastic.

Sensing the party's breaking up, Lloyd quickly walks toward Frank, who is holding the door for Mercy. Putting his hand on Frank's arm, Lloyd looks at him.

"Hey . . ."

"What?" Frank says, annoyed, as Mercy walks out.

"We both messed up. The two of us made some bad choices, but I think I can help you now if you help me."

"Thanks for the pie, Lloyd."

"Bones," Lloyd says, and something in his voice, a subtly commanding tone he's acquired since running a TV show, makes the other man turn around. "The last time I saw you, you were bleeding to death on my living room floor. I never busted you for nearly knocking my house down, never pressed charges, never did anything, and believe me, there were people who wanted me to. So maybe you could cut me a little slack."

Frank takes this in silently. Then he walks out the door, down the steps of the diner, and to the parking lot, where Otis and Mercy are waiting. Lloyd debates whether to follow and determines he's shown enough belly for one night. He goes back to the table for his credit card.

Shit! I played that completely wrong. Frank's madder at me than I thought. I shouldn't have sat down with them. I should have just kept my distance and watched. No, that's wrong, too. What I should have done is gone back to the motel. There's going to be plenty of time to buttonhole Frank. They're probably talking about me now. Frank's telling that bartender girl and his lawyer that he thinks I'm an asshole. Why didn't I go back to the motel? Shit!

By the time Lloyd gets to the parking lot, they're gone, but he has ceased his recriminations for a moment and is comforting himself with the thought that for once he has not taken the easy road. He wants to write a serious book, he's flown to Oklahoma to do research, and it's going to work out if he follows it to the end. He can play cat and mouse with the Notorious B.O.N.E.S. if that's what Frank wants. The point is, he's not on a soundstage with a bunch of whiny actors anymore. No, this is really happening, the murder, the comic, the girl; as if it were something from one of the pulp fictions he collects. Only he can't close the book, curl into his luxurious sheets, and drift off to his usual NyQuil-induced slumber because now it's swirling around him.

Otis is dropping Mercy off first, but when the car pulls up to her house, she asks Frank to come in with her, telling him she knows a twenty-four-hour car service and he can get a cab home, so the two of them get out. As Otis drives away, Frank says, "Your husband's not coming back tonight?"

"Not unless he wants a bullet in his useless ass." He likes this woman more and more.

The inside of the small house is decorated with thrift-shop furniture. The kitchen has a Formica table and a couple of vinyl chairs, the living room an old sofa and two wing chairs, one of which is losing its stuffing. Frank notices a catalog for Broken Arrow Community College. He picks it up and flips through it.

"I'm taking some courses," she says. "Trying to improve my standing in life."

"What are you studying?" Frank asks, genuinely curious.

"Basic psychology right now. They call it 'Nuts and Sluts.' I figure I could teach the course but the faculty didn't see it that way."

"So you wanna be a shrink?" Frank says, moving closer.

"I dunno, I just want to find out what makes people tick," she says, sticking her tongue down his throat.

The streetlamp outside the window throws soft light into the bedroom where Frank and Mercy are making love. On a shelf above the king-size bed are a row of little ceramic houses: a cabin, a manor house, and a lighthouse among others equally fanciful. As the bed rocks into the wall, the houses shake slightly.

When they are finished, they lie naked side by side. "I got your new CD, Frank," Mercy says. "I bought it this afternoon. I wasn't gonna tell you 'cause you already think I'm some kind of comedy slut."

"No, I don't."

"There's a lot of pain in some of those stories you tell. I mean, they're funny, but there's pain, too."

"I'm the Pain Queen."

"Lucinda Williams is the Pain Queen, son. But you're not bad."

"I can die now that I've been compared to Lucinda Williams. Who is . . . ?"

"The greatest songwriter and singer alive today, you ignorant man, you. Think you know everything, doncha?" she says, propping herself up on her elbow and stroking his chest. "I felt bad today so I played it."

"And it made you feel better?"

"It made me feel worse."

"Did you visualize me?"

"I did."

"Was I naked?"

"You were wearin' a red dress. The lesbian inside you was leapin' out."

Frank gets out of bed to go to the bathroom, and when he comes back, she asks, "What's that scar on your back?" so he tells her the whole story of Honey's implants and his dalliance with Candi Wyatt and her cat, no reason to lie now.

"You're a cheatin' man," Mercy says, not without amusement. "I coulda told you that."

"Never had the incentive not to be." Frank looks into her open face, and for the first time in what feels like years a woman's eyes aren't working like spotlights, lighting a stage, *Ladies and gentlemen, Frank Bones!* He's not performing with Mercy, he's *being* with her, and it's a new and soothing feeling for him.

Mercy kisses him on the mouth, then says, "Frank, I want you to stay, but you better go."

"I thought you said he wasn't coming home."

"He's got a set of keys."

"I guess a threesome is out of the question."

"Are you gay for Creed?"

"If I have to explain when I'm joking, there's no future here, babe," he says, getting back up and starting to dress.

"That's good to know because I was plannin' the church wedding, coupla kids, house in the suburbs with you, Frank Bones, accused killer," she says, smiling. He tells her he'll settle for conjugal visits in the big house and is laughing when he leaves.

The next morning Robert tells Frank, "There's a lot of heat on you. We've been getting a major amount of calls. Everyone wants to know what's going on. If you beat this thing, the net career effect is going to be very positive." Frank is still struggling to wake up. It's just after ten and Robert's call was his alarm clock. "You're gonna do all the talk shows, we'll tie it into publicity for the new CD, and listen to this, Harvey Gornish called. They're thinking about developing something new for you at Lynx."

"They could put me away for life, Bobby. How am I going to do a television show?"

"We're in spin control mode right now. All four network morning shows called. We're giving *AM America* an exclusive tomorrow, and when you do it, please, no sunglasses."

"Why them?"

"Because when people see you make Patty Sullivan laugh while they're eating their oatmeal, it's gonna help buff your image, which between you and me has taken a few hits lately." Patty Sullivan was the preternaturally perky, blond hostess of *AM America* and was the breakfast nation's prom queen, beloved by all. The notion of Patty Sullivan and Frank Bones, gone denizen of the night city, unrehabilitated rehab patient and indicted criminal, together was preposterous, Beelzebub with Bo Peep. But if by the end of the interview she behaved as if he were not radioactive, it would influence the perceptions of millions of Americans, many of whom were swimming in the prospective jury pool. After listening to Robert expound on how being cleared of a murder charge is exactly the shot in the arm his career needs, Frank hangs up, shaves, showers, and heads out to find breakfast.

"G'morning."

"Jesus Christ, Lloyd, you're like a bad cold. What are you doing?"

What Lloyd is doing is leaning against the wall outside Frank's room reading a copy of that morning's *Variety,* which he has downloaded from the Web.

"*Variety* liked the show. They called it"—he reads from the print-out—"'audacious, reckless and very funny. Vintage Bones.'"

"Let me see that," Frank says, grabbing it out of Lloyd's hand and scanning it himself.

"Can I buy you breakfast?"

"What do you want from me, Lloyd? The one time I asked you for anything, you made me walk the plank, so why should I do anything for you?"

"I never asked you to apologize for wrecking my house."

"You want an apology, Lloyd?"

"No, I don't because I think I understand what you were doing."

"You do?"

"It was an irrational act. You were pissed at me, sure, but it wasn't like you could have been thinking you were going to accomplish anything. It sprang from the same place you get your material, you know? The rage, Bones. The blistering rage! I didn't take it personally."

"I appreciate it," he says, turning over Lloyd's analysis in his mind.

"A lot of people are going to be weighing in on you. I want to write something sympathetic. I want to write about the two of us and the business and how the most talented people, the ones who really deserve to succeed, are so often the ones who don't because—"

"I'm brilliant but misunderstood?"

"More or less."

"Do I get a cut?"

"Fifty-fifty. It's not about money for me, Frank. I want to do something good."

This sits in the air between them for a moment, Frank thinking, *Maybe I misread this guy.*

"How are you getting around town?" Lloyd asks.

"Cabs."

"I rented a brand-new Cadillac. You want to drive it?"

So with Lloyd in the passenger seat, Frank drives the two of them back to the diner to get breakfast, and over pancakes and multiple cups of coffee he agrees to let Lloyd be his shadow for his time in Tulsa. In exchange, Lloyd agrees to let Frank read the manuscript before he submits it and also promises to help with whatever creative endeavor next manifests itself; legal briefs excepted.

★   ★   ★

"He can't be in the meeting," Otis says, taking a putter from his golf bag and looking at Lloyd. It's around eleven o'clock in the morning and the November sun warms Otis's office in downtown Tulsa.

"Lloyd, this is confidential, okay?" Frank says.

"Sure," Lloyd replies. He's been looking out the window at a billboard across the street that says REMEMBER WAYMAN.

The walls of the office are covered in Civil War memorabilia and several sepia-tinted photographs of black soldiers. A large sword hangs on one wall above the set of golf clubs from which Otis has removed the putter. Otis presses the button on a tape recorder, then lines up a putt, aiming at a tennis-ball can lying on its side. Frank continues to stand while Lloyd sits silently on the couch, scribbling away in a leather notepad, enjoying his new status as accredited observer.

"Let's get the fat out the way," Otis says. "They pulled your fingerprints off the rental car."

"That's the fat?" Frank asks.

"No biggie. Drivin' without a license. But here comes the gristle. The results of the ballistics test are in. The gun they found in the glove compartment was the one killed Tino." This is a nuclear detonation. Frank takes the news stoically, the inner beast quiescent, exhausted, but Lloyd has to keep from making involuntary noises. Not only has he found himself in the middle of a murder investigation, now he is privy to its internal workings. Frank is on the receiving end of some deeply unpleasant news and Lloyd is observing his reaction from a privileged perch. How will he describe the unfortunate comedian's response? Indifferent? Apathetic? And Otis's manner in delivering the body blow: matter-of-fact? Casual? Cavalier? His luck is a thrilling gift.

"You know they planted it. Christ!" Frank slumps on Otis's desk.

"You play golf?" Otis asks. Casually? Cavalierly?

"No," Frank says. Lloyd resists the urge to say "I do."

"See that sword on the wall?" Otis asks. "Belonged to my great-great-granddaddy. Used it in the Civil War. I laugh when I think of him watching me play golf. Stupid game, chasing a little ball all over a goddamn cow pasture. Good for the image, though. I get my picture in the paper playing golf, I double my price, no one asks why. People say, 'Otis Cain, the famous golf-playing attorney. He's worth the money.' I'd try polo but I don't want anyone seein' me step in horseshit."

Lloyd nearly laughs out loud, struggling to get down all of Otis's words.

"They didn't find your fingerprints on it," Otis continues.

"Why would the cops want to plant a gun?" Lloyd asks, having wrestled his urge to laugh into submission.

Ignoring the question for the moment, Otis hands Frank the putter. "Try it. After I get you off, we'll play in one of those celebrity pro-ams." Then in the voice of a golf announcer, he says, "Now on the fourth green, Frank Bones and Otis Cain."

Frank, to diffuse the tension that has begun to work its way from his neck to his shoulders, lines up a putt. He hits the ball and misses the tennis-ball can by a foot. "Why would they plant the gun?" Frank asks, repeating Lloyd's question.

"You're a perfect patsy. Passing through town, witnesses see you have a fight . . . and baby, you got some résumé. Menacing in Cleveland, resisting arrest and the high-speed chase in Cali . . . Frank, you had a band called Killer Bones and none of that's gonna help."

"It's not like my whole life's been leading up to this moment."

"But it has," Otis tells him. "It has. So you might want to watch your back, 'cause whoever it was smoked Tino . . ."

"What do you mean 'watch my back'?"

"If you get killed while you're under indictment for murder . . . case closed."

Lloyd can't believe he isn't watching a television show.

"What should I do?" Frank asks.

"Lloyd, don't write down what I'm about to say. If I see it in print, I'll kill you in your sleep." When Lloyd nods in assent, Otis says to Frank, "As your attorney, I'd advise you to buy a gun. Oh, and, Frank, do you have a will?"

"No."

Otis slides a document across his desk toward Frank. "This gives me power of attorney in the event of your death."

Frank is more than a little shocked at both Otis's request and the intimation of his own mortality.

"I'm not signing anything."

"Look, Frank," Otis says patiently, "if we're gonna bring this thing to trial, I need you alive. I didn't get lucky with Wayman and I don't want to be unlucky twice."

"Wayman? What do you mean, you didn't get lucky?"

"I was his lawyer. We grew up together. The police killed him."

Lloyd looks at the billboard across the street, REMEMBER WAYMAN. That answers his question.

"Why do you need power of attorney?" Frank asks.

"Have I talked price with you yet?"

"No."

"Well, what do you think? I'm the welfare office? I win with you alive and the publicity is going to be worth more than you could ever pay me. You get killed . . . it's my insurance policy."

"So you would actually profit from my . . . ?"

"You don't trust me, Frank, don't let the door hit your ass on the way out."

Frank signs the document.

"Where are we going?" Lloyd asks from the passenger seat of his rented Cadillac, as Frank drives in light traffic on Highway 244 near the Tulsa State Fairgrounds.

"You got a police record, Lloyd?"

"Not to my knowledge."

"No history of mental illness or psychiatric confinement?"

"I had a crazy aunt in Queens. My mother's sister."

"But not you?"

"As far as mental health? Nothing obvious."

"Clean as a whistle?"

"Fresh as milk."

"You're buying a gun."

"Excuse me?"

"You're going to walk into a sporting goods store, buy a gun, and give it to me. I'll feel a lot safer."

"Frank," Lloyd says, choosing his words carefully, "I can't do that. You've got a couple of felony convictions . . . I could get in very big trouble buying a gun and giving it to you."

Frank hits the brakes and pulls the car to the side of the road, cars shooting past. He stares at Lloyd for a moment before saying, "Get outta the car."

"Bones, this is *my* car. The reason we're riding in it is you don't have one because you're not eligible to rent one because you've got a criminal record."

"Babe, get outta the goddamn car."

"No."

"Fine. We'll sit here." Which they do for a few moments before Frank says, "Lloyd, you're never gonna be real because you won't take risks. You can hang around with me, you can try to write about my world, but you'll never understand anything on a bone level unless you learn to stick your neck out, pal." Frank gives Lloyd a moment to take this in, then continues, "You don't like your life, right? I mean, you told me as much, and when Honey and I went out with the two of you I could see you should have been with someone cooler. How long you married to her?"

"We're in double digits." He says it dully.

"I'm thinking about you that morning at Duke's with the fuckin' fabric samples. That's the life you want, okay. You're at a fork here, man. You want to leave the suburbs behind and step out onto the highway? Now's the time."

Frank watches Lloyd's reaction and sees his expression darken slightly, indicating the armor has been pierced. Lloyd believes what Frank reported to be true, but hearing it spoken aloud simply compounds the wound. "You're gonna be hanging around, right? You heard what Otis said. Someone might want to take a pop at me and knock the case right off the docket. When that guy comes looking, if I'm not packing, I'm dead, Lloyd. And those are usually take-no-prisoner situations, so you gonna make me draw you a picture?"

"What do you mean?"

"You're dead, too."

Every so often a moment comes when a person is forced to make a decision so momentous it could affect him for the rest of his life, stick to him like bad credit. Being asked to buy a gun for a man under indictment for murder fits neatly into this category.

"What if I carried the gun?" Lloyd asks.

"What do you mean *you* carry the gun? Like a bodyguard?" Frank actually laughs out loud. "Babe, I want a bodyguard, I can hire one."

But Lloyd is undeterred. "For an all-access pass, I'll buy the gun. But *I* carry it."

"No dice. I saw you shoot. You couldn't hit the water from a boat."

"I told you I went back to the Gun Club and took a lesson. Don't worry about me," Lloyd says a bit rashly. "I can take care of myself."

Frank waits in the car as Lloyd walks into Chet's Sporting Goods, a large barn of a place near the Oral Roberts University campus in south Tulsa. After a tall Cherokee with a lazy eye does a background check that takes less than five minutes, Lloyd returns to the car with a Beretta 9mm handgun. He settles back into the passenger seat feeling like an old-school gangsta until Frank, who sees the gun jammed into his waistband, says, "Don't blow your dick off." Lloyd wants to say something clever back to Frank, something to put the unlucky comic in his place, but remembers his last performance with a firearm while in Frank's presence and decides it is perhaps best to keep quiet right now. So he smiles tightly.

As Frank pulls out of the parking lot, he answers his ringing cell phone. It's Otis saying, "I got great news."

"They dropped the indictment?" Frank asks, hope swelling his chest like oxygen.

"You're gonna be in *Rolling Stone*! They have a photographer passing through on another story, and they want her to shoot you, but she's on a very tight schedule so you're gonna have to do it tomorrow."

"Rolling Stone?"

"I told you I was working on a few things."

Frank hangs up and turns to Lloyd, saying, "Give me the gun."

"I can't give you the gun, Frank."

"Babe, don't think I'm going to rely on you for protection."

"You don't have a choice," Lloyd says in the noirest tone he can manage, a vocal timbre meant to summon images of neon-lit bars, smoke from a Lucky Strike, and several days gone without shaving.

"Did you remember to buy bullets?"

Five minutes later, Lloyd emerges from Chet's Sporting Goods again, this time fully supplied. He has told the clerk he is protecting someone and then asks if the guy's heard of Frank Bones. The guy has heard of Frank.

The Trade Winds has been overrun by the College Christians, a group of boisterous, clean-cut kids in town for a convention of like-minded youth. They are partying in large Caucasian numbers by the pool below Lloyd's second-story room. With their innocent evening cries echoing in his ears, Lloyd, after recording the day's events in copious detail on his laptop and e-mailing them to Tai Chi, with whom he had made arrangements to print and collate the material, stands in front of the mirror in his room looking at his bad self in profile. He wears cream linen pants purchased the day of his shopping spree with the shiny-faced Kevin, a dark blue T-shirt, and a loose-fitting, summer-weight sport coat whose billowing cottony folds perfectly conceal the Beretta, which is resting comfortably in his newly purchased shoulder holster. On the desk next to Lloyd's open laptop is an open bottle of Cuervo Gold from which Lloyd has been swigging.

332

The son of Estelle and Bernie, husband of Stacy and father of Dustin, denizen of Brentwood and the Lynx Network, ten-year member of the Writers Guild of America West, tries out a series of facial expressions. First comes the silently sneering *Can I help you?* followed by a condescending *Sorry, but for a second I thought you wanted to fuck with me.* This is then replaced by the supremely confident *Keep walking,* accented by a slight upward tilt of the head indicating the direction in which the carbuncle should move if he doesn't want Lloyd to unload a world of trouble upon him. Lloyd then reaches for the gun, rips it out of the holster, pivots, gripping the handle with both hands, and imagines himself ending the miserable life of whatever poor bastard has been hassling him. He finds it satisfying to hold a gun now, away from the judging eyes that beheld him on the range back in Los Angeles. The piece comes out of the holster again and again as Lloyd repeats the movement, as if memorizing a dance step: dip, lift, pivot, grip, point; dip, lift, pivot, grip, point. Lloyd could be back in L.A. now, standing on a soundstage addressing whether Jacy Pingree's top reveals enough cleavage to keep Harvey Gornish tumescent, but instead he is here in Tulsa, learning to pull a gun out of a shoulder holster and cogitating on how to describe the feeling some way other than *it's dead good.*

Mercy spends the night in Frank's room at the Trade Winds, and over the course of making love four times to the ever-decreasing background clamor of the cavorting College Christians, she tells Frank her life story, which goes like this: Her family were Kentucky hill people who came to Oklahoma to work in the oil fields in the 1940s. Her mother, also named Mercy, was one of twelve kids. Her father, a luckless petty criminal named Tom, married her mother because she was pregnant, although not by him, and a judge gave him a choice of marriage or jail. When Frank asks her if she knew who her real father was, she glibly says, "Some tickpicker named Marvin," and then loudly laughs in a way intended to convey she dealt with that shit a long time ago.

Mother Mercy ditched her when she was three and headed down to

Panama with the second of four husbands. When Frank asks her whom she was left with, she tells him, simply, she was sold to a Tulsa couple, a preacher and his wife. Her new father had a taste for pornography and read a lot of sex novels, which he would carelessly leave lying around the house. She liked to read, and when there was nothing else around, she would pick them up and flip through them herself. This provided an unusual educational environment for a prepubescent girl. One day, the local bookmobile was parked out front and Mercy hopped on. A title caught her eye: *Of Human Bondage*. Believing it to be a sex novel, she picked it off the shelf, brought it home, and read it. She tells Frank the words of Somerset Maugham changed her forever, and tonight Frank is falling in love with her and her crazy life. After the story they make love one more time and Frank sleeps well for the first time in days.

Early in the morning, Lloyd drives them to the studios of WKNS, a local television station where Frank is going to sit alone in a studio and do the *AM America* interview with Patty Sullivan, who will be ensconced behind her desk in New York. Lloyd, who has parked the gun in the trunk of his car, watches from behind a pair of recently purchased Ray-Ban sunglasses as Frank sweeps into the station with Mercy at his side, shaking hands and signing autographs. In the studio a technician attaches a lavalier microphone to Frank's lapel. Frank motions for Mercy to stand next to the monitor, and she obediently slides over while Lloyd settles himself at the side of the studio, writing furiously in his notebook.

At 8:32 A.M. Patty Sullivan, whose seriousness of purpose is continually upstaged by her pageboy haircut, endless legs, and a perky smile that won't stay down, announces, "They call him the comedians' comedian, but now the state of Oklahoma calls him a killer. Frank Bones is with us today, live, to tell us his side of the story . . ."

The red light on the camera facing Frank illuminates and he smiles easily. "Good morning, Patty," he says, looking at Mercy, who smiles back.

"How're you feeling today, Frank?"

"I don't usually do the breakfast shows so now I'm a cereal killer,"

Frank banters as his interlocutor's hand flies to her mouth choking back a laugh, no slouch at grokking the shtick, Patty a Georgetown University graduate and former White House correspondent, "which is actually something that would work better in print since it's cereal with a *c* for the viewers staring at your million-dollar gams instead of hanging on my every ejaculation, and by *ejaculation* I mean the verbal kind with the words."

Mercy is enjoying herself greatly as Patty giggles in appreciation of Frank's double anatomical reference and says, "So you're comfortable joking about it?"

"Hey, I'm not O.J., I'm a comedian. If I didn't joke about it, I'd look guilty."

For the next two minutes and thirty seconds he is allotted, Frank is so charming and entertaining, the viewing audience could be forgiven for thinking he was there to promote a new television show rather than assert his innocence of a capital crime, and at the end of the interview he tells Patty he'll be happy to come back on the show when he is acquitted and tell her all about how he got off, still making with the double entendres. The red light vanishes, indicating Frank is no longer on camera, and after the soundman removes the lavalier, Frank walks up to Mercy and kisses her on the mouth as Lloyd writes it all down.

Then Lloyd drives them to the police station so Mercy can pay her parking tickets. Frank, having had enough of the police lately, waits in the car while Lloyd accompanies Mercy inside. In their morning together she had casually mentioned the amount in her checking account did not begin to cover what she owed the city of Tulsa for parking violations, and Lloyd, eager to be helpful, has offered to give her the money. She takes it reluctantly and only after insisting he understands it's a loan. While Lloyd was off getting a drink of water at the television station, Mercy mentioned his generosity to Frank and this served to soften Frank's stance toward him.

★   ★   ★

"What do you think?" Robert Hyler says to Jolly De Meo. The two men are seated on a white leather sofa in Jolly's office where they have just finished watching a tape of Frank's performance on *AM America*.

"Guy's a complete *gavone*," Jolly says, employing the word Italians use to describe their low-rent brethren, never mind Frank isn't Italian. Jolly would have preferred Robert drop Frank long ago.

"Come on, man. Give him a break. He's not crazy." Robert considers what he's just said and continues, "Okay, maybe he is crazy. But I don't think he could kill anyone."

"I don't know how a guy in his situation can look so relaxed, like he had a Valium enema or something," Jolly observes. "If he was that good in *Kirkuk,* Harvey would have picked up the show."

"Frank's a very charismatic guy," Robert remarks, his mind now elsewhere. He's thinking of how Frank summarily rejected the services of the high-powered lawyer Nada had arranged for him. Did this indicate a crack in his loyalty to the company? He had rarely questioned a decision of Robert's before, and never before had Robert made a decision with such far-reaching implications. If Frank didn't trust his judgment any longer . . .

"How's his CD doing?" Jolly asks, stroking his beard contemplatively.

"Sales tripled since the indictment."

Tessa sticks her head in the door, interrupting their discussion. "Quentin Tarantino is on the phone. It's about Frank."

"Relax, Frank."

"If I was any more relaxed, we'd be dancing," he says to Jane Lee, the *Rolling Stone* photographer. Frank stands against a white backdrop in a rented studio in the warehouse district of Tulsa as this itinerant chronicler of contempo cool points a Nikon with a lens the size of a cucumber at him and snaps viciously. Jane is dressed head to toe in black, her spiked hair chopped short. Between shots, Hiro, the young, male Japanese assistant, flutters around behind her adjusting the silver umbrella-like reflector they've set up, Frank tricky to light since he's wearing the traditional all-black as well, and if not photographed correctly it will appear as if he's clad in a finger-painted charcoal glob. Seated in adjacent folding chairs off to the side are Otis and the newly strapped Lloyd, who has actually produced more sperm cells in the past twenty-four hours than he has in the last week.

"This might go on the cover, so make it good," Jane says. "Give me something . . . I don't know . . . show me some killer."

Frank is a little surprised by the directness of her request but wants to be game, so he tries to subtly coax his features into something suggestive of sexy homicide, feeling not a little absurd at doing so.

"Yeah, yeah, that's right, good," Jane says, her Nikon spraying shots like a drive-by.

Lloyd is watching the two of them, committing every detail of their interaction to memory and feeling the weight of his gun against the side of his chest. Actually, to say Lloyd was simply *feeling* the weight would be understating things. More accurately, he is savoring it, relishing it, delighting in the sense of indescribable heft the weapon provides his battered psyche. The man whose wife had given away his entire wardrobe against his will, and who could only respond by leaving the house in a fit of inarticulate pique, now sits confidently with a piece of death-delivering metal nestled against the curve of his lean chest. Liberated from Los Angeles with its constraints and expectations, he doesn't feel at all ridiculous about it.

After tossing off fifty exposures, Jane stops suddenly and turns to Hiro. "Could you touch up his hair?"

Hiro pulls out a brush and gently coifs the alleged killer as Otis asks, "How much do you charge for a shoot?"

Looking up from her camera where she has been adjusting a setting, Jane fixes him with a bemused gaze. "This is free," she says. "The magazine pays."

Otis, equally bemused, responds, "No, no, no, baby. I mean for me."

★   ★   ★

That night at the Trade Winds Motel, Frank and Mercy are slow-dancing to a Lucinda Williams CD she bought for him earlier in the day. They're each holding glasses of Jack Daniel's, the bottle in Frank's hand for convenient refills. Frank kisses her, then puts his glass and bottle down on the dresser. Taking Mercy's glass, he puts it next to his. Then he pushes her down on the bed. She lies on her back and puts her hands behind her head, and Frank unzips her jeans and pulls them down over her ankles, tossing them to the floor. He removes her white cotton thong and places a hand beneath the small of her back. Leaning over, he slips his tongue between her legs, and as she groans with fresh pleasure, he quickly brings her to orgasm. Grabbing her by the hips, he turns her over. She pushes herself onto her elbows and knees, and Frank enters her from behind. As he is making love to her, his face buried between her soft hair and lightly freckled shoulder, he realizes he wants her to come to Mexico, to live with him down there, make some kind of new life. His orgasm arrives in shuddering spurts, and pressing hard against her pelvic bone one last time, he heaves off her, lying on his back. Mercy rolls over on her side, facing him. They stare into each other's eyes, and Frank, his mind clearing, knows it's a ridiculous idea. Despite this, he says, "I could love you."

"You better not," she murmurs. "I'm not the sentimental type," and he inches further in that direction.

Mercy watches Frank getting dressed as she climbs back into her own clothes. She's doing what she swore she wouldn't do with this guy. Reaching into the pocket of her jeans, Mercy pulls out the knife she was waving at Tino when Frank walked into her life. She flicks it open and he doesn't speak or flinch when she lightly traces the blade from his groin to his stomach, past his nipple, over his chest, and to his throat. She rests it there, says, "I want you to have this." Then she closes it with a snap of her wrist and hands it to him.

"You *are* sentimental." Accepting the offering, the onyx handle, the pearl inlay. "It's a wonderful knife," he says, and the ghost of Frank Capra feels it slipping through his ribs.

"Think of me whenever you stick it in someone," she says.

He knows he'll miss this woman more than the rest of them put together.

While this is going on, Lloyd stands in his room holding a bottle of tequila and yelling into his cell phone, "Because I don't know when I'm coming back, okay? That's why!" He is communicating with Stacy for the first time since he'd left Los Angeles three days earlier and he is distracted by the College Christians, who have once again colonized the pool area and are having a party featuring a plethora of young, lithe, unpierced bodies and barrels of soda. Someone has set up a boom box and the sound of Christian rap floods the area, bouncing hard off the poolside concrete and into Lloyd's open window.

Ordinarily, when he was on the road, he and Stacy would talk several times a day and their conversations would essentially be a competition as to who was suffering more. If he said he had had a bad day because he'd missed a plane connection and had to sit for five hours in the Minneapolis airport, she would say, "*You're* having a bad day? Let me tell you about the day *I'm* having," and regale him with the story of how their son had had a meltdown that began in the frozen foods section of Gelson's Supermarket and lasted a full hour, causing her to miss her appointment with the manicurist, and now she thought there was a gas leak in the house. "So don't tell me about *your* bad day." That is how their conversations usually went. This conversation is not going like that.

Tonight, when Stacy says, "So I'm just supposed to wait here while you pal around with the guy who destroyed our house?" Lloyd's response is "No, you don't have to wait around. Get a facial, get your legs waxed; plan a benefit with Daryl. I don't really care what you do." He says this walking around the room and periodically looking at himself in the mirror, his jacket off, the gun in the shoulder holster. He takes another swig from the bottle. He would have said the same things to Stacy even if he had not been drunk. Being drunk simply allows him to enjoy saying them.

339

"Lloyd . . ." is all Stacy can manage at this point, unaccustomed to full-frontal hostility, so deft had he become at concealing it. The great reserves of antagonism Lloyd had accrued while married to Stacy remained in storage largely due to his fear of her own withering anger. He would inwardly cringe at the thought of her simmering rage being unleashed and so took great pains not to provoke it. But the idea of Stacy is receding now, along with the *Happy Endings* experience and the rest of his Los Angeles life, so the sting of her nettles, particularly at a distance of over a thousand miles, has dissipated and is unable to produce its former effect. Stacy senses this and, realizing she will get a lot more in the divorce if Lloyd returns home and serves out the rest of his contract, modulates her tone. "Everyone at Lynx has been calling you. Harvey Gornish, Pam Penner . . . Bart Pimento called here, Lloyd." She's trying to plead without sounding as if she's pleading.

"Okay."

"*Okay?* All you're going to say is *okay?*"

"What I really want to say is, they can all go fuck themselves, but that would be gratuitous."

Outside the room the loud report of a string of firecrackers sounds *pop pop pop pop pop.*

"Lloyd! What is that, gunfire there?"

"Some college kids are having a party. Those are firecrackers."

"It sounds like you're in a battle zone. Listen, it's not okay, what you're doing."

"What else do you want me to say?"

"You walked off your own show. It's very bad. Your lawyer called and he says Lynx is going to sue you, so it's not really okay at all." Realizing this sounds judgmental rather than seductive, she adjusts her approach. "You have to get back to L.A. and apologize to everyone." Another *pop pop pop pop pop* of firecrackers fills the background. "It sounds like those kids are in your room."

"You think I'm going to crawl into Lynx on my hands and knees and beg them to let me back? They're replacing Dede Green with Honey Call!"

"So what?"

"You hate her! You said she was no better than a hooker!"

"Our mortgage is eight thousand dollars a month, Lloyd!"

"They're not letting me do my show!"

Stacy finds it unbearable now that Lloyd has started to climb on the art horse. It is with the greatest concentration that she remains calm and intones, "You signed a contract. You can write your book when it's over. Right now you have to come home and get back to work, hon." It kills her to call him hon and she grits her teeth while doing it, but she knows if she is to lure him back, it will take Circean wiles.

"I'm not gonna do that."

"Oh, yes, you are!" That comes out wrong. She realizes this and follows it up with a shrill "We really miss you!" which does not fool him for a second.

"I'll come home when I'm done."

"And that's going to be when?"

"I'll let you know." He snaps the phone shut, jamming it in his pocket without saying good-bye and, inwardly lamenting the years he has spent married to his wife, feels his body temperature rising to an unacceptable level. Stacy could do that to him. There were times Lloyd was convinced being married to her was literally killing him, and when he experienced that, it incensed him further, the whole dynamic a nasty circle.

Since Lloyd arrived in Tulsa he has been looking for ways to connect with Frank and appear to the other man as something more than an opportunistic hanger-on with literary pretensions. It is important to Lloyd's endeavor that Frank view him as a peer in a personal way, Lloyd calculates, since then Frank will be more inclined to reveal aspects of his inner self. Sensing he can use his recent discussion with Stacy as a way to connect on a primal male level, Lloyd decides to share the story while it's still popping fresh. He knows his ire is great comedic fuel, and he's never more amusing than when genuinely pissed off about something. If Frank is in his room, Lloyd is confident he will be able to work himself into an aggrieved lather the comedian will find highly entertaining. Getting Frank to laugh would be a great victory and allow Lloyd to further insinuate himself into the life of the other man. Now, he is feeling at once elated and agitated. He goes into the bathroom and grabs the bottle of Paxil sitting on the sink. *Shit! Only one left.* He takes it, chasing the pill with chemically overloaded tap water, and makes a mental note to get the scrip refilled tomorrow.

Hastily pulling on his jacket, Lloyd walks down to Frank's room accompanied by the cacophonous sounds of the firecrackers, which uncannily reflect his own troubled interior landscape. He has finally succeeded in fully objectifying Stacy, now more a source of material than a spouse. Like his emotions, his wife has become important primarily for her comedic value.

The door to Frank's room is caught in the jamb and is not closed entirely, so Lloyd assumes no sex is taking place and he is free to cross the threshold. Ordinarily, he would knock and wait, but eager to do his material and wanting to make an entrance, Lloyd knocks and doesn't wait, pushing the door open.

He is immediately confronted with an alarming sight.

Frank is kneeling on the floor of the motel room with the barrel of a revolver in his mouth. Clay Porter stands in front of him holding the gun. Both of them look at Lloyd, and of the three men now in the room it is a toss-up as to who is most surprised.

Two minutes earlier, Mercy had just gone to the bathroom. Frank was lying on his bed watching the Shopping Channel when there was a knock at the door. "Come in," he said, having had four shots of Jack Daniel's, his normal level of paranoia lower than it should have been. Clay Porter stepped into the room, closed the door behind him, not noticing when it caught in the jamb and didn't close all the way.

"Hi, Frank," he said blandly. "Nice to see you."

342

Frank looked at Clay with unconcealed disdain and said, "Didn't I scrape you off my shoe yesterday?"

"Get up from the bed, please. I'm gonna have to frisk you." Cool, didn't want to get into a snapping contest with Frank.

Frank hesitated, looked toward the bathroom, where Mercy had gone to take a leak. "Don't you need a search warrant to be here?"

"This is just a friendly visit. Tell you the truth, I'm not sure it was you . . . I think we may have moved too quickly. The wife said Mercy pulls a knife on Tino the day he croaked, and Mercy told us the wife and him were going at it like cobras the same day . . . Come on, just let me pat you down."

Frank thought about what Clay was saying. Could these things be true? Were the police about to move their investigation into another area and deliver him from the purgatory in which he'd been living? He inwardly cursed Robert, whose tender mercies had sent him on this ill-starred comeback, and shifted his weight, buying time. Then, he rose from the bed and glanced at Clay, now what? With an upward tilt of his chin, Clay indicated Frank should put his arms against the wall, but Frank wasn't looking at him any longer so Clay had to say, "Assume the position," which Frank did. He wanted this encounter to be a bad memory as quickly as possible. Clay patted him down and said, "Sorry, just a precaution." Now Frank turned to face him. His slack features radiated a strange brew of hope and contempt. "We're looking for a videotape and we think your friend Mercy might be holding it. Now you talk to her and get us this tape, and I'm gonna pretend you didn't buy a gun this afternoon."

"I don't know what you're talking about."

The firecrackers banged away in the background, *pop pop pop pop pop*.

"You're sitting in a car when Lloyd Melnick comes into Chet's Sporting Goods over by Oral Roberts and buys a Beretta. We ran Melnick, Frank. He's some kind of Hollywood asshole, probably can't find his dick with his hand."

"What do you mean you *ran* him? Guy's got no record."

"I Googled the guy, Frank."

"You Googled Lloyd? That's what you've been doing? Googling?" Frank had to strain to keep from laughing.

"Never mind how I spend my time. We know who the gun was for and we want to talk to your friend Mercy about that videotape."

"I don't know anything about a videotape."

"I want you to talk to her and find out where she's got it."

"Why don't you Google her? Maybe the information's on the net."

"You think this is funny?"

"Why would she tell me?"

"A gun's a serious thing, Frank." As if to underscore this point, Clay removed his own police-issue sidearm from its holster and looked at it. "Guy like you, two-time loser . . . don't think this isn't going to interest the judge at the trial." Clay noticed Frank had looked away again and, suddenly, without warning, smashed the gun into the side of his head and sent him sprawling to the floor. Frank's hands went up in a belated and useless effort at protection. "I ain't here to have a discussion," Clay said as he stood over him. "If you don't get it, you can go back to jail until your trial."

"I'm not going back to jail" came from the quivering heap on the floor.

"Then please pick up the phone and call her."

Frank rose unsteadily to his feet. The pain on the side of his skull was acute, but the alcohol made it more bearable than it would otherwise be. He realized it was not inconceivable he could be beaten to death in this motel room. Frank looked at Clay and said, "No."

Clay whipped a punch into Frank's face that snapped his head back and caused him to fall once again to the floor, where he noticed the metallic taste of blood in his mouth.

"Want another love tap?" Clay thought he was being clever.

Frank got up to his knees and through bloody lips told him, "Blow me, as Noël Coward said in another context." The room not being up to his level never something that stopped Frank.

Clay Porter's response to this mid-twentieth-century theatrical reference was to shove the barrel of the gun into the kneeling man's mouth. He said, "Think about it. I got all night."

This is the tableau Lloyd beheld when he opened the door prepared to regale Frank with some fresh material about his crumbling marriage.

Now he stands there, his eyes and mouth widening, tequila tamping his fear and allowing the irritation he's feeling to intensify at the sight of Frank's victimization. Clay removes the gun from Frank's mouth and says, "Well, well, well, Mr. Melnick," which freaks Lloyd completely, since he has no idea how this guy, this armed thug, whoever he is, knows his name. "Come on in!" the man tells him with a feral smile. Lloyd hesitates a moment, thinks about backing out, but knows if he does, the all-access pass to Frank is revoked in perpetuity with no hope for appeal. Hesitating only long enough to draw a shallow breath, he steps into the room, closing the door behind him. Lloyd watches Clay contemplate the next move. He feels the weight of his gun in the holster, his jacket open. "So you bought a gun for Mr. Bones here. You could be in a lot of trouble, son."

"Why don't you go home, Clay?" This from Mercy, who has stepped out of the bathroom. Clay's head swivels to get a look at the latest arrival. "There's nothin' you want here," Mercy says.

"I want you, girl," Clay says, still affecting the cool.

"Drop the gun." Now Lloyd is pointing the Beretta at Clay, holding it with two hands and trying to keep them from shaking, the tequila running through his veins, his mouth cotton, still wondering, *Who the hell is this guy?*

Clay smiles at Lloyd, completely in charge of the situation. "Don't do that, son, it's a bad idea. Put down the weapon." Clay slowly turns from Frank and Mercy and walks toward the panicking Lloyd, whose twitchy response to this ratcheting up of the tension level causes a spasmodic tightening of his muscles that leads to the unfortunate result of the gun discharging, the blast deafening in the small room. Clay looks considerably surprised when the bullet from Lloyd's gun rips into his chest with a force that knocks him to the floor. The sound of the gunshot is immediately followed, a call and response written in gunpowder, by another round of *pop pop pop pop pop* celebratory firecrackers detonating at poolside.

Chapter 16

Lloyd's left leg begins to shake uncontrollably, and it is this sensation he is most aware of when Frank's dead-calm voice intrudes on the silence that has enveloped the shrinking room in the wake of the gunshot.

"I think it's time to go."

The three of them look down at the prostrate Clay, whose eyes are rolling back in his head in a way that does not portend good news for anyone. Mercy grabs the gun from his now open palm and quickly checks the load. Safe to say, if the currently recumbent Clay had pulled the trigger a moment ago, he would have blown off the back of Frank's head.

"It was self-defense," Lloyd says, trying the thought on for size. Looking at the trembling man on the floor, he is fleetingly reminded of how he feels when he utters something particularly hurtful or insensitive and wants to retract the words as soon as they're out of his mouth, that sensation one has of sliding down a muddy hill unable to stop the inexorable descent toward a sticky and unavoidable end. Alas, bullets, unlike words, cannot be retracted. Shooting someone cleaves to the neurotic perpetrator like bad reviews, which is why someone like Lloyd, a ditherer in far less charged circumstances, should never carry a firearm. "Should we call the cops?" Lloyd hears himself say.

"He is the cops," Mercy informs him. "A detective."

This fact smacks Lloyd in the face and a weak "Oh, God . . . " gurgles up from the depths of his throat. It's all he can manage upon being apprised of the exact nature of his current situation, the Paxil powerless against this kind of reality.

★　　★　　★

None of the College Christians look up from their uncorrupted revels as the three Children of Mammon quietly leave the room, walk along the balcony unmolested, and disappear into the stairwell that delivers them to the parking lot and the safety of Mercy's car, the one determined to be least likely to attract unwanted attention.

Mercy's in the driver's seat, Frank's in the passenger seat, and Lloyd's squeezed in back. She starts the engine, then says, "Where are we going?"

"Dinner and a movie?" This from Frank, to Lloyd's amazement, the man shticking in the tempest.

"Oh God, oh God, oh God, oh God, oh God, oh God" emanates from the churning vortex into which the creator of *Happy Endings* has been sucked. It is mumbled like an incantation and marks the totality of Lloyd's contribution to the conversation up to this point.

"Frank?" Mercy's voice intrudes on Lloyd's cataleptic daze. "What are we gonna do?" The car is still idling. They haven't moved from the parking lot. Firecrackers can be heard through the open windows.

"We're going to Mexico," Frank says.

"Do you have any money on you?"

"About nine bucks."

"That's more than seven million pesos. We're in clover."

"Are you gonna come?"

"Hell, yeah."

"You don't have to. You can just lend us your car. If we get caught, I'll say we stole it."

"I wanna come."

"Mexico?" Lloyd inquires, snapping out of it. "Is the cavalry chasing us? We're making a mad dash for the border? What are we, Butch and Sundance? Who goes to Mexico anymore?"

"If you got a better idea, let's hear it," Frank says.

At the moment, Lloyd does not have a better idea, which deflates him. Looking out the car window as they leave the parking lot, he sees streetlights, fast-food franchises, service stations feeding lines of big gas-guzzling American cars with their lurid colors, reds, blues, yellows, greens, purples, oranges, on down the unnatural rainbow softened by the late hour but still vivid in the night, and has the thought that this could be the last time he sees any of this. For all of his caterwauling about the degree to which he is not savoring his existence, it is not a thought he finds himself embracing.

The back door of Club Louie opens and a hard beam of light illuminates the interior of a hallway. Mercy is holding a flashlight and steps quietly into the club, followed by Frank, who has taken the gun, and Lloyd, who has no desire to be left in the parking lot with his morbid thoughts. The guys, Frank on a bold new adventure and Lloyd trying to keep from imploding, flow in Mercy's wake as she leads them to the bar area, saying in a whisper, "Tino's wife was always bugging him about money so he used to give me envelopes full of cash to hide."

"How come you didn't split to Vegas and book yourself into a suite at Caesars with a male escort?" Frank asks.

"Because I'm an honorable person," she replies, kneeling behind the bar and pulling up a floorboard.

Lloyd peers around the bar, remembering his first night here, seeing Frank's act, making notes for his book. His book! The ludicrous memory of his aspirations! The cloak of innocence and naïveté that has led him to this terrible moment has now completely unraveled and blown away, leaving him to face his true self, naked, blanching at what he sees.

Frank's helping himself to a bottle of whiskey, saying, "You know, when I'm about to be indicted as an accessory to murder, I like to take a nip. Lloyd?" Frank extends the bottle to Lloyd, who can only shake his head mutely, ruminating on how his life could possibly have reached this juncture. Mercy pulls a manila envelope, the one Tino had given her the day Frank arrived, out from under the floor along with a handgun. She jams the gun in her belt with an ease that indicates she's put that kind of hardware in this particular place before. Holding the flashlight in her armpit, she aims it at the envelope, which she tears open with both hands, then pulls out the videotape Clay Porter died for, showing it to Frank.

"Where's the money?" he asks.

"All's that's here is this tape."

An hour later, most of which has been spent in silence, Frank, Mercy, and Lloyd are passing through Bristow on I-44 headed for Oklahoma City. Once there, the plan is to sprint due south on I-35 for Mexico, rather than drive in the direction of Frank's house on the Pacific coast, the thinking being just get the hell over the border as quickly as possible. Frank looks back at Lloyd, saying, "I like how you brought it back there."

"Where?"

"The way you smoked that guy, Lloyd. Mothafucka had a gun barrel kissing my tonsils, coulda taken me out right then, but my man Lloyd . . ." He says *my man Lloyd* with the blaccent he uses when intending to convey singular approbation and continues in the same vein, liking those three words so much he repeats them. "My man Lloyd smoked the mothafucka! Wouldn'ta guessed ya had it in ya, but, dang, you dropped his ass like a sack of potatoes!" which comes out like *pah-tay-tuhs*. Now Frank reaches toward his new hero in the backseat with his fist, offering it to be tapped in the current universal sign of hipster solidarity. Lloyd says nothing and halfheartedly reciprocates.

I shot a cop and he's acting like I just won a People's Choice Award, congratulating me! Frank is giving me the Black Man Fist Tap because I accidentally—and please let me stress that word accidentally, please!—I shot someone, a cop no less. I don't care that he was acting like maybe he's had one or two civilian complaints filed against him. Is this the functional definition of irony? Am I being consumed by an irony so grand it will literally kill me? For days, no— months—months? Who am I kidding—years! Yes, years—I have craved the approval of the Bones, this sociopathic miscreant, who I glorified in some adolescent way, as if I were fifteen years old, zit-faced and stupid and didn't know any better, and now that I've shot someone I've earned it? What kind of cosmic joke is being played on me? I've just sailed off the edge of the world at a terrible velocity with someone who inhabits an alternate universe, and I have no idea how I can possibly get back on solid ground. Would death be a relief right now? I may need to think about it. I can't think like that. I have to get to Mexico; Mexico's a good idea. I'll get some clarity down there. It was an accident. I didn't mean to pull the trigger. The man had a gun in Frank's mouth. Who puts a gun in a person's mouth? I didn't know he was a cop. For all I knew it was some kind of shakedown. Why couldn't I have stayed on the phone with Stacy? The only time in my life I cut one of our phone conversations short when I'm out of town and I walk into someone else's bad dream with a loaded gun. I'd let her yell at me for a thousand years if it would get me out of this disaster. I wonder if an insanity defense will fly? I'm out of Paxil. I took my last Paxil right before I shot that guy. That should count for something, along with the tequila. A good lawyer, a five-hundred-dollar-an-hour guy, should be able to make something out of a tequila and drug combination. I want to see my kid. Maybe I should turn myself in. No, that's a bad idea. I shot the sheriff. But I did not shoot the deputy, no, no, no. Stop it! Stop it! What are Bob Marley's lyrics doing here? I want to be back in Jamaica. I wonder if Dustin would like it there? Maybe we could . . .

While Lloyd's mind is whirring, fracturing his thoughts like some kind of demented Cuisinart, Frank looks over at Mercy, who's driving.

"You didn't shoot him, did you?"

"Who?"

"Tino."

Lloyd glances toward the front seat from between spread fingers, roused from his downward spiral by this exchange. He's trying to unravel the puzzle of recent events, using Frank's situation as an anchor for his own free-floating anxiety. He didn't believe Frank had done Tino; despite his violent history, a killing didn't fit. But Mercy? He hadn't even considered the possibility. Trying to sort this out would give him a break from his own miserable projections.

"Damn, are you outta your mind?"

"You were waving a knife at the guy when we met," Frank points out.

"I'm not the one with the colorful rap sheet, Frank. I didn't pull a gun onstage or drive a Hummer into Lloyd's living room after a high-speed police chase. I'm not the one Tino pulled a gun on that night and the cops didn't find a weapon in a car I was driving. If anyone should be suspicious . . ."

"You think I did it?"

"Hell, no! But jeez Louise, give me a break, all right? I didn't shoot him!" When this is met with silence, she says, "Look, Frank, I'll get out of the car right now if you don't trust me. No one's gonna be looking for me anyway. They're gonna be looking for Frank Bones. So you and Lloyd can take the car and—"

At this, Lloyd leans forward and places his hands on their shoulders. "Mom? Dad? No fighting. It upsets me."

"I mean, what the hell's the matter with you?" she asks, ignoring Lloyd, who is impressively masking his perfervid mental condition. "I got the milk of human kindness running in my heart and you're treating me like I'm a suspect. It's like you've never seen someone who's true."

Frank thinks about this a moment and quickly realizes she's right. He hasn't seen someone who's true. Lloyd is now true, of course, since he's shot a cop on Frank's behalf. But he correctly assumes Mercy is talking about women. He looks at her, chastened. "I'm sorry" is all he can manage, but from the slight smile she gives him he knows it's not bad. Sensing an opening, he says, "I'm a little upset is all. I didn't move to New York City when I was a kid so I could die in Texas. The idea was *not* to die in Texas."

Touching his arm, Mercy says, "You won't."

Lloyd, for his part, is not so sure as the car rolls south through the increasingly black night, toward Texas, toward Mexico, toward . . .

Mercy's car is flying down I-35 south of Waco as dawn creeps in on bobcat feet. Mercy is driving, Frank in the passenger seat in a fitful sleep. Lloyd has been wide-awake all night ruminating on how he has arrived at this point. If his sojourn in Tulsa was a way to put distance between Stacy and himself, it has worked far better than anticipated. Lloyd had not simply left his wife and son but left his life entirely. What had been a quiet suburban existence marked by children's birthday parties, backyard barbecues, preschool fund-raisers, lunches with guy friends where they would complain about their wives and their work, dinners with couples, the conversations focusing on kids, vacations, and real estate, long days at work ending in silent evenings of desperate contemplation; in one brief moment, all that had become a hellish plunge into a bottomless pit. If they are caught, Lloyd realizes, his life is effectively over. The bullet in Clay has his name on it, and Lloyd knows he does not possess the tools to evade the highly motivated police dragnet that ensues whenever an agent of social control buys it in the line of duty. He will certainly be apprehended in short order, and after a quick trial during which he will spend a gigantic sum of money on a phalanx of well-known lawyers, the best he can reasonably hope for is life in prison. No one will care that he gave generously to charity; that he is a respected professional in an important industry will carry no weight; that he tried to be a good husband and father will mean nothing. All that will matter is the terrible crime he committed.

Life. In. Prison.

Prison clothes, prison food, and worst of all, other prisoners. Lloyd can only imagine the murderous dregs, the scum, the malodorous human flotsam with whom he would be consigned to spend the reminder of his years on earth doing penance for a crime he had never intended to commit. He thinks about his purchasing the gun, his ridiculous posing in front of the motel-room mirror, his deeply unfortunate decision to remove it from its holster, and he sinks further into his seat. However evil Clay Porter was, he was still a cop, Lloyd had shot him, and if he was caught, he was going to pay—unless they made it to Mexico. And yet . . .

What am I supposed to do in Mexico? Work on my tan? Don't know anyone, can't speak the language. The tourist areas are out. That's where they'll be looking for me. Is it possible to eke out some kind of marginal existence doing menial work? Yeah, that's a good plan. Dig ditches. My back would go out the first day. So how am I supposed to eat? The food's no good anyway. I can't live on it. The food in

Oklahoma was bad enough. I think I'm getting nauseous. Probably just nerves. Nerves and a parasite. Won't be able to contact Stacy. Can't trust her. Can't see Dustin. If I try to reach him, I could be traced and they could catch me. I'll never be able to stop running, a gringo nowhere-man lost in some vast, violent Catholic country I'll never begin to understand.

What if I get sick? It's not really an if proposition, more of a when. They have diseases down there no one's even heard of. Flesh-eating, intestine-ingesting, brain-devouring microbes that will do unspeakable things to my organism while I'm still alive! I'll die slowly, racked with pain, chills, fever, vomiting, shitting, befouling myself, guts turned inside out and no one to help me, everyone I know thousands of miles away.

Still, that's better than prison.

Do I even want to go back? What's there for me anyway? What was it Phil Sheldon said the last time I saw him? It's all a shiny penny. I can't breathe. I feel my chest constricting.

Paxil!

I need to take my Paxil right now. I can't handle this level of anxiety. But I took the last one! Now I don't have any. How can I get it in Mexico? Can I find a doctor to write me a scrip without telling him who I am? Do they even have it down there?

Look at Frank. Sleeping like he's on vacation. Guy's got a beach house, probably people to send him money. And Mercy, driving. They're outlaws. I'm not an outlaw. I'll be the guy who pointlessly pissed it all away, one more self-important hack deluded enough to think he was destined for something more, another putz who gazed at the moon and tumbled into the gutter.

Around seven-thirty that morning they're at the Quik Stop in Mingo somewhere in the wasteland northeast of Austin. The fugitives have determined that for the time being Mercy is the least likely to be identified, so she has been selected to go into the convenience store and cater the getaway. They've been driving all night, first Mercy, then Lloyd, Frank, the most recognizable of the bunch, deciding on the off chance they're pulled over his face shouldn't be the first one the cop sees.

A souped-up blue Chrysler with a FOR SALE sign in the window is parked nearby. Lloyd's pumping gas when he sees the clerk, a kid, maybe twenty, grease-stained jeans and a T-shirt that says DEATH BY METAL, following Mercy out of the store, and he asks him, "You want to sell that car?"

Frank's walking back from the bathroom and the kid, noticing him before he can quote a price, says, "You're Frank Bones!"

"I get that all the time." Easy, not skipping a beat.

"Hey, I seen you on TV. I know it's you," the kid says, looking around, as if someone might be listening in the dry vastness. "It's cool. I ain't telling no one." The kid eyes Frank appreciatively, unaccustomed to having celebrities, much less fugitive ones, at his Quik Stop. "Dude, you're in some serious shit! Are you going to Mexico?"

Mercy and Lloyd are nervously watching this exchange. They've been traveling in darkness most of the ride, and now, after less than an hour of daylight, someone has already identified Frank, Lloyd thinking, *We might as well be in Pasadena.*

"Why do you say that?" Frank asks the kid, genuinely curious.

"You're on the run. Where else would you go?"

"Canada, babe."

"Well, you better head to the bathroom first."

"I just went."

"Dude, I mean to hide. There's a state trooper car a mile down the highway," the kid says, squinting in the distance. Lloyd looks down the highway, wondering what to do.

Jail? Mexico? An accident?

Frank, Mercy, and Lloyd are huddled in the bathroom ten seconds later. The strong smell of disinfectant does not entirely hide the piquant odor, providing a further disincentive to breathe. Frank and Mercy face one another, gallows smiles. Lloyd stares at a wall where some highway R. Crumb has taken the time to draw a Magic Marker cartoon of a man whose eyes are visible over a toilet bowl, the rest of him having been sucked in.

"Stay cool," Frank says, as if it were a mantra.

"Where's the gun?" Mercy asks.

Frank lifts his waistband, shows it to her, whispering, "I'm gonna die in a bathroom, just like Lenny. He had a needle in his arm but the parallel is un-fuckin'-canny."

It was self-defense. It was self-defense. It was self-defense.

Lloyd says, "I'm going to surrender. You two can stay here." Reaching for the doorknob, he feels the chill of cold metal against his neck.

Frank says, "Lloyd, don't." The disconcerting feeling of a gun barrel pressed against the area below his ear has the desired effect and Lloyd lowers his hand. Then he feels something sharp in his back and sees Mercy is holding a knife against his spleen.

"Stay with us," she whispers, and now Lloyd is getting angry.

In another minute the cruiser pulls into the station. The kid has moved the Camaro to the side of the lot. He's behind the counter of the Quik Stop when the trooper enters, a short, muscular guy with a bristly crew cut.

"Whose car is that out there?"

"You want to buy it?" the kid replies, unflappable.

"The other one," the trooper says.

"This guy and this chick were here like ten minutes ago. Asked if they could park it, then started hitchhiking east. Tomato truck picked 'em up. You could catch 'em prob'ly," drawls the kid, feeling that he's in a movie and playing his role to perfection.

"You're sure?" The trooper narrows his eyes, dubious.

"Oh, yeah, Officer," the kid says, pulling a twenty out of his pocket. "They gave me this for looking after their car."

The trooper walks out, peering in the garage adjacent to the Quik Stop. He circumnavigates the building, then comes back inside. "What about the bathrooms?"

"They're locked. I got the keys right here," the kid says, holding up a couple of random keys he spots on the desk.

Handing the kid a card, the trooper says, "Them people come back, you call me." The kid nods and watches the trooper approach Mercy's car, open the driver's-side door, and look around. A moment later, he is gone, speeding east in pursuit of the phantom tomato truck.

When the trooper's car disappears, the kid walks to the back of the building, calling, "Red rover, red rover . . . ," and is delighted to see Frank, Mercy, and Lloyd emerge from the bathroom.

"So I'm a hostage now?" Lloyd says, spilling into the sunlight.

"Until we get to Mexico," Frank replies, shocked beyond measure when Lloyd sucker punches him in the side of the head. Frank staggers a few steps, then trips and falls. Lloyd swoops down and grabs the gun, which has rolled out of Frank's waistband, and before Mercy can do anything with her knife, Lloyd trains the gun on the two of them, tired, nervous, and pissed off.

"I think the ride's over," Lloyd says.

"Excuse me, people. You mind telling me what's going on here?"

"Mind your own business," Lloyd growls—*where'd that come from?*—the kid slinking away, marveling at what the larger world has visited upon him this day. Frank gets up from the ground, rubbing the side of his head, Lloyd really drilling him a moment ago. Turning to Frank and Mercy, Lloyd says, "I shot the guy. *I* shot him. Me. It's my responsibility and I want to . . ." Here he hesitates, as if reconsidering what he is about to say. "If I examine the situation . . . I want to turn myself in."

Frank shakes his head. "Lloyd, you are dumber than a stump. They'll fry you for *shooting* a cop, even if *didn't* kill him. And . . ." Frank pauses, considers an even more disturbing thought. "Never mind *you*. They could pin it on me. I'm the one with the motive."

"But I could testify—"

"I'm the one they're trying to get!"

"You're makin' a mistake," Mercy weighs in. "Folks in Oklahoma, they don't like boys who shoot police officers."

"Babe, you're not gonna get a Bronx jury," Frank informs Lloyd, the obscure reference being to the presumed unwillingness of majority-black juries to convict black defendants, Lloyd's skin color irrelevant to the larger point, i.e., that the jury was not going to regard this Los Angeles malefactor in a friendly way. "Just a bunch of angry white people."

Lloyd is starting to waver, but before he comes to a decision, he hears the kid saying, "Drop the gun," and turns to see a sawed-off shotgun pointing at him. "Just put it on the ground."

The feeling of having a presumably loaded weapon pointed at you with the strength to blow a cantaloupe-size hole anywhere it's aimed is unsettling, and Lloyd immediately does as he's told. Frank picks up the gun. "Now calm down and let's get back on the road. You're not surrendering." When this observation is met with silence, Frank says, "Lloyd? No surrendering, right?"

"Not today."

"Right. Not today. Now, no hard feelings, okay? Everyone's stressed-out. Chillin'?" Frank says, the blaccent again.

"Yeah" comes Lloyd's aggravated reply, although he has inwardly admitted there is no use acting precipitously.

"I'm sorry about pokin' you with the knife, Lloyd," Mercy says. "I didn't break the skin, did I?"

Lloyd's done with the moment. "Can we please just get out of here?"

The four of them are next to the Chrysler with the FOR SALE sign. "This speed machine yours?" Frank asks.

"You can have it if I can come with you," the kid says. "I'll be your roadie."

"Maybe another time," Frank tells him. The kid is so thrilled to have his car taken by a celebrity he offers them the entire contents of the cash register, over four hundred dollars, which Frank is only too happy to accept.

They were going to cross the border at Laredo, less than five hours away, but heading down I-35 they get caught in morning traffic. Frank takes care to slouch in the backseat so no eagle eyes will spot him. Lloyd has thought little about what happened to Clay, preoccupied as he is with the logistics of his own future, but as the traffic eases and they sprint for the border, past Pearsall, Dilley, Cotulla, and Artesia Wells, he tells himself he will deal with the incipient guilt he is feeling in a less hectic moment; and he fully expects to be overwhelmed. It is early afternoon when they reach the muddy Rio Grande.

Two international bridges link Laredo, Texas, with Nuevo Laredo, the Mexican border town right over the river. Twenty miles to the northwest is the Puente Solidaridad for those wanting to bypass the town altogether, and it is there that they go.

If you're an American citizen, all you need to get into Mexico is a valid driver's license, which Mercy has. Cars going north to south are rarely searched since most of the criminal activity (illegal immigration, truckloads of pot, whatever happens to be the felony du jour) is headed in the opposite direction. For this reason, it is decided Frank and Lloyd should ride in the trunk while their Oklahoma Charon ferries them across.

On a Laredo side street in a Mexican neighborhood, Mercy pulls the car over in front of an empty lot. There's a beauty shop across the street and a bodega about fifty yards away. No one's paying any attention to the gringos with the Chrysler. All three of them get out of the car. Mercy opens the trunk as Frank and Lloyd look at each other.

"After you, Mr. Melnick," Frank says, as if they were stepping into the lobby of the Plaza Hotel instead of a car trunk.

The trunk is remarkably dark and smells of gas vapors. Old rags are scattered around, with some tools and empty beer cans. Both men struggle to get comfortable, pushing hard things out of the way and curling up, trying not to touch each other. It's hot. No one has showered or washed in over twenty-four hours. Lloyd feels a tightening in his back as Mercy puts the car in gear and they start moving.

A back spasm now? That's perfect. They'll bust us at the border and I'll do the perp walk on national television bent at a forty-five-degree angle.

Concentrate.

Release tension. Yeah, release tension in the trunk of a car lying next to a guy with felony priors while being driven over the border by someone who was holding a knife to my back a few hours ago. Very relaxing. What is that rank smell? Is that Frank? What does prison smell like? I don't like being this close to another man; especially this one. A stinking fugitive. A dysfunctional, self-destructive, narcissistic . . . I loathe the man. What he represents, what he represents about me . . . And I killed to protect him, which is something I'll endlessly pay for. Am I going to be a target in the showers or am I too old? Why did I want to write that book? What am I trying to prove? That I exist? As if words on a page no one will read in a hundred years will somehow deliver me from this emptiness. If I shift my leg, maybe the pain in my back will go away. There, that's better. Those are gas fumes, aren't they? And they're toxic. Maybe I can fall asleep. Maybe I can die in my sleep. That would solve everything. It's so hot in here, so incredibly hot. Why am I blaming Frank? It's not his fault; it's mine. If I die in the trunk (am I dying?), I don't want my last thoughts to be angry ones (could I be dying?). Just get through this. Frank has a beach house. Think of beaches. White sand, blue sky, cold beer, white sand, blue sky, cold beer . . . I killed someone . . . I'll never fall asleep and not have that be my last thought . . .

They feel the car turning a corner and Lloyd has to brace himself to keep from rolling onto Frank. The car lurches and rattles. A pothole. Neither man says a word during the entire ride, fatigue catching up with them in the fetid darkness of the fume-stinking trunk. The car slows, then stops. They hear an American voice asking, "What's the purpose of your trip?" The remaining oxygen in their tiny pod continues to dissipate. Their lives are coming to an end now, the lives they know. They will either be fished out of the trunk by a lucky border guard, JACKPOT! CELEBRITY FUGITIVE CAUGHT FLEEING INTO MEXICO, or they will pass through this border place and cross the stygian line separating them from the Underworld, where they will be reborn into some strange new life neither man can conceive of at this moment.

A hard hand suddenly slaps the trunk, causing them to tense. Neither man dares to breathe, the wait interminable. One, two, ten seconds. Nothing. Then, voices. And once again, silence. Although the darkness is complete, Lloyd closes his eyes. Frank quietly rolls onto his back. If the trunk opens, he doesn't want to be caught looking fetal, always conscious of how to make an entrance.

Then just like that the car starts to roll. Slowly at first, then gathering speed. They've been waved through and they're gliding over the bridge and across the border. Mercy had to answer a few questions about where she was going, telling the guards with a flirty smile she was just day-tripping. They told her to head into Nuevo Laredo to get a tourist card and a vehicle permit, which she does, pulling over behind an abandoned building to let Frank and Lloyd, both sweating profusely, climb out of the trunk and get into the car. After Mercy procures the vehicle permit, which takes all of ten minutes at the immigration office, she heads back out to the parking lot. Frank and Lloyd are sitting in the car with the weak air-conditioning on, Frank in back, Lloyd in front, low-profiling it. Even though they made it across, no one's smiling. Mercy climbs in behind the steering wheel and puts the car in gear.

"Mercy, stop the car," Frank says. They're cruising down the commercial strip in Nuevo Laredo, past a market.

She pulls over and says, "*Please* always helps."

"And leave the engine running. We need some bottled water for the trip. You want to go in and get it, please?" Frank says, smiling now.

"I'll get it," Lloyd offers.

"You stay here, Lloyd. You and me need to talk." Lloyd shrugs, whatever. "Mercy . . . please?"

"Alright," she says, shaking her head and laughing as she gets out of the car. "But once we're away from the border, you're workin' for me."

Frank watches her walk toward the market feeling a twinge of regret for what he is about to do. The second she disappears into the store, he jumps out of the car, goes to the driver's side, yanks the door open, gets behind the wheel, and floors the gas before the door's even closed.

"What are you doing?" Lloyd asks from deep inside his own fear, the burst of acceleration pushing him against the seat, looking over his shoulder to see if Mercy is chasing the car.

"We're leaving her here. For her own good. She didn't do anything back in Tulsa. If we get nailed, or the cops start shooting . . . it's better if she's not with us." Frank's looking in the rearview mirror now, and for the first time in his life he's feeling guilty about something. But it's a strange sort of guilt because what he's feeling guilty about is doing the right thing, which is also a new sensation for Frank. The light catches a piece of silver on the front seat and Frank looks down and sees Mercy's knife, the pearl inlay, the onyx handle.

Now Lloyd's at the wheel and they're traveling toward Frank's beach shack in Playa Perdida, a couple of hours out of Puerto Vallarta. The car heaves along the highway, heading south on Highway 85 toward Monterrey, where they plan to spend the night before heading to the Pacific Coast the next day. There they intend to reconnoiter and weigh their limited options, which for Lloyd consist of finding a good lawyer and negotiating his return to Oklahoma and eventual reintegration into society.

"You think we should have taken Mercy along?" Frank asks, running his finger along the now-open blade of Mercy's gravity knife.

"Nah, you did the right thing. Send her a postcard."

From Frank's look, not only can Lloyd tell he doesn't agree; he's actually a little put out by the response. "We made a mistake," Frank tells him. "I did, anyway." Lloyd does not answer for a moment, so surprised is he at what his traveling companion has said. The Bones admitting to a misstep? The Bones displaying incipient signs of pining? Hasn't this day been strange enough already? Lloyd feels the need to take the nascent melancholy blooming in Frank's breast and strangle it before it manifests in some behavioral way.

"You didn't make a mistake. No mistake was made. Taking her would have been a mistake," Lloyd says, not having fully forgiven Mercy for sticking the knife in his lower back. He wishes Frank would put the thing away.

★　　★　　★

362

"Dustin, if you don't eat your chicken fingers, Mommy's going to turn off the television."

"I'm not hungry."

Stacy and her son are facing off in the breakfast nook of the Brentwood kitchen, where a bright midday sun pours through the windows and coats the room in a flat light. Dustin, riveted to the cartoon he is watching on the wall-mounted combination TV/DVD/VCR, is ignoring his food despite his mother's harangue. Stacy is wearing her exercise clothes and is desperately wishing she were in her two-thirty Pilates class right now. Instead, it's just afternoon and she must endure another couple of hours of Dustin's company before she can drop him off at a friend's house for a play date. She is particularly eager to get to class this day since her last telephone conversation with Lloyd so upset her that she consumed most of a quart of Cherry Garcia ice cream last night and is desperate to perform sweat penance.

"Dustin," she says, irritated, but before she can formulate some kind of threat, the telephone rings. Stacy picks it up, checking the caller ID: MARISA PINSKER. What could she possibly want? Stacy hadn't talked to her in months. Well, it would be a relief from dealing with her recalcitrant son. "Hello?"

"Stacy, it's Marisa."

"How are you?" Stacy chimes, hoping she has effectively feigned interest.

"So are you watching TV?"

"Dustin's got cartoons on," she replies, wondering why Marisa would ask this.

"Put on CNN. They're talking about Lloyd."

Stacy grabs the remote and, over Dustin's effusive protestations, changes the channel to CNN, which is where she learns that her husband is wanted for shooting a police officer.

"Are you watching? Stacy? Hello?" But Stacy can't hear Marisa's voice emanating from the receiver she is now holding at waist level. She can't hear Dustin's yammering. She can only hear the sound of her life crumbling.

"Lloyd, let me ask you something," Frank says, still playing with Mercy's knife, the car speeding through the wastes of northern Mexico. "Why didn't you help me out back in L.A.?"

"What are you talking about?"

"When I was doing the pilot."

"Aren't we done with that?" Lloyd looks at Frank and can see from his expression that they are clearly not done with that so he says, "Because I had my own problems." Lloyd suddenly feels the intense heat cutting through the feeble air-conditioning, the dryness of his lips, his mouth. Involuntarily presses harder on the gas, then catches himself as the car shoots forward, lets the juice ride out, not wanting to touch the brakes. A semi blows past them in the other direction carrying a cargo of melons to Texas.

"I'm just asking because if you had done me a solid . . ."

"If I had . . . what?"

"Maybe we wouldn't be here."

"You're kidding, right? You think if I had punched up that script, the show would have been picked up? That's so ridiculous, I don't know what to say. And how can you even think about it now? I mean, Frank, for godsakes! We're in some kind of traveling dreadfest and you're ragging about a pilot?"

"Because if you had, maybe I'd be a TV star instead of on the run in Mexico with a wannabe badass like you."

"Now I'm a wannabe badass? Who shot the guy when he had a gun in your mouth, Bones?"

"You said it was an accident."

"Considering you were about to get your head blown off at the time, I'd say you're splitting hairs."

"You'll never be me, Lloyd. No matter what you do, no matter how hard you try, until you can take the risks that get you there. You're always going to be skating on the surface, Brentwood Boy. You're just a careerist. You got nothing, no philosophy, nothing at all . . ."

"*I* have no philosophy? What, I'm on the run with Descartes now? I'm fuckin' Hegel's copilot? *You* have a philosophy?" Lloyd feels his body heat rising, the anger center in his brain starting to flex.

"Burn till there's nothing left but the bones," Frank says, looking at Lloyd in a way meant to end the exchange. "Put that in your book."

Lloyd had to admit it was an impressive articulation of Frank's animating principle. But he does not say so. Instead, he retorts, "About an hour ago I was lying next to you in the trunk, Frank. I was human cargo," which does not articulate any philosophy at all other than survival.

"Because you were with *me*. I made you do it."

"Hey, you didn't fuckin' make me, Frank, okay? I did it to help you out because I was ready to turn myself in back at the gas station, remember? Just like I helped you out by not pressing charges when you destroyed my house or like I helped you out by shooting the cop or like I was trying to help you out by writing the book, but I'm done with that now, Frank. I'm done with it because I see what you do is confuse extreme behavior with being an artist, as if acting like a madman somehow justifies the creative result, which in your case is pretty slim pickings if you want to know the truth." Here Lloyd takes a breath and looks at Frank, calculating the effect of his words. Frank remains quiet, staring out the window, his face impassive. Sensing his blows are landing, Lloyd presses on, nothing to lose now. "I used to envy your talent, but whatever chops you had?—they went up in crack smoke a while ago. Not that you can't still be funny or say clever things, but you drove your life into a tree and you've been lying on the hood of the car for years now, looking just the way you did in my living room with the broken glass and the blood, and by the way, did I ever send you a bill, which is obviously a rhetorical question because the answer's no since I had too much respect for the talent you pissed away. I'm sorry the pilot didn't work out for you, because you got nothing left. It's over, man. You're lucky you're in Mexico."

Lloyd's spent now. He looks away from Frank and out the windshield, wonders how long he's taken his eye off the road. Frank is too exhausted to respond but knows in his soul everything Lloyd says is true, and the sudden and overwhelming sense of loss and futility he experiences almost makes him stop breathing. As for Lloyd, if he could have consistently harnessed the energy he'd just expended and tapped the emotions he was feeling, his career might have gone in an entirely different direction, but Frank was not the only one for whom it was too late. Trembling now, not from fear but from agitation, Lloyd looks at the Bones, sees the target of his diatribe fingering the knife blade, wonders if he's going to stab him, almost not caring, not realizing Frank is likelier to stick it into his own neck because if a fraction of what Lloyd said is true, what's the point? Then Lloyd feels something in the vicinity of his heart. A tightening? A pulsation? Is this the warning sign of a massive coronary that will end his life in the middle of this ridiculous situation? Snapping out of his dark meditations he realizes his cell phone is vibrating in his breast pocket. His cell phone! Vibrating! Still in his own life! He reaches into his pocket and quickly opens it, greedy for the ordinary, loving the simple familiarity of the act.

"Hello?"

"Thank God you're all right." It's Stacy. Lloyd, an astronaut getting a buzz from Houston, never happier to hear a friendly voice. "Where are you?"

"Somewhere in Mexico," he manages in a near whisper, spent from his explosion.

"Lloyd, they're saying on TV you shot a policeman. Did you?" Her voice crackling with anxiety for their future, her future.

"It was an accident!"

"They're saying you're lucky he's not dead."

"He's not dead?"

Could he have heard that correctly? *Not* dead? Was this a second chance, an opportunity to rewind, reedit, re-everything the worst moment in his life, to adjust if not the facts then the ramifications? Did he just slip away from the shadow of the hangman?

Frank hears *He's not dead* and nearly levitates through the car roof, the bitter aftertaste of Lloyd's words momentarily evaporating. "He's not dead?" Frank asks, unable, due to the enormity of the implications, to recast the information more elegantly.

"Are you sure?" Lloyd asks his wife.

"According to CNN, he was wearing a bulletproof vest."

"Oh my God!" Lloyd exhales, almost expiring from relief.

"He's not dead?" Frank repeats, his ordinarily silvery wordcraft having entirely departed.

"They're saying on TV he was wearing a vest," Lloyd tells him.

"Are you with Frank now?" Stacy wants to know.

"He's right here."

"If you had written that show when Robert Hyler asked you, you probably wouldn't—"

But Lloyd cuts his wife off before she can finish the thought, saying, "Can we not talk about this now?"

"Sorry, I'm a little upset," she says justifiably.

"You think *you're* upset? Let me tell you about *my* day."

But this time it's Stacy who calls a halt to the familiar marital conversation pattern and asks, "Where are you?"

"I don't know."

"What do you mean you don't know?"

"I mean I don't know. We crossed the border a while ago and right now I have no idea where we are."

"When you get a bead on it, I want you to call me, and don't call on the house line. They could get a tap by then and trace you. Call me on my cell."

"What are you going to do?"

"I'm coming down there and I'm going to get you out of this mess."

"But you hate Mexico."

"Your life is on the line, hon. I'll deal with it."

As Lloyd hangs up, he has no idea how she intends to do this, but he knows that when Stacy is determined to effect something, woe to those who stand in her way.

Up in Otis's office, the lawyer is saying, "I haven't seen him since yesterday." He smiles at the camera being wielded by Jane Lee, who is in the middle of a shoot. Otis shifts in his chair, giving Jane a new pose.

"If he gets in touch with you for any reason—" Faron says.

"I'll be sure to let you know," Otis leaning back in his chair and putting his hands behind his head, smiling at Jane's lens.

"Perfect, give me more of that," she says, unconcerned with Faron, who is walking out of the office without saying good-bye.

Manny Escobar, who is seated on the couch, watches Faron disappear. Removing a red, Western-style kerchief from his jacket pocket, he wipes his perspiring brow and says, "That guy doesn't like me."

"What cop would like you, Manny? You put criminals on the street." Manny nods; can't argue with that. "You hot, Manny? What's with the do-rag?"

"I sweat when I lose money. You gonna cover it, Otis? You guaranteed me he wouldn't skip."

"You're in a high-risk field, my brother. Got to take the bitter with the sweet."

"I got a kid in college, you cocksucker!"

"There's a lady present," Otis reminds the hostile bondsman.

Jane, who is changing rolls of film, looks up, saying, "I've heard a lot worse. Otis, you want to change clothes while I reload?"

"Yeah, I brought two different sports coats." Then, to Manny: "You ain't the only one holding the bag. I was gonna try this case and get my name in every damn newspaper in the country."

"Don't worry, Otis," Manny says, wiping his forehead again. "I know a skip tracer, new to the business, guy I bailed out one time. He's gonna find Frank and drag him back by his balls." Manny distractedly chews the inside of his cheek as he thinks about the depredations that will surely be visited upon the elusive comedian when he is once again behind bars. Then he dabs his sweaty forehead with his increasingly rank handkerchief and looks at Otis. "This skip tracer? He's very motivated."

Stacy and Dustin are the only two passengers in the Hylers' Learjet, which Daryl generously offered as soon as Stacy called her with the news. They're headed for Mexico, and as Dustin watches a Monster Truck video with a look of slight discomfort, Stacy ignores the turbulence they're flying through and assiduously works the phones. She has already lined up one of the top criminal lawyers in Los Angeles and is now putting teams together in Mexico and Oklahoma. Stacy agonized over what to wear since this is not a circumstance in which tastemakers generally weigh in, and she has settled on a tasteful Dolce & Gabbana pantsuit worn with a cream silk shirt, simple gold earrings, and black pumps she purchased at the Barneys spring sale. Her hair is freshly washed and her makeup subtle and refined since she knows she could wind up on television before the day is over and it is important that the wife of any potential defendant display a pleasant and sympathetic mien. Stacy is clearly in her element. Like many intelligent, nonworking wives of successful men, she has felt an unacknowledged absence of intellectual challenge in her life, an absence that book clubs do not address, and now, despite the potential dangers that lie ahead, she is enjoying the task at hand. Lloyd's foolishness has clearly come to a screeching halt, and she is going to help him ease back toward the small pleasures of day-to-day life upon which he has so cavalierly turned his back. Stacy is convinced that with some clever lawyering, he will be back to his old high-earning ways within a year or two and they will be able to pretend this entire unfortunate business has never occurred.

The plane suddenly dips and judders in an oncoming wind. Stacy has just dialed Lloyd, in an attempt to ascertain a more precise location so she will be able to tell the pilot exactly where in northern Mexico they are going. She is waiting for his phone to ring.

"Mommy?" Dustin asks plaintively, and before she can answer, he has vomited today's lunch all over her suit.

Lloyd's driving, and Frank, still reeling from the tirade and enervated from the recent events, has decided to lie down in the back. The silence in the car has been oppressive. When Lloyd's phone rings, he answers it with palpable relief.

"Lloyd, your son just threw up on me!" From Stacy's tone, you would have no idea the current situation is anything out of the ordinary. In fact, it's the exact tone she would use were she admonishing him for working on a weekend when there were errands to do. Then he hears her say, "Honey, talk to Daddy. Mommy needs to get cleaned up."

Then: "Daddy?"

"Hey, pal," Lloyd says, the simple three-word communication producing in him an awe you would associate with hearing a voice transmission from another galaxy, a fundamental stirring of the emotions that is impossible to counterfeit. Stacy may be difficult, but Dustin? Frankly, he's difficult, too, but by virtue of his age *he* has potential. "How ya doing?"

"I feel sick."

"Yeah, me, too."

"We're coming to see you, but now Mommy's mad." In the plane Stacy has been furiously wiping herself off with bar towels.

"I'm not mad, I'm not mad," she says, taking the phone from Dustin. "Okay, where are you?"

"We're headed for a town called Monterrey. Keep your phone on and I'll call you when I know exactly where we are."

"Lloyd?"

"What?"

"It's going to be all right," she says, picking an errant piece of regurgitated chicken off her lap with a cloth napkin and placing it in the silver trash receptacle. Then, quietly, so the pilot doesn't hear: "Just don't shoot anyone else."

★ ★ ★

370

Las Casitas Motel is on the main drag outside Monterrey, between a taquería and an auto body shop. It's a tired-looking two-story building built in the shape of a horseshoe with a pale blue swimming pool surrounded by a Cyclone fence. Frank and Lloyd have each rented a room.

In the late afternoon Lloyd lies on the bed. Taking a shower, conscious it could be his last private ablution in a while, he was no less resolute about his desire to head north. Now he is watching *Judge Judy* (in Spanish) and imagines himself on her docket. He runs through his defense in his head: *accident, Paxil, tequila, accident, no criminal record, remorse, Paxil, accident, accident, accident, Paxil,* and feels reasonably confident that he will not be sent away for life. Looking over, he notices the phone is bolted to the night table, confined, shackled. Ditto the television and VCR. He wants to see his son, spend more time with him; do father/son things. Jail looms. Stacy looms. He needs to address the subtle daily rumble he discerns beneath his life, the one that has taken him on this quixotic journey that is culminating in a motel outside Monterrey, Mexico. He'll have time. There will be time.

If they don't kill me.

Am I being naïve to think this could turn out well? I did shoot someone after all, a cop. Are they going to take us down? Are they going to look for an excuse to shoot us? Frank said it didn't matter I didn't kill the guy. Should we have kept driving until we got to his house? The beaches? The blunts? It's a holiday paradise for him but I don't even smoke dope anymore. Did I remember to ask Stacy to see if she could find any Paxil in the medicine cabinet before she left? I don't think I did. Why did she bring Dustin? Things could get hairy. I could die in custody, killed while trying to escape, which is what the cops say after they bang your head into a wall a hundred times. I want to see Dustin . . .

Just after five in the afternoon, Lloyd opens the door to his room and beholds an apparition, his wife and son. Stacy has changed into tight jeans and a white tank top, Dustin's stomach having foiled her sartorial planning. "You couldn't have found a nicer place?" Stacy asks as he ushers them in, quickly closing the door behind them. When she sees his face, she says, "I'm joking, okay? I'm glad you're alive."

"That's two of us," he says, looking her over. Stacy's arm muscles are supple and defined, her whole body torqued and ready for combat with whatever's on the way. Lloyd can't help noticing she looks terrific.

"I'm hungry," Dustin says. He's in a new outfit as well.

"Hi, pal," Lloyd says, picking up his son and hugging him, placing his face in the crook of the boy's neck and inhaling the boy smell, sweet and once again sticky, even after having been cleaned up at the Monterrey airport. Having considered the possibility he might never see his son again, Lloyd watches him for an extra moment as the boy explores the room. He feels a slight tightening in his throat.

"We'll get you some food in a little while, sweetie. Mommy needs to talk to Daddy."

"Can I watch the SpongeBob video?"

"We left it on the plane." Sensing the strain of the day could shortly lead to a meltdown, Stacy adds, "But we'll buy you two new ones as soon as we get home."

"Three." A talented negotiator already.

"Fine." She turns to Lloyd. "So, where's your friend?"

Lloyd has summoned Frank to his room and deposited Dustin in front of the television in Frank's so the adults can reconnoiter. Stacy has had to keep herself from recoiling at the sight of Frank, whom she blames for her current troubles, Lloyd in her mind a cult member in need of deprogramming, Frank the sinister guru now reclining on one of the beds. Lloyd is seated in a chair and Stacy stands facing them. It's her meeting. "I talked to the most prominent criminal attorney in Los Angeles this morning, he's a friend of Daryl's," she says, looking at her husband knowingly, proud of her access. "He can't try the case since it's out of state, but he's willing to co-counsel pending a meeting. He'll fly to Oklahoma and arrange the surrender so the cops don't come looking for you. All I need is the go-ahead and he's on a plane," Stacy concludes, looking around as if expecting to be congratulated. But Lloyd is the only one who's impressed.

Frank's response is "Fuck that, I'm staying down here."

Stacy looks at Frank and exhales through her nostrils. This is all such a trial for her. Ordinarily, she'd be in her marble-countered kitchen now giving Dustin his dinner and waiting for Lloyd to come home from work. That she is in a cheap Mexican motel room discussing the surrender of her husband and his accomplice is an absurdity not lost on the woman whose wedding china was purchased at Bloomingdale's. This keeps her from becoming annoyed with Frank's reaction.

"The Bones can handle Mexico," Frank says, lapsing into the third person, a distancing device, to prepare himself for the difficulties that lie ahead.

"Hey, the Bones can do whatever the hell the Bones wants to do, okay? I could give a shit what the Bones wants to do," is Stacy's coolly delivered reply. Lloyd looks at his wife, shocked. He's never heard her talk to anyone other than him this way, and he finds it curiously inspiring, implying, as it does, that someone is taking control of the situation. Indeed, Stacy has left no doubt what's going on here. She is engaged in a surgical extraction, a virtual military rescue mission. If Frank wants to get on the Chinook, fine, he's welcome to come along for the ride, but what truly matters is that Lloyd is pulled out, dusted off, and somehow eventually deposited back in his Los Angeles life.

Dustin's frantic entrance interrupts the conversational flow, and in the torrent of words and tears the leitmotif is "The bad video! The bad video!" A moment later the four of them are in Frank's room standing in front of the television on which can be seen a boxy room shot through the lens of what appears to be a ceiling-mounted security camera. In the room a black man, big guy, maybe thirty-five years old, is handcuffed to a chair. Clay Porter and Faron Pike stand next to him, Faron saying, "Just tell us where our share is, Wayman."

Wayman answering, "I don't know," his voice higher than you'd expect, given a man of his size. Clay slugs him in the face, causing his head to jerk back, his nose breaking.

"What is this horrible thing?" Stacy asks, hiding Dustin's eyes.

"Those are cops," Lloyd says. "The short one's the one that got shot."

On the television Faron's saying, "We're trying to be nice here, Wayman."

"I told you it got stole," Wayman says, blood running down his face and onto his shirt.

"Someone just helped themselves to ten pounds of our crystal meth?" Faron asks rhetorically.

"Wayman, that is bad business," Clay says, smashing him on the head with a blackjack.

Lloyd clicks off the VCR. "I've seen enough of that," he says as Frank and Stacy watch mutely, Dustin whimpering against his mother's stomach. The room is dead silent until Frank says, "Where'd this come from?"

"I found it in a bag! I'm sorry!" Dustin wails.

"You did a good thing, pal. Don't apologize," Lloyd tells his son.

"It was good?" Dustin says, looking up at his father through wet eyes, his sobs abating. Lloyd smiles at him. "Can I have a present?"

"I will definitely get you a present."

Stacy is now morbidly fascinated by the circumstances of the tape and wondering if this could somehow be exculpatory in Lloyd's case. She has actually watched enough police shows on television to know what *exculpatory* means so she says, "Maybe this is exculpatory." As Lloyd watches his buffed and cut savior, his wife of over ten years and the mother of his child, plan his deliverance, he vows to love her more, to reclaim his old life with enthusiasm, to remain untroubled by whatever is roiling him, but in a dark corner of his furtive mind a splinter of consciousness recognizes this will forever be a vain hope.

Frank and Lloyd are saying good-bye in the darkened motel parking lot as Stacy and Dustin watch from their rented SUV, Stacy's environment-alism conveniently retired for the day.

"You still want to write that book?" Frank asks.

"I think so."

"If you sell it to the movies, make sure you let me know. Maybe I'll come out of hiding to play myself."

Lloyd looks at Frank and marvels at the promise of his gift, now largely wasted, his time onstage nearly over. Still, even now he wishes the other man's talent were something he could grab on to, hold, place in his soul's hard drive like a diskette whose contents he could access to render himself something he will never otherwise be. As for Frank, he just wants Lloyd's money, not for the purchase of glittering baubles, the spangled treasures by which success is measured in America, but to give to Mercy so as to assuage the remorse he's feeling about having decided once again to recast the part.

"Keep in touch," Lloyd says sardonically, turning toward the car.

"Patronize me more, babe."

Frank drives slowly toward the Pacific Ocean and wonders what led the two Tulsa cops to tape their tea party. He thinks about the kind of country that produces people whose overwhelming desire is to see their image on a television screen. He reflects on the armies of suburban couples shooting bedroom pornography and the increasingly common phenomenon of criminals videotaping themselves committing crimes. He realizes these are among the disparate elements which have combined to create a culture where the exalted place reserved for people who command attention through actual talent is smaller all the time. He knows everyone's an entertainer now. Finally, the whole world is in show business.

As Frank flows along Mexican roads toward the distant sea, Stacy, Lloyd, and Dustin fly to Tulsa where, in an elaborate minuet choreographed by the Los Angeles lawyer Stacy retained, Lloyd surrenders to the police and immediately posts a quarter-million-dollar bail. A trial date is set for several months hence, and Lloyd is allowed to return to Los Angeles.

★   ★   ★

375

Three days after Lloyd left Mexico, Frank is in Playa Perdida seated in a lawn chair on a bluff overlooking the Pacific Ocean. He hadn't been to his house in almost a year and was not surprised to find that it had been broken into in his absence. Unfortunately for the thieves there was nothing to take besides a cheap television and an old boom box, and after helping themselves to those they left the place more or less intact. Now, Frank is sipping coffee and contemplating what to do with the rest of the day. He considers calling Robert Hyler back in Los Angeles to let him know he's all right but worries the police may have been in touch, and Frank doesn't want to put his old ally in a compromising position. He doesn't have much of a social life in town. Having bought the house on a whim a long time ago, he would only get to Mexico sporadically, and the purpose of those trips was to get away from everything anyway. He's heard there's a group of people down here wanted for serious crimes north of the border, but doesn't suppose they have meetings and a clubhouse. He's read about a priest on the run from the usual child molestation charges and the scion of a major industrial fortune wanted for multiple rapes in Arizona where he drugged and videotaped his victims (another vile *auteur*). Both of these men had drawn the attention of certain elements that led to their arrest and forced departure from the world of tropical dreams. Frank knows enough to keep a low profile. There was a local boy, a teenager, who spoke some English, and Frank paid him to go into town and do some food shopping for him. He had most of the four hundred dollars that came out of the till at the Texas gas station and, local prices being what they were, figured that would last him until he could come up with a way to access some cash. A couple of weeks, a month, he'd think of something, the man always a survivor. If only he had the energy.

Before landing on this Pacific bluff, when he flowed through the New York streets, snapping and popping through his early days and then rolling down the Western boulevards after he'd reached the level of success at which he'd become so annoyingly stuck, there was a reason to rail against the elements of his life that were conspiring to impede his rise, to plot, to plan, to devise ways to keep going so when his time came, as he knew it surely would, he'd be ready. But now his time, his moment, his place, had announced itself and he is regarding it over his shoulder, moving from light to shadow, speeding toward the long night. It had already happened. He's had his eyes on the glittering lights for so long he's not sure where to focus them now. Having wanted something for his entire life, the letting go is not entirely smooth. Now he hasn't seen a newspaper in three days and it's about all the cold turkey he can do.

Playa Perdida is a small town but not so small it doesn't have two Internet cafés, one on the main street and another, more modest one on a side street. It is here two teenagers play a video game, blowing the heads off intergalactic invaders. Frank is next to them, sipping strong coffee in front of a computer screen. He had done a search on his name and come up with over a thousand hits, more than he would have had at any time in his career. This is something about which he is understandably ambivalent. He has examined what has been written about him on many of the major informational Web sites and finds himself distressed at some of the coverage with its promiscuous use of words like *formerly popular* and *has-been*. If only he were dead, he thinks. Perhaps then the tenor of this coverage would be different. If only his drive through the Melnick living room had ended in the extinguishing of his neon lights, perhaps then the perception of what Frank Bones was would be different. He thinks about Jimi Hendrix. What if Jimi Hendrix had lived? Probably in and out of rehab for the next four decades, and then corpulent and arthritic, dragged out on some 401(k) Tour sponsored by an adult-diaper company. If ever anyone should have ascended toward the heavenly spotlight young, it is Frank Bones.

Now he is reading the following article on the Web site of a major American daily.

Melnick Denies Knowledge of Bones Whereabouts
The man who confessed to the accidental shooting of a Tulsa police detective in a packed courtroom two days ago denied he helped comedian Frank Bones elude a

police dragnet. Flanked by his lawyers, Los Angeles comedy writer Lloyd Melnick claimed not to have seen Bones in four days. "After the gun went off and we left the motel room, I got out of town," Melnick claimed. He went on to say, "I have no idea where Frank went or where he is."

Mercy Madrid, who is also believed to have been in the motel room when the shooting took place, has maintained her silence. Her lawyer, Otis Cain, issued a terse "No comment" on her behalf when asked if she knew Bones's whereabouts. Ms. Madrid is expected to be charged with being an accessory to attempted murder. Through her lawyer, she has denied this allegation.

Frank feels a twinge of regret upon reading about what Lloyd and Mercy are going through, but he is confident it will not turn out too badly for them. He even appreciates that Lloyd has, once again, covered for him. Taking a final sip of his coffee, he places the cup on the saucer, brings it to the counter, and saunters into the late-afternoon light. He considers whether to risk a stroll down the main street, but decides against it. Thinks about what he's going to have for dinner and realizes he hasn't been hungry all day. He is starting to wonder if he's depressed.

When the videotape of Faron Pike and Clay Porter came to light, those charged with administering the judicial system in the state of Oklahoma took a dim view of everything having to do with the two brutal police detectives. Further sullying their reputation was the surfacing of the tape player Frank used to record his act the night Tino Suarez was killed, which preserved a conversation between Clay and Tino where they were conspiring to distribute illegal substances. So, upon looking at the Wayman French home video, listening to the nefarious plotting backstage at Club Louie, and hearing all the testimony from the parties involved, the jury in the case of the People vs. Lloyd Melnick voted unanimously to acquit the titular defendant. As for the case against Frank, Faron Pike, in an attempt to negotiate a plea bargain in the Wayman French situation and save his own skin, turned state's evidence against Clay Porter, claiming Clay had actually shot Tino Suarez and then planted the gun in the car. For his cooperation, Faron Pike received twenty-five years to life, which is exactly what Clay Porter got. They are currently serving their time in McAlester Correctional Facility in McAlester, Oklahoma, where they do not speak to one another.

The murder case against Frank Bones was dismissed. What remained was a charge of jumping bail and a rather large debt to his bondsman, Manny Escobar.

A little over two weeks after arriving in Mexico, Frank is feeling a certain longing, much the way a recovering alcoholic does. But it isn't a drink he craves. The man who has spent his entire adulthood in front of groups of people has begun to chafe at the enforced solitude he is experiencing, the personal Elba he has come to inhabit. He's been back to the side-street Internet café several times to follow the progress of the legal cases against Lloyd and Mercy online, and at moments he thought he might actually go back and turn himself in. But he recognized these thoughts as manifestations of weakness and vowed he would not capitulate to them. Today he is feeling he can fight these nefarious urges, wrestle them into submission. As for tomorrow . . . the tidal pull is strong on a weakening constitution.

Late one afternoon (he's already forgotten what day of the week it is) Frank is taking a nap, something he'd gotten into the habit of doing soon after getting settled. It's been a warm day and as he's lying on the couch in the living room of his house facing the wall and struggling into wakefulness, he's thinking about money. Getting himself set up in Playa Perdida has caused him to go through about half of the cash he had brought down here, and it has occurred to him that it may be time to pay more serious attention to procuring funds for his future endeavors, however modest they are currently projected to be. He has a few thousand dollars in a Los Angeles bank account, but to access that he must reveal himself to people who will be legally obligated to inform the authorities, so that is a nonstarter. He could call Honey and ask her to send him some money, but they didn't part on the best of terms, and he isn't sure he can trust her. Lloyd's name briefly swims to the surface, but

Frank realizes even had he not completely decimated whatever goodwill his erstwhile traveling companion had previously felt toward him, he could never again approach him as a supplicant. The fact is, Frank has foreclosed his financial options. The anxiety this is causing as he eases toward wakefulness, though low-grade, has the potential to grow into something far larger and more troublesome. He consciously finds himself pushing it back toward his subconscious and replacing it with sexual thoughts about Mercy. He knows if he is thinking about sex, he can't be depressed, so he forces himself to think about sex and he's not enjoying it. He is perspiring and wants to get up from the couch and get a beer from the cooler he bought when he realized the refrigerator was not going to come back to life, but he doesn't have the energy.

"Don't move, asshole."

Still not entirely awake, Frank wonders if he's left the television on, then remembers the thieves stole the television. Who, then, just said that? With no little trepidation, he moves his head from the cushion on which it is resting and turns toward the room, where he sees Creed Baru standing and pointing a gun at him. This is something he has not anticipated, and it wakes him up quickly.

"What do you want?" Frank asks, more irritated than scared.

"I believe you owe my client a big pile of money, Bones."

"Your client? What are you talking about?" Frank racks his brain, tries to recall some obscure gambling debt, wondering if he's not dreaming.

"The name Manny Escobar ring a bell?" Frank has already forgotten the bail bondsman, but now a tsunami of bad memories hits the beach. "Dude, he is pissed."

Three hours later in the folds of darkness, Creed sits in the passenger seat, his gun pointed at Frank, who is driving his captor's beat-up Toyota Tercel east toward Durango, his wrist handcuffed to the steering wheel. They turned off the coast road about an hour ago and now they are climbing in elevation. The night air blows cool through the open window, chilling the inside of the car. Since technically this is a kidnapping, Manny has told Creed to bring Frank to Durango, and Manny will get down there on a friend's plane and fly him back to Tulsa to settle their accounts. Frank knows regardless of how his other case is adjudicated, the bail jumping is certain to land him in a numbered orange jumpsuit. In the meantime, Creed is saying, "I'm figurin' with the money I'm gonna make bringin' your ass back, I can get out to L.A., maybe get into stunt work or somethin'. Can't be too hard right? Drivin' fast, fallin' outta windows? I can do that . . ." Creed watches Frank as he runs his mouth, but Frank only stares through the windshield, looking at the two-lane highway rolling through the Mexican night and wondering whether he should talk to his captor about show business. Creed, getting no response from Frank, heads in a different conversational direction.

"You like doin' it with my wife?"

Frank knows this can't end well so he keeps it neutral. "She's a good person."

"Fuckin' whore is what she is, dude. First thing I'm gonna do when Manny pays me is wave the money under her face and say, 'You coulda had this, girl. *You coulda had this!*'" Silence for a few moments while Creed collects himself. He shakes his head, barely perceptibly, and continues, "Then I'm gonna tie her to the bed and take that knife of hers and I'm gonna heat the point, you know, make a brand, like? Then I'm gonna burn my initials on her ass so every time she gets fucked again the dude's fuckin' her gonna know Creed Baru was there first." Frank swallows, still not looking at Creed. Wonders if he's serious, the guy scum, probably capable of most felonies. "What do ya think of that, Bones? Then I'm gonna have a party, buy ten cases of tequila, invite everyone I know. Next day, I'm gonna pack up and move to Hollywood. That's the only thing keepin' me from shootin' you in the neck, the money an' all. Otherwise . . ." Here he cocks the pistol as if he just might pull the trigger, and Frank wishes he would. He remembers finding his father in the basement and the rainy night in Los Angeles with the Hummer, and he tries to recall his exact state of mind at the time, what he was feeling as the rain streaked the window of the monstrous vehicle and he hurtled toward wet, verdant Brentwood lawns, blackhearted and deeply, deeply sad, and Creed continues to talk about Mercy and money and what he's going to do to her and his own tawdry fantasies of American success as Frank twists the steering wheel. When the violent motion of the car causes it to heave and take flight, rolling off the highway and into a culvert, he thinks, *Yes, I've finally done it, oblivion, it's over, yes, one more second and then* . . .

Chapter 17

The car lies upside down, some distance from the road. Inside a veil of twisted metal and broken glass, Frank's feet are above his head, but even from his compromised position, he can see Creed is already dead, his skull crushed, presumably from its impact with the dashboard; never would have been much of a stuntman. He is slightly disappointed at finding himself alive, but being no stranger to surviving horrific car crashes (and pretty much everything else), he is not entirely surprised. A sense of invincibility briefly suffuses him and just as quickly recedes as a dull pain appears in his shoulders and neck, informing him that his body does not absorb a beating the way it once did. He disengages himself from his seat belt, rolls on his sore shoulder, then sits upright. His morbid expectation makes the proximity of a dead man no big deal, and he reaches into Creed's pocket, removes the keys to the handcuffs, then releases his wrist from their malign grip. Rotating on his side he uses his elbow to punch out the remaining shards of glass from the window and crawls out of the car. Frank has no idea where he is. He notices there is not a lot of traffic on the road, although it appears to be a highway. The headlights of a car drift past but the driver doesn't stop.

Frank walks away from the wrecked Toyota as if in a trance, then turns, half expecting to see it parked on the side of the road with Lloyd standing alongside, waving for him to get in. For less than a second, it occurs to Frank he may actually be dead, but he quickly realizes the metaphysical absurdity of that notion. He runs a quick checklist of his systems and finds everything to be functioning. But the death of this other man, this member of the audience, is undeniable. Does he say a prayer for the soul of the petty dreamer who had come to effect his return to Babylon? Frank doesn't believe in that kind of religion. Yet he feels remarkably small, standing by the ruined car near the spectral highway beneath the infinite night sky.

He knows there are bandits on these Mexican roads, a lawlessness that could swallow him whole. Drivers are advised to avoid traveling at night. People set off and disappear, vanish in the hills, no traces left behind. He is stranded, alone. The night is chilly, but clear. Looking up, he sees stars. Some time passes, he's not sure how much. No cars stop. He's thirsty but there is nothing to drink.

The idea comes to him as if he were in a fugue state, open to messages temporal and celestial. He knows if he listens, something will lead him where he must go if he is to survive. Picking up a rock, he walks back toward the car and climbs in the driver's-side window. Seeing Creed's still-warm body pitched over itself, he sticks his hand in the man's pocket and fishes out his wallet. The driver's license will come in handy. Frank is starting to feel queasy, but he knows what must be done, and less than ten sharp strokes with the rock breaks every tooth in the dead man's mouth, which bleeds profusely since the body was pulsing with life not long before. Then he crawls back out of the car and collects some dry brush from the side of the road. Unscrewing the cap of the gas tank, he stuffs the brush in, making a wick. He takes a lighter out of his pocket and ignites the brush, then steps back to watch it smolder. There having been no rain for weeks, the brush, baked in the unforgiving Mexican sun, quickly burns down and Frank has to quicken his pace to avoid being hit by flying debris when the car explodes. An angry fireball of hellish oranges and reds plumes upward, creating a sound alternately whooshing and crackling. A moment later there is a secondary explosion, probably the engine, Frank realizes, the flaming fuel having moved back to front and the car burning hotter, more intensely. The flames seem to lick the stars now as if daring them to come closer and watch what a man will do to survive once he realizes nullity is not his answer and the void can wait. Only when Frank ascertains that the luckless man's body is burned beyond recognition does he climb onto the road and flag down a truck heading east, ride into Durango, phone the local police from a gas station, and report his own death. When the police ask his name, he says, "Mí llamo Creed Baru." Then Frank hangs up, calls Otis, and tells him everything that happened.

Otis was on a plane the next morning flying from Tulsa to Houston, where he caught a flight to Mazatlán. There he rented a car and drove to Durango. He made contact with the police and after some judicious greasing of palms was in possession of Creed's charred remains. Although the forensic examiner who looked at the body did note that all its teeth were missing, no one was particularly motivated to find out why, and Otis arranged for the corpse to be cremated by nightfall, which was only two hours after the news of Frank's death hit the Internet. By the time the story was making the rounds in Los Angeles, the body thought to be Frank's had turned to DNA-less dust, and officially, Frank Bones was no more. No one could definitively prove the festively decorated urn Otis possessed contained Frank's ashes; but no one could prove it didn't.

A week after Frank's presumed death there was a memorial service at the Comedy Shop on Sunset Boulevard. The four hundred seats in the main room were filled before it started, and arrangements were made to pump the show through loudspeakers set up for the overflow crowd in the parking lot. Robert spoke eloquently about his friend and colleague, telling the assembled crowd the most talented among them might never achieve the success they deserved because they were blazing the path everyone else would follow. It was exactly the kind of pabulum people say at memorial services, since Frank hadn't really been doing anything anyone hadn't done before. It was only because things had become so tame in the early years of the new century that he looked like a revolutionary. But the show business audience, all of whom were either working for or aspiring to work for the multinational conglomerates that controlled the game, needed iconoclastic heroes they could hold to and tell themselves they would emulate, and they ate it up. Frank, it was agreed all around, was a great talent, and if he was unappreciated in life, he would be venerated in death. With this in mind, Jolly De Meo, not one to miss a bandwagon, announced he was endowing a chair in Frank's name in the field of comedy studies at USC. Candi Wyatt sobbed through the service because she knew in her heart that even though she was not yet twenty-three years old, she had already had the peak experience of her life. Honey Call wanted to be there, but she and Bart Pimento were leading a PETA demonstration that day because Honey believed life was about the living, and publicly mourning Frank was not going to be any help to the laboratory animals she and Bart were trying to liberate by chaining themselves to a research facility in San Luis Obispo. She did, however, send a large, horseshoe-shaped carnation wreath to be displayed onstage at the club.

As for Lloyd, he stayed away, not wanting to have to answer any more questions about Frank. And he'd had just about all he could take of him anyway. To Lloyd, Frank had forever been a distant yet brilliantly shining light, a fascinating planetary object representing a vastly more exciting way of life, a man whose sparkling, crackling effervescence allowed him to exist on a rarefied plane. That he had ultimately failed to live up to Lloyd's image of him, crashing and burning (literally!), his early promise unfilled, allowed Lloyd to feel better about the results of his own exertions. Bones flew too close to the flame, his thinking went; *let him be the legend; at least I'm alive.*

The day after the memorial service Robert Hyler is seated at the desk in his office talking on the phone. He has interrupted his meeting to take the call, and he lets an imperiousness creep into his voice so his guest will get a sense of how he deals with people. "We control the estate," he says. "The whole thing, okay? You cannot use his likeness in the advertising unless we approve it. Now think about it and make me an offer this afternoon." Hanging up, he returns his attention to his guest, who had been in the office less than five minutes before Robert took the call. "If only he'd been this hot when he was alive," he says. "So, the famous Otis Cain. What can I do for you?"

"You can start by calling those people back and telling them you no longer represent Frank Bones," Otis says neutrally, no point provoking anyone.

"What are you talking about?"

Otis takes a piece of paper out of the briefcase on his lap and slides it across the desk, saying, "I have power of attorney over Frank's estate. I also hold a brief for every other individual in this story not currently under indictment, Mr. Hyler. Mercy Madrid and Vida Suarez are both my clients. So the deal is . . . no deals get made without Otis Cain."

Robert examines the document, takes a close look at the signature. "I've represented Frank for over twenty years . . ." More sorrow than anger. "Why would he . . ."

"It's all legal," the lawyer says, his way of comforting. But when Otis gets the sense that it was more than business to Robert, that there was something in Frank he responded to and it had nothing to do with dollars, Otis drops the hard cool for a minute and tells Robert, "Hey, Frank was about Frank."

Unless one is talking about Jesus or Marilyn Monroe, brands that can be milked well into eternity, in the exploitation of celebrity death there is a short window during which commercial opportunities can be maximized. Otis was indefatigable in his pursuit of Frank's interests, and in short order deals were struck for a new CD, T-shirts, shot glasses, two books (one an authorized biography, the other a coffee table book of photographs), and a video game, which consisted of Frank in a car being chased by the police. Then there was the feature film, which had some of Hollywood's biggest stars fighting for the role of Frank Bones, a man who couldn't get his pilot picked up when he was alive.

Belize is a paradise for most of the year but never more than in the spring. The jungles, bursting with vines and flowers, edge down to the white sand beaches peopled by locals and the occasional European and

Canadian tourists, Americans for some reason preferring other Central American countries. On a Sunday morning in early May a slender man, well into middle age but looking fit, lies on a double bed in a modest bungalow. Otis managed to sell the house in Playa Perdida and buy this place with the money he got for it. It's not fancy, three rooms and a kitchen, but Frank's not planning on doing much entertaining. He's grown his beard out and is surprised at the gray streaks, but when it occurs to him his fiftieth birthday has come and gone while he was down here, the face looking back at him in the mirror doesn't seem so incongruous. Taking stock, Frank realizes that for a man who's lived the life he has, he's feeling pretty good. He's been swimming, gotten some sun; never felt more serene. The beast that once rampaged through his head with such malevolent energy appears, if not exactly a spent force, to have quieted down to a degree he never would have anticipated.

He had thought about going up north, back to America, because all charges had posthumously been dropped. That cleared the way for a return-from-the-dead comeback (he was calling it The Frank Bones Easter Tour—He Has Risen!) and all the ensuing publicity, should he choose to work that angle. But after thinking it over, he has decided to remain on the beach at the edge of the jungle. What was it he wanted up there now anyway? He'd had the bright lights and some money, too, although it was never really about money for Frank. Rather, it was simply about being his deepest, purest self and having that self validated by the largest possible number of people. Now he had finally come to understand the futility of trying to wring something truly human from the connection between a performer and an audience. They had been amused by him, but it was when he was in serious trouble that they loved him, and his perceived death will solidify that love, at least for a time. If he were to return he knows what would happen when the collective memory of his travails began to fade, as it surely would, and he was once again a man who couldn't get his own television series. Would he go back on the road and tell the story of his life again and again? Hardly. What, then?

Rising from the bed, Frank walks into the kitchen and opens a drawer. He pulls out a gravity knife, onyx handle with a pearl inlay, flips it open. It's not meant for kitchen use, but he likes the association, the memory it brings back. Runs his finger along the blade, still sharp. Taking a fat orange from a ceramic bowl on the wooden counter, he deftly slices it in quarters. Puts one in his mouth, sucking the juice out. A little of it runs down his chin and he wipes it away with the back of his hand; looks at the phone for a moment, feeling as if he's about to go onstage. Then he remembers it's changed, he's not performing anymore, and he's been thinking about this moment almost since he got here, Frank never one to dwell before, to live in anything but the eternal present. But this time it's been different. He's recalling a link, a bond, and he's been speculating about it, two molecules colliding, the heat, the evanescence, the flickering firefly light, then darkness again. And in the distant night, a glimmer?

It's been said that when a man reaches fifty, he has the face he deserves, and from that it can be extrapolated that he gets the life he deserves as well; perhaps not the recognition he is worthy of, or the riches, but certainly the quality of existence. So it often follows that once someone reaches a certain age, it isn't difficult to discern what fate has in store for the remainder of his days. But occasionally, in those rare moments when we are able to truly see our behavior and at last recognize the patterns that have ineluctably shadowed us through the years, leaving sorrow and pain in their wake, we can derive strength from the resultant knowledge, allowing us to burst their seemingly immutable shackles and begin life anew. On the dazzling day when that occurs, we are free at last.

Frank picks up the phone and dials. One ring, two, then a voice on the other end, a little sleepy, still early.

"Hello?"

"Mercy, it's me."

Silence on the other end. Frank hears a bird singing outside the window, looks at the blue water kissing the sand. Two fishermen pull their small boat ashore. Then: "Frank?" Complete shock, her voice a smoky whisper. Disbelief, a choked sound. Laughter, floating through the wires, or was it a sob, perhaps both? More silence. It's an effort for her to get a word out, but she's trying. The fishermen are unloading their catch now. Mercy collects herself, and she doesn't let him down when she clears her throat and asks, "How's my favorite dead man?"

"You like the beach?"

"If Oklahoma had one, I'd never have to leave."

The conversation goes on like this, as if it's an ordinary occurrence for a man the whole world believes to be ashes in a jar to call up someone he's been wondering about and ask her to fly south. To Frank it feels like the most natural thing in the world.

In the late spring, a little over a year later, Lloyd and Dustin are spending a Saturday afternoon at the Los Angeles Zoo. Lloyd tried to move back in with Stacy, but after weeks of halfhearted attempts at communication inevitably followed by ruminative silences, it became apparent that it was no longer going to work, and he got a place in the Oakwood Apartments, a well-known Los Angeles way station for lonely men leaving failing marriages. Lloyd has made a conscious effort to spend more time with his son, and the boy, who had often been skittish when alone with his father in unfamiliar surroundings, has started to look forward to their outings, which have included a Dodgers game, a trip to the Long Beach Aquarium, and of course Disneyland. Lloyd has grown to enjoy these times with Dustin far more than he could have anticipated. Now he holds his son's warm hand in his as they walk through dappled shadows toward the chimpanzee area, a remarkably well-landscaped environment of boulders, tall grass, crags, and water, all designed to foster the illusion in the simian mind that nothing is amiss.

Once Lloyd put his legal difficulties behind him, he returned to Los Angeles to face a new professional world. True to Harvey Gornish's word, Lynx declared him in breach of his contract and his deal was abrogated around the same time *Happy Endings* was canceled. Not long after the Lynx checks stopped arriving, they were forced to sell the Brentwood house, and to Stacy's immense chagrin she and Dustin are currently back in Mar Vista, where she suffers like a White Russian exiled to Paris by the arrival of the Bolsheviks. Lloyd has recently joined the writing staff of a long-running sitcom, one he would not watch if he were not working on it, and so continues to responsibly provide for his fractured family. He is well regarded in the writers' room, and what transpired in Oklahoma has supplied him with the patina of boundary-breaching eccentricity so prized by his comfortable colleagues, whose own glaring violations of the social order consist of activities like turning up in the express checkout line at the Whole Foods market with eleven items when they *know* they're only allowed ten. The result of Lloyd's journey into the shadow world is that he is slowly beginning to feel less uncomfortable in his own life, more accepting of his limits, and finally, grateful for his luck. Upon receiving an invitation to the publication party for his former assistant's novel, something that would have once sent him over the edge, he reacted with a level of equanimity only partially attributable to the increase in his Paxil dose.

Now in odd moments at the office and occasionally in the evenings in his one-bedroom apartment, he labors over his still-untitled book about Frank with lowered expectations. After having written more than a hundred pages, he showed it to a few people and, upon discussing the manuscript with them, decided to throw it out and start over, the consensus being it lacked an animating idea or philosophy. But Lloyd considers himself an artist and has decided to persevere in his quest to prove it to the larger world.

"Daddy, look," Dustin says, pointing in the direction of the ersatz jungle in which several primates are capering. Lloyd gazes in the direction indicated by his son and notices one of the chimps has an impressive erection, which he is absentmindedly fondling. At the same time this happy chimpanzee is contentedly nibbling a banana. A Mexican family—mother and father with three kids—watches the spectacle, pointing and laughing, enjoying their time together. Lloyd envies the chimp, his desires basic and easily met, untroubled by the need to be more than he is, to foist himself again and again upon an indifferent world. While this paragon of nature continues to simultaneously consume his banana and masturbate, Lloyd wonders if this irreducible act might conceivably suggest some kind of unifying credo, which he could elucidate and render as a worldview, the notion that we are at the mercy of our basic immutable nature, whatever it happens to be, and are only truly contented when fulfilling the destiny it foretells. For the monkey, it's easy enough since his needs are of a purely physical kind: to have a sated libido and a full stomach. Sex and Bananas, as it were. But for Lloyd, who is only beginning to understand the degree to which self-knowledge figures into the human aspect of this equation, it is not quite so blissfully uncomplicated. He realizes if a worldview is to have any actual resonance in the life of the person who posits it, it must not simply be explicated but embodied, enacted, lived fully each day, for it is only then that one's destiny can be fulfilled.

Having had enough of the chimpanzees, Dustin takes his father's hand and leads him toward a new adventure, his six-year-old mind unbowed by experience, alive with possibility. As they walk past the reptile house and toward the big cats, Lloyd once again finds himself thinking about Frank. Despite the passing of time, the memory of the other man remains a beacon that, while dimming a little more with each passing day, will abide with him forever.

Burn till there's nothing left but the bones.

Late that afternoon, when he drops Dustin off at the house in Mar Vista, he gets out of the car and hugs the boy, holding on to him for an extra second (is he bigger than he was two weeks ago?). Although still in his forties, Lloyd knows he is no longer young and his already attenuated time with Dustin is fleeting. He watches his son run up to the front door and ring the bell. In a moment, Stacy appears and Dustin vanishes into the house. Stacy waves at Lloyd and gives him a half smile. She has learned to temper her anger about the dissolution of the marriage, comforting herself with the knowledge that Lloyd had disappointed her in every way that mattered, so she's going to be better off in the long run. As for Lloyd, now that he isn't expecting anything from Stacy, he no longer has to hate her. He waves at his soon-to-be-ex wife and gets back in his car. Then he drives through the gathering twilight to his apartment, where he will prepare a simple dinner and watch television until it's time to go to sleep.

Thanks, you've been a great crowd. Please remember to tip your waitress.

ACKNOWLEDGMENTS

Thanks to Dick Lochte, Tom Teicholz, David Kanter, John Tomko, Billy Diamond, and Larry David for generously reading early drafts of this book.

Thanks to my excellent agent Henry Dunow. His enthusiasm and myriad skills have been a boon to me from our first conversation.

Thanks to my editors Colin Dickerman and Panio Gianopoulos. Their insightful suggestions improved the manuscript significantly.

Thanks to Leo Greenland and Drew Greenland for unstinting encouragement.

And finally, thanks to my wife, Susan, and our children, Allegra and Gabriel, for everything.

A NOTE ON THE AUTHOR

Seth Greenland is an award-winning playwright. He has written extensively for film and television. A longtime New Yorker, he lives in Los Angeles with his wife and two children. *The Bones* is his first novel.

A NOTE ON THE TYPE

The text of this book is set in Bembo. This type was first used in 1495 by the Venetian printer Aldus Manutius for Cardinal Bembo's *De Aetna*, and was cut for Manutius by Francesco Griffo. It was one of the types used by Claude Garamond (1480–1561) as a model for his Romain de L'Université, and so it was the forerunner of what became standard European type for the following two centuries. Its modern form follows the original types and was designed for Monotype in 1929.